The Given Sacrifice

A NOVEL OF THE CHANGE

S. M. STIRLING

A ROC BOOK

ROC
Published by the Penguin Group
Penguin Group (USA) LLC, 375 Hudson Street,
New York, New York 10014

USA | Canada | UK | Ireland | Australia | New Zealand | India | South Africa | China
penguin.com
A Penguin Random House Company

Published by Roc, an imprint of New American Library, a division of Penguin
Group (USA) LLC. Previously published in a Roc hardcover edition.

First Roc Mass Market Printing, September 2014

ISBN 978-0-451-41732-9

Printed in the United States of America
10 9 8 7 6 5 4 3 2 1

continued . . .

"*Tears of the Sun* engages fans of the saga who will anxiously await the next Change."

—Genre Go Round Reviews

The High King of Montival

"Filled with plenty of action, intrigue, and a touch of romance. . . . S. M. Stirling provides another fabulous postapocalyptic thriller to his Change saga."

—Alternative Worlds

"Stirling's series combines the best of fantasy and post-apocalyptic genres but rises above them both with his long vision and skill in creating compelling characters, no matter how large or small their role."   —Fresh Fiction

The Sword of the Lady

"This new novel of the Change is quite probably the finest by an author who has been growing in skill and imagination for more than twenty-five years."

—*Booklist* (starred review)

"Well written. Stirling has the ability to make the commonplace exciting and to dribble out the information needed to complete the tapestry of understanding . . . a good tale."   —SFRevu

The Scourge of God

"Vivid. . . . Stirling eloquently describes a devastated, mystical world that will appeal to fans of traditional fantasy as well as postapocalyptic SF."

—*Publishers Weekly* (starred review)

"Stirling is a perfect master of keep-them-up-all-night pacing, possibly the best in American SF, quite capable of sweeping readers all the way to the end."

—*Booklist* (starred review)

The Sunrise Lands

"Combines vigorous military adventure with cleverly packaged political idealism. . . . Stirling's narrative deftly balances sharply contrasting ideologies. . . . The thought-provoking and engaging storytelling should please Stirling's many fans."   —*Publishers Weekly*

"A master of speculative fiction and alternate history, Stirling delivers another chapter in an epic of survival and rebirth."   —*Library Journal*

A Meeting at Corvallis

"[A] richly realized story of swordplay and intrigue."
—*Entertainment Weekly*

"Stirling concludes his alternative history trilogy in high style. . . . [The story] resembles one of the cavalry charges the novel describes—gorgeous, stirring, and gathering such earth-pounding momentum that it's difficult to resist."
—*Publishers Weekly*

"A fascinating glimpse into a future transformed by the lack of easy solutions to both human and technological dilemmas."
—*Library Journal*

The Protector's War

"Absorbing."
—*The San Diego Union-Tribune*

"[A] vivid portrait of a world gone insane . . . it also has human warmth and courage. . . . It is full of bloody action, exposition that expands character, and telling detail that makes it all seem very real."
—*Statesman Journal* (Salem, OR)

"Reminds me of Poul Anderson at his best."
—David Drake, author of *What Distant Deeps*

"Rousing. . . . Without a doubt [*The Protector's War*] will raise the bar for alternate-universe fiction."
—John Ringo, *New York Times* bestselling author of *Citadel*

Dies the Fire

"*Dies the Fire* kept me reading till five in the morning so I could finish at one great gulp. . . . Don't miss it."
—Harry Turtledove

"Gritty, realistic, apocalyptic, yet a grim hopefulness pervades it like a fog of light. The characters are multidimensional, unusual, and so very human. Buy *Dies the Fire*. Sell your house; sell your soul; get the book. You won't be sorry."
—John Ringo

"A stunning speculative vision of a near-future bereft of modern conveniences but filled with human hope and determination. Highly recommended."
—*Library Journal*

To Jan, forever

ACKNOWLEDGMENTS

Thanks to my friends who are also first readers:

To Steve Brady, for assistance with dialects and British background, and also natural history of all sorts.

Pete Sartucci, knowledgeable in many aspects of Western geography and ecology.

Thanks also to Kier Salmon, unindicted co-conspirator.

To Diana L. Paxson, for help and advice, and for writing the beautiful Westria books, among many others. If you like the Change novels, you'll probably enjoy the hell out of the Westria books—I certainly did, and they were one of the inspirations for this series; and her *Essential Ásatrú* and recommendation of *Our Troth* were extremely helpful . . . and fascinating reading. The appearance of the name Westria in the book is no coincidence whatsoever.

To Dale Price, for help with Catholic organization, theology and praxis.

To Brenda Sutton, for multitudinous advice.

To Walter Jon Williams, John Miller, Vic Milan, Jan Stirling, Matt Reiten, Lauren Teffeau and Ian Tregellis of Critical Mass for constant help and advice as the book was under construction.

Thanks to John Miller, good friend, writer and scholar, for many useful discussions, for loaning me some great books and for some really, really cool old movies.

Special thanks to Heather Alexander, bard and balladeer, for permission to use the lyrics from her beautiful songs, which can be—and should be!—enjoyed by all. Run, do not walk, to do so at www.heatherlands.com. or visit her heir, Alexander James Adams, at http://faerietaleminstrel.com/inside

Thanks again to William Pint and Felicia Dale for permission to use their music, which can be found at www.pintndale.com and should be, for anyone with an ear and salt water in their veins.

And to Three Weird Sisters—Gwen Knighton, Mary Crowell, Brenda Sutton and Teresa Powell—whose alternately funny and beautiful music can be found at www.threeweirdsisters.com.

And to Heather Dale for permission to quote the lyrics of her songs, whose beautiful (and strangely appropriate!) music can be found at www.heatherdale .com, and is highly recommended. The lyrics are wonderful and the tunes make it even better.

To S. J. Tucker for permission to use the lyrics of her beautiful songs, which can be found at www.skinnywhitechick.com, and should be.

And to Lael Whitehead of Jaiya, www.jaiya.ca, for permission to quote the lyrics of her beautiful songs.

Thanks again to Russell Galen, my agent, who has been an invaluable help and friend for more than a decade now, and never more than in these difficult times.

All mistakes, infelicities and errors are of course my own.

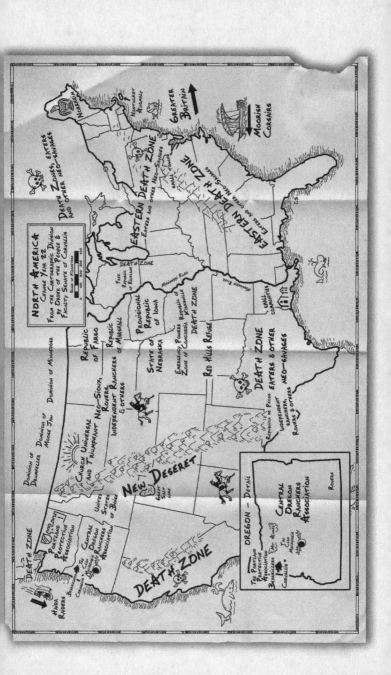

PART ONE

THE HARVEST KING

CHAPTER ONE

I am so fucked, Pilot Officer Alyssa Larsson thought, as the glider hit a pocket of cold air, shocking and utterly unexpected.

The nose went down and she had a feeling like her stomach was floating up into her throat, like skiing down a steep slope and going over a bump into a jump.

Like falling, in other words.

Get out of this pocket, fast! Dive out! training and reflex said.

She did. Her hands and feet moved on the controls of the glider with delicate precision, coaxing the last ounce of performance out of the Glaser-Dirk 100. Air whistled by, the loudest thing in the profound silence of the sky; the cockpit was paradoxically stuffy and smelled of lubricants, ancient plastic and fresher leather and fear-sweat. The falling-sled sensation went away, but she'd gone down three or four hundred crucial feet. Her head whipped around, and she saw uncomfortably high ground all around her, a situation that had gone from *chancy* to *bad* all at once. This was unfamiliar territory, known only from the map—that was the whole point of reconnaissance flying, but it made things a lot more dangerous. Over the country she knew well the spots for likely lift were all as familiar as the feel of her bootlaces. Here, not so much.

Of course, I know where the nearest three landing points are. Only now I can't get to any of them.

She was over dense forest, with a saw-toothed ridge of nearly vertical rock directly ahead; she could get to it, but not over it to the steep river-valley beyond. Alyssa shoved the goggles up on the forehead of her leather helmet, hiding the snarling face-on bear's head worked into the hide there. Her eyes peered at the air over the ridge.

Shit. No birds.

Birds were a good way to find air moving upward; lots of them didn't like to flap if they could avoid it. So probably no updraft directly ahead. She was sweating and her mouth was dry, but there was no *time* to be afraid. Her hand moved on the stick, very gently, no rudder, just the shallowest of banking turns to cruise along the face of the ridge looking for a spot where there *was* an updraft.

No joy.

The aircraft was losing one foot of altitude for every forty it went forward towards a sheer slope, and there weren't that many feet left before you ran into the trees and rocks below. She was moving faster than a galloping horse, faster than a pedalcar on rails, faster than virtually anything else in the world except a peregrine falcon stooping or a catapult bolt, and when hundreds of pounds hit at speed . . . the gentle floating of the glider would abruptly transition to nasty un-Changed calculations of kinetic energy release and the strength factors of human bone and tissue. *Her* bone and tissue. The only good thing was that this wasn't happening over enemy-held territory; it was pretty well uninhabited around here these days.

If I can get this thing down in one piece, we can bring in a horse team and pack it out.

They'd been built to disassemble, and been modified since to do it more thoroughly.

"All right, my beauty, let's *do* this," she muttered.

Some of her older instructors had been pilots before the Change, when powered aircraft could just bull their way through the air. Most of the time she agreed with the modern school which held that dancing with the invisible currents of the sky-ocean was preferable, but right now something to just *push* would be welcome. And aesthetics be damned.

"Well, shit, Bearkiller," she told herself as she leveled out again, sparing a quick glance downward.

"OK, the Bear Lord was aloft in something a lot less aerodynamic and with a lot higher stall speed than this over mountains not all that far from here when the Change hit. With Dad and Aunt Signe and all in the back-seats. Uncle Mike walked away . . . well, swam away . . . from a real hard landing, the rest of the family survived too; so will you if it comes to that."

Although he just barely *survived. Holy Mary Mother of God, if he hadn't—*

Since she'd gotten her wings a little while ago she had a much better grasp of what a combination of blind luck and superlative piloting had been required at the very beginning of the Bearkiller legend. Her mind blanched at the thought that the whole world she knew including her personal self wouldn't have existed if her aunt's future husband been just a *little* less skillful or fortunate.

So I've got to live. Maybe as much depends on me!

She turned away from the ridge to try and get closer to base. That ridge ahead was going to be *really* close, looking like a fanged jaw reaching for her. Her gut tightened in an involuntary effort to haul the sailplane upward by sheer willpower. She absolutely needed to climb at least a bit, but she *couldn't* put the nose any higher. If she tried she wouldn't climb, she'd just drop below stalling speed and fall out of the sky like a leaf in autumn as the wings lost lift.

Like a leaf in autumn except for the last crunchy bit. Just a little more, then slam the stick down once I clear the crest to get some margin back, then go looking for an updraft—

Speed was dropping. Dropping fast, *too* fast. Reflex tried to make her turn the nose down again, but that would mean diving into the mountain slope so bloody damned close below.

Just another hundred yards . . .

Stalling felt like slipping backward an instant after the controls went mushy.

Oh fuck *me, what utter brass-assed moron came up with this mission in the first place—*

The left wingtip brushed the top of a tall larch less than a second later. Whirling impact, battering, tossing, the scream of tearing metal. She shouted and flung her arms up in front of her face.

HIGH KING'S HOST, BOISE CONTINGENT HQ
COUNTY PALATINE OF THE EASTERMARK
(FORMERLY EASTERN WASHINGTON STATE)
HIGH KINGDOM OF MONTIVAL
(FORMERLY WESTERN NORTH AMERICA)
JUNE 1ST, CHANGE YEAR 26/2024 AD

Fred Thurston was dickering with a would-be defector from what remained of the United States of Boise's army. Rudi Mackenzie stayed in the shadows at the back of the tent, arms crossed on his chest, ignored after a single startled glance and a jerk of Rudi's head towards Fred. The man who was now High King Artos of Montival kept silent; he was scrupulous in not interfering in the chain of command without very pressing need, and with Fred such was very rare indeed.

Though there's need more often than I'd like with others.

Artos the First was a young man, a Changeling as it was called here—he'd been born near Yule of that year— but the High Kingdom of Montival was far younger. Its armies were cobbled together from what had been a dozen separate realms, many of them with a history of mutual suspicion or outright battle. Everything was a makeshift of constant improvisation.

You fight with what you have, not what you'd wish, Rudi thought.

Even if you were fighting the biggest war since the Change. Certainly the biggest in North America since then, if you didn't count the desperate scrambles in the months after the machines stopped. Not the biggest in the world, probably; Asia still weighed heavily in the nine-tenths-reduced total of humankind. Rumors trickled in now and then across seas pirate-haunted when they weren't empty. They spoke of warlords fighting each other and invaders from Mongolia and Tibet across the ruins of China, and the bloody rise of *Mahendr Shuddhikartaa hai*—Mahendra the Purifier—carving out a new empire called Hinduraj on the Bay of Bengal. . . .

The world is wider and wilder than we can know. But this is the part the Powers have set me to ward.

The defector and Fred had gotten down to cases more rapidly than Rudi would have considered tactful at first, which was another reason he was leaving this in his friend's capable hands. Someone who'd grown up among Boise's folk would understand them in ways that Rudi never quite could, even bearing the Sword of the Lady. The officer wouldn't be his subject unless and until he came to an agreement with Fred, and even then only indirectly.

He and Fred had gone all the way to Nantucket and back together on the Quest; they were comrades and allies, but lord and sworn follower as well. Fred had come to understand the relationship those words implied, but most Boiseans didn't. Worse, they thought they *did* understand it.

Being ignorant is truly bliss compared to being misinformed, especially if you're aware of the depths of your own ignorance. As Mother says, it isn't what you don't know that will kill you, it's what you think you know that just isn't so.

"Yes, sir, Mr. President," the officer said at last, saluting; he hadn't been invited to sit.

"I'm not President yet," Fred replied sharply. "There's a little matter of elections first. I expect to win them . . . but I also intend to do it fair and square."

The man looked very slightly anxious; he was in his thirties, with Brigadier's insignia on his loose olive-green linsey-woolsey field uniform of boots and pants and patch-pocketed jacket. Fred wore the same kit, the uniform of the realm that called itself the United States of America and ruled much of Idaho from its center at Boise, but without marks of rank at all apart from the Stars-and-Stripes badge on the shoulder. That ostentatious plainness was a statement in itself.

"But we have an agreement, sir?" the man said.

"Certainly, Brigadier Roberts. Unless you insist on having the personal parts in writing? That could be embarrassing down the road, unless we altered some of the details."

So you'd better hope *I win the vote* went unspoken between them. *And use what influence you have to make sure I do. Someone else might not consider themselves bound by our negotiations here.*

The man licked his lips; they were thin, like his face, and together with his cropped blond hair and pale yellowish eyes gave him the look of a wolf that had gone a little too long without a meal. Those eyes flicked towards the back of the big tent. The High King had never made any secret of the fact that one of the things the Sword gave him was the ability to tell truth from falsehood. By now, nearly everyone believed it.

Or more precisely, I can sense the intention to deceive, Rudi thought. *The which means my simply standing here keeps him . . . relatively . . . honest.*

Though with a man as fundamentally untruthful as this, whether *anything* he said was true at heart would be a matter for philosophers to split hairs over.

"Of course not, sir. I wouldn't be here if I didn't trust your word."

And oddly enough, he does trust Fred's word. Wise enough not to judge others by himself, at least.

Fred nodded. "Report to my chief of staff, and we'll slot your men into the overall TOE. He'll show you where to plant the eagle."

He stood and returned the brigadier's salute, then shook hands. The man left, his stride growing brisker with relief, and there was a clank as the armored guards outside the tent's entrance brought their big oval shields up and thumped the butts of their long iron-shod throwing spears to the hard-packed earth. Silence fell for a long moment, amid the smell of hot canvas and dust and horses and woodsmoke from the encampment beyond. There were sounds—voices, someone counting cadence, the massed tramp of booted feet, iron on iron from a field smithy—but they were curiously muffled.

"I don't like that deal at all," Fred said quietly, when the defector was well out of ear-range, looking at his right hand and turning it back and forth. "I'll do it for three-and-a-half-thousand men . . . to *save* three-and-a-half-thousand men . . . but I don't like it at all."

Rudi Mackenzie smiled wryly as he came forward and sat across from him.

"I don't *like* it either, Fred. And neither of us *likes* fighting battles, but you do as you must, not as you would. You must have seen it with your father; I certainly did with Mother, by Nuada of the Silver Hand who favors Kings! It may mean *dying* for the people. . . ."

Fred ran a hand over his hair, which was cut short in a

cap of soft black rings. "I think I'd actually prefer that, sometimes."

"We're all *going* to die sometime, to be sure. More often ruling well means we have to do things like shaking hands and breaking bread with men we'd rather put face-down in a dungheap with a boot to the back of their necks. The which hand-shaking and bread-breaking is nearly as unpleasant as death and wears harder on the soul."

Fred grinned in weary agreement and kneaded the back of his neck. "Thor with me, this sort of thing wears you out worse than a march in armor. And that's an attractive image. The manure pile and the boot and his face, that is."

Rudi nodded. "And you can wash muck off your boot, but it's harder to get clean of *that* sort."

He jerked his head towards the entrance, the long copper-gold hair swirling about his shoulders. Fred sighed and nodded.

"Should I have been more . . . tactful?"

"No, you were about right, I'd say. He'd smell a trap if you were all hail-fellow-well-met and inviting him to sit down for a yarn and a tankard of beer with a slap on the back in good fellowship. And he'd despise you if he thought it was genuine. Best to make it a matter of business and advantage on both sides."

The king and his ally were both big young men only a year apart in age, with similar broad-shouldered, long-limbed builds, both with the smooth graceful movements of those raised to the sword and the tensile wariness of those who'd also lived by it in lands beyond law. In other ways they differed. The younger son of Boise's first ruler had bluntly handsome broad features and skin of a pale toast color, legacy of his sire's part-African blood.

"Well, it is to our mutual advantage," Fred said. "And he does have *some* virtues. He's smart enough to treat his men well enough that they'll follow him. Especially now that he's leading them in the direction they want to go."

"That always makes it easier, to be sure," Rudi said.

The High King's eyes were a changeable blue-green-gray, brighter by contrast now as the setting sun turned the big command tent into a cave of umber gloom. He wore the pleated kilt of a Mackenzie in the Clan's green-brown tartan, with a plaid pinned at his shoulder over a loose-sleeved saffron-colored linen shirt cinched at wrists and throat with drawstrings.

A sword hung at his right side from a broad belt, in shape a knight's long cut-and-thrust weapon with a shallow-curved crescent guard and a double-lobed hilt of black staghorn inlaid with silver knotwork. Its pommel was a globe cradled in a web of antlers, at first glance a perfect sphere of moon-opal. Then if you looked closer it was like crystal, and within it curves that drew the vision deeper and deeper—

Fred's eyes flicked aside from it, though he was a brave man, and not just about physical danger.

"Was Roberts telling the truth?" he asked.

Rudi's hand fell to the pommel in a gesture that had become habit. "What do you think?" he asked.

I try to keep from being too dependent on this, Fred. You should too. The more so as neither I nor the Sword will be with you whenever you might need them.

"That he was reasonably sincere, and he'll keep his

word—as long as he still thinks we're the winning side," Fred said.

Rudi flipped up his hands in a gesture of agreement. "See, you don't need the Sword of the Lady to tell you *that*."

Fred looked at it again, obviously forcing himself a little.

"That thing is useful. It had better be, after we went through hell and high water to get it—"

Rudi chuckled; that was uncomfortably close to being literally true.

"But . . . better you than me, Rudi! I can judge men pretty well, I think, but it would be sort of stressful to *know* what I read was true. And I'd hate to be incapable of half-believing some little white lie."

Rudi laughed; he'd been born late in the first Change Year, but there were already a few faint lines beside his eyes that showed he was a man who laughed often.

"My sentiments exactly and in precise measure, Fred. But I'm stuck with it; worse, my children after me."

Fred's smile died quickly. "Speaking of an inheritance . . . what I really hate about making deals with Roberts and the others who backed Martin after he killed Dad is that he gave them *land*, land from the public reserve that should have been kept for division into more family farms. Dad always said yeomen are the bedrock."

"More than they deserve, sure and it is," Rudi said. "Though finding folk to work it for them . . . that'll be another matter."

Land—who held it, and on what terms; who worked it, and how; and for whose benefit besides their own—

was what most of modern politics, and much of modern life for that matter, were *about*.

"They deserve what Martin got, what you gave him," Fred said.

Which had been the Sword through the gut. Though at the last that had been a mercy, freeing his soul even as he died.

Fred's face hardened as he spoke. Rudi reflected that the younger man normally wasn't much of a hater, which was a very good thing in a ruler for more than one reason. But Fred had hated his elder brother Martin, for parricide and killing their father's dream of a restored United States and allying Boise with the malignancy that was the Church Universal and Triumphant.

Possibly most of all for killing the love they must have felt once, he thought sympathetically. *I have no brothers, but of my sisters I am most fond.*

Fred went on: "And I have some ideas about tax policy on unused land. . . ."

A cough at the entranceway brought their heads around with a caution ground in by short but extremely eventful lifetimes. Hands relaxed from weapons as they saw who stood there, a young man of middling height but broad-shouldered and thick-armed, with a square face and oak-colored brown curls beneath his Scots bonnet.

"Merry meet, Edain," Rudi said to his guard-captain.

Edain Aylward Mackenzie put down the trays of food he was carrying. They looked a little incongruous with the outfit of the High King's Archers anyway. That was the Mackenzie kilt and plaid and the green brigandine the Clan's warriors usually wore, though the outer layer of leather bore the Crowned Mountain of Montival rather than the Mackenzie crescent moon cradled in antlers. He had shortsword and buckler at his belt, a dirk, and a sgian-dubh tucked into his knee-hose.

Across his back was a quiver of gray-fletched arrows, with a great yellow yew longbow thrust through the carrying loops on its side. The Mackenzies were a people of the bow, and old Sam Aylward their first teacher had been known as Aylward *the* Archer in his time. His son bore that nickname these days, for very good reason.

Right now he prodded a thick callused finger at the food. "Merry meet, and merry part, Chief; and you, Fred. Now eat, both of you."

Rudi blinked in surprise. "*Arra*, and is it that time already?"

"It's sunset," Edain said.

Then with a show of thought, tapping a thumb on his chin: "It happens nearly every day in these parts, and then most often it grows dark!"

"And how would I remember such things without you to remind me, blood-brother?" Rudi grinned.

Edain snorted. "The Lord and Lady may know, but I don't even ken how I got you to Nantucket and back alive. I'm here because Fred's batman came to me near weeping, *Not now they tell me, not now, we're too busy . . .* and to think a crew of fancy cooks have toiled and moiled all the day to whip up this feast for you, sure and they did like Lughnasadh come early, what with the well-basted roast suckling pig with the honey-garlic glaze and the spiced meat pies with their fragrant flaky crusts and the succulent fresh-picked asparagus and steamed sweet peas and glazed carrots and stuffed eggplant and four types of bread hot from the oven and sweet butter and the cakes and ices and whipped cream and all!"

Rudi chuckled; the food consisted of two bowls containing chunks of mutton stewed with dried beans and desiccated vegetables, a stack of tortillas and a block of ration-issue cheese the size, shape and consistency of a cake of soap. It was the same food anyone in the US of Boise contingent would be eating tonight, officer or enlisted.

"Sit, man," he said to Edain, as he pulled the little knife out of his sock-hose and shaved rock-hard dry cheese onto the bowls of stew. "There's work to be done and I'll need you to hear and speak. You've eaten?"

"Aye, Chief. Asgerd saw to it."

Fred uncorked a wine bottle and poured three glasses as Edain unhooked his baldric and hung the longbow and quiver from a peg on one of the tent poles.

"You should have gotten Asgerd pregnant, the way Rudi and I did our wives," the Boisean said, then looked at his King.

"And I won't have to envy you much longer, Rudi. I wouldn't have your *job* on a bet, but that, yeah. To hold our daughter—"

The longing was naked in his face for an instant, and the remembered joy in Rudi's own.

"Son," Rudi said absently. "For you two it'll be a son, first."

All three men looked at his hand on the pommel of the Sword.

"You're going to name him Lawrence," Rudi went on. "And Dirk after Virginia's grandfather. He'll go by Dirk, mostly . . . sorry! I should have left you to find that out; it comes on me unawares, betimes."

Fred's face unfroze. "Well, in the old days they had machines . . . x-sounds, did they call them? To tell you ahead of time." His smile grew wide. "A son! Our son!"

Then he laughed. There was a silver hammer on a chain around his neck; he touched his jacket over the spot where it lay.

"Son or daughter, Freya knows it's the only way I was going to stop Virginia coming on campaign with me," he said. "Freya keep her and our kid both safe, too."

"They're a fierce lot in the Powder River country," Rudi acknowledged, drawing the Invoking pentagram over his bowl of stew. *"Hail and thanks to the Mother-of-All who births the harvest, to the Lord who dies for the ripened corn, and thanks to the mortals who toiled with Them,"* he went on, before taking up the first spoonful.

The Powder River plains in old Wyoming were where Fred had first met his spouse, when she stumbled into their camp on the run from the followers of the Church Universal and Triumphant who'd taken her family's ranch. She'd ended going to Nantucket and back with the Quest.

Fred hammer-signed his bowl, murmured: *"Hail, all-giving Earth,"* and went on: "And Mathilda's meek and retiring, Rudi, yeah, right, she certainly wouldn't be here even if she hadn't gotten knocked up. And I've *never* seen her charging over a barricade into a mess of Saloum corsairs right beside you, shield up, visor down and sword swinging and screaming *Haro, Portland! Holy Mary for Portland!* at the top of her lungs."

He tasted the stew. "Damn you, Edain, you actually

made me hungry as hell with that description and now I have to eat *this*."

Rudi chewed and swallowed. It was . . . fuel, slightly enlivened by the chilies some camp cook had dropped in to disguise the fact that the contributing sheep had probably died of old age. He'd eaten much worse, and the tortillas were even palatable when fresh; he rolled one, dipped it in the stew to spoon some up, and took a bite before he spoke:

"Matti fights from duty and necessity. Virginia actually likes it. The fighting, I should be saying, not the killing as such, though to be frank she also minds that less than you or I."

"Yeah," Fred acknowledged. "And she's got a powerful hate on for the Cutters, and just between me and thee, Rudi, sometimes she doesn't grasp the difference between leading a country and owning a ranch, not deep down. At least this way she's got a chance to get to know Mom and my sisters better. And Mom will do anything she has to with a grandchild to protect, even keep Virginia in line."

"And if Asgerd's not blessed by the Mother-of-All yet, it's not for want of trying on our part," Edain said cheerfully. "And there'll be time enough."

Like Fred he'd met his wife on the Quest. Asgerd Karlsdottir had been born in what was once northern Maine, and was now the Kingdom of Norrheim. Edain had come away from their time there with a new wife. Fred had found a faith, one that spoke to his soul as his family's nominal Methodism never had.

Rudi used the half-eaten tortilla to gesture. "Look you, we just took . . . what, a tenth of Boise's remaining strength this last hour? And without an arrow or sword-stroke, and it was the fraction of it blocking our way at that. Took it from their line of battle and added it to ours."

"Yeah," Fred nodded, soberly. "I've got as many men as the junta has now, infantry at least, and mine *want* to fight. Or at least to get the job done so they can go back to their farms without worrying about the Cutters threatening their families."

Rudi nodded, but it wasn't completely a gesture of agreement. "I want to pick up the pieces without killing any more of your people. Corwin is the real enemy."

"Damn right. It's not *their* fault Martin screwed them over and got them on the CUT's side."

"True, but morals aside . . . two things a king can never have enough of: one is money, and the other is good troops. And good soldiers will get you gold more often than gold will get you good soldiers, as my foster-father Sir Nigel is fond of saying. I want those men fighting for *us*."

"But we have to hammer past Boise as fast as we can," Fred said; he'd been trained in Boise's staff schools, where playing devil's advocate was a standard technique. "Before the passes are snowed in again and while there's still grazing. Otherwise the League of Des Moines and the Canuks will get to Corwin before we do. And you . . . we . . . Montival . . . don't want that."

"No, though the Lakota will be with them, and they're part of Montival now, keeping our spoon in that stewpot across the Rockies. Also our allies may not *get* to Corwin this year, being naturally less eager than we; if they tie down the bulk of the Prophet's men on the high plains, I'll be satisfied. But when Corwin falls, the war is over bar the mopping up."

"*When* being the operative word," Fred observed dryly.

"Exactly. Fighting into next year means fields unplanted or unharvested, and there's been too much of that already."

"So . . . '*if it were done when 'tis done, then 'twere well it were done quickly,*'" Fred quoted.

Rudi nodded, barring his teeth in what was not quite a smile. That was from *Macbeth*, and that tale of ambition and treachery and death seasoned with ill-wreaking magic was all too apposite.

"The city of Boise itself . . . that may be tricky. Your father built strong walls and gates."

"Not if they're opened from the inside."

"That would be . . . difficult."

Fred hesitated, obviously reluctant. "There's . . . a way. Dad told me about it. I'm pretty certain that he told Martin, too . . . but I don't know who *Martin* told."

"Ah, so?" Rudi said softly. "Now that is most interesting. If . . . those Powers . . . thought to ask him, he would have told. Told anything. But they have a weakness; they don't *like* the world of matter. They might not have."

"And anyway, the fortifications . . . it's the men that count, in the end. But the number of officers coming over to us is slowing down. Even though the writing's on the wall."

Rudi nodded grimly. "The Cutters can compel men's minds, if given even the slightest opening. Notice how bitter Roberts was against the CUT? Somethin' they did frightened him badly, and he's a bold bad man. We need to bring as many waverers to our side as we can while they still own their own souls. That'll be easiest if they're facing you in particular rather than Montival in general, not least because they know the common soldiers will hesitate to fight their own. That may well have turned the Horse Heaven Hills fight in our favor."

Fred mopped his bowl with a tortilla and chewed on it thoughtfully. When his mouth was clear:

"There are a lot of Cutter horse-archers still loose; if I run into them . . . there's nothing like some plate-armored lancers riding barded destriers on your flanks to give you peace of mind. Say what you like about the Associates, they can *fight*. I won't be sorry to have the Grand Constable leading them either, she may not be the most charming person on earth—"

"An acquired taste, yet worth the effort."

"—but she knows her trade and then some."

"Very true indeed, and I'll be glad when she's back. But the propaganda the enemy is putting out paints me as lusting to divide Idaho into fiefs for my supporters and build castles on it, the way my black spalpeen of a dead father-in-law did with the lands he took in his day . . . which admittedly was a great whacking amount of territory, which now sprouts noblemen and castles like toadstools after rain."

"Yeah, if I ride in trailing a *menie* of armored Associate lancers with pennants streaming and gold spurs gleaming it'll make that look sorta convincing," Fred acknowledged. "Dad never slugged it out with Portland, but for a long time everyone *expected* that to happen, and there were some pretty bloody skirmishes before we split the Palouse with them. What's your plan?"

"I'll use them at need, but I'd like to keep the chivalry

of the PPA in reserve as far as I can, until we're east of Boise into lands where there's no memory of the wars against the Association. Or of the days when Norman Arminger was the . . . what was the phrase . . . the *big bad*."

Fred frowned. "I see your point. And they can be an arrogant bunch, and come across as even more arrogant than they are, to people who aren't used to their, ah, ways. But from a strictly military point of view—"

"War is the means, Fred. Victory is the end, and that's always about politics. We need to separate the remaining Boise troops in the field against us from the Cutters; the Grand Constable and the barons can trample *them* under-hoof in finest feudal style with my hearty cheers. So I want air reconnaissance as far as Boise itself. For that we need good launching sites, say in those mountains south-east of here for a start—"

"The Seven Devils. Hmmm. There were old airstrips up there before the Change . . . probably a lot of ther-mals and updrafts . . . I suppose you want me to turn my field engineers loose on the approach roads? 'Cause I don't have any glider squadrons to spare, to put it mildly. It's harder for the Air Force to defect, oddly enough. As units, at least."

"Right you are. Forbye we can use Bearkiller pilots and ground crew, and Mackenzies to guard and skirmish down towards the lowlands, if you supply the transport. With luck we can draw some of the Cutter cavalry off, too, and make them fight us in terrain that gives us the advantage."

Edain stirred from where he'd been holding his glass between two palms and listening silently.

"And you'd be wanting to go up and supervise yourself,

Chief," he said wearily. "Not leaving it to those whose *proper* business it is. That's the ill news you had for me."

"How well you know me!" Rudi said. "Get the Archers ready. I'll not try to go alone, lest you sicken with worry and do yourself an injury."

"Or put the toe of me boot to the stony arse of you, that being the way to get sense into your thinking parts, Chief," Edain said. "Now you've eaten, I suggest you seek your tent, unless you've decided to do without sleep as well. *Something* is making your judgment worse than it might be."

Rudi nodded good-bye to Fred and rose. "*You* try presiding at meetin's and reading reports all day, Edain, and see if you don't seize any excuse to get away!"

More soberly, and looking out into the fire-starred darkness beyond the tent: "And I'll be sending those pilots into peril. They can at least see the face of the man who's asking them to do it."

CHAPTER TWO

Private Cole Salander (1st Special Forces Battalion, Army of the United States) suppressed an impulse to dive for cover as the glider whipped by close overhead, just beyond the tips of the firs. He hadn't had any warning; walking in tall conifer woods meant the only sky he could see was right overhead and the flying machines were as quiet as a ghost.

Instead of moving he froze, just turning his head down towards the ground to hide his face. Jumping for concealment made you more conspicuous. He'd had that well enough drilled in during the last couple of years for it to be reflex; he was a solidly built and broad-shouldered young man, with a snub-nosed face, pale eyes and sandy hair cropped in the Army's high-and-tight, now still as a statue.

In the old General's day you had to spend several years in the ranks with superior fitness reports and then qualify for the Rangers before they let you volunteer for the Special Forces, and they washed out most of the applicants even so. He knew standards had probably slipped and training had certainly gotten compressed since the war against the western powers started, and over the last eight months since President-General Martin Thurston was killed at the great and bloody cluster-fuck known as the Battle of the Horse Heaven Hills everything had started unraveling for sure.

I wouldn't be pulling this mission on my own otherwise, and me just out of training. This is a job for a four-man team with at least an experienced leader.

But he was stubbornly determined to prove that he was as good as any of the old-timers.

Once the glider was out of sight he dropped his field pack, slung his crossbow so that it lay right down his back and deployed his climbing rope in a loop around the rough barked trunk of a big column-straight pine that must have been growing here when his great-grandfather left Värmland still in his mother's womb. That and a scramble from branch to branch above the clear section got him sixty feet up in less than a minute, amid a spicy sweet sap-scent.

From there he had a magnificent view through his binoculars, though he made a note to rub the sticky residue off his fingerless gloves before touching his crossbow again. Forest, a slice of green meadow starred with red Indian paintbrush, even a herd of elk grouping together on a ridgeline against the menace of wolf-packs. What he couldn't see was the glider, which meant . . .

Which means it crashed, and probably pretty hard.

He grinned as he half-slid and half-fell down the big tree and hit the ground with a grunt and a squat. There wasn't much in the way of landing sites around here; mountains had lots of updrafts, but not many flat smooth places. Gliders were useful, but they had short working lives. So did their pilots.

Cole had noted the bearing of the aircraft against three landmarks, one of them a high snow-topped peak to the west. He got out his compass, checked against the map and his memory of how the terrain lay, and started through the woods at a trot.

"*Bearkiller* is sort of *symbolic*. There's no need to take it personally," Alyssa Larsson said, her voice a feeble rasp in her ears. "It was a black bear Uncle Mike killed, anyway. I've seen the head on the Bear Helm. Big, but not a grizzly like you, no sir."

The bear beneath her didn't respond, except to sniff more energetically. She reached for the clasp of the seat belt and whimpered slightly at the jagged rasp of pain through her left forearm. Then she shook her head—which itself hurt badly enough to notice any other time—and decided that would have been a lousy idea anyway. This wasn't the time to operate on pure reflex, no matter how bad the hurting was or how dizzy and nauseous she felt.

The glider had snapped off one wing and come to rest more or less upside-down, twisted to the side just enough to make her position the most awkward possible. The bubble canopy was about seven or eight feet above the ground, and spotted with the blood that was still dripping from cuts and a squashed nose. She didn't think *that* was broken, and none of her teeth felt loose despite the way her lips had been mashed against them, but it was unfortunate that she was bleeding. The boar grizzly sniffing around under the crashed aircraft probably found the scent far, far too appetizing.

They had a very keen sense of smell.

It was young but fully adult and big even for a silvertip. About the size of a medium horse, say nine hundred to a thousand pounds. One of the many wandering down into all their old range now that humans were scarce and didn't have guns, following in the pawprints of the faster-breeding wolves. It was sniffing the ground carefully; their eyesight was bad, and the glider probably too strange to assimilate readily into its mental vocabulary of shapes and smells. Then it realized where the blood-scent was coming from and reared. Suddenly the gaping roaring red mouth and white fangs were far far too close, only an arm's reach from the canopy.

Skrreeeetch.

A massive paw tipped with five long claws swiped across the tough synthetic. The whole fabric of the glider bucked and twisted; the bear outweighed it by a considerable margin, machine and pilot together. Alyssa smothered a scream of pain as her battered body was flung back and forth against the buckled metal of the cockpit like the clapper of a monastery bell with a mad monk hauling on the end of the rope.

Slap-slap-slap, and the bear's giant paws were working like pistons in a water-powered factory, tossing the glider back and forth the way a piñata at a posada party in Larsdalen swung under the sticks of shrieking blindfolded children. She'd done that herself as a kid.

The image wasn't as pleasant with herself as a meaty treat inside instead of hard candy and dried fruit and nuts. Metal buckled and tore with screeching sounds. Suddenly cold air and the rank scent of the bear flooded in as the canopy came off, torn from its hinges by a massive blow.

Alyssa snarled back at the animal, fumbling out the utility knife from its sheath on the leg of her leather flying suit and using her teeth to open the blade. The important time to show *sisukas* was when it was hard, which made this the absolutely ideal moment.

The four-inch knife was razor sharp. Maybe if she could slash the beast across the nose it would give up—

The grizzly stopped, peering at her with its massive barrel head cocked to one side. Its tongue came out like a red flag, sweeping over its nose.

You could see its mental processes working behind the little piggy eyes: *Smells like fresh meat. Injured, bleeding, helpless. Worth the trouble, yes-no? Yes. Go for it. Yum!*

Then it slouched back on its haunches, preparing for an upward lunge at the prize temptingly just out of easy reach. She swiped the air with the knife and shouted:

"Come *on*, you piece of fuzzy dogshit! Come get what Uncle Mike gave your second cousin once removed! I *am* a bear killer! *Haakaa päälle!*"

The monstrous humpbacked brown shape was unmistakable, Old Ephraim his every own self. Even these days grizzlies weren't common in the open sagebrush country Cole had grown up in, but he'd hunted black bear, and he'd talked to men who'd tackled Old Eph. Their advice had been heavy on the *don't try it alone*, but needs must.

Whung!

The crossbow kicked back against Cole's shoulder. He'd been aiming for the spine; the grizzly had its back to him as it reared on its hind legs towards the shouting pilot brandishing her pathetic little cheese-knife. Even with the x3 scope on his Special Forces model that was a chancy shot at a hundred yards and uphill. It *hit* the bear, he'd have put the next bolt into his own head if he'd completely missed that big a target with a scope and time to take careful aim and nice still air. But it struck just to the left of the backbone, slamming into the beast's massive body and probably smacking a rib loose along the way.

The bear staggered and twisted under the impact before it whirled to find what had struck it, bawling in rage with every hair bristling. Even the end cap of the twenty-inch bolt disappeared into the dark fur. This was an Army model built to drive through armor, not a hunting weapon; it had a thick steel prod made from salvaged leaf spring across the business end, and it could send a heavy shaft out at three hundred and fifty feet per second. He'd had a three-edged broadhead in the groove and more in the quiver, rather than just the standard-issue pile-shaped points. Men-at-arms in plate weren't the most likely targets in the mountains and the slashing effect made for a quicker kill.

One of the good points about being in the Special Forces was that you had wide latitude to tailor your gear to the mission.

For an instant the bear spun in place, convinced that something had bitten it. Then its nose went up for an instant, it caught his scent, the head went down and the whole mass headed his way in a shambling avalanche of fur, fangs and claws. Cole's hands were steady as he reloaded, but his mouth was a little dry, and he didn't waste any time admiring the first shot or wishing it had been two inches to the right and dropped the beast with a severed spinal cord. Instead he pumped frantically at the lever set into the forestock. Six seconds was the standard rapid-fire rate for cocking a GI crossbow; he managed to cut it to four, with another two to slap the next bolt from his belt-quiver into the groove under the holding clip and bring the weapon back to his shoulder.

Even so the beast's roaring muzzle was shockingly close through the scope. Old Eph could move faster than a galloping horse over short distances. They were nearly as quick as tigers for all their size. Cole let his breath out as his finger gently squeezed the trigger, with the cross-hairs on the base of the beast's neck. Then he turned and ran full-tilt along the path he'd picked out beforehand, slinging the weapon across his chest and cinching it tight as he went.

There was no need to look back. He knew exactly what was there, and he could hear its guttural bawling roars of pain and rage as it galloped. It was undoubtedly going to bleed out, but it would have plenty of time to catch Cole in a straightaway run first.

Up ten yards of steep rocky slope, and he could hear stones spurting from under the grizzly's paws. A forty-foot Douglas fir had fallen against a rock-face years ago, its trunk bleached white and hard as bone. He leapt onto it and ran along it at speed, preparing to jump to a ledge in the nearly vertical slope of dark basalt beyond. Even if it could walk on something this narrow, there was no way the log would carry its weight. Heavy animals were cautious about falling, since they hit a lot harder than men if they did.

The grizzly cast caution to the winds and tried to follow him up the tree-trunk anyway.

Cole pitched off with a yell as the far tip of the trunk broke away where it rested against the cliff. He curled himself into a ball around his crossbow as he fell ten feet or better, landing loose. Rocks punched at him as he landed and bounced and rolled, including one with stunning hurt over the kidneys and several glancing blows on his head; luckily the hood of his battle-smock took a little of it. Behind him the bear was scrabbling at the wood before it followed him in a slide that was half-fall, but he didn't waste any time looking at it or feeling his hurts.

Instead he came out of the roll running, leaping for a handhold in a rock-fissure. He went up four feet in the first jump, scrambled as much again as he grabbed frantically for plants and knobs of stone, then nearly fell again as something heavy slammed into the cliff below him. His hands clamped on a wrist-thick pine rooted in the cliff's face and jerked him upward. Instinct made him pull his feet up too, which was fortunate as something hit his right boot hard enough to tear the hobnailed heel half-loose.

The glancing impact of the bear's claws nearly twisted him free of his grip. Operating on reflex he used the momentum of the blow to swing himself upward and did a loop-over he couldn't have duplicated on a base gymnasium's equipment if he'd practiced for months. Pain jagged at his groin as he got one leg across the trunk of the pine and levered himself upright to stand on it.

"*Got* you!" he gasped down at the frenzied animal, almost inaudible even to himself beneath the bear's rasping battle cry.

Adrenaline fizzed through his body, and now his hands shook a little. The raving face of the bear was below him with the fletching of the second bolt just visible at the base of its neck. The open mouth sprayed blood and slaver, and it tried to scrabble up after him again. The claws swiped a foot beneath his boots.

"Here's where weighing half a ton and not having fingers is a drawback, Eph," he gasped. "Christ, if I ever get grandkids they'll never *believe* this one and they'll roll their eyes every time the old fart has one too many after dinner and trots it out."

He braced himself against the rough rock behind him, took several deep slow breaths, and began to reload the crossbow. The bear was moaning now as well as roaring, blood coughing out of its open mouth in gouts. He felt a slight twinge of pity, which was easier now that he was more or less safe.

"Sorry, Eph," he said, slipping in another bolt.

It was dying, but there was no point in letting it suffer. You could get killing angry at a man who plain chose to be an evil son-of-a-bitch, but a beast just . . . did what it did according to its nature. There was nothing personal in it, any more than there was in bad weather hammering a wheat-field ready to harvest or hoppers eating bare the pasture your sheep and cattle needed.

"But better you than me, and the brass will want that pilot alive to question," he finished, snuggling the butt into his shoulder and aiming downward.

Tung.

This time the head of the bolt was only six feet from the target. It flashed into the bear's open mouth and he could hear the bone crunch as it drove into the palate. The huge animal toppled backward and struck with an earthshaking thud, paws outstretched and belly up. Now he could see the head of his first bolt, the tip just show-ing; it must have traversed the whole width of the ani-mal's body.

When he reloaded and reached for his water-bottle his hands really *were* shaking, enough to spill water over his face. Cole stopped for a moment to just think himself steady, while he made doubly sure that the great limp furry form below him really wasn't breathing anymore. He suspected that the vision of the bear's face as it seemed to be right on the other end of the scope was going to come back to him at night for a long time.

One of the instructors who'd taught his class was a grizzled old coot who looked like he'd been carved out of ancient roots, and he'd been a Ranger back when the old General was a pup before the Change. He'd told them *adventure* meant *someone else in deep shit, far away.* Cole was beginning to appreciate what the man had meant.

Getting down from the ledge was a lot harder than going up had been, and his body felt like strong men had worked it over with baseball bats and bicycle chains from toe to chin. Each movement revealed some new bruise or nick or scrape, none of which had seemed important with Old Eph at his heels and all of which hurt like hell now. He walked back upslope towards the wrecked glider, keeping carefully alert and limping a little where the claws had taken the heel off his boot and wrenched the leg. Bears usually didn't travel in pairs, but you never knew. He'd do a quick fix on the footwear when he had some time.

When he arrived the pilot had managed to get herself out of the glider and down to the ground, probably by cutting herself free with the knife and falling. Her left arm looked to be out of commission, and her face was a mask of blood from a pressure cut on the forehead and a nose that was swelling after being smacked into something hard.

Curly leaf-brown hair peeked out from beneath a leather flying helmet with goggles pushed up on her brow; her eyes were light blue-green, but what he could see of her skin was a sort of pale toast color, save for a little bluish scar between her brows. The whole ensemble was probably exotically pretty in a pixie sort of way when she wasn't bleeding and beat-up. And, he judged by the way she'd been facing that bear, she was fully capable of chewing nails and spitting out rivets.

She'd just managed to get up on her feet when he arrived and stopped a couple of yards away, and she dropped into a fighter's crouch with the knife held in an expert grip. Cole started to laugh. She was also about a thumb's width over five feet, and skinny with it, confronting his five-ten and hundred and eighty pounds, not to mention his crossbow and hatchet and bowie and sword. Her scowl got more ferocious at his mirth, but she wasn't any more daunted by him than she had been by the bear that had been about to scoop her out of the cockpit like a nut out of its shell.

"You are one tough scrappy little bitch, I'll give you that," he said admiringly.

He was also careful to stay out of reach. Nobody was safe if they had a knife and were determined to use it.

"That's Pilot Officer Bitch to you, soldier," she said.

Briefings and rumor had it that westerners talked funny, but apart from the effects of her nose swelling shut she sounded pretty much like people from his part of the world, maybe a little rounder on the vowels. He looked at the glider caught in the rocks and trees, at the pilot, and thought hard. While he did he also looked at his left hand; one of the fingernails was standing up from the quick, mostly torn away. He absently stripped it loose with his teeth and spat it aside.

"Dang, that smarts," he said mildly. "Look, girl . . . Pilot Officer . . . what say we call a short-term truce while we fix ourselves up? That bear near enough got a piece of me and I don't think he meant you any good at all, likewise. I'd feel sort of stupid if I had to kill you now after going to all that trouble."

"You're Boise, aren't you?" she said; it wasn't really a question. "Not a Cutter."

"Yup, US Army," he said. "I'm a Methodist, more or less, if that matters to you."

"All right," she said grudgingly.

There was a spring seeping out of the rock not far away. He ended up donating some material from his medical kit, and then slitting the sleeve of the leather flying suit she wore along the seam to examine her left forearm. It was thin, though the slight muscles on it were like wire cords, and he couldn't feel any gross break. She hissed as he touched one spot.

"Ulna," he said. "Not a compound, and the elbow isn't dislocated. Nightstick fracture, I'd say, right about midway. Doesn't feel bad."

"Doesn't feel bad to *you*," she said. Then: "Yeah, that sounds about right."

He trimmed some deadwood branches into a set of immobilizing splints, bound them on, and arranged a sling. After that she sat sullenly brooding while he used his climbing rope and a half hitch around a tree to pull the glider down, breaking off the other wing in the process. The cockpit was disappointingly bare of anything useful; there was a map, but the only things marked on it were the suspected locations of *his* side's troops. Two that he knew about were pretty accurate.

Cole wasn't surprised at the lack of data, since whoever was in charge of enemy glider doctrine would have anticipated something exactly like this. If the enemy were stupid they wouldn't be winning. There wasn't anything in the way of emergency gear, either. Every single ounce of weight was precious in these things.

"Look . . ." he paused to give his name and rank.

"Pilot Officer Alyssa Larsson, on the A-List of the Bearkiller Outfit, flying for the High Kingdom of Montival," she said.

"OK," he said, organizing his thoughts. "Name, rank and serial number, right? You're not one of the castle freaks."

"A PPA Associate? I should hope *not*."

He nodded. "We've got two options here. I can just let you go, in which case you'll starve or get et by something or die of exposure. Unless your base is close—"

He lifted an enquiring eyebrow, and she laughed sourly at the invitation to fall into an elementary trick.

"OK, or you can surrender and I'll take you back to *my* base."

"How far, and in what direction?"

He snorted a chuckle. "I'm not an idiot either," he said, then nodded when she just smiled.

It was a wry expression, but then, it had to hurt with those injuries. He went on:

"Right. If you come with me, I want your word you won't try to backstab me or give me away to your people."

"I'm not going anywhere near the Cutters," she said flatly. "I'll take my chances with the wolves and bears and tigers first."

He kept his face neutral; his impulse was to say *well, of course, the Cutters are fucking mad weasel lunatic neobarbs*, but it wasn't something you could say to the other side about your sort-of allies. For that matter most of the westerners were officially neobarbs too. Instead he thought hard, and went on slowly: "My CO . . . Captain Wellman . . . ah," *Hates the Cutters like poison*, he didn't say.

They'd tried to put a Church Universal and Triumphant chaplain in with Battalion about three months ago, now that Boise didn't have a President to keep them at bay. The man had just disappeared two days after he arrived, and nobody had known a thing. He suspected that Wellman and the sergeant-major had taken care of it personally and buried the body in a latrine about to be filled in.

". . . ah, the CO is an absolute stickler for the rules."

Which had the advantage of being true; scuttlebutt said it was the reason Wellman hadn't switched sides, which some of the men thought he *should* do. Cole hadn't wanted to believe the stories about Martin Thurston, but with his own mother and his *wife*, for God's sake, defecting to the enemy and screaming that they were true . . . and he was dead now anyway, which left Fred Thurston as the old General's only living son, and *he* was on Montival's side.

Fubar squared.

The glider pilot looked at him searchingly for a long moment, then nodded slowly.

"My chances right now with a busted arm and no gear aren't much," she said. "OK, but I *will* take off if I get a chance and think the odds are good. I'm not giving a general parole. We're not allowed to, anyway."

"Fair enough, neither are we," he said. "Now, what about something to eat?"

She snorted and pulled out a paper-wrapped something from one of her many pockets. The wrapping had *Rat. Bar* stenciled on it.

"This is the sum total of my supplies. As the label suggests, it's made from dried rats."

Cole did a double take before he was sure she wasn't serious. He had a couple of pounds of hardtack and some dried fruit in his pack, along with some salt and half a bag of dried chili flakes his mother had sent him. He grinned anyway and felt the edge of his smaller knife, the one he used for general camp work, including skinning. Special Forces were supposed to live off the land in the field—they were known as *snake eaters* for that reason—but right now he didn't have to settle for reptile meat anyway.

"We won't starve today; pity the rest will go to waste and we can't take the hide, but the coyotes have to eat too. Bear tastes like pork."

"I always thought it was a little gamy unless you soak it in vinegar a while," she said. "Or beer."

The pilot started to smile, then winced as scabs pulled. "Not a feast at Larsdalen or Todenangst," she said. "But sort of . . . fitting."

CHAPTER THREE

Castle Todenangst, Crown demesne
Portland Protective Association
Willamette Valley near Newburg
(formerly western Oregon)
High Kingdom of Montival
(western North America)
June 15th, Change Year 26/2024 AD

Squire Lioncel de Stafford's muscles still ached very slightly from the morning's run in armor up and down the endless flights of stairs, with a shield on his left arm and a weighted wooden practice sword in his fist. Just enough that it felt good standing at parade rest behind the Grand Constable's chair, where she sat with the document-and-plate-laden table between her and the Lord Chancellor of the Association, Conrad Renfrew, Count of Odell.

The Silver Tower had the exotic luxury of a functioning elevator, powered by convicts on a treadmill in the dungeons, but Baroness Tiphaine d'Ath didn't believe in letting her *menie* go soft merely because they were stationed at HQ for a week.

She'd led the run, of course.

A confidential secretary from the Chancellor's office

took notes in shorthand, with an occasional *no, not that!* to halt the pen about to render permanent an embarrassingly frank opinion about some exalted personage. One of the Count's squires stood behind his wheelchair, and the Grand Constable's pages were serving a working lunch when they weren't standing silently against the far wall out of earshot; still, it was a sign of the trust attached to Lioncel's position that he was present as the two most powerful officials of the Association conferred in private.

Just now Tiphaine tapped one finger on a note signed in crimson ink:

"Sandra's gotten a complaint from the Seneschal's wife at Castle Oliver and passed it on to me with a flag for action after consulting you, Conrad."

Both the nobles lifted their eyes slightly at the mention of Sandra Arminger, formerly Lady Regent of the Association and now Queen Mother. There was nothing above this level save her apartments, the crenellations, cisterns, a heliograph station, a detachment of the Protector's Guard and the roof. The Queen Mother was doing pretty much the same work that she had as Lady Regent, and from the same places.

Lioncel carefully didn't look up. Lately she'd actually been noticing one Lioncel de Stafford a little beyond the pat-on-the-head level. Not in a bad way, but it could be alarming when things shifted like that.

"Castle Oliver . . . middle of the Okanagan . . . barony held in Crown demesne . . . twenty-two manors, the castle and a lot of grazing and woodland. The Seneschal would be Sir Symo Herrera," the Chancellor said. "His wife . . . Lady Aicelena of the Chelan Dennisons. Aicelena's running the place while Sir Symo's away, the usual."

Conrad of Odell was nearly sixty and built like a squat muscular toad, with a face that would have looked coarse-featured and rugged even if it hadn't been terribly burned long ago. A bit gaunt now, without the spare flesh he'd had before the Battle of the Horse Heaven Hills last year. He'd been smacked off his destrier there and suffered a hairline fracture of the pelvis. He was out of traction, but still wearing a long embroidered robe with wide sleeves, informal garb for an invalid, which looked rather odd with the massive gold chain of office.

Tiphaine nodded. "Sir Symo's at the front with the Oliver levy . . . he's been doing quite well, too."

"So has she," Conrad said thoughtfully. "Deliveries on time, no major complaints, the books balanced last time I send auditors around, and she doesn't keep asking to have her hand held. What's her problem, and why didn't it come direct to me? Why does the military side need to get involved?"

"Apparently a party of men-at-arms on their way south from County Dawson, seventy-three lances and followers plus some light horse, stopped there. Lady Aicelena quite properly invited the chevaliers and esquires in for dinner and had an ox-roast put on in the courtyard for the rest."

"Ouch," the Chancellor said. "I think I can see what's coming."

Another nod, this one short and curt. "They repaid her by dropping the drawbridge and then emptied the storehouses in the castle bailey and the barns in the home manor of everything a horse could eat. Nobody hurt and nothing else taken except for a couple of chickens, but from the description it was as near as no matter robbery at spear-point."

Conrad nodded in turn. "After the Crown emergency requisitions, that was probably the last surplus the area has," he said thoughtfully. "Except what can be bought in at wartime prices."

"Right. That cupboard's going to be bare when the next *legitimate* call comes."

The Lord Chancellor and the Grand Constable both had suites on the level just below the Queen Mother; it made conferences like this easier. Much of the Portland Protective Association's government was handled from here in the great fortress-palace of Todenangst, and the hierarchy of status was quite literal; the higher up the massive ferroconcrete bulk of the Silver Tower you were, the more exalted the rank and the less there was of the tomb-like gloom usual in castles. This high there were pointed-arch windows and balconies, letting in a flood of afternoon light through the Gothic tracery along with plenty of fresh air slightly laden with smells of woodsmoke and flowers.

Lioncel still felt a slight chill at the tone of his liege's voice; calm and even and . . . angry. There were reasons her title of *Lady d'Ath* was usually pronounced *Lady Death*.

"That was also Royal property they took, especially if they didn't pay," the Chancellor said.

"Not a penny. Our northern heroes just made noises about military necessity and hightailed it on down the main rail line towards the Columbia, radiating innocence and dribbling stolen alfalfa-pellets and cracked barley."

"Who was the Dawson commander?"

"Sir Othon Derby," Tiphaine said.

Conrad Renfrew closed his eyes, consulting some inner file before he spoke:

"He's the second son of Lord Hardouin Derby, Baron

de Taylor, one of Count Enguerrand of Dawson's major vassals. Arms: *Argent, on a bend azure three buck's heads cabossé d'or.* With a crescent of cadency, of course. Twenty years old, reputation as a hothead, engaged to one of the Count's daughters. Bit young for an independent command, I'd have thought."

"Temporary command; Enguerrand sent him back north to bring in this bunch as replacements for others we're letting go home for one reason or another. The new levy were mostly men who've come of age since the Prophet's War started."

"How long since they were called up?" the Chancellor asked.

"When they arrived at Oliver it was twenty-three days since they took the oath at Castle Dawson's muster-yard," Tiphaine said, a hint of satisfaction in her voice.

Ah, Lioncel thought. *That's the official start of their period of service.*

Landholders, from counts and barons down to footmen holding fiefs-minor in sergeantry, were liable to war-service whenever their overlords or the Crown called. That was what being an Associate was *about*, after all—fighting to protect the realm, which was why a special dagger was the mark of belonging to the Association. The first forty days after a summons to the *ban* were at the fief-holder's own expense, though. Only after that was the Crown obliged to furnish maintenance, with a right to draw on Royal storehouses.

So they wouldn't be able to plead even a shadow of law-fulness, he thought.

Unexpectedly Tiphaine turned slightly. "Lioncel," she said. "Your opinion—concisely."

Lioncel gulped; having questions like that shot at you was one of the less attractive parts of moving up from page to squire.

"Umm . . . definitely unchivalrous conduct towards a gentlewoman, my lady, unworthy of a knight. And a violation of the terms of service. This Sir Othon *was* obliged to see to his men's provisioning, but that doesn't mean he can act like a bandit on Association territory . . . or anywhere in Montival. Plus it will leave a hole in our supply plans in that area, and it's a major north-south corridor. My lady."

"Correct," Tiphaine said, making a small gesture that stiffened him back into anonymity.

"Sandra *so* does not like getting ripped off," Conrad of Odell said, looking upward. "We used to call it *an aggressive zero-tolerance policy.*"

"You don't say," Tiphaine said dryly, glancing in the same direction. "She *is* my patron too, Conrad."

She snapped her fingers without looking around. "Boy! The Count of Dawson's status reports," she said.

The Baroness of Ath was forty and looked ageless in the way people who spent their days outdoors in all weathers often did, a tall woman with a build like a swordblade, her sun-faded silver-blond hair cut in a bob much like those worn by pages, and eyes the gray of sea-ice. Her male-style court dress of curl-toed shoes, hose, shirt, jerkin and houppelande coat were as plain as ceremony allowed and mostly shades of rich dark fabrics, relieved only by her chain of office and the small golden spurs of knighthood. A round chaperon hat hung on one ear of her tall chair, the liripipe dangling.

Lioncel slid the logistics file she'd called for forward

and stepped back behind her chair, standing in the formal posture with one hand on the hilt of his sword and the other over the heavy cut-steel buckle of the sword belt. That let him feel more than hear the rumbling of his stomach. He'd had a very substantial lunch and he was hungry *again* hours short of dinnertime; everyone laughed and told him it was being fourteen and shooting up like a weed.

"Oh, by Our Lady of the Citadel," Tiphaine said after a moment, flicking pages.

Odd, Lioncel thought. *I've never heard that used as one of the Virgin's titles before.*

She went on: "Did the man seriously expect to ship fodder all the way south from *Dawson* for his destriers? Without the railway draught teams eating everything they were pulling by the time they got to the Okanagan country? Enguerrand's a Count these days; it doesn't give him supernatural powers."

Conrad flicked through the same file and grinned, an alarming expression as the thick white keloid scars on his face knotted.

"They've got a lot more oats than money in the Peace River country and Dawson levies haven't fought down here in the south much. At a guess, back when the *ban* was called out at the start of this war my lord Enguerrand told his quartermasters to get the fodder wherever it was cheapest and then forgot about it. Then *they* tried to draw on his own elevators full of nice cheap tribute grain before they realized how shipping costs would screw their cash flow, and ever since then they've been robbing Peter to pay Paul. Coming up short now and then, which was where young Sir Othon found himself, I'd wager. And there's not much coin circulating up there even now, too remote. Just not used to paying cash for grain."

"The Count will pay for this, and a fine, plus compensation-money to Lady Aicelena for the abuse of her hospitality," Tiphaine said flatly. "Or Baron de Taylor will. And the bold Sir Othon can see how he likes a month of attitude adjustment in Little Ease."

Lioncel winced behind an impassive face as the older nobles smiled, or at least showed their teeth. *Little Ease* was a dungeon oubliette beneath the Onyx Tower, a cramped cell carefully designed to make it impossible for an inmate to either lie or stand or sit properly, not to mention the rough knobby surface and utter blackness and total silence and cold and filth and damp. Sending people there was done by the prerogative Court called *Star Chamber* . . . over which the Queen Mother would preside.

"Oh, a month . . . that's a bit much, unless you want a gibbering madman," Conrad said cheerfully. "A week would be about right. It'll just *feel* like months. Like forever and a day in Hell, in fact."

"All right, a week. You're getting soft, Conrad."

Conrad's smile grew more alarming. "You can be a bit . . . drastic . . . when you're peeved. That's probably why Sandra had you consult me, you know. We want to *discipline* Sir Othon and his lieges, not drive them to desperation. Besides, we've reformed. We're the good guys these days. Sorta."

"Sorta, kinda." Tiphaine rubbed one hand across her forehead. "I don't have time for this crap. Our command structure is still scrambled six ways from St. Swithin's Day. I'm being bounced back and forth from here to

Portland to the front like a Ping-Pong ball. Trailing files and letters like a comet's tail. And you would be too, Conrad, if you weren't in that wheelchair."

Conrad Renfrew shrugged.

"If the High Kingdom of Montival were a human being it'd still be in diapers," he said. "And His Majesty is trying to run a war with what used to be six or seven separate armies two years ago. Us, and six separate armies built to *fight* us plus bits and pieces of odds and sods. It's not *our* command structure, even if we're the biggest single element; it's *Montival's* command structure. And yes, it's fucked."

The Lord Chancellor chuckled like gravel shaken in a bucket.

"And *Ping-Pong*? Pre-Change metaphors are *so* twentieth century for a near-Changeling like you. You're dating yourself, Tiph."

"Dating myself? Doesn't that make you go blind?"

Didn't dating *also mean something like* courtship *before the Change? Then—*

Lioncel suppressed a startled giggle with an effort that made him cough as he struggled to maintain adult *gravitas.*

Lioncel had the same fair hair and blue eyes as his father Lord Riobert de Stafford and a similar bold cast of features, and his hands and feet gave promise of equal height, but so far a lot of it was adolescent gawkiness and his sire's easy natural dignity was only an aspiration. It was like your voice breaking occasionally and having impure thoughts about girls every thirty seconds, about which even his confessor had to work to keep the smile out of his voice. Evidently it all just went with his age.

At least I don't have pimples. Well, not many.

"I wouldn't like to be in Sir Othon's boots when the Count learns how he avoided asking for money. Over and above what we're going to do to him," Renfrew said.

"His own damned fault and a valuable life-lesson for the lot of them."

"At least my lord Enguerrand isn't complaining about stripping his eastern border anymore. They're still paranoid about the Canuks up there," the Chancellor said.

As the Grand Constable's squire—and before that as a page, and before that simply as the son of Lady Delia de Stafford, who'd been the Grand Constable's Châtelaine since before he was born—Lioncel had been in and out of these rooms for years. He found himself more self-conscious about their function now that he was older and knew more about it. It was no longer simply a place he lived sometimes, like Montinore Manor back in the barony of Ath that he thought of as *really home*, or the townhouse near Portland.

Tiphaine spread the long callused fingers of her right hand slightly, half a gesture of agreement, half a motion like touching a swordhilt.

"Taking Dawson wasn't really cost-effective, no matter how much plowland it has or even how many extra workers we got. I remember distinctly at the time Sandra thought Norman was getting Big Eyes syndrome again, pushing our frontier that far north," she said. "Risky. We were overstretched."

Renfrew shrugged. "Our big advantage was getting organized first, and at least *suspecting* where the pointy end of the sword went, not to mention *having* swords and not just kitchen knives on sticks. That was a wasting asset. Norman knew we had to use it or lose it."

"Norman just liked looking at the map and rubbing his hands and saying: *Mine, all mine! BWA-HA-HA-HA-HA!*"

"Yeah, that's him to the life, but it worked. And half the time back then we hardly had to fight at all to take over, people were so glad to see someone who knew what they were doing and had a plan. Later . . . later it got a whole lot harder."

"We had to fight for Dawson, all right," she said. "And then fight *seriously* to keep it when the Drumheller government got their act in gear and decided to restore British Columbia."

Conrad spread his massive hairy spade-shaped hands. "By then we had some castles built, and they never did manage to cleanse us from the sacred soil . . . or permafrost . . . of Canukistan."

"They certainly tried. The Yakima is a lot warmer and closer, and we could have rolled up the rest of the towns there after the Tri-Cities fell, if we hadn't had so many troops chasing Canuks through the snowdrifts and getting frostbite, also arrows in the rump."

The Count nodded. "Remember the February campaign? Back in . . . Change Year Five, or Six, wasn't it? You were doing scout work there with . . . mmm, Katrina Georges? She died four or five years later, in that ratfuck rescue attempt with Eddie Liu after the Mackenzies kidnapped Mathilda? Dawson would have been your first real war, apart from all that black-bag and spec-ops work you two were doing as Sandra's Teen Ninjas."

"Change Year Five *and* Six," Tiphaine said, her voice softening a little. "Kat and I were doing scouting, right . . . we actually *were* scouts before the Change, you know. Girl Scouts. It's the main reason we didn't die."

The Chancellor frowned. "I thought you were a gymnast? Olympic hopes and all that?"

"Gymnastics first, but Kat talked me into the Scouts in 'ninety-seven, my mother pitched a fit . . . Sandra pulled some strings to have us attached to the reconnaissance element for the Dawson campaign. Norman thought we were a joke, but she wanted us to broaden our skill-sets. And get some mojo with the regulars."

"Ah, right. I remember you two mousetrapped that Mountie deep-penetration patrol. A nice change from all the times the sneaky bastards did it to us. Yes, and you marched up and plopped the heads down on the breakfast table and said *Pray allow us to present some friends, my lord*. He didn't think *that* was a joke!"

"He laughed, Conrad. He laughed so hard he snarfed his porridge and you had to pound him on the back. Kat offered to do the Heimlich on him and then he turned blue."

You can always tell when older people are reminiscing, Lioncel thought indulgently. *They start using that old-fashioned way of speech, even my lady isn't quite a Change-ling that way.*

"He didn't think *you* were a joke anymore. The heads, yes, that hit him right in the funny bone."

"We did think it would cheer people up," Tiphaine said, a little amusement in her tone.

"That was when I really first noticed you. *That girl will go far*, I thought, and now you've got my old job."

Conrad shivered reminiscently and crossed himself before he went on:

"I also thought I'd never feel warm again, and it was so damned dark all the time. . . ."

Tiphaine gave a half-snort: "I remember trying to pee and my armor being so cold that skin stuck hard to the metal *anywhere* it touched," she said. "That and the way the Canuk ski troops kept working around our flanks through the woods. If they'd had more body armor and cavalry it would have been impossible."

Conrad sighed as he referenced a letter and murmured to his clerk. "Enough about the old days, let's get the rest of these supply projections sorted."

"All right, let's start with the barges and that elderly hardtack we have stockpiled at Goldendale—"

Watching the Chancellor and my lady the Grand Constable do their work is . . . educational, Lioncel thought as he stood and directed the page boys with flicks of his hand. *Well, I'm the Grand Constable's squire; I'm supposed to be learning.*

They went through the rest of the stack of documents at a pace that made him blink, usually talking in an elliptical compressed way that showed how many years they'd worked together and stopping just long enough to chew when they took a bite of the lunch collation.

"That's all for now, Mistress Brunisente," Conrad said to the senior clerk when they came to the bottom of the stack. "Get me a typewritten transcript by tomorrow and do a précis."

"Copies, my lord?"

"No carbons. We'll circulate it under seal to the Queen Mother and Chancellor Ignatius after we go over it. No need to bother Their Majesties with this unless the Chancellor-slash-Questing Monk says so. Rudi and Mathilda have enough on their plates."

The clerk took the hint, bobbed a curtsy and left.

"Good enough," Tiphaine d'Ath said.

She leaned back, stretching her arms far behind her and tilting her head to one side and then the other until there was a sharp *click*.

"As far as the Association contingent goes we're golden on the supply situation for the rest of this campaigning season," she said. "Especially since His Majesty's letting a lot of our infantry go back to their villages and plow."

"The downside of that is that we're cutting the size of the field force because we can't feed that many so far from the Columbia, not because Rudi couldn't use the men," Conrad grunted. "Anyway, it's time the rest did their share, and their foot soldiers are just about as good as ours. Nobody else has anything like our men-at-arms, though."

"The Bearkillers come fairly close. Nobody else has anything like the Mackenzie Archers, either," Tiphaine said and shrugged. "Our knights are more use on campaign than they are back home beating on each other at tournaments and hawking and boozing, and only a little more expensive."

"*You* don't have to find the money to pay their stipends," Renfrew said. "*Or* pay to replace their beloved destriers when the bloody things die in the field—you wouldn't think something so big would be so fragile. Those damned gee-gees cost more than a suit of plate and they wear out a whole hell of a lot faster."

Lioncel was mildly shocked at the way the Count was talking about the noble beasts. Nearly everyone he knew loved their destriers and coursers, but you had to make allowances for the older generation. It took six years to breed and train a charger fit to bear an armored lancer into battle wearing armor of its own. He'd been unpleasantly surprised to find out that their average life expectancy on active campaign was around ten months. Even the High King's fabled steed Epona, who'd gone all the way to the Sunrise Lands and back with him on the Quest, had died at the Horse Heaven Hills.

"The knights pay war-tallage anyway," Tiphaine said. "So it's out of one pocket and into another. And the Crown owns a lot of the horse-breeding farms, plus we have insurance. The Counts aren't complaining really seriously either, it's just the usual moaning bitchery and mine-is-bigger bickering. Ah, the delights of feudalism."

"If you think this is bad, you should have seen what SCA politics were like before the Change. Truly murderous, at least as far as emotions went."

"Society politics? With so little at stake?" Tiphaine asked.

"*Because* so little was at stake by modern standards. And notice that the Counts bitch to *me*," Conrad said. "Not to you."

"They're not as afraid you'll kill them, my lord Chancellor. And you *are* a Count, of course."

"Nobody likes paying taxes . . . also of course. Wait until they see what Matti plans to levy on them for the reconstruction program," Conrad said, using the familiar form of High Queen Mathilda's name.

Of course, he's been around her since she was a baby, Lioncel thought charitably. *And the older generation . . . well, you have to make allowances.*

The Count of Odell shuddered slightly for effect, then rubbed his hands together and grinned. "Sandra's drawing up one of her little *lists.*"

"You seem to be working well with Father Ignatius, by the way," Tiphaine said.

"He's very capable," Conrad Renfrew said, nodding and running a spade-shaped hand over his head, mostly naturally bald now rather than shaven as had been his custom for decades. "Even if he disapproves of me."

"Ignatius disapproves of me a lot more," Tiphaine said. "I can't say he's my favorite person in all the world either, though he and Matti are close. And he'd *better* be able, with his job. He gives it everything he's got, I grant him that."

The Knight-Brother was a Lord Chancellor too, but of the whole of the new High Kingdom of Montival. The warrior cleric had won great glory and ringing fame for himself and his Order of the Shield of St. Benedict at the High King's side on the quest to Nantucket. He'd had a vision of the Virgin, too, which was awe-inspiring.

But Their Majesties gave him high office for his talents, Lioncel thought. *The Order are scholars as well as warriors.*

They'd also been leaders in the old wars . . . on the side *against* the Portland Protective Association, despite the Lord Protector's championing of the Faith. Of course, technically the Protectorate had been in schism in those days; all contact with Rome had ceased on the day of the Change and for better than a decade after, and Norman Arminger had found a bishop willing to claim the Throne of St. Peter. Rome was a haunted ruin now, but a legitimately chosen Holy Father ruled the universal Church from the Umbrian city of Badia.

Curiosity as to why the Lord Protector's chosen anti-pope Leo had survived him by less than a month was *strongly discouraged* in the Association lands. Officially it was a heart attack, providentially easing the task of re-union.

Unofficially, from things overheard at home, Lioncel knew Sandra Arminger had sent one Tiphaine d'Ath to untraceably turn him from a problem into a memory, though it had been before he was born. That sort of thing didn't happen nearly as often nowadays. . . .

Conrad laughed. "Though unlike me, Ignatius only has to bust his ass for the Crown *metaphorically*."

"That joke was funny the first seventeen times, Conrad," she said in a coolly neutral voice. "And you started the min-ute the field medics told you what the problem was."

"Not until they got the morphine into me; before that I just screeched and swore. And I paid for that *joke* with months of my ass being *literally* in a sling and I'll use it as often as I damned well please," he said cheerfully. "Still, it's all more fun than it was in the old days."

He nodded out the pointed-arch window that lit the dayroom. That looked south across the courtyard to the glittering gold-tipped black height of the Onyx Tower, the Lord Protector's old lair.

Tiphaine snorted slightly, but Lioncel thought it had a wealth of meaning.

"Granted Norman blossomed into a tyrant's tyrant when he got the opportunity, but he wasn't *all* bad," Conrad said a little defensively.

Conrad of Odell had also been a fixture of Lioncel's life—besides his duties, his Countess and her daughters were good friends of Lioncel's mother—but at times like this you remembered that the unofficial uncle who'd played "bear" with you in front of the hearth had also been the Lord Protector's right-hand man. He was beginning to suspect that being disconcerted that way by sudden shifts in perspective was another . . . disconcerting thing about being his age.

Mother told me once she'd heard from the Countess of Odell that the Armingers stood by him when he got those burns on his face, way back before the Change.

"Ninety percent absolutely rotten bad," Tiphaine said shortly.

"Except that we'd all have been gnawed bones without him. *I* sure as shit had no earthly idea what to do when the Change hit and the machines stopped, and he *did*. Ah, well, it's ancient history. I think we've wrapped up all the essentials and you've had a chance to look over the replacements we're sending forward. They're eager enough."

"They're ironhead macho imbeciles who need to be bled, to correct the balance of their humors," she said crisply. "Which I will see to. Not to mention learning that there's more to war than couching a lance and sticking spurs in a horse's ass."

"Better to restrain the noble steed than prod the reluctant mule. Give my regards to Rudi . . . His Majesty . . . when you're back in the cow-country."

"The Prophet's men did a good cloud-of-locusts imitation out there to slow pursuit. It's *gnawed bones* country, since you brought up the phrase, with cows pretty scarce. The buzzards there have to carry their own rations," she said.

"Speaking of which, here's the grant," he said, pulling a last formidable-looking document out of a folder and tossing it in front of her. "That'll keep you travelling out there the rest of your life!"

"Joy," she said. "Thank you . . . I suppose."

"Hey, it's free! That's always a bargain."

"Like getting fifteen million tons of undelivered Arizona sand for sixpence ha'penny," she said dryly. "Don't work yourself to death while I'm gone, Conrad. I'd rather snog wolverines in a confessional booth than be saddled with the job you've got *now*."

The Count of Odell picked up the ebony cane that leaned against his wheelchair, tapped it on the marble tiles of the floor and waved it forward as he cried:

"En avant!"

There was a ripple of bows as his squire wheeled him out.

"Clear this up, Tasin," Lioncel said, when nobody was left but the Grand Constable's household.

The senior page—he was Tasin Jones, one of the younger brothers of Count Chaka of Molalla—slid forward and helped the younger pair clear the remains of lunch. His square brown face was intent; he'd entered the d'Ath household barely six months ago. Lioncel had been a page himself until last August, and he remembered how anxious you could get at the thought something would go wrong while you were attending the lords. It would be worse for Tasin, since he hadn't grown up with the Grand Constable, just knew her fearsome reputation.

He was shaping well, though, now that he'd gotten

over homesickness. Lioncel gave him a discreet wink and a thumbs-up when the job was done, and got a brief broad smile in exchange.

The plates held the remains of a lunch of cold spiced pork loin, a long loaf of white bread, sharp Tillamook cheese, sweet butter, a green salad and fruit tarts; the sort of plain good fare Tiphaine d'Ath preferred even at court. At a gesture, Tasin poured her another glass of watered wine and one for the squire and left the carafe. The pages made a little procession as they took the plates out to hand off to the castle staff; they were eyeing the uneaten blueberry tarts too, since those were their lawful prerogative . . . though as he remembered it the staff would get them as often as not.

One of the points of page service was to teach young noblemen humility, learning to obey among strangers before they commanded at home. And that good things didn't simply appear by magic when you waved your hand.

"Lioncel, attend," Tiphaine said.

They were about as alone as you ever got at court. A tinkle came from a wind chime near the windows, and one of the interior walls of the big room was mostly bookshelves and map-racks, with a trophy of crude spears taken in some skirmish long ago crossed over a shield made from a battered-looking *STOP* sign above the swept and empty hearth. The furniture was understated and strongly built, mostly rubbed oak lightly carved and brown tooled leather held by brass rivets; a tapestry showed Castle Ath across a landscape of forest and vineyard and huntsmen bringing in boars, and the rugs were patterned with birds twining through vines.

The decor suited the Grand Constable perfectly, down to the hunting trophies—a stuffed boar's head, tiger and bear-skins—but she wouldn't have bothered about it herself. His mother had furnished the place, part of her duties as Châtelaine. In effect, general manager of the whole civilian side of the barony, from interior decoration to keeping the reeves and bailiffs honest and arranging apprenticeships for deserving youngsters. In the last few years he'd started to realize just how much *work* that involved, something that had taken a while not least because his mother always made it look either effortless or enjoyable. And how not only the baron's interests but the comfort and livelihoods of hundreds of families depended on it.

"My lady?" he said.

"Time for a little question-and-answer, boy."

It had also been just recently that he really realized what it meant that Lady Delia de Stafford lived with the Grand Constable, and that his father was perfectly content with the arrangement. It hadn't made all that much difference, though he was a good Catholic himself. They were the people he'd grown up around, after all, the ones he knew and loved.

His liege jerked her thumb towards a stool. Lioncel de Stafford was a dutiful young man. He bowed and sank down with a perfectly genuine expression of alert interest. Squirehood involved a lot of lectures, if your liege was conscientious; it was the aristocracy's equivalent of apprenticeship. His liege-lady was always worth listening to and didn't just talk because she liked the sound of her own voice.

"What did you gather from all that?" she said, inclining her head towards the door the Lord Chancellor had used.

Tiphaine had always been kind enough to Delia's children, but the Grand Constable wasn't a woman who had much use for youngsters. As he got older she was paying more and more attention to him, which was intriguing and disturbing in about equal measure. They were a long way from equals; he didn't know if they ever would be that, since she was terrifyingly capable at all of a noble's skills save some of the social ones. But he'd put his foot on the bottom rung.

"That some of the great families are starting to bicker and complain, my lady. Even though the war isn't over!" Lioncel said, trying to keep the heat out of his voice.

He'd had a ringside seat the last few years, old enough to no longer assume victory was automatic, and things had often looked . . .

Very bad indeed, he thought. *Before the Quest returned with the High King and the Sword . . . very bad.*

"We won the decisive battle at the Horse Heaven Hills, and Rudi killed Martin Thurston to put the brandied cherry on the whipped cream," Tiphaine said in a cool even voice, wine-cup between her long fingers. "That leads to . . . premature relaxation. Mistaking *are winning* for *having won.*"

"Last year the enemy *were winning,* and look what happened to *them.* The Prophet isn't dead yet! Are these people *stupid?*" Lioncel burst out. "My lady," he added hastily.

"Some of them are. The rest . . . just arrogant and shortsighted and obsessed with who's getting precedence. And in love with their own supreme awesomeness, particularly since it was a classic chivalric bull-at-a-gate charge with the lance that finished off the battle, like something out of a *chanson*. They tend to forget the rest."

Lioncel looked down at his glass. He'd always loved the songs and still did, and the great charge *had* been like one of the *chansons* about Arthur or Charlemagne and their paladins come to life.

When eight thousand lances crested the ridge in a blaze of steel and plumes and rearing destriers . . . and then the oliphants screamed the charge *à l'outrance* . . .

It would be a thing of pride for the rest of his life to have taken part, even in a junior squire's place behind the line . . . but he'd seen enough of real war now to realize that the troubadours tended to dwell on a very narrow part of it.

And to leave out things like what a man looks like after a conroi's worth of barded destriers have galloped over him. Or maybe it was a man and a horse to start with, I couldn't tell for sure in a single glance.

Tiphaine raised one pale brow, as if she was following his thoughts.

"When we were desperate, politics got damped down," she said. "Now, not so much."

"Yes, my lady," Lioncel said. He thought for a moment, then: "Still, it's better to have the problems of victory than those of defeat."

She gave a thin small smile. "True. You're learning, boy."

And high politics is a lot less boring than classes in feudal law, he thought.

Then she handed him the vellum folio that the Lord Chancellor had given her.

"Your lady mother will be handling most of this, but give me your take."

He picked it up and read. The snowy material of split lambskin smoothed with pumice and lime was reserved for the most important documents, ones that went into the permanent record for reference and had lots of brightly illuminated capitals. The text was bilingual in English and Law French, which he could follow after a fashion, even done in the distinctive *littera parisiensis* Fraktur typeface of the Chancellery of the Association. It included a map and references to the cadastral land survey.

The familiar forms leapt out at him; every nobleman took a keen interest in land grants. There was going to be a new entry in the next edition of *Fiefs of the Portland Protective Association: Tenants in Chief, Vassals, Vavasours and Fiefs-minor in Sergeantry.*

His eyebrows went up and he stopped himself from whistling softly with a conscious effort at the acreage listed.

The signatures were *Conradius Odeliae Comes, Dominus Cancellarius Consociationis Defensivae Portlandensis* and *Mathilda, Dei Gratia Princeps Regina Montivalae et Domina Defensor Consociationis Defensivae Portlandensis,* complete with all three privy seals in red wax over ribbons.

That translated as Conrad, Count of Odell, Lord Chancellor of the Portland Protective Association and Mathilda, by the Grace of God—

And marriage to Rudi Mackenzie, Artos the First, of course.

—High Queen of Montival and Lady Protector—

That in her own hereditary right.

—of the PPA.

"That's . . . that's a *very generous* fief you've been

granted, my lady. Much bigger than the Barony of Ath! Congratulations!"

His warm glow of delight was entirely unselfish; Lioncel was heir only to Barony Forest Grove. As adopted son of the Grand Constable his younger brother Diomede would inherit the title and lands of Barony Ath, the original fief in the Tualatin Valley west of Portland and the new grant too. His sister Heuradys was an adopted daughter of d'Ath, too, for similar reasons; it left House Stafford and House d'Ath each with one son to inherit and one daughter to dower, a perfect set for succession purposes.

Tiphaine nodded, her long regular face tilting a little to watch his, her ice-colored eyes considering as they met his bright blue. They looked enough alike in face and feature and build as well as coloring to be close blood kin, though they weren't.

"Not quite as generous as it looks at first glance, boy," she said. "It's in the Palouse out east, not the Willamette."

Lioncel frowned. He'd been too young then to really follow things, but . . .

"Didn't we—the Association—split the Palouse with old President-General Lawrence Thurston of Boise just before the war, my lady?"

"Right, and a couple of armies have passed that way since, so the only other living claimants are pronghorns and prairie dogs. Good wheat and sheep land, though; it's near a rail line when we get that fixed, and there's water enough given work and money. By the time Diomede's my age, it'll be valuable."

"Their Majesties are generous," Lioncel said, thinking

hard. "But you certainly deserve it, my lady. You've been a, ah, a pillar of the dynasty"—that had started with her working as an assassin for Lady Sandra, early on. Right after the Change, during the Foundation Wars, when she was only a little older than he was now—"since the beginning!" he concluded, tactfully.

She'd also been a duelist in the Crown's interest, and still had a chest full of expired *lettres de cachet* signed "Sandra Arminger" and inscribed with the dreaded phrase: *the bearer has done what has been done by my authority, and for the good of the State.*

"And you commanded the rearguard on the retreat from Walla Walla last year, and led the charge at the Horse Heaven Hills. A good lord rewards his most faithful vassals with land. It's the only wealth that's really real."

My lady wants me to pick something out here. What is it? What am I missing?

"OK, Lioncel, look at it as if *you* were on the throne. What's the reason *not* to spill land grants wholesale like candied nuts out of a piñata?"

"Ummm . . . well, God isn't making any more land, my lady. Fiefs are hereditary so it's a lot easier to give it out than to get it back into the Crown demesne."

"Right. Now, specifics: Sandra Arminger already sponsored me into the Association in the first place, knighted me with her own hands, and gave me everything I have. She was your mother's sponsor too. And I was one of Mathilda's tutors for a long time. I . . . and your parents . . . owe everything to her family."

"Well, yes, my lady. Put that way, House Arminger have been extremely generous already."

"So even if you didn't know me personally, can you imagine me *not* being loyal to the Crown?"

"Ah . . . put that way, no, my lady. It's sort of proverbial, in fact."

They call you the Lady Regent's Stiletto, actually. Or just Lady Death. Which is a pun on d'Ath, but they mean it.

"And apart from the fact that I *want* to be loyal, there's the additional fact that I'm disliked by the Church, and hated by a lot of lay nobles whose relatives I've killed. I've been generously rewarded with land and office, and I . . . and your parents . . . need the Crown's ongoing protection. Why give me more?"

"Well . . . it's good lordship to reward service with an open hand," Lioncel said, beginning to sweat slightly. "It's not supposed to be a *bribe*, after all. It's *recognition*, it bestows honor, not just revenues."

"True, and with Matilda . . . and Rudi . . . good lordship means a lot. They like me personally too, oddly enough, and more understandably they like Delia . . . your lady mother."

"Ah . . ." Greatly daring, Lioncel cleared his throat. "My lady? Do *you* like the High King?"

He'd seen them working together, but his liege wasn't a demonstrative person. He was fairly sure that she regarded the High Queen as something like a younger sister, but he couldn't tell with Rudi Mackenzie. The ice-gray eyes considered him, and there was a very slight nod of approval.

"Yes, I do," she said. "And as you may have learned by now, I'm not given to easy likings."

He nodded. A couple of hours would be enough to

learn *that*, much less a lifetime. It took him an instant more to realize that Tiphaine was making a dry joke.

As if I were a grown man, he thought with a mixture of pride and, oddly, a faint sadness.

"More importantly, we . . . respect each other. While he was living up here part-time—"

That had been part of the peace settlement after the Protector's War; the Mackenzie heir had come north, and Mathilda Arminger had spent time every year in Dun Juniper.

"—I helped teach him the sword, among other things. You'd be too young to recall most of that, and mainly it was at court, not Ath."

Lioncel nodded; he had vague memories of visits, no more. Tiphaine's face went a little distant, as if looking into time.

"He's really extremely good. Mathilda always tried her hardest and she's better than average. But Rudi . . . he's a natural, and he soaked up technique like a dry sponge does water. The only man I ever sparred with as fast as I was. A bit faster, now; he's at his peak and I'm a little past mine. And even experts usually can't strike full force without losing either speed or precision. I can, but so can Rudi . . . and he's *extremely* strong."

Another pause, and Lioncel nodded soberly. He'd had glimpses of the High King fighting with his own hands during the tag end of the great battle, the savage scrimmage around Martin Thurston's banner, and it had been . . .

Frightening, he decided. Even on that field of wholesale butchery, even if you'd been raised among swordmasters. *Like some pagan God of war come to life.*

"Most men remember grudges; Rudi never forgets anyone who does him a good turn," Tiphaine went on. "And he always returns loyalty. That was obvious even when I first met him, when he was younger than Diomede is now."

Her eyes met his. "You'll start out with his favor, for my sake and your parents', but to keep it, you'll have to *earn* it. Never forget that."

"I won't, my lady," Lioncel said seriously.

"Good. Because when he has to be, the High King is . . . well, you've heard the saying: *Mercy to the guilty is cruelty to the innocent*? He won't spare himself in the kingdom's service, and he won't spare *you*, either. Which brings us back to the grant. What's the *realpolitik* reason? Remember that that usually coincides with good lordship, if you're thinking long-term. The higher your rank, the more careful you have to be about decisions, because the easier it is to break things."

He resisted an impulse to adjust the collar of his jerkin, suddenly grown a little tight.

"Ah . . . well, that grant, it's just idle land right now, not settled manors. No annual revenues, no knights or sergeants owing service. The Crown will get the Royal mesne tithes without having to pay anything upfront if *we* develop and settle it, full tithes since we're tenants-in-chief. And we'll have to see to the roads and rails and patrols at our own expense, too, which means more trade and the dues on that. What did they say in the old days . . . all gain, no pain?"

Tiphaine almost smiled, which startled him a little. She went on:

"Good points, but those are basically reasons to grant

the land to *someone*, eventually, not necessarily to me and Rigobert right now. Speaking of whom, my lord your father is getting an identical tract next to this"—she flicked a finger at the parchment—"which means we'll be neighbors out there, too. On the same terms, just the names and map changed. So?"

"And because it's important to be *seen* to reward good service? That's a big part of a lord's repute and good name, and that's part of what makes people eager to take service with you and do their best, and ready to stick with you if things go badly."

"Another point. I actually am grateful, too . . . not least because this means I can reward some of *my* landless followers."

She visibly took pity on him.

"Lady Sandra used to grill me like this, and she did it to Matti, too. The less obvious part is about *your* generation of House Ath and House Stafford."

Lioncel blinked a little, startled. Then he nodded slowly. It made sense that the Crown would start thinking about him . . . though it was a bit . . .

Nerve-wracking. Exciting, though, too. Someday not too long from now I'll *be someone who does important things.*

Tiphaine spoke, echoing his thoughts closely enough to startle:

"Rigobert and I will be out of the picture in a few decades, but you'll be in your prime when Crown Princess Órlaith is as old as you are now, and Diomede not long after. This means the Crown thinks you and your brother will likely be assets for *her*. Plus . . . take a look at the tenures those manors are held under."

He reread the document, frowning in concentration; this *did* involve questions of feudal law.

"Ummm. Parts of it . . . three manors out of twenty . . . are held in free and common socage, not just by knight-service and tallages like the rest."

That was unusual and meant they could be alienated, unlike ordinary land held in fief by a tenant-in-chief, which descended undivided by primogeniture whether held in demesne or subinfeudated. It didn't escheat to the Crown in default of natural heirs, either.

A light dawned. "Those parts in socage are an inheritance for Heuradys and Yolande!" he said delightedly.

His young sisters were a bit more than two and less than a year old respectively. When he had thought of it at all he'd expected that they'd be dowered by charges on the revenues of the baronies of Forest Grove and Ath, sunk in government bonds or town properties or the like.

Actual manors in their own names would improve their prospects considerably, whether they wanted to marry, go into the Church, or make some other choice. Right now the "manors" were each just big chunks of rolling bunchgrass, but his sisters were very young.

Wait a minute, if my lord my father got a grant like this, a hell of a lot goes to me, *too,* he thought for the first time.

Which meant raising him as well as Diomede into the top rank of tenant-in-chief barons; there were Counts with less, though not many. That was a distant enough prospect to seem pretty theoretical, but it was agreeable enough too.

"Right," Tiphaine said. "And—"

She stopped, cocking her head as if to listen. "That's

odd . . . did you hear that owl? Sounded like a big Harfang."

Lioncel looked at her blankly; he knew all the birds of prey well, from hawking and hunting.

"Owl, my lady? It's the middle of the afternoon!"

It was, and a bright one in early summer; the sunlight was a thick glowing bar across the table, patterned where the Gothic stone tracery of the window cut it, and even the corners of the room showed a bit of glitter on the metallic threads of the tapestries.

"That does make an owl unlikely, eh?" Tiphaine said. "And you've got youngster's ears."

He'd rarely seen her indecisive. For a moment her face went utterly still, and she touched her right hand to the base of her throat; she wore an owl pendant there lately, he remembered.

Then her eyes opened and she looked upward, crossing her arms and tapping her fingers thoughtfully.

"So, logically . . ." she murmured. Then, oddly: "Thanks!"

The next floor was the Lady Regent's . . . no, now the Queen Mother's . . . chambers; some sort of do was on for this afternoon, ostensibly a tea party, with the High Queen and his own mother and a clutch of countesses settling privately what would be supposedly *debated* publicly later. Tiphaine didn't raise her voice—she rarely did—but there was a crispness to it when she spoke.

"Tell Sir Armand and Sir Rodard to turn out the *menie*, everyone on hand right now. Then arm me, half armor, no more."

Putting on a suit of plate complete took about fifteen minutes with expert help, and couldn't be done alone at all.

"*Move*, boy!"

He did. Nobody stopped him to ask for explanations, just started doing what was needed. And by the time he dashed back with the flexible plate cuirass of lames in his arms and the other equipment slung around him Tiphaine had already tossed her houppelande aside and hung her sword belt over the back of the chair. The steel would be a little loose without the padded arming doublet beneath, but he latched it quickly and stood by to hand her the articulated steel gauntlets, sallet helm and the four-foot knight's shield shaped like an elongated teardrop with its arms of sable, a Delta Or upon a V Argent.

"What are we going to do, my lady?" he asked, proud that his voice was steady.

"Head straight in, yelling alarm and murder," she said absently.

"That will . . . look strange, my lady."

She shrugged to settle the harness, and put both hands up on the sallet's low dome to press the broad-tailed flared helmet with her palms so that its circuit of internal pads were snug in exactly the right place before she buckled the chin-cup. The visor was down. Without a bevoir attached to the breastplate her mouth and chin showed beneath, and the long narrow blankness of the vision slit in the smooth curve gave a look of merciless detachment and power to her glance.

The armor the *menie* of Ath wore wasn't black like the harness of the Protector's Guard, because that color sucked up heat in the sun and sometimes stood out against a background. It wasn't white—bare and brightly polished—like that of many baronial fighting-tails, either, because that was even more conspicuous.

Instead it was a pale neutral gray like her eyes, the finish very slightly roughened so that it wouldn't glint, though in fact you rarely tried to hide in plate. Lady Death was meticulous about details.

Mom is that way too, Lioncel realized suddenly. *Only she does it about other things.*

"It'll look very strange, my lady," he added, and didn't go on to say: *Charging into the Queen Mother's quarters with drawn sword and armed men at your back.*

"Lioncel, have you heard the saying that you can do wonders if you don't care about who gets the credit?"

"Yes, my lady. My lord my father is fond of that one."

She smiled, a chill stark expression. "Well, you can do even more if you don't give a damn how crazy it makes you look."

As she spoke he went down on one knee and buckled the sword belt around her waist while she pulled on her gauntlets; that took three extra holes on the belt in armor, and he tucked the tongue neatly beneath. Then she drew the sword, a yard of tapering watermarked cross-hilted steel. That slid the honed edge within an inch of his ear, but it didn't occur to him to flinch. Tiphaine d'Ath's sword went exactly where she wanted it to go, neither more nor less. He'd seen her flick flies out of the air, neatly bisected with a twitch of the wrist, something he *still* couldn't do in practice.

With the curved top of her shield she knocked the visor of her sallet up. His own vision disappeared for an instant as he pulled his light mail shirt over his head; when he settled the familiar weight and belted on his own sword the two household knights were there.

"Lioncel, get your helmet on," she said. "And stay behind the shields when we move."

"What's up, my lady?" Rodard said as he strode briskly in, blinking at the naked sword, his brother Armand at his heels. "I have six men-at-arms including us—"

All knights were men-at-arms, full-armored and capable of fighting as lancers on horseback among their other skills. Not all men-at-arms were knights, though most hoped to be some day.

"—and as many more of spearmen and crossbowmen. I could recall men from other duties or rustle up some more from the Lord Chancellor's household—"

The Georges brothers had been given the accolade last year; Rodard had been wounded at the Horse Heaven Hills and was just back on full service. Both young household knights were armored cap-a-pie with their shields slung point-down across their backs; they'd been on duty. Usually there weren't more men than that up here in the Silver Tower; most of the *menie* of Ath was still at the front, or at work on half a dozen assignments.

"No, no time for explanations," his liege replied.

Lioncel felt himself nodding, under a tight-held excitement. His liege-lady was fond of the maxim that it was better to react in good time with a small force than too late with a larger one. He used the moment to get his own crossbow and hang the quiver of bolts to his waist; he was still too young to match a grown man with the sword, but he was a good shot and his quarrels hit just as hard as a veteran's.

"I think the enemy are going to try something underhanded and we need to move *now*."

She flicked the point of her blade towards the ceiling, and the steel-framed faces of the knights changed; they pulled on the guige straps that slung their shields and ran their arms through the loops. Armand spun on his heel and began calling orders.

There was a rustle and clank as the command party came through into the outer chambers, and the ranks of the *menie* stiffened the way a cat did at the beginning of its stalk. This part of the Grand Constable's suite was interlinked reception rooms; in normal times they were spacious and airy, despite the massiveness of the structure around them. Even a small force of armored men in a bristle of shields and spears and glaives made them at least *feel* crowded. Honed metal winked and glinted as the pole arms shifted into beams of light from the high windows, amid a smell of leather and male sweat and oiled steel.

"There is a plot against the Crown," Tiphaine said without preliminaries. "Some officers of the Protector's Guard must have been suborned or replaced and we may have to fight the Guard."

Which would mean being grossly outnumbered, for starters.

"Anyone who isn't ready to follow me on this had better step aside right now. Fall out if you care to."

Fists and swordhilts thumped on breastplates and shields. There was a short crashing bark of:

"D'Ath! *D'Ath!*"

Lioncel wasn't surprised; he'd have been shocked if anyone *had* dropped out. These were all men who'd sworn fealty to Tiphaine d'Ath of their own will. Nobody became a personal vassal of Lady Death because they longed for a quiet life.

"The cry is *Artos and Montival*. Follow me!"

Then they all trotted towards the stairwell; there were two on this level, spirals set in the east and west thicknesses of the tower. A slam of boots and a clatter of harness, men-at-arms and spearmen settling their shields and crossbowmen loading as they ran.

Mother! Lioncel thought suddenly with his hand on the cocking lever. *And the girls, and Huon! They're up there with the High Queen!*

The war was *here*, with shocking suddenness, not just out at the front. It was like running down a staircase in the dark and expecting another step when there wasn't one, a blow running up into his chest and squeezing even as his hands fumbled through the loading routine.

This is Castle Todenangst, not some gulch out east!

CHAPTER FOUR

SEVEN DEVILS MOUNTAINS
(FORMERLY WESTERN IDAHO)
HIGH KINGDOM OF MONTIVAL
(FORMERLY WESTERN NORTH AMERICA)
JUNE 15TH. CHANGE YEAR 26/2024 AD

Cole Salander was under a fallen tree, sweating and baring his teeth in an unconscious rictus of tension. The first warning had been a covey of blue-gray upland quail taking off, and then a Cooper's hawk perched in an aspen had turned its mad red eyes upslope and discovered business elsewhere without trying for one of its natural prey. And then something that could have been a dog giving tongue . . . that was when he'd gone to ground in a hurry.

Cole glowered at the POW lying to his left out of the corners of his eyes. Alyssa was the reason he couldn't just try to outrun the pursuit. The enemy glider pilot smiled at him—with poisonous not-real-sweetness—and lay quietly with her splinted arm cradled against her chest. A distant sound . . .

Yup. A hound belling. Shit.

Somewhere the damned dog bayed again, and closer, the sound echoing against rock, startling the woods into silence. All that could mean only one thing here in the Seven Devils Mountains of western Idaho. Nobody had lived here even before the Change, and few had even passed through since the machines stopped. It had to be soldiers in this time of war. More than one or two, and he didn't think they were soldiers of the US Army. Normally that wouldn't be an insoluble problem; he could cover forty miles a day or better if he really pushed it, even in mountain country like this, and the same terrain made a cavalry pursuit impossible. There might be individuals in the bunch combing the area who could equal his best pace, but no *unit* of any size could.

I should have just bugged out when I found where the glider crashed but no, I had to be a hotshot.

Soldier and captive were both well-hidden, in a hollow covered by a hundred-foot lodgepole pine that had fallen across the mountainside sometime in the winter just over, surrounded by a thick scrum of blue lupine taking advantage of the light let in by the gap in the canopy. The rootball wasn't totally broken off, and the needles had mostly stayed on the branches as the wounded tree struggled for life. He could smell his own sour sweat under the sweet pine and flower scents, and hers—though he had to admit she was a lot less rank even now. You had to be borderline insane to be a military glider pilot and the last chaotic tumbling smashing crushing moments of your short terrifying life were likely to suck bigtime, but until then you lived better than a foot soldier, with cooked food and hot water available every night.

The soil in the declivity was shaded and damp, and the wet had soaked through the mottled green-brown-gray linsey-woolsey of his battle-smock and pants, chilly and uncomfortable. Summer came late and reluctantly to these heights. The forest was open here, big old-growth conifers widely spaced, with thickets and aspens around the occasional clearing where fire or geology had kept the climax vegetation at bay. Fortunately the wind that bore the sound of the dogs wouldn't be carrying their scent back to the animals.

Unfortunately, good hunting hounds can follow a ground trail regardless of the breeze, once they've cut across it.

And while he was confident he could outrun men, even without an injured prisoner he couldn't outpace dogs; over short to medium distances four legs just plain beat two. But there was a mountain stream running strong and cold with melted snow downslope. If he could just get there and use it to break trail . . .

But I'm tasked with getting Ms. "That's Pilot Officer Bitch to You, Soldier" back to our lines. And I'm doing it alone because we're losing the war and everybody's trying to do three men's work so I can't fight even if it's a small patrol. The enemy don't have to send their men out alone.

She won't run away or shout, she gave her parole and I think she'll keep it, but I can't make her move . . . not all-out, and anything else would be a waste of time if there's a pursuit. To be fair, that arm has to hurt if she moves fast.

He still felt like he'd fought a grizzly himself.

Mainly because I did.

It wouldn't stop him from moving fast or fighting hard, he hadn't actually cracked bones or torn ligaments, but it would make it a lot more painful. He wasn't at quite ten tenths of capacity.

And if I just cut her loose, then her parole is over and she can shout her lungs out with a clear conscience and then I am so fucked. Unless I just kill her, which isn't going to happen. Shit. Maybe trying to get her back to base wasn't such a good idea even if she'd be a valuable intel source.

He had a good view through a little gap in the branches of the open forest across the broad slope. He brought his crossbow to his shoulder and peered through the telescopic sight, careful to move slowly and keep the lens well back; he might be just out of the accelerated SF training course, but he *had* done well in it, and he'd been a hunter since he was old enough to take a slingshot out after rabbits to help fill the family stewpot and guard the truck garden. The downside of a scope was that it narrowed the field of view but that was all right if you kept switching back between the scope and naked eyeball.

Two shaggy gray-brown dogs bounded into sight, big ones—as big as he'd ever seen, and looking to have mastiff and Great Dane and deerhound and a bit of timber wolf in their ancestry. Or possibly a donkey in the woodpile, if you concentrated on the size alone. They wore leather collars with steel studs, and they quartered the ground in an efficient-looking pattern. Fortunately there weren't any tracks for them to find right there; he'd come in from the north, trying to loop around the latest known enemy activity . . . which was now evidently much closer than anyone had thought.

Alyssa Larsson had just smiled every time he asked her where the base was. Now he knew why: he'd been headed straight towards it all by himself.

I was giving her an armed escort home!

One of the dogs bayed again, a deep-chested sound. That was a signal, it wasn't just making noise because it liked to hear the sound of its own voice. Four minutes later a human figure came loping through the woods. Doll-tiny at this distance, around three hundred yards, but the scope brought him close enough to see the knee-length kilt and the long yellow yew bow in the left hand with an arrow held on the string.

Shit. Clan warrior.

They weren't exactly the enemy's equivalent of the Special Forces. Those were the Dúnedain Rangers who were supposed to be *even weirder*. But the Clan Mackenzie were rumored to be neobarb headhunters and they were most definitely and by hard objective evidence very bad news. He'd talked to men who'd made it back from the battle at the Horse Heaven Hills. Sometimes in conversations that carefully excluded officers. They'd all featured profanely emphatic warnings about the reach and punch of those arrows and the uncanny rate of fire.

They're sneaky, too, had been common.

Closer, and he—

No. It's a she. *Christ, aren't there any* normal *women out west, looking after babies and working in the fields and fighting off bandits while the men are away at war?*

—leapt easily onto a jut of rock that stood out from the slope and stood with arrow half-drawn. That was close enough that her face filled the scope. A young woman, early twenties like Cole.

It took him a moment to see the details, because the face was *painted*. Not makeup, real lines of black and white like a mask of dark wings starting on the forehead and sweeping over eyes and cheeks and then curving in along the jaw to the chin. It gave the countenance an eerie alien aspect, like something you saw in a dream.

OK, the briefing said Mackenzies wear war paint. *Nice to know we get information right sometimes.*

She wasn't wearing a helmet, which was good practice doing a scout in the woods; the protection wasn't worth the way it restricted your hearing and peripheral vision. Instead she had on a sort of beret-like thing, with a clasp that held a spray of raven feathers standing up above her left eye. Brown hair hung in plaits at the front down either side of her face, and then the scalp was shaven above the ears to leave a braided roach falling down her back with a length of cord wrapped around it.

He shifted the scope slightly. Pleated kilt and plaid over the shoulder in a green and brown tartan with slivers of dull orange, a broad leather belt, buckled ankle boots and knee-hose. A short sword a lot like the one he carried except that it was on the left hip and not the right, with a green-painted steel buckler the size and shape of a soup-plate clipped to the scabbard; a long dirk; a smaller knife tucked into her hose; and a green brigandine over her torso. On it in dark outline was a crescent moon cradled between antlers, and a big war-quiver stuffed with gray-fletched arrows jutted up over her right shoulder.

Eyes scanned back and forth, patiently, not hurrying or narrowing in on any one spot yet, instead sinking into the landscape and looking for the break in the pattern. He recognized the technique, and was thankful he'd taken the time to break up the outline of his crossbow with scrim and little bits of vegetation. Straight lines and too-regular curves drew the gaze in the wilderness.

OK, that's extreme range, but I'm a really good shot and there's not much wind, so I could almost certainly put one through the center of mass . . . of course, there's the armor, those brigandines are nearly as good as a solid breastplate . . . and the dogs would go for me . . . nah, better be cautious, this is an intelligence mission not a hot op; I'm trying to get away, not *fight.*

His training had emphasized focusing on the mission. And that aggression was a means, not an end. Those were the differences between an army and a *neobarb* mob.

At last she made a short chittering noise that would have passed as forest background if he hadn't been watching her, and a man in the same gear appeared. Cole blinked; he hadn't seen the second Mackenzie at all, and it made him very glad he hadn't chanced a long-range shot at the first one while someone unseen was covering her. The man was slender and of medium height, looking wiry-strong, with a brown mustache and short chin-beard. The rest of his head was apparently shaven, except for a lock at the back that spilled down in a braid. His face was painted as well, though more lightly, and somehow looked astonishingly like a cat's, and there was a tuft of gray-brown fur in the clasp of his : . . Cole blinked . . . *Scots bonnet*! That was what it was called!

These people are seriously strange. *Those knights and castles and things they've got out west are bad enough, but* this?

There was nothing eccentric about the way he quartered the ground, though, with the dogs trotting at his heel and his gaze scanning the pine-duff and old aspen leaves ahead of him. Occasionally he would go to a knee and peer more closely. Cole recognized that too—an experienced tracker looking for sign. He lay and sweated and thought he heard an *almost* entirely inaudible snigger from his prisoner.

I don't suppose it matters what they do with the head after they kill me . . . I should be able to take out whoever stumbles across me first, but that's one bolt and I can't reload as fast as an archer can shoot . . . they're too far apart to shoot one and rush the other with my sword before they get me and there are the dogs but maybe if I'm really fast and even more lucky . . . and if this *time there's nobody in reserve I can't see yet . . .*

They could just be not finding him; he was *good* at concealment. Or it could be a trap. At last the newcomer turned to the woman on the rock and shook his head. They gestured at each other—military sign language, he thought—and then she nodded. Cole forced himself not to blow out his breath in relief as she took an oxhorn slung at her waist and put the silver-mounted mouthpiece to her lips.

Huuuuu-huuuuu-huuurrrrr!

The sound was surprisingly deep, and it seemed to resonate in his chest for a moment, but it meant they thought nobody was around. It brought a dozen more kilted archers loping through the woods. He lost sight of some as they continued on past the coffin-tight hiding place and the rest shook out into a skirmish line. If they didn't walk right into him and they assumed this area was clear afterwards, he had a good chance of staying hidden until they all went on about their business. And after they'd checked the area once they probably wouldn't be back. There was a *lot* of forested mountain around here.

Go away, he thought, clenching his stomach muscles in an involuntary attempt to project the thought that was half a formless prayer. *Nothing interesting here, you gave it a once-over, much more important stuff elsewhere, move along now. . . .*

One halted, a dark-skinned woman with her hair in a multitude of tight braids tipped with little silver balls.

That's not a bow she's carrying, he realized as she came closer. *That's a staff.*

A six-foot length of carved rowan-wood, topped by a circle flanked by two silver crescents.

What the hell is she *doing? That's not a weapon. Focus, Cole, focus, you're missing something.*

He narrowed his attention. Through the sight he could see the dark woman blink and frown, looking like someone trying to remember or catch a nagging thought at the edge of perception. She halted and drew a circle in the forest floor with the butt of the staff and inscribed lines within the figure in some complex pattern of angles and curves. Then she began to *spin* the staff, first over her head, then touching the end down with what looked like careful precision on the figures she'd drawn. The circle on its end was a disk of silver-rimmed crystal, and it caught the morning sun in a flickering glitter as she whirled the wood at arm's length again. After a moment she began to walk outward in a spiral, still turning the staff wrist-over-wrist like a quarterstaff.

What the hell . . .

It all made no sense that he could see, but there was something fascinating about the movement of the staff. The way it cast sun-blinks, the rhythmic *intensity* of it, the swooping grace, the humming song that went within it. Moments later he realized she actually was singing. A wandering tune, hauntingly strange, yet somehow re-

minding him of how his mother sang while she was working the churn or getting the harvest supper ready . . .

> *"Sleep of the Earth of the land of Faerie*
> *Deep is the lore of Cnuic na Sidhe;*
> *Hail be to they of the Forest Gentry*
> *Pale dark spirits help us see!"*

So soothing, not scary at all. She took something from
a pouch at her belt and held up her bunched fingers,
blowing across them sharply like someone getting rid of
flour or cat-hair. He sighed and let his head drift downward, onto the deep pine-duff, cool and damp and
friendly, comfortable as his own bed in the attic up under
the roof on the farm as the song went on . . .

> *"White is the dust of the state of dreaming*
> *Light is the mixture to make one still*
> *Dark is the powder of Death's redeeming;*
> *Mark that but one pinch can kill—"*

Something hard rapped him on the forehead, just under the hood of his battle-smock. He started awake with
a strangled yell and an icy thrust of fear as the butt of the
staff withdrew, reflex sending his hands snatching up his
crossbow . . .

. . . and then freezing at the glitter on the honed edges
of arrowheads pointing at him. Six arrows, drawn past the
jaw, ready to nail him to the ground.

It had to be his imagination that he heard the thick
yew staves of the longbows creaking, but the barred-fang

growl of the dogs was like millstones turning as they crouched and stared at his throat with fixed intent. The dark woman was leaning on her staff and panting a little as if with hard effort. She blew out a breath and grinned down at him, her full lips curving away from white teeth.

"Who's the naughty laddie, then?" she said, in an accent that held a strong pleasant burbling lilt. "So, would you be puttin' your hands on your head the now, or would you rather be pierced, perforated and sent off to the Summerlands for a wee bit of a rest before you try life again?"

Shit, he thought. *So much for my glorious military career and a general's stars by forty. Shit twice and on toast.*

"Your choice," one of the archers added helpfully.

"I surrender," he said, laying down the crossbow, coming up onto both knees and clasping his hands across the top of his head.

"Now that's a sensible lad," she said cheerfully, extending her hand so Alyssa could stand and move out of the line of fire. "Better not to kill without strong need, for aren't we all alike children of the Mother? Merry meet, Lady Alyssa; who would this likely youngster you're travelling with be?"

"I'm Cole Salander, Private First Class, United States Army, serial number A3F77032," he said sourly, staring ahead.

"Toss the sword belt, number-on-a-list-man," one of the archers said. "Undo it with your left hand, mind, and keep the other on your head."

He unbuckled it and did, which put his sword, bowie, utility knife and hatchet out of reach; he supposed it was a compliment of sorts that they were being cautious about getting close to him while he was armed. Another Mackenzie extended the horn-sheathed tip of his yew stave and snagged the sling of his crossbow, dragging it cautiously away before firing the bolt into the ground with a *whap* and examining the weapon with professional curiosity.

"And is there any more cutlery, ironmongery or things of a sharp and pointy or otherwise harmful nature?" the first bowman said. "Produce, man, and no monkey-shines."

He was a little older than the others, with a cropped blond beard and only a few touches of war paint and no weird haircut except for it being a lot longer than was common for men in Idaho, his thick yellow braid tied into a clubbed bunch at the back of his head. A piece of wolf-tail dangled along with it. A thin collar of twisted gold lay around his neck, the ends fashioned into the heads of wolves meeting muzzle-to-muzzle.

"Steady now, boyo, and don't try to befool us," he said, his voice hard. "That would not put us in a better mood. You get a whap alongside the head for every one we find when we search."

Cole had two holdout knives, one in his boot and a little one sewn into the jacket behind his neck. He tossed the blades and his sentry-removal wire garrote and black-jack after the crossbow, removing them from their hiding places with two fingers and great caution but no undue waste of time. He didn't know how long they could hold the draw on those heavy bows and didn't want to find out if it meant fingers slipping off the string and a thirty-six-inch arrow heading his way at several hundred feet per second.

What the fuck happened? he thought, dazed and unre-sisting amid the painted faces grim or grinning. *How the hell did I go to sleep with an enemy patrol all around me? Please tell me I'm not that much of a noob screwup, God. Or . . . did she do something to me?*

That was almost as scary as the arrowheads, more so if you thought about it for a minute. Pilot Officer Alyssa Larsson *was* snickering now. The Clan warriors took the tension off their bows, though several kept their arrows on the string until he'd been quickly and expertly searched. There were a few happy chortles and whoops as they found and appropriated the more handy items in his light field pack as well as his stash of silver coins.

Yeah, OK, you're happy, he thought with resigned irri-tation.

That was one of the perks of capturing someone; every-one knew the (unofficial) rules. They left him his sleeping bag and some of the really essential gear, and conscien-tiously returned the personal letters and family pictures after a glance to make sure what they were, which meant they *were* playing by the rules. His paybook, map and the other official documents went into a sack. Alyssa took back the map, papers, knife and compass he'd appropri-ated from *her.*

The wad of green paper money they tossed back with a jocular suggestion that when it ran out he could just use leaves and grass like anybody else. They had a point, with the way prices had gone haywire since the President bought it at the Horse Heaven Hills. His last letter from home had cautiously mentioned that people were *swap-ping a lot again,* which said volumes in a way the censor couldn't object to.

"Merry meet," Alyssa said to the Mackenzies.

The senior archer looked at her, the splinted arm and the spectacular and now colorful bruises on her face, then back at Cole. His eyes narrowed.

"Merry meet, and merry part again, Lady Alyssa," he said. "Now, would you want the whole corp of this one to come back with you still walking upon the ridge of the earth, or just the ugly head of him in a bag, to be pickled in cedar-oil and nailed above your door?"

Alyssa chuckled. Cole didn't think the suggestion was funny at all, and decided he disliked her sense of humor. Despite her lack of accent she seemed to know a fair bit about Mackenzies.

"No, he's been a perfect gentleman, Sèitheach," she said. "Strictly according to the laws of honorable war."

He nodded and took the hand off his swordhilt and looked grimly at Cole, who was trying hard to hide his relief.

"Well, and doesn't that demonstrate the Law of Threefold Return, boyo?" he said. To Alyssa: "Where's your machine?"

"Twenty-odd miles that way, most of it up and down, as of three days ago," she said, pointing northeastward. "What's left of it, which isn't much. Thought I could catch an updraft but hit still air instead and I used a couple of trees and a boulder as a landing strip. He came along while I was still dizzy. I'd have been in a really bad way otherwise. I was upside down and couldn't get at the belts because of the arm and there was a grizzly sniffing around and I don't think it was on my side. I'm a Bear-killer, after all!"

"What happened to the bear?"

"We ate some of it."

She cocked an eye at Cole. "He put two bolts into it and then took off like a squirrel. I don't think I've ever seen a man run up a rock face so fast. Then he shot it dead while it was trying to climb up and get him."

"More of them?" the blond archer said.

He ignored chuckles from his followers. Several of them nodded respectfully at Cole, and a few even murmured something like *bravely done*, but the Boisean's snap judgment was that their commander was a notable hardcase.

"He didn't say, but from the way he acted no, not within a couple of days' travel minimum. Be careful with him. He knows his way around the woods and he's quick. No fool, either."

The dark woman with the staff used it to swat the bowman in charge on the backside before she added sharply:

"And taking heads is forbidden. That's *geasa* for all the Clan as you know perfectly well, Sèitheach Johnston Mackenzie. It's even *geasa* for McClintocks, the which is saying a great deal!"

"Well, I was just jokin', so I was," the man replied a little sheepishly.

"No you weren't, Sèitheach-me-lad. Not about taking the head, at least, if not the pickling and nailing."

Gurk! Cole thought, restraining an impulse to take one of his hands down and rub the back of his neck with it. *OK, she's a witch.*

There were rumors about that, too. He hadn't believed them until now. Of course, there were also rumors about the Cutters, the Church Universal and Triumphant, and what their High Seekers could do. Officially *they* were supposed to be friends and allies who just absolutely *loved* the reconstituted United States centered in Boise and wanted to bring their stamping ground out in Montana back under the Constitution. Cole most certainly didn't believe *that*. He'd met a couple, and the only way they loved anyone else was the way Cole loved a ham sandwich with mustard and a pickle. Witness the way their cavalry bugged out at the Horse Heaven Hills when everything went to shit, and left the infantry-heavy US forces in a world of hurt. Two of his brothers hadn't come back from that fight, and nobody knew what had happened to them.

So OK, the westerners really do have witches. But it sounds like she's a good witch. Anyone who's against chopping off my head is pretty damned good as far as I'm concerned. Christ, this all just gets better and better, doesn't it? "Sorry, sir, they took me prisoner 'cause a witch cast a spell on me, which is why I went to sleep, really it is, honest." That's sure going to go over well, assuming I ever get to report in. Sergeant Halford will ask me if their dogs ate my homework, too.

"And don't jest on things the Goddess-on-Earth made *geis*!" the woman continued. "We may be Gaels, but this isn't Erin in the ancient times and you're not the Hound of Ulster nor yet one of the Red Branch."

"Yes, *fiosaiche*," the man named Sèitheach muttered.

She frowned. "I . . . there's something strange about this one. That's why he caught at me like a wrong note in a song. I'd not have found him otherwise, not if this were just a matter of humankind. Yet I can't say precisely what. It's not that he's a banewreaker himself, I do not think."

"What should we be doing with him, then?"

"Why, I'm but a *fiosaiche*," she said blandly, stepping back. "You being the bow-captain here, it's your decision, not a matter of brehon law. War's for a warrior, not a priestess or a foreseer."

A couple of the archers grinned and Alyssa snickered. Then the *fiosaiche* started looking at her arm, probing gently along the splint. She hissed slightly and her eyes went blank at the pain.

The witch-woman nodded. "Thin break, right enough. It should heal well, and that's a good job of splinting. Provided you get some rest and don't put any strain on it!"

When the bow-captain—

Whatever the hell that is. Some sort of rank, probably. I think this guy's a platoon sergeant or something like that.

—snapped orders the Clan archers went on grinning, but they obeyed promptly too and without argument. Presumably a *fiosaiche* was something like a chaplain or a political officer or both. Though she looked a lot nicer than any of the zampolits—what were officially called morale officers—he'd ever met.

"We'll sweep along the river until dark and lie out tonight, forbye there may be some of this one's friends about," the bow-captain said. "Remember how well he was hidden. The next one may be more twitchy with his trigger, so keep an eye out for sign unless you want a bolt in the back. Caillech—"

That was the girl with the wings painted on her face.

"—you and Talyn—"

The guy who'd been covering her and bossing the dogs.

"—take the lady and the prisoner back to camp. You're

up to the walk, Lady? It's a fair bit of a way and nothing but deer-tracks, and those of an exceeding steepness."

"That's Pilot Officer, bow-captain; I'm no lady among Mackenzies. And it's walk or crawl, isn't it? War isn't a hunting trip. I broke my arm, not a leg."

The man named Talyn nodded to Cole as he took his hands down and got to his feet. It felt strange not to have a sword at his waist or a crossbow in his arms, like being naked in public. The Mackenzie's voice was not unkindly as he pointed southwest with his longbow.

"That way, Cole Salander of Boise. If the Lady needs assistance, give it, and do it well. Oh, and just so we understand each other about any thoughts of skipping off into the woods with rude unseemly haste like a Jack in the Green—*urghabháil dó*!"

The two great dogs had been at his feet, heads on paws. They sprang in a blur of speed, and Cole froze again as the gruesome jaws closed on his wrists; they were tall enough at the shoulder that they didn't have to bend their heads upward to do it. They didn't clamp down, which he suspected would have cut right through bone and sinew with a single bite, but they weren't letting him move either. Those growls like millstones grinding came from each deep chest again, and their eyes cocked up at him in warning. Or possibly hopeful anticipation. The feel of the fangs was like the teeth of a waiting saw, and between them they weighed as much as he and half over again.

Alyssa was grinning at him. Which was understandable; turnabout was fair play, and being a helpless prisoner was no fun.

"*Urghabháil dó!* means 'grab him,' pretty much, soldier," she said. "You don't really have to worry until he says *mharú air*! Which means 'kill.' Though he'd most likely just shoot you instead."

"Loose him, Artan, Flan!" the Mackenzie said to the dogs, and they obeyed, backing away but looking at Cole with suspicion anyway. "Now, off we go!"

"You guys are weird," Cole said resignedly.

"Oh, you have no idea," Alyssa said cheerfully. "What you've seen so far is nothing. Try Dun Juniper sometime. Or even better, Castle Todenangst, I've visited there a couple of times with Mom and Dad. *That* place is weird."

CHAPTER FIVE

Castle Todenangst, Crown demesne
Portland Protective Association
Willamette Valley near Newburg
High Kingdom of Montival
(formerly western Oregon)
June 15th, Change Year 26/2024 AD

"*Mom!*" the High Queen of Montival said.

Sandra Arminger looked up from where she had been kneeling at her prie-dieu. The padded prayer-stool—rather like a reversed legless chair—stood before a triptych of the Madonna and Child flanked by Saints Edgar and Olaf, the patrons of rulers. The gold leaf of the halos in the icons glowed in the beam of light from an ocular window set high up under the carved plaster of the coffered roof.

She smiled at her daughter, the dark-brown eyes dancing. "Honestly, Matti, you needn't goggle as if you'd caught me doing something nasty with a pageboy. I was *praying*."

Mathilda opened her mouth and closed it as Sandra crossed herself, returned her rosary to the embroidered purse at her belt and stood. That still left her six inches shorter than her tall daughter, a smoothly pretty and slightly plump woman in her fifties, in a cotte-hardie of dove-gray silk elaborately jacquarded with ribbons and swallows and a white silk wimple bound with silver and opals. A Persian cat yawned and padded out from beneath the prie-dieu, its gaze as blandly self-satisfied as that of its mistress.

People who don't know better underestimate Mother.

Though nowadays you had to go a long way to find someone so utterly uninformed. She'd seen very hard men start to sweat when Sandra Arminger smiled at them in her let's-share-a-joke way. The joke might be very pointed, or give you indigestion.

Mathilda shook her head. It wasn't the first time she'd seen her mother pray, of course; it was just the first time she'd seen her doing it strictly in private, where there wasn't any political benefit to be gained by conventional piety. Previously she'd used this little room off the Regent's suite for confidential interviews, though it *was* the sort of place a noblewoman would set up a private shrine. Now, besides the prie-dieu and images it had a big carved rood on one wall and a small shelf of devotional books.

"What . . . were you asking?" she said at last.

"I was praying for your father," her mother said.

"Oh, good!" Mathilda said with a rush. "I mean, for both of you."

They looked at each other silently for a moment in the incense-scented gloom. She'd told her mother much of what she'd seen in the . . .

Visions, Mathilda thought. *That's as close as you can get to a word for things there aren't words for. What did Father Ignatius say when I made my confession? That some realities make language itself buckle and break when we try to describe them instead of just living them.*

. . . the *visions* she'd seen at Lost Lake, when she and Rudi had joined their blood on the blade of the Sword of the Lady and thrust it into the living rock of Montival.

Or perhaps where Artos *and I did.*

Rudi carried the Sword again now, but in another sense it was still there beside the infinitely blue waters with their hands clasped on the hilt . . . and always had been and always would be. She could still feel a little of the curious *linking* that had started then, the sensation that the whole of Montival was like her own body. Since then her dreams had been odd; not so much fantastic as . . . *real.*

Like vivid memories but of things she had never seen. Perhaps of ragged men stalking deer in a clearing fringed by redwoods, or wild horses running in a desert with dust smoking around their hooves and manes flying, or gulls on a cloudy beach beneath the enormous rusted hulk of a wrecked freighter, or the empty tinkling clatter of glass falling from the leaning tower of a skyscraper as wind-blown rain hooted through the wreck of a dead city . . .

Either it had faded a little or she'd grown accustomed to it; Rudi thought it was the latter, though he felt it much more as bearer of the Sword.

But for a while at Lost Lake she and he had walked outside the light of common day, their footsteps carrying them on separate paths across all boundaries of space and time. One thing *she* had seen was her own father, Norman Arminger, in a place where he did penance. And there she had met . . .

Her eyes went to the supernal peace on the Virgin's face as she looked down upon the Christ Child.

"*She* said . . . She said that because he loved us, he could receive love now," Mathilda said softly. "And choose to . . . to make amends. I think that works both ways."

Her mother sighed. "Here I receive positive proof of an afterlife, and instead of being reassuring it's *frightening*."

"Well, of course," Mathilda said. "That's *much* worse than death. Potentially. Worse than oblivion, I mean. It raises the stakes of *everything*."

They looked at each other with perfect mutual bafflement for a moment.

Sandra broke it with a laugh. "You know, darling, I have exactly the opposite problem with this than many people *used* to have with religion. When I was your age."

Mathilda raised an eyebrow, and Sandra made a graceful gesture with one small well-manicured hand, tapping her own temple with a finger that just touched the white silk of her wimple.

"Now I know up *here* that it's all true. Including the parts that are flat-out mutually contradictory, but leave that aside. Oh, well, a great many very intelligent people always *did* believe it, and I'm not going to reject the evidence of my own senses."

She put the hand over her heart. "But the difficult part is making *this* part of me believe it . . . integrate it into my worldview, as we'd have said in the old days . . . my heart rebels against my mind. And here I thought I was a complete rationalist!"

"You are *impossible*, Mother!" Mathilda laughed.

"Not impossible. Improbable, yes. Anyone who's lived

my life and done what I've done would have to be *highly* improbable at the very least, my darling. Now let's go. It wouldn't do to keep people waiting, even now that you're Lady Protector."

"*Particularly* now that I'm High Queen too," Mathilda said, with a slight quirk in her smile. "I always knew that the higher your rank the more firmly you were bound by custom. I hadn't quite realized . . ."

"Just how *high* a High Queen is," Sandra finished for her. "But there are compensations, dear."

They walked out through the semipublic part of the Regent's suite arm in arm. Technically Mathilda was Lady Protector now; the peace after the Protector's War had provided that she'd come of legal age at twenty-six. In practice . . .

In practice, being High Queen of Montival in the middle of a great big war doesn't leave me the time to be Lady Protector of the PPA! And being a new mother, which cannot be completely delegated and I won't anyway . . . having Mother handling the administrative routine and a lot of the politics in the north-realm territories not only lets me do other things, it buffers me from Associates who'd presume too much. I don't want to alienate the Protectorate's nobility. But I'm High Queen of all Montival, not just the PPA, and I have to be seen to be so people will know I mean it. Ruling is as much about seeming as being. If there's a difference at all.

So she'd firmly turned down her mother's pro forma offer to relinquish the suites that occupied the upper stories of the Silver Tower and shuffle off to some manor. Sandra Arminger had been the *Spider of the Silver Tower* for far too long. Even her virtues were a political problem; everyone knew how effectively she'd rebuilt the PPA after the shock of Norman Arminger's death in the Protector's War and the Jacquerie rebellion and the reforms and purges that followed it. If the Prophet hadn't come along that might have caused real trouble with fearful neighbors.

Mathilda would have felt uneasy calling these her own chambers anyway, though of course her bedroom had been here before she turned twelve and got her Associate's dagger and her own household and retinue. Like much of the great fortress-palace they'd been designed by Sandra, or at least she'd directed the terrified architects and interior decorators and artists she and Norman had swept up after their coup.

They were well over a hundred feet high here, and on the side looking out southward over the central keep, so the windows could be large—sets of triple pointed-arch portals at intervals, their upper fifth filled with stained glass and stone tracery in the Protectorate's version of Venetian Gothic style. The sashes below were thrown open on the fresh early summer afternoon amid a scent of roses and Sambac jasmine from the planters. A torrent of light shimmered on walls and floors of pale stone, on tables of inlaid rare woods and mother-of-pearl, the carved surrounds of arched open doorways or tile above hearths, on spindly chairs and sofas upholstered in cream silk and on tapestries of war and the hunt and high ceremony.

The vivid colors of the hangings and those of the rugs on the floor were a deliberate contrast. Walls and niches held art commissioned new or scavenged from museums and galleries all across the west of the continent. Some were as familiar as her own face: Leighton's *Pavonia* for instance, which had been there in the background so constantly she'd assumed for years it was a modern portrait of Delia de Stafford until she embarrassed herself by saying so at a reception here. But there was always something that surprised even her: this time it was a bronze statue of a youth, a slimly perfect athlete standing hipshot and about to crown himself with a wreath of laurel vanished twenty-four hundred years ago.

Classical but not Roman, Mathilda thought. *Greek, and of the great years. And undamaged except for the feet. Oh, my . . .*

"That's new," she said. "Well, you know what I mean."

"Not so very," Sandra said, stopping for a moment and seeming to caress the figure with her eyes. "This one is . . . probably . . . by Lysippos, Alexander the Great's court sculptor. But it was in storage for a long time, since that last expedition I sent to southern California just before the war . . . my goodness, three years ago now! I've had some experts working it over and mounting it on that pedestal. It's amazingly fragile, for something that's lasted so very long."

Mathilda looked at it and sighed, then sighed again rather differently as they walked on. She'd gone through a phase of guilt about her mother's art-collecting activities when she'd been a teenager and in the first incandescent sureness of her faith. Some of the men in the teams sent to retrieve these treasures had died horribly in the desolate Eater-haunted ruins of the lost cities, in Seattle and Vancouver, San Francisco and Los Angeles and places like San Simeon and the Getty Villa. And the revenues to finance it all came out of the incomes of peasants and craft-folk and traders, eventually.

When you were in a position to spend the fruits of

other people's sweat, not to mention their blood, prudent thrift became a cardinal virtue.

But should we be concerned only *with food and shelter and the weapons to protect it?* she thought. *Mom saved so much that was beautiful. And she made it fashionable for the other nobles and the wealthy guildsmen to do the same thing;* and *to give patronage to our own makers. That kept knowledge and skills alive through the terrible years when everything might have been lost. How many generations will thank her for both? And if she did it so she could have this . . . stuff . . . does that matter? The realm gets it just the same, and all the people in times to come. That's good lordship too.*

Two separate holy men had pointed that out to her— Father Ignatius had used Sandra's art collecting as an example of how God's plan turned all things to good in the end. The Rinpoche Tsewang Dorje had phrased it a little differently, but it amounted to the same thing. Though her private confessor at the time had simply and sternly admonished her that her own sins were a heavy enough burden to carry up to Heaven's gate without adding the spiritual pride of assuming someone else's.

I've never quite understood why my confessors and tutors were all so sincere. *Not since I realized . . . or let myself realize . . . that Mother wasn't, that she was playing at it. Which I only* really *accepted when she stopped playing and started trying it for real. And now I'm High Queen—*

She asked the question bluntly, and was a little astonished when her mother wiped at one eye until she caught a glint through the tear that was neither entirely false nor altogether genuine.

Absolutely Mother, in other words.

"My little girl is all grown up, and just as smart as I am!" she said.

Then, in utter seriousness: "Because I wanted you to *fit* in this world, darling. I can fake it . . . sometimes for days or weeks at a time, I don't notice . . . but then everything, all this—"

She waved a hand.

"—is suddenly like a dream, and I expect to wake up and pop another tape in the VCR."

Mathilda looked around and shook her head. Todenangst was about the most solidly real place she knew. Her mother went on:

"I *survived* by playing a game in deadly earnest I'd always liked to pretend to do for fun—I was in the Society but not the type who pulled their persona around them like a security blanket after the Change and never let go. Possibly I could play it so well *because* something deep down in me never entirely believed it, which meant I could be more objective. But it's your *life* and you deserve to live it with a whole heart."

Mother is troubling, but she's rarely dull, Mathilda thought. Then with a rush of anguish: *Oh, Rudi, I wish I was with you! Not safe here, but there where things are happening!*

She couldn't tell if it was normal worry, or her new sense of being linked to everything, but she could *feel* peril approaching, and that had to mean Rudi was in danger far from the strong walls that surrounded her.

SEVEN DEVILS MOUNTAINS
(FORMERLY WESTERN IDAHO)
HIGH KINGDOM OF MONTIVAL
(FORMERLY WESTERN NORTH AMERICA)
JUNE 15TH, CHANGE YEAR 26/2024 AD

Cole Salander and his captors moved mostly in single file through mountainside meadow and forest, with the dogs weaving back and forth to keep an eye and nose on the surroundings. Occasionally he caught one cocking an eye at *him* in a considering manner, as if to remind him of something.

After a while Talyn pulled out sticks of jerky from his sporran and handed them around. Cole got one, which surprised him slightly, though Artan and Flan weren't left out either. It was a not-too-odd variation on the usual fibrous salty not-much, better than nothing, and it made him thirsty.

They'd left him his canteen, and they all stopped to fill up at a spring-fed pool. He noted that they used water purification tablets like his, too; no matter how clear and cold and inviting it looked, any open water could have giardia in it, or for that matter a dead animal under a rock or dollops of dissolved deer-crap. You didn't drink it untreated unless there was no choice, and the slight chemical tang was the taste of safety. The dogs didn't drink at all until their master gave them a nod of permission.

The Mackenzie held out his hand before they started out again: "Talyn Strum Mackenzie, of Dun—village, you'd say—Tàirneanach; the totem of my sept is Lynx. And this fair but tight-lipped warrior maid is Caillech

Carlson Mackenzie, a neighbor of mine and oath-sister. And a Raven like the *Ard Rí* himself, as you might be guessing from the paint."

"*Ard Rí?*" he said.

"High King," Alyssa said. "That's what it means. Artos the First, High King of Montival. AKA Rudi Mackenzie, my cousin, sorta."

Whoa, wait a minute, a cousin, "sorta"? What's that mean?

"And you talk too bloody much, Talyn, the which is beyond question or doubt," Caillech said, but smiled.

Cole shook the offered hands; to his surprise Alyssa extended hers, too. Then he hesitated. You weren't supposed to talk . . . but nobody had asked him any military secrets. Plus there were things *he* really wanted to know. And after all, they were all Americans. That was the official line too, which enabled him to feel a slight glow of virtue about not keeping his mouth completely shut. Talyn and Caillech might be the children of people who'd gone so batshit insane after the Change that they just barely managed to hang on to the side of the planet with suction cups, but they were also working countryfolk caught up in the gears of war even if they were on the other side. Very much like him.

"I'm Cole Salander—"

What the fuck is the equivalent of what he said?

"—and, uh, I'm from Cottonwood Ranch, about half a day's walk from a town called Bruneau. Which is a little pimple of a place with thirty, forty people a hundred-odd miles west of Boise City. My folks run a few cattle and sheep and crop a little bit, they and my brothers . . . before the war . . . and sisters and a hand or two."

They were probably having a hell of a time just getting by, with his elder brothers missing in action and him away in the Army, but he tried not to think about that too much. There wasn't anything he could do about it, anyway, except try to keep foreign armies away from them.

"You might say the same of us, in reverse," Talyn said cheerfully. "Adding in a bit of smithing and weaving and the like. Save that her ladyship here is by way of being a princess and above such low and mean pursuits."

Alyssa snorted. "What he means is that my dad is Eric Larsson. And we're Bearkillers, not Associates, Talyn; I've done chores all my life and I made the A-list on merit, not birth."

After a moment Cole missed half a step. Eric Larsson was the military commander of one of the western outfits in the enemy alliance. They were from the Willamette valley near the Mackenzies and called themselves the Bear-killers. His sister Signe Havel—née Larsson—was their civilian leader. Though from the briefings, they didn't make much of a distinction that way, they'd been founded by a former Marine right after the Change. And Eric Larsson was related by blood or marriage to a whole clutch of other VIPs including the enemy's big bossman, the one calling himself High King Artos these days.

I am a toad, Cole thought mournfully. *I am one dead toad. I didn't just miss handing over an intelligence asset, this is high-up political stuff. I am a dead toad that got run under a road-roller and left in the hot sun. Oh, I am such a dead, flat toad.*

"And my mom is Luanne Larsson," the glider pilot went on gloomily. "Who is going to have an absolute *cow* when she hears I crashed and got banged up. She didn't want me to be a pilot."

"Instead of a lancer so shiny in armor and all?" Talyn asked innocently. "Your mother being Horsemistress of the Bearkillers."

That got him a scowl from Alyssa and a laugh from Caillech; the Bearkiller woman was obviously much too slight for fighting in plate armor on horseback, though quick and very strong for her size. The briefings said the Bearkiller elite force were most of them cavalry, as good as the knights of the Portland Protective Association and more versatile and better disciplined. They called them the A-List.

"Mom thought I'd be more useful to the war effort helping with the remount program. But I took the Gunpowder Day barrel-riding cup," Alyssa snapped. "*And* the mounted archery prize for the under-eighteens, one year. I could have made cavalry scout, easy. I just . . . like flying."

Being a shrimp wasn't a handicap for a glider pilot, of course; the opposite, if anything. Cole was a bit above medium-sized. He'd asked about pilot training himself when he turned eighteen back just before the war started, in the old General's day, and had been told that the only way to make the weight limit would be to amputate both his legs above the knee. Or his head.

"And if I was stuck-up, would I hang out with lowlifes like you two?" Alyssa said.

"Ah, it's the bonny long curling golden locks, the lassies can't resist 'em," Talyn said.

He took off his Scots bonnet for a moment to run a

hand over his shaven head and waggle the ordinary brown pigtail at the back.

"Beating them off with sticks I am three days in four, a trial and a troublement and a weariness."

The women looked at each other and mock-kicked in unison towards the bowman's backside. Cole stepped unobtrusively forward to let Alyssa steady herself against his shoulder. Having an arm in a sling interfered with your balance; he remembered that from his own experience with cracked bones.

"Wait 'til we get back," Caillech said. "I'll punish you good and proper then."

"Something to look forward to! Or I might be the one making you beg for mercy, eh?"

Caillech laughed and winked. Cole reflected gloomily that all *he* had to look forward to now was a POW camp. He supposed it was easier to be cheerful when your side was winning. Talyn might be a friendly sort, but he didn't relax his vigilance one iota; neither did his companion, or their dogs, and Alyssa was keeping an eye peeled too. Cole hadn't given any parole, so he kept his eyes open without being too conspicuous about it, and—

I am a skilled wilderness scout. It says so right there in my paybook that they took away from me after I fell asleep.

That meant he could expertly evaluate his chances of making a break, and the probability of getting anything but an arrow in the back and/or two sets of really large fangs ripping bleeding chunks out of his ass were somewhere between absolutely nothing and fucking *zip* right now.

And the fact that I'm feeling a little relieved at that analysis is neither here nor there. Or that I don't want to be the last man to die in a lost war.

Surrendering on your own was risky—everyone knew that even if both sides were playing by the official rules you were as likely as not to be finished off if you just put up your hands one-on-one at the point of the spear. When the other guy's blood was up or he'd just lost a buddy rules were a thin way to avoid becoming another anonymous body.

But Cole had made it past that stage, and the grapevine, as opposed to official propaganda, said the enemy treated POWs pretty well. Better than his own side did, these days. He was prepared to risk his life for the mission. But there was a distinct difference between a hero's honored grave and a hole in the dirt for a damned fool.

Mrs. Salander hadn't raised any fools.

"Ah . . . OK if I ask a question?" he said.

The three looked at each other. "Ask away," Talyn said. "I won't promise to answer, mind."

"That lady with the staff . . . she's a witch, right?"

Unexpectedly they all laughed. "They're *all* witches, Cole," Alyssa said.

"That we are," Caillech said, striking a mock-spooky pose and making passes through the air for a moment with her free hand. "My other horse is a broomstick!"

He absently noted that Alyssa had used his first name instead of *private* or *soldier* or *Salander* or combinations thereof; evidently shaking hands made it all right. He shook his head.

"You know what I mean. That lady with the braids and the staff *did* something to me, didn't she?"

"Meadhbh Beauregard Mackenzie is a priestess of the triple cords and the first degree, right enough," Talyn said, more solemnly than his usual bantering tone. "But for the most part she's our healer back in Dun Tàir-neanach. That's her trade."

"Doctor at home, field medic with the levy," Alyssa amplified.

"She said she felt the need to come along on this patrol," Talyn said. "She's a *fiosaiche* as well—"

"Seer," Alyssa said, or translated. "Prophet, sorta. Irritating, all those odd words, aren't they?"

"Says the *sisu* lady. And the kettle cried out *awa' with yer grimy arse* to the pot," Talyn said pointedly, then continued: "Meadhbh is a *fiosache* of note, and it's bad luck to disregard the feelings that come to such. And she found you, right enough!"

"She didn't just *find* me."

Caillech nodded. "She cast a slumber on you," she said. "I've heard of such things—Lady Juniper, the Mackenzie, the Chief herself herself, did it to a whole warband of your folk two years ago. There was a High Seeker of the CUT with them."

Cole had heard rumors about that; he'd figured it was a cover story for a defection. There had been a lot of those, especially recently.

But maybe not . . .

"But I've never seen such with my own eyes," the Clanswoman said. "It was . . . just a wee bit alarming."

"Yah *think*?" Cole said with feeling.

"And not in the usual run of things at all, at all," Talyn said.

Caillech nodded again, her face absolutely serious for a moment.

"It would recoil on the doer, so, unless there was a . . . a provocation of the same sort," she said. "So that it was in self-defense, you see? Even then it's not something to be done lightly. When a *fiosaiche* . . . a seeress or a priestess . . . calls upon the Powers, then They're all too likely to answer . . . but you're never quite sure *how*, for They are greater and other than we and Their minds are not as ours. Whether the glass bottle hits the iron cauldron, or the cauldron hits the bottle, it's often bad news for the bottle. Hence not something to be done lightly."

"Best not speak too much of it now," Talyn said warningly, and made a sign in the air.

Yeah. It's creepy.

The walk took most of the day and by the end of it they were treating him like an old friend—albeit one they were ready to shoot on the instant if he tried to run or make trouble, and one they never let into a position where he might seize a hostage. Which was flattering, if you looked at it right.

The sun was sinking behind the white peaks to the west before the first challenge came from behind a rock. Well-camouflaged sentries passed them through to a camp not far from a mountain lake. The heart of it was a long sloping flower-starred meadow of twenty or thirty acres that dropped off even more steeply southward.

A curved launching ramp of lodgepole trunks had been built down the center of the open space, with a counterweighted catapult system for throwing gliders into the air along it; it was a neat, solid piece of field engineering and differed only in detail from the ones the USAF used. As he watched a lever was tripped, the boxcar full of rocks slid down the short section of wooden rails below the ramp, gears and winches whined, and a glider swooped down and then soared into the air with a throw *just* short of the speed that would have ripped its wings off. It banked back in, came into the breeze and landed, probably testing the launcher after some repairs.

Alyssa followed the brief flight with her eyes and sighed. "No chance for me to break my neck again for a while," she muttered.

Four of the slender-winged tadpole shapes of sail-planes were staked out with technicians working around them, and flags and a wind sock marked the landing area. He even recognized the type; pre-Change Glaser-Dirk 100s, one of the Air Force favorites, or modern copies so close to the original that a nonexpert like him couldn't tell the difference. A set of big tents flew a banner that showed a snarling bear's-head, face-on in black and red and white on a brown background, and they contained a portable forge and workshops with treadle-powered lathes and presses.

The rest of the encampment included a corral for draught animals, mainly big mules, and a thick scattering of bell-tents grouped in threes around a somewhat larger one; the flag there was the moon and antlers of the Mac-kenzies. A taller pole in the center bore the Crowned Mountain and Sword—what the new "kingdom" of Montival used.

Folk gathered around, about half in pants and the rest in the Clan's kilt. There must be more than two hundred here all up, but he'd gotten used to crowds since he started his military service. Though so many strange faces still seemed slightly unnatural, to someone who'd grown up on a little family ranch where you could go a month or more at a time without seeing a single outsider and a year without meeting someone from out of the neighborhood.

Alyssa exchanged salutes just like the one he'd learned in school with a hawk-faced woman in her thirties with brown hair in the same shortish bob cut.

He looked around. *OK, Bearkiller women in the army wear it that way, like our high-and-tight.*

She was dressed in a practical-looking brown uniform that included a basket-hilted single-edged sword. There was a small blue scar like Alyssa's between her brows and what would have been a Captain's bars in the US Army on her shoulders.

"Don't tell me. A write-off, right?" the officer said.

"Yes, ma'am."

"Did you see any sign of the enemy *before* you totaled it?"

"Nothing, ma'am. I didn't get that far."

"How did you manage to pile up your ship?"

"I relied on getting lift somewhere it wasn't and then I was lower than the terrain all around me. Then I was lower than the terrain *under* me."

The officer sighed. "If you had a sane approach to risk management you wouldn't be a pilot, Larsson."

"No excuses, Captain Sanders. Nothing salvageable in my estimation, the terrain's not suitable even for mules, you'd have to backpack the wreck out in pieces. Plus there's a *really big* dead bear lying next to it."

A shrug. "It might be worthwhile going after the instruments, later. You're a good pilot, Larsson, and they're harder to produce than gliders. Don't make a habit of it, but combat-lossing these things occasionally is a cost of doing business. We'll just show some *sisu* and suck it up. Written report including map data by fourteen hundred hours tomorrow."

"Yes, ma'am. *Haakaa päälle!*"

"Hack 'em down! The arm?"

"Hairline fracture of the ulna, according to the Mackenzie *fiosaiche*."

"She's a qualified field medic," the officer said—a little reluctantly, Cole thought.

Alyssa nodded. "No need for a plaster cast, just time. I don't think there was much of a concussion, none of the symptoms, except that I was woozy for a while. No recurrence of headaches, or blurred vision or loss of balance. Didn't even lose any teeth."

"Right, have our doc take a look when he's got time but you're on restricted duty until the arm heals anyway, four to six weeks if nothing goes wrong. I'll unload some of my paperwork on you."

Alyssa gave an almost imperceptible wince, and the officer returned a slightly disquieting grin. "I know, you can interrogate your cutie of a POW here. You are now in charge of that, seconded to Intelligence until you're fit for unrestricted duty again."

I'm a cutie? Cole thought, torn between feeling flattered and insulted.

"He's technically the Mackenzies' prisoner, ma'am."

"I doubt they'll be competing for the privilege of talking to him."

"That we will not," Caillech said. "No offense, Cole Salander."

Alyssa chuckled. "He's not going to talk much anyway. Not at first, at least."

"SOP, we have to jump through the hoops." She looked at Cole. "Interested in switching sides? We've got a lot of Boiseans on our side now, and Frederick Thurston leads them, your first ruler's son."

Cole shook his head, keeping private doubts off his face. "No, ma'am," he said. "Captain Wellman's always been straight with me, and as long as he says it's the right side I'm on it."

"Fair enough, private. A man's obligations are his own to judge. You're between a rock and a hard place and I don't envy you that position one little bit. You may change your mind when you're further back and get a chance to talk to more of your own folk who've come to different conclusions. Larsson, ask the usual questions, write 'em down, and we'll send the report on with him when we have time and personnel to spare to move him out. Carry on."

A swatch of Mackenzies had gathered around, along with some of their enormous dogs. Apart from the hair-cuts and whether or not they'd painted their faces they looked more uniform than he'd expected, given their wild neobarb reputation . . . but then, according to the briefing they wore the kilt and plaid all the time anyway, so this was probably their ordinary clothes apart from the war-gear. Alter the clothes and such and keep their mouths shut and they'd pass for his neighbors easily. Nearly all of them were Changelings of around his age give or take a few years. There were some adolescents doing chores and standing in back, and a few slightly older ones were officers, most of whom wore a neck-torc of thin twisted gold.

Right, that's the Mackenzie equivalent of a wedding ring, only they wear it around the neck. And there are so many women! he thought.

Then, after he did a deliberate count: *No, not as many as all that. Well under half the total. It just looks like more to my eye, I guess. What the lecture called perception bias. Got to watch that if you want to make an accurate report.*

Talyn and his comrade made *their* report to a big scarred man pushing thirty, with freckles on a ruddy pale face, rust-colored hair in a queue and one of the torcs around his bull neck. After drawing them aside out of earshot for a few sharp questions he gave Cole a long look, then turned to Alyssa.

"Is this one's word good, Lady?"

Alyssa looked at Cole herself. "Is it?" she said.

He scowled and nodded. A man whose word *wasn't* good was a toad—no, a worm—and he instinctively resented the question. But to be fair she wasn't a neighbor who'd grown up knowing him down to the bootlaces in the usual way. Dealing with strangers could be hard, without reputation to guide you. Nobody trusted people they didn't know the way they did kin and the folks from over the next creek.

"I break any promises to you, ma'am?" he said.

"No." She turned to the Mackenzie. "And our acquaintance was brief, but intense, Bow-captain Luag. I'd say he was honorable but I can't take oath on it."

Luag looked to Cole for a long green-eyed moment. "Give us your oath not to fight nor to try escaping while you're in this war-camp, and we'll let you walk free, though watched. Deny it, and we must keep you bound save when you're on the latrine, the which would be uncomfortable and would do your cause no good at all or whatsoever. Suffer uselessly or not, as you please."

A pause, and he went on flatly: "If you give your word and break it, then we'll kill you sure. As an offering to Lugh Longspear."

Cole thought carefully while the Clan warriors leaned on their great bows and watched him, moistening his lips a little as he did. On the one hand, standing orders said if you were captured you had to escape if possible. On the other, the New UCMJ said you had to escape *if possible* not *get yourself killed trying* when it wasn't possible; his chances of that were much better when he was being moved and was far away from an enemy encampment.

OK, giving a general parole is out, but a temporary one . . . possible.

Especially if he stayed here a couple of days with liberty to walk around he could probably learn something valuable, and he *was* specifically tasked with getting information about bases like this, so it was aiding his mission to be able to ask questions and watch things. He could try for a break when they moved him—they couldn't spare much effort to guard one prisoner, and in any army things got looser as you moved away from the sharp end. On the third hand—

"Unless US forces attack this camp," he said. "If they do, all bets are off."

There were grins and chuckles at that. *Such a lot of merry lighthearted jokester bastards,* he thought. *Goddammit.* It was probably a lot easier to laugh when you were winning.

The redhead raised an eyebrow. "Or unless the sky fall and crush us, or the sea rise and drown us, or the world end," he said sardonically.

"And my parole to last three days from sunset today and no more. After that I'm free to escape and to do anything necessary to carrying out my duties. And you're free to shoot me if I try and if you can."

A short, crisp but somehow respectful nod. "Good. A man careless of his oath would likely make fewer conditions, so. Swear then, in the sight of whatever Gods you follow and on a fighting-man's honor."

"I'm a Methodist, I guess . . ." He thought for a moment, then raised his right hand and swore *so help me God*.

Luag listed the specifics carefully, and drew a sign in the air before finishing:

"So witness all the Gods of my people, and the Mother-of-All in Her form as the Threefold Morrigú, who loves a warrior's faithfulness, and the Lord Her consort as Lugh of the Oaths. You're free of our camp, but don't go beyond its bounds—those white wands you see planted about."

He hadn't noticed the peeled sticks, but they were obvious once the bowman's thick finger pointed them out.

Luag went on: "What the Bearkillers do is their affair, but I wouldn't go among them alone either, if I were you, for all that they're blood brothers of ours, so to speak. They're a suspicious lot about outsiders and quickly fierce with their blades."

Raising his voice slightly:

"To harm this man is *geasa* so long as he keeps his oath. Watch him close, but put no slight nor insolence on him while he's bound helpless by his pledge. Or I will most assuredly kick your arse until your teeth march out of your mouth like little Bearkiller pikemen on parade, and you will be mocked by all and the bards will make a tale of it at the next festival and ill-luck will dog your tracks. This is a war, not a blood feud. Treat him as you would wish on one of our own if they had the misfortune to fall captive. Understood?"

There was a murmur of assent.

"Then spread the word. About your work the now, Mackenzies."

"Ah . . . that's it?" Cole said.

"Is anything more needful?" Talyn said. "Ah, here's our tent, the which you are welcome to share. Though we usually sleep under the stars unless it's raining or much colder than this. Stow your gear."

He and Caillech spent a few moments removing each other's war paint, with a mixture of flaxseed oil and goose grease that smelled of herbs—sage and rosemary, Cole thought—and then soap and water. Most of the Mackenzies just nodded at the prisoner and walked away, going back to working on their gear or shooting at wooden targets and flinging disks with truly alarming dexterity or sparring or towards some cooking pits where an agonizingly good smell was drifting with wafts of bluish smoke to remind him that he'd been working hard on light rations. Others simply napped, played flutes or guitars, read or wrote letters, played games with dice or cards, or . . .

He blinked, and blushed a little. Soldiering tended to erode your sense of privacy, but he was used to it being all guys. His army had stopped recruiting women after the old General died a couple of years ago, and hadn't had many even then. Cole averted his eyes.

Bearkillers seemed to do things more or less the way he was used to. The Mackenzies . . .

"They're sort of informal, aren't they? But it works for them," Alyssa said. "*God* knows why."

"Hup-one-two, and a lance up the arse to keep your back braced straight," Caillech said. "The Bearkiller way."

The two young women stuck out their tongues at each other, and Talyn rolled his eyes.

"I smell that a sounder of wild pig were guided our way by Cernunnos," he said, rubbing his hands together. "Rather than the over-stewed muck of infamous memory we get nine days in ten, when it isn't jerky and trail mix and dog biscuit instead, *ochone*, the sorrow and black pity of it. Let us prepare for the sacred rite of eating ourselves full and drinking what's to be had while we have the chance, for it won't happen often."

Cole smiled a little. The general awfulness of military food was something everyone seemed to have in common, weird or not.

CHAPTER SIX

Castle Todenangst, Crown demesne
Portland Protective Association
Willamette Valley near Newburg
High Kingdom of Montival
(formerly western Oregon)
June 15th, Change Year 26/2024 AD

The last series of windows came down to the floor, opening out in French doors. Beyond was a fan-shaped open platform the size of a largish room, held by curved girders of cast aluminum alloy whose ends reared up into stylized eagle's heads all around its rim. Between them along the edge was a border of waist-high marble sheets carved into fretwork. Not at all coincidentally, they were exactly the right height to lean on comfortably for a rather short someone named Sandra Arminger.

Most of the balcony was covered by an arched pergola of thin wrought bronze rods thickly grown with vines, the last of the late-blooming violet-blue Shiro Noda wisteria hanging in foot-long clusters interwoven with golden Rêve d'Or roses. The heady Noisette perfume of the roses mingled with the fainter, more delicate scent of the Japanese wisteria. Hummingbirds flitted among the blossoms like living jewels of ruby and malachite, and the eyes of several of Sandra's Persians tracked them with bright wistful interest.

And a low feline chittering of teeth accompanied by a murmur of *ah ahnt ahnt ahnt*, which meant something like: *Chew toy! Chew toy!*

"I wonder, was that excessive?" Sandra murmured, looking up. "Roses *and* wisteria? Did I do it just because suddenly I *could*? I'm afraid that happened a fair bit back then. It was as if we were both a little drunk with possibilities, your father and I. From impecunious academics to gaming with kingdoms."

Laughter came from the space beyond the doors, and then the bright tinkle of a metal-strung cittern, and a woman's voice raised in song:

> *"I waited for a sunny day to launch my grand design.*
> *The clouds would loom—*
> *The wind would turn—*
> *It happened every time!*
> *Until at last it struck me:*
> *I should just let it all unfold*
> *The sun is shining somewhere . . .*
> *And fortune loves the bold!"*

Mathilda smiled at the sound of Lady Delia de Stafford's clear alto voice; she supposed she didn't *approve* of Delia, but she certainly *liked* her and always had. She turned the smile into one of greeting and nodded to the squire who stood beside the entrance with a white rod of office in his hand. He'd been chatting with Lady Jehane Jones de Molalla, her mother's amanuensis—confidential secretary—a sleek young woman in a rose-and-gold cotte-hardie and a gold wimple, which set off her chocolate skin.

"Lady Jehane," she said, smiling and extending her hand for the kiss of homage. "God give you good day, Huon," she went on to the squire.

"And God and the Virgin be with you, Your Majesty," Huon Liu de Gervais said, bowing gravely, a flourish of the baton in his right hand and the left on the hilt of his sword.

He was in court dress: Ray-Bans, tight hose, ankle-shoes with upturned toes tipped with little golden bells, loose shirt of soft linen, doeskin jerkin and a houppelande coat with long dagged sleeves. And a roll-edged chaperon hat with a broad liripipe tail hanging to one shoulder; that was a mark of near-adult status as opposed to the brimless flowerpot style all pages and most squires wore. At sixteen he was young for it, but he *had* charged with her *menie* at the Horse Heaven Hills when the chivalry of the Association broke the Prophet's elite guard.

If he'd been a little older she'd have knighted him on the field, and not because his elder brother Odard had been one of the companions of the Quest and died for her on the far cold shores of the Atlantic.

Well, not only because of that. Plus his sister Yseult is getting to be really useful in the Household. No flies on that girl at all, as Mother would say, and she's been invaluable with Fred's sisters. And I like them both.

The colors were the black-lined-scarlet of House Arminger, which suited Huon's dark tilt-eyed good looks. She hadn't had time to put the Household into the High Kingdom's forest green and silver yet. . . .

And I'll still be an Arminger, anyway. That doesn't change.

"Have you and Lioncel had any time for hawking, Huon?" she said.

Delia's eldest son and Huon had become fast friends during last year's campaign; she knew it roweled him to be here behind the lines while his comrade was mostly off as the Grand Constable's squire in the east.

"Yes, my lady," he said eagerly, looking less solemn—and he was allowed to entitle her so in an informal setting, since he was her personal liegeman. "We're going to have some time to fly tiercels along the river tomorrow, we think. Diomede can come along—"

Who was Delia's *younger* son, a page in the household of Countess Anne of Tillamook, and just a little too junior to take the field as yet at all. And green with envy, though too good-natured to be a real pest about it.

"The Grand Constable and Lioncel and my lord Rigobert his father have been winning great honor!"

"So have you, Huon Liu de Gervais," Mathilda said gently. "For I trust you with my life, and more, my daughter, the heir of the Kingdom."

He flushed a little and bowed again as she and Sandra swept past. Her mother was fighting to keep the smile off her face as she concluded a low-voiced exchange with Jehane that had the girl packing up her lap-desk and gliding off on some errand.

"He'll remember that," Sandra said approvingly, and *sotto voce*.

"It's *true*," Mathilda replied, very slightly indignant. *Even though there's no actual* danger *here—stone smooth* as polished glass above and below us, and miles of guards between here and the gates. It's one of the few places we can really relax.

"Truth? All the better!" her mother said happily.

She'd practiced good lordship by sheer political calculation all her life.

And if she weren't my mother, her approval would make me doubt myself, sometimes! But a ruler must be a good politician too; it's a duty. So many lives and livelihoods depend on it! It's when politics fail that the swords come out and homes burn.

The others were sitting around the tables as the dappled shade played across the pale cream and blue Redondo tiles in patterns that shifted with the breeze. They rose as Huon announced her, calling out *The High Queen!* and *The Queen Mother!* briskly but without the annoying bellow heralds used sometimes.

The Associate ladies sank in deep curtsies, the skirts of their cotte-hardies spreading in a display of colors brighter than the flowers overhead and the long sleeves touching the tile. The combination of their own high rank and the relaxed social setting meant they didn't have to kneel. That sort of thing was one reason why sometimes more could be done during a tea party than at an official council-meeting.

Though this is rather formal dress for a tea party . . . I know, I'll get Delia to start drawing up a manual of court etiquette and costume for the High Kingdom. Something more relaxed than Association protocol. We can call it a political compromise to make the non-Associates feel more at home.

"Lady Delia, Lady Ermentrude, Lady Anne," she said—deliberately informal modes, as she extended her hand again. "Lady Signe."

Signe Havel gave her a stiff salute with a little frost in it.

No hand-kissing there! Mathilda thought, as she returned it with a Protectorate-style gesture, right fist to chest—which looked a little odd when you were wearing a cotte-hardie since it was usually accompanied by a clash of armored gauntlet on breastplate, but she couldn't think of anything more appropriate.

Signe *wasn't* an Associate, of course. The Lady of the Bearkillers was a handsome blond woman in her forties, in the plain practical brown uniform her folk wore in the field and with a basket-hilted backsword leaning against the arm of her chair. She'd never really forgiven any member of House Arminger for the spectacular and mutually fatal public duel between Norman Arminger and Mike Havel that had ended the Protector's War.

"And Virginia! You're glowing . . . and looking uncomfortable. Believe me, I sympathize."

Virginia Thurston was in a housedress, of very expensive printed cotton but cut simply, what a well-to-do woman in Boise would wear though she'd never yet seen the city. It was a maternity style, though, and she looked every day of her seventh month.

"I feel like I've swallowed a pumpkin," she grumbled; her face was still narrow, framed by her yellow-brown hair. "And my ankles hurt and I have to pee all the time. Least I ain't . . . I'm not puking so much."

"Don't worry. It gets better," Mathilda said.

Delia chuckled. "But not before the birth. And that's

anything but comfortable, let me tell you. The pumpkin has to come *out*."

All the mothers present laughed, which meant everyone except Countess Anne, who winced slightly in sympathy. Juniper Mackenzie was still grinning as she came forward and hugged Mathilda. Countess Ermentrude blinked slightly, showing that she knew more of the theory than the practice of Court etiquette. Everyone made allowances for Mackenzie irreverence, and Juniper was a sovereign herself as Chief of the Clan, albeit one in vassalage to the High Kingdom now. Plus after the Protector's War Mathilda had spent months every year in Dun Juniper with her and her family, just as Rudi had come north. That made Juniper her second mother as well as mother-in-law.

"My darlin' foster girl!" she said, and Mathilda squeezed her back through the fine soft wool of her *arisaid*.

"Your unrecognizably *fat* foster girl!" she murmured into the older woman's ear.

"Nonsense. Just a few healthy curves; the Maiden becomes Mother."

Mathilda hugged her again, and felt that little familiar shock that she was so much taller than the Mackenzie.

She and Mother are about the same height. One of the few things they have in common, besides their wits. And that you forget it because they both feel bigger in your mind.

Signe's face turned a little chillier. She'd also never completely forgiven Juniper Mackenzie for meeting Mike Havel and bearing his son, who was now Mathilda's husband and High King. Not just for the usual reasons a woman would, even though that had been a single night and before Signe had married him, but because Rudi *was* High King, instead of one of *her* children.

The wet-nurse—an Associate herself, a younger collateral of the great Jones family who were Counts in Mollala and who'd lost her own child not long after birth—brought Órlaith to Mathilda. Objectively Mathilda's daughter looked like any three-month-old . . .

But by the holy Mother of God, she's beautiful! Mathilda thought.

For a moment the feeling clenched her eyes shut like physical pain. When she opened them again her daughter was baring her gums in a broad smile and kicking within the linen smock, reaching for her.

"Órlaith," she said as she picked the solid little weight up. "My golden princess!"

"*My* granddaughter," Sandra said.

"*And* mine," Juniper Mackenzie said.

"But my *only* granddaughter, so far. Your fourth."

"Give me time, Mom!" Mathilda said.

She was that post-Change rarity, an only child. Juniper had what she thought of as a more typical middle-of-the-road total of four.

Mathilda kissed her daughter on the forehead and handed her over to Sandra, who gave a short odd laugh as she took her competently in the crook of an arm. Juniper looked a question.

"I was just thinking," Sandra said, "of how often I've wondered what the world will be like when the last of us oldsters have shuffled off to our—literal, as it turns out—rewards and the Changelings like Mathilda are left to run things without us."

"And I've had the same thought, many a time," Juniper said. "But?"

"Just now," Sandra said, tickling the tip of the baby's nose with one finger as she smiled and kicked, "it struck me that I should wonder what the world will be like when *Órlaith's* generation is in charge . . . people who never knew the people who knew the world before the Change. When she's my age it will be . . . Good Lord, it'll be Change Year 84! Nearly a century! Will they really believe anything about our world by then, except as myths? And of course *her* children . . ."

Juniper's face froze for a moment, though the Change-lings showed polite incomprehension. Then she said, slowly:

"It never fails; in a conversation with you, something truly *disquieting* will be said. Now I'll be having that thought every time I look at a baby, instead of just enjoying the little ones. *Thank* you, Sandra."

"You're welcome, dear Juniper."

Mathilda sat with a slight snort; talking to Mother *did* keep you on your mental toes, the way sparring with Rudi sharpened your reflexes with the sword. She arranged the skirts of her cotte-hardie and nodded to the others as a maidservant offered a tray.

Everyone occupied themselves pouring tea and passing plates of tiny sandwiches and pastries—potted shrimp and cucumber and deviled chicken and little glazed things with raspberries and cream. The tea was the real luxury, even more expensive than coffee. Local equivalents were still experimental, and this was the genuine article, imported by a profoundly unreliable chain of middlemen through desolate pirate-haunted seas from the few revived plantations in Asia to Maui in the Kingdom of Hawaii and then to Astoria. The world was a very large place, these days. Even larger than it had been in the Jane Austen novels that were so popular among the female nobility, and which probably helped keep the beverage so prestigious.

"Please, no formality, Mesdames," Mathilda said, and picked a pastry off the chased silver, making herself nibble graciously rather than bolting it. "Speak freely, and don't worry about precedence."

I'm hungry. *Getting back into shape is* brutal *but I don't dare go anywhere near a battlefield until I do. Even commanders end up fighting with their own hands at least occasionally, God knows I have often enough, and if you get tired first you die. I want to help Rudi the way I did on the Quest, not burden him.*

She'd managed to hack out a two-hour session every morning from her impossible schedule, and sparring in plate armor with a fifteen-pound shield on one arm and an oaken drill-sword in the other hand was about the best overall exercise there was. The changes in her body during pregnancy had been . . .

Interesting, she thought. *And certainly worthwhile. Though the mood swings . . . poor Rudi! He was probably glad to get back to the field.*

Her lips thinned a little as a muscle-memory of her sword-edge hammering into bone ran through her fingers and up into her gut. That was the sort of thing you remembered in the middle of the night sometimes; that and the faces.

She worked her right hand, the way you did to get the kinks out after a fight. Unexpectedly, she found herself crossing eyes with Signe Havel, who nodded very slightly with a small wry smile. They'd never be friends, but for that instant across the gulfs of family and rivalry they shared something—something incommunicable to anyone who hadn't been in the place they'd both visited and from which you never *entirely* returned.

The hardest part now was that unlike a lot of warriors she had never really *enjoyed* the utterly essential life-preserving process of keeping in tip-top shape. She enjoyed the results, the feeling of strength and capacity, she was a pretty good natural athlete and sparring was fun in limited doses, but it wasn't the passion for her it was with—say—Rudi. Or for that matter Tiphaine d'Ath, whose idea of *rest* was flipping through a back issue of *Tactical Crossbows* between bouts in the salle d'armes. And if she was better than average with a sword, it was because she'd pushed it doggedly all her life with the finest tutors.

Not least of that had been Rudi. Just trying to keep up with *him* made you do things you hadn't imagined were possible.

God, I miss him, seeing him smile and touching him and even the way his hair smells. Oh, well, at least my sword-calluses are recovering so my hands don't hurt as much. For once I'm not sorry to be in a cotte-hardie; I still feel shapeless without lacing.

Delia de Stafford exchanged a glance with Sandra; she was in her thirties and smoothly beautiful, with raven-black ringlets hanging artlessly from under an open lace wimple topped by an embroidered cap. Baroness Forest Grove by marriage to Baron Rigobert and Châtelaine of Ath because of a rather less . . . orthodox . . . arrangement with the Grand Constable, as the two sets of ceremonial keys at her belt indicated. Sandra had always been her patron—she had an Associate's dagger because of the then Lady Regent's favor, as well as the Grand Constable's—and the whole rather complex quasi-family were pillars of the throne.

"It's wonderful that the news from the east is so good," Delia said. "Not only more victories, but so far *bloodless* ones. Well, mostly bloodless. As far as *our* blood goes."

"Thanks to Fred! Ah, General Thurston," Virginia Thurston—née Kane—said. "President Thurston, soon."

"He's certainly done a wonderful job," Mathilda said. *And truthfully again!* she thought, and went on:

"We both saw what he could do on the Quest."

Though we also saw him grow up a lot getting there and back again. Or at least I did. You *never saw him in his father's shadow.*

Delia's eight-month-old daughter Yolande was with her, and a very active toddler named Heuradys in a lace-fringed shift and mob cap controlling unruly mahogany hair, both playing quietly to one side under the direction of a nanny. Though Heuradys had apparently learned the word *no* and liked using it with lordly insouciance. Mathilda chuckled at the sight, not least because of the names.

Yolande and Heuradys, Lioncel and Diomede . . . all of Delia's children were named from a set of books her mother had always liked, set in a skewed version of France seven hundred years ago. Mathilda liked them too; they were far more realistic than most pre-Change fiction, even Austen or Mallory. They fitted in perfectly with the archaic-French naming pattern the PPA nobility mostly favored anyway; Spanish was the second choice. The

Grand Constable, Tiphaine d'Ath, had taken her Associate name from them too, long before, when Sandra had taken her under her wing and recognized her . . . unique . . . talents.

The Countess Anne of Tillamook looked at the children wistfully. She was in her twenties and handsomely strong-faced, a pale blonde with sea-green eyes; and she ruled that coastal holding by her own hereditary right as her father's heir, as yet without a consort. She was more or less betrothed to Ogier, the youngest son of Count Renfrew of Odell. Young Sir Ogier was with the host, of course; another thing to resent about the war was the way it *delayed* things you were looking forward to.

The other noblewoman was Countess Ermentrude of Walla Walla, a slim dark-haired willowy woman in her mid-twenties, still looking a little uncertain in this company but hiding it well. By birth she was from County Dawson on the Association's far northern border, and her husband's holding—the County Palatine of the Eastermark, centered on the great fortress-city of Walla Walla— was on the PPA's far frontier eastward, what had been the border march with Boise before the war. Neither she nor the young Count Palatine, Felipe de Aguirre-Smith, had been much at court, beyond the essentials.

She was making a strong effort to be gracious to Delia, too; the last year had given her and her spouse good personal as well as military reasons to be grateful to Tiphaine d'Ath and Rigobert. And Ermentrude herself had won considerable troubadour-spread fame by commanding the defense of the city of Walla Walla during its siege by the enemy, while the Count led his vassals in the field with the High King. She'd commanded the all-important political side at least, which included keeping the city's guilds and her lord's war-captains in order, and that despite being heavily pregnant at the time.

It's breaking out all over, Mathilda thought whimsically. *Well, replenish the earth and all that. At least this miserable war is cementing a lot of new relationships between the noble houses who support the Crown. Delia and Anne and Ermentrude between them have connections all over the Association, and their opinions really matter on the manor-house grapevine telegraph. If they're all pulling in the same direction, it'll make things a lot easier.*

Signe looked down at the heir to the crown of Montival and chuckled as she tickled her, a little unexpectedly . . . but she was a mother as well as a political leader, of course.

"They're so cute at that age," she said. "They have to be, or we'd strangle them. After two sets of twins and a singleton I should know." She looked around. "Aren't the Thurston kids here at Todenangst? Fred's sisters?"

"Shawonda and Jaine? They're at their lessons with my lady-in-waiting, Yseult Liu," Mathilda said.

"Studying falconry, was what I heard," Juniper said. "Diomede is giving them a tour of the mews."

Delia smiled fondly at the mention of her younger son. "Diomede is just getting to the age when showing off to girls is something a boy likes," she observed.

Mathilda nodded. "I'm keeping them close for security reasons, but this is going to be a bit boring for teenagers, they're good friends of Yseult, and . . ."

"You don't want them too closely identified with Court," Signe said; she was a politician too, after all. A wolfish grin. "Especially with *Associate* court stuff."

Sandra nodded coolly and sipped at her tea; partly in recognition, partly an unspoken *tsk, tsk*. She would never have said that *aloud* at a public gathering, even a small one like this. Not that she'd give Signe any notice of it, either.

Mathilda could read her thought: *those with wit enough will realize, and why point out to the gullible and dim what they can't see for themselves? Part of being clever is not needing to prove it all the time.*

Juniper snorted and rolled her eyes.

"They're nice kids," Virginia said. "And their Mom is one smart lady."

Everyone nodded and took a sip of their tea. Anne of Tillamook had been visibly waiting to speak, but she deferred gracefully to Ermentrude. The flat, slightly drawn-out vowels of the Peace River country were still audible in her voice as she spoke slowly:

"Thank you for inviting me, Your Majesty. I've written, but it's always better to speak face-to-face if you can. And Felipe . . . well, he's very busy with leading the County's contingent in the field, of course. The thing is . . ."

She took a deep breath. "I've been touring all the areas of the County Palatine the enemy overran, helping with the reconstruction. It'll be years . . . we lost so much livestock and equipment. Though we're not actually facing famine thanks to what you've shipped in. And the damage to the manor houses and villages was very bad . . . the castles held, almost all of them, but . . ."

Her calm broke a little. "A generation of work wrecked in a year!"

"I said after the Horse Heaven Hills that the Association looks after its own," Mathilda said. "We've already sent a good deal."

Everyone nodded. About a quarter of the Protectorate's manors had been damaged in the war, ranging from *cattle raid* level to *burned to the ground*. Castles were nearly invulnerable if well provisioned and strongly held—that was the whole point—but villages and manor houses were easy meat to an enemy who held the open country. The untouched ones farther west had agreed to doubled mesne tithes and even better had mostly actually paid them, with no more than a token amount of grumbling. That was over and above the lawful reliefs they owed in war anyway and the lost labor when the full levy was called out, and it was going to hurt. That response had made her proud to be an Associate and an Arminger.

"We're grateful. But?" Ermentrude said. "Your Majesty, I can hear the *but* in your voice. My father always said that *but* is the killer."

Mathilda sighed. "Have you seen the reports from south of the Columbia? The CORA territories?"

She pronounced the acronym in the usual way, as if it were a woman's name. Technically it stood for the Central Oregon Rancher's Association, the ad hoc group that had gotten the area west of the Cascades through the first years of the Change down there.

Ermentrude winced a little. "Yes. There's . . . really not much left, is there? We were hurt, they were wrecked."

Juniper sighed, suddenly looking older. "The people got out two years ago, the most of them, and some of their stock, and what they could carry with them on packhorses moving fast through the Cascades to the Willamette. Nothing else."

The Mackenzie chieftain nodded to Signe. "You Bear-killers helped cover the retreat well, after the lost battle at Pendleton."

Signe shrugged. "From what Eric tells me it's a total mess there."

Her brother Eric Larsson had led the Montivallan forces following the retreating enemy south of the Columbia; he was a hard man, but there had been an undertone of horror in his reports.

"Pure meanness," Virginia Thurston said with deep sincerity. "Christ . . . or the Aesir . . . but the CUT needs to be burned off the face of the earth."

She obviously sympathized with the Ranchers; she was fierce, but not vicious. And the CORA were very much like her own folk, though perhaps a little less . . .

Rustic, Mathilda thought charitably. *The Powder River country is very . . . rustic. Or within wiping distance of the arse-end of nowhere, as Edain put it.*

"Most of the CORA fighting-men are with the host," the High Queen said aloud. "And the King will need them badly in the east, they're fine light cavalry. But they're also proud folk, the Ranchers and their cowboys both. They've fought well, and their guerillas did good service tying down enemy troops south of the river. They don't like being refugees living on the charity of others.

"They want to go *home,* and make a start on rebuilding, even while their warriors are away."

Looked at coldly, it would make more sense to resettle the folk elsewhere. Morality and practical politics both made that out of the question, of course. Her own consciousness of the land—all the land of Montival—made that part of it feel like a raw bruise.

Some of the conversation that followed was by prearrangement. The Mackenzies had always had close links with the CORA, and she suspected it hadn't been too hard for Juniper to get the Clan's *Óenach Mór*, the Great Assembly, to agree to more help; Father Ignatius had assured her that Mt. Angel would do the same. Signe offered to join the effort, and hinted that she'd get Corvallis to cough up too. They all promised longer-term aid to the County Palatine as well.

"Lady Ermentrude?" Mathilda said, when they'd gone around the subject long enough.

"I . . . yes, we'll accept that some of the aid from the western and northern parts of the Association goes to the CORA rather than immediately to the County Palatine. Felipe will agree, after he shouts and kicks the walls a little." More firmly. "Yes. Ruling means setting priorities and you can never satisfy everyone."

Juniper handed the little princess to Sandra; Mathilda smiled to herself at her mother's well-concealed eagerness. The Mackenzie went on:

"I'd suggest that we find some excuse to take folk . . . including some of yours, Lady Ermentrude . . . on a wee bit of a tour of the CORA lands, to see for themselves what's been done there. Forbye that will show them the extent of the damage and that they weren't the only ones to suffer. And remind them why we're fighting, to be sure, to be sure."

Sandra nodded. "Excellent idea, my dear Juniper. Now, about the details—"

Halfway through the discussion Mathilda found herself standing at the edge of the balcony, making a tactful withdrawal of her High Queenly presence and sipping her fourth cup of tea and nibbling a scone rich with hazel-nuts. She smiled a little as she looked out over the great castle. The Association's barons affected a plate-armored machismo; the unkind said they tended to be solid iron from ear to ear whether their helmets were on or not. But it occurred to her, not for the first time, that this group here was making a lot of the real decisions among them-selves . . . and every single one of them was female.

From here you could see most of Todenangst, the south side at least. The great circuit of the outer bailey, a tall granite-faced wall studded with machicolated towers bearing tall witch-hat roofs of green copper, lined on the inner surface by a linear town of tiled homes and work-shops, barracks and stables and armories and inns and churches. A ring road and terraced gardens marked the bailey's boundary; the gates there were tunnels into the hillside that bore the inner keep, and could be blocked by portcullis-like slabs of steel falling at the push of a lever. Inside access was via spiral roadways that were death traps to an invader in themselves.

Then the keep itself, itself far larger than most castles, a hill topped with wall and tower, courtyard and cathedral and endless little nooks and surprises, all the way down to the dungeons below and the secret passages that laced the whole. Above them all the Silver Tower and the Onyx, rearing sheer hundreds of feet into the air and flaunting their banners beneath the blue cloud-speckled sky. It had been so all her life that she could remember—the main structure had been completed by ten thousand men working in round-the-clock shifts and finishing when she was about five, though furnishing and fitting was still go-ing on in some parts, and probably always would be.

Mother kept that copy of Gormenghast *close at hand when she was designing the place. Though it's much prettier than Steerpike's stamping grounds. Gormenghastian but not Gormen-ghastly. And say what you like about father, he had a will like forged steel, and he dreamed grandly.*

Perhaps it was what Juniper and Sandra had said earlier, but it struck her now that virtually everything in the landscape she could see save the bones of the earth—things like the tiny perfect white cone of Mount Hood off to the west, the lower blue line of the Coast Range westward— was not much older than she. Todenangst *looked* as if it had reared here for centuries amid its surroundings of river and woodland, manors and the multihued green of field and vineyard, woodlot and orchard, the spires of churches, railroads thronged with horse-drawn trains, dusty white roads thick with oxcarts and peasants on foot, monks and men-at-arms, merchants and bicyclists or Tinerant caravans.

In fact the lower bulk of the castle was steel cargo-containers from trains, and from barges and freighters stranded in the Columbia by the Change, filled with crushed automobiles and rubble and cement and all locked together and set in cast mass-concrete. The heights were girders and lead-coated rebar and more concrete; the very stone sheathing had been stripped from skyscrapers in Portland and Vancouver and Seattle. Only the roofing-tile and some of the woodwork and textiles had been made for it. Parts of the enormous complex were still faintly warm with the heat of curing cement.

I don't think this way very often, Mathilda reflected, sipping at the delicate acridity of the tea.

She'd received a good Classical education, including

elements of the pre-Change sciences. Some of them were still useful, but it had all never seemed really real to her until she'd been whirled through the depths of time at Lost Lake. Still . . .

Will any of this ever occur to Órlaith at all? she thought.

Something hit the bronze bars of the trellis with an enormous *whung* sound. Mathilda whirled around in a flurry of skirts and dagged sleeves. A man had flung himself out of a window sixty feet above the balcony, spread-eagled to distribute the impact. It should still have broken half his bones, but his face was as empty of expression as an insect's as he rolled off the metal and onto the tile of the floor. He wore a servant's tabard and livery, but a curved knife glittered in his hand, with the rayed sun of the Church Universal and Triumphant etched into the steel.

The mark of the CUT's assassin-priest-mages.

Two more figures were hurtling downward even as he shambled erect, lurching away from her towards the tables with one leg turned at an impossible angle.

Now she could *feel* them. As an emptiness, a lack of presence, a hole in her link with the land.

"Órlaith!" she shouted.

Mathilda snatched up the silver tea tray, the pot and cups flying over the edge of the balcony unheeded. She gripped it by the edge, twisting and flinging it with a snap that sent the disk skimming through the air. It struck the assassin in the back of the neck with a heavy *chunk* that would have been instantly fatal to any normal man. The cultist staggered, fell . . . then twitched and began to rise again.

A fourth figure fell, and a fifth. Her heart froze,

though these were in armor. One was just dead; the other managed to draw his sword and push it towards her before his head fell slack.

"Guard Órlaith!" she called, snatching up the heavy blade as she ran, taking it in the two-handed grip.

CHAPTER SEVEN

By the time the lingering summer sun was well down behind the peaks, Cole Salander had had a chance to wash and get outside a satisfactory amount of cowboy beans, some sort of griddle biscuit and a couple of pounds of strong-tasting pork with a very satisfactory BBQ sauce. Someone opened a sack of nuts and dried fruit that was quite tasty too, and there was wine though nobody was drinking very much.

"Sip, man, sip! Don't swill it! That's a Larsdalen red!" Talyn said as a small straw-covered jug went around the group by the little fire not far from the tent-flap. "It's not beer!"

There were only the two Mackenzies, the Bearkiller pilot and him; the Clan used a nine-man squad, but the rest of Talyn and Caillech's outfit were still off on their scout. Evidently they and Alyssa were old friends.

"Alyssa gets treats from her parents, and it makes up for the sharpness of her personality, so to say," Talyn said.

Caillech threw a dried apricot at him, which he caught and ate, and Alyssa made a rude noise with her lips.

Cole sighed. He missed his friends and buddies, too, although he hadn't been in the special-ops unit enough to make really close ones. Still, sitting round the fire eating BBQ ribs and drinking wine after a ten-mile hike on mountain tracks was a hell of a lot better than some of the other things that could happen to a prisoner. He hadn't ended up full of arrows this morning, for example, which was also a definite plus, and he wasn't sitting in a cage in chains.

And it *was* good wine, or at least a lot smoother than Army-ration issue or what you got in the bars around base camps. Cole had grown up on water and milk, with beer once he was past his mid-teens and diluted whiskey on special occasions, but there were vineyards closer to Boise City.

"Good ribs," he said.

He wiped the back of his hand across his mouth and tossed the stripped bone to Talyn's dogs. They'd looked towards their master for permission to take the treat the first time. It made him slightly homesick; he'd had a dog before he reported for duty, one he'd had since they'd both been pups and hand-trained up himself and let sleep on the foot of his bed despite his mother's scolding. They'd been inseparable until poor creaky smelly half-blind old Bob ran into a catamount that had been sniffing around the sheep-pen and died doing his valiant best. He'd hunted the cougar down with his crossbow, blind with rage, and its hide was now gracing the floor in front of the fireplace back home, but even at a heedless eighteen he'd known a milestone in his life when it happened.

"Not bad, but the sauce is a bit mild," Alyssa said, wiping her face with a cloth—eating them one-handed was messier than the usual way. "Mackenzie cooking is pretty good but they go lighter on the peppers than most Bearkillers like."

It had been about as hot as *Cole* liked. When he raised his eyebrows at her she went on:

"My grandmother . . . on my mother's side, Angelica Hutton . . . was the Bearkiller quartermaster while Mike Havel led the first of us back to Larsdalen. She's *Tejano*. We got a war-cry from Finland from the Bear Lord's family, and Tex-Mex cooking from her. From what the books say about Finnish food it was a hell of a good bargain."

A hair-raising squeal brought Cole's head and attention whipping around. Talyn laughed and tilted back the flask.

"The pipes!" he said, toasting the harsh droning sound as it modulated into something resembling music.

"They're not torturing a pig or biting a cat's tail, honest," Alyssa said. "Mackenzies are a tuneful bunch, always playing something. Including bagpipes, if you can call that a musical instrument. Especially the *Píob Mhór*, the war-pipes."

"And a war-camp is the place for war-pipes," Talyn said. "But it's true, we're a musical lot, having Brigid's blessing."

Cole nodded, a little puzzled. Everyone but the very rich made their own music or did without most of the time; he'd heard a wind-up phonograph once at a county fair, but hadn't been impressed and anyway they and the records to play on them cost the earth. His parents had complained all his life about how you couldn't just snap your fingers and have first-class music in the modern world, which was even more annoying than the rest of the stories about the old times.

He understood more of what Alyssa meant when half a dozen flutes and stringed instruments and little hand-held drums played with a stick came in faultlessly, weaving around the hoarse wild song of the drones.

Cole could pick out "All You Need Is Love" or "Old MacDonald" or "Riders on the Storm" with a six-string guitar and one of his uncles was pretty fair with a lute and he had an aunt who played a mean fiddle at barn dances, but everyone he could hear was better than that. As good as the professionals you heard at county fairs or parades, and better than the neighborhood favorites who played weddings and funerals.

"Sure, and wasn't the Chief, the Mackenzie herself, herself a bard by trade before the Change?" Caillech said. "I've often heard the oldsters saying how her music kept their hearts up, in the terrible years. And the songs taught us all the ways of the Lord and Lady, of course."

"Gillie Chalium!" someone shouted. "Let's dance the blades!"

Which apparently meant something. Talyn whooped, and Caillech grinned as she got up and hitched at her plaid.

"Sword dance," Alyssa explained.

More of the clansfolk put out circles of swords in the open spaces between the campfires—eight blades each, set with one edge down in the dirt and the other up, points-in. Talyn and Caillech faced each other in one circle, bowing and then standing with hands on hips. Another pair joined them. . . .

"Pretty," Cole said, as the dance began. Then: "Gurk!"

It started slow, and seemed to involve keeping the upper body fairly straight; the hands switched up from hips to over the head from time to time. The *feet*, though, were moving quicker and quicker—and it involved skipping and stepping over those swordblades, while keeping the eyes locked on the other dancer, and all four taking a leap to the left at intervals combined with a high kick so that the whole ensemble moved in a circle counterclockwise.

All done in the dark by flickering firelight.

"Care to give it a try, Private First Class?" Alyssa asked slyly.

"*Christ* no!" Cole blurted.

He was quick and agile and liked a barn dance or a waltz, but the thought of maybe stamping his foot down on the business edge of a solidly grounded swordblade made his toes curl in reflex. Those were fully functional swords, too; good steel salvaged from leaf-springs, and *sharp*.

"My thought exactly," Alyssa said. "Nice to watch, but I've never wanted to try it. It's one of those things the Mackenzies do because they enjoy freaking out the *cowan*, too."

"Cowan?"

"Ignorant, benighted infidels like you and me."

"You're not, ah—"

"Of the Old Religion? No. Quite a few of us Bearkillers are, say one in every two or three, we and the Mackenzies have always been neighbors and allies. My branch of the family's Catholic—"

She pulled on a fine chain around her neck, showing her crucifix and kissing it before she replaced it.

"—but I wouldn't claim to be a very *good* Catholic. My aunt Signe and her kids are pagan, though. She's Asatruar, to be technical, which is sort of different from the Clan's version. I don't think Mike Havel . . . the first Bear Lord . . . was religious at all, from what people say."

"I know what you mean," Cole said, and nodded

That sort of thing had been more common in the old days. He didn't know anyone at home who didn't go to church at least occasionally, though. The world had been a strange place before the Change.

"We Bearkillers let people make up their minds about that sort of stuff pretty much as they please. What really matters to us is doing your duty to the Outfit. Mackenzies . . . well, they're tolerant as all get-out, but if you were cowan it wouldn't be a really comfortable place to live in the long run, you'd feel left out. A lot. Left out of pretty nearly everything."

"So that's a religious sword dance?" Cole said, watching with interest.

He'd stopped expecting a scream and blood to interrupt, and he could see that this would be useful training in situational awareness and swift movement. Probably more fun than drill, too, but it still put his teeth on edge a bit. Mackenzies seemed nice enough folk from what he'd seen, nothing like the propaganda apart from being on the other side, but they certainly weren't what you could call timid. At all.

"*Everything* is religion, over there in the Mackenzie stamping grounds. Even peeling an apple. Even sex. In fact, *especially* sex . . . how does it go . . . *All acts of love and pleasure are My rituals.*"

"What's that?"

"From the Charge of the Goddess. They take it pretty seriously, too. Which can be dangerous to anyone who doesn't abide by their rules."

"How?"

"Well, let's just say their *dùthchas* is about the safest place in the whole world to be a woman on her own, even at a Beltane feast when everyone's drinking hard and running around buck-naked except for wreaths or masks or antlers on their heads and yelling *Evoe! Io, Io, Bacchios!* and believe me they *totally* know how to let their hair down at a party. Oh, my, yes. But they don't take any excuses at all for someone who doesn't understand the word 'no.'"

"Head-chopping for offenders?"

"More likely burial at a crossroads with a spear in you. Possibly burial alive with the spear in the dirt if they're *really* angry or afraid the Goddess is going to smite the vicinity, or both. You ask me, they pick the right things to be completely *intolerant* about."

"Gurk! And I though the *dance* was scary."

She grinned, then winced a bit as a scab on her lip pulled.

"If you think the *Gillie Chalium* is scary, you should see the *Dannsadh Bhiodaig*."

"What's that when it's got its pants . . . or kilt . . . on?"

"The dirk dance; a dirk is what they call those long daggers they wear. Sort of like a knife-fight set to music. Actually it's as much a training *kata* as a dance, but the Clan loves mixing stuff up like that. Real experts do it with live steel and *fast*."

The dance ended with a leap and shout; there was a bit of shuffling around, and then the pipes started up again.

"Hey, I know that tune!" Cole said happily as the pipes sounded through the humming rattle of the bodhran drums. "That's *Lord of*—"

The music faltered a little, and heads turned. Cole did too.

A tall man stood on the jut of rock near the fire, in kilt, saffron-dyed loose-sleeved shirt and a plaid pinned with a broach of silver and turquoise knotwork. His bonnet had Raven feathers in its clasp. A long sword whose pommel shone and glittered hung at his right hip; the firelight gleamed on the bright red-gold hair that fell to his shoulders and the dense short-cropped beard on his sharp-cut regular features. A grin lit his face, and the blue-green-gray eyes sparkled. A ripple and murmur went through the crowd, a chant—

"Ard Rí! *Ard Rí!*"

"Holy crap, could that really be—"

"Yeah," Alyssa said. "My cousin Rudi! Or His Majesty Artos the First, High King of Montival, to you lowly peasants."

"Here?" Cole blurted.

Alyssa grinned. "He shows up everywhere. It's . . . notorious!"

The chant changed: "Artos! *Artos!*"

Cole shivered a little despite himself; Rudi Mackenzie's name had become a thing of fear to Boise's survivors. And here he was, like something out of an old old story, like one of his great-grandfather's illustrated books: *Tales of the Round Table* and those. There had been a great big tin box the family had discovered when they fled back to the old ranch house after the Change, and he'd read them after chores all his childhood. Good stories, and a lot more realistic than most pre-Change stuff.

Then the newcomer threw back his head and sang, in a strong deep tenor that wasn't quite a bass, and the musicians took the tune up again:

"Dance, dance wherever you may be!—"

"Well, whoever he is, like I said, I know the song. Something familiar at last!"

"I wouldn't count on that," Alyssa said, and uncorked another jug. "Here."

He took a swig and hugged his knees as she sat beside him, using his shoulder to lower herself with her good hand. He sighed inwardly at that. Cole Salander wasn't quite twenty-three yet, but he was old enough to tell when a woman was interested in him. Maybe fighting off that bear that'd been about to eat her had something to do with it. It had been a large and very determined bear, or very hungry, or both.

Unfortunately, it's an interested woman on the other side of the war, and a banged-up woman with a cracked arm who I'm probably not going to see again after a couple of days from now. Dang, I really have the luck, don't I? Maybe I should hunt up a dice game, I've got to start beating the odds on something soon or lightning will hit me out of a clear blue sky.

The dancers began to move, left hand on hip, the right above their heads; the beat started slow, but every time their feet brought them to the edge of a blade there was a lightning-quick step.

The man called Rudi Mackenzie sang on in a slow

rhythm, voice carrying effortlessly through the music and the crackle of the fires:

> *"I danced at a Beltane with the pole standing tall,*
> *And ribbons flowing 'round the dancers all.*
> *I danced in the morning of the Midsummer Feast*
> *As the day dawned pink with the Sun Lord's heat!"*

"OK, maybe I *don't* know this one," Cole muttered to himself. "But, what the hell, it's the same tune."

He joined in the clapping and the chorus:

> *"Dance, dance—"*

The tall man went on, quickening just a little:

> *"As Lughnasadh came and the corn shone gold,*
> *Moonlight brought the kiss of Samhain cold.*
> *I danced about the balefire, late at night,*
> *And turned the Wheel against all fright!"*

The Mackenzies all joined in the chorus; evidently this was an old favorite with them. Then:

> *"As the world turned black, I lighted the log,*
> *With Yule burning bright and piercing the fog.*
> *I lay with my Lady in the dark of the year,*
> *And I'll be reborn when Beltane draws near!"*

Rudi Mackenzie leapt down from the rock as the song ended, and the dancers crowded around him. There was

a whoop and they tossed him high and set him on his feet
again.

Kill.

Panic seized Cole. Something was *talking* to him.
Something was *talking him*, and he was watching it like a
play.

Kill.

Emotion came with it, a cold malevolent hate, a rancid
disgust at . . . everything. Himself included; himself especially. He was alone in a prison of rotting meat, he had to
get out, get *out* into the dark warm *rightness*.

His hand stripped the knife out of a belt and he lunged
up. The tall man's laughing face loomed before him, a
brightness that made an intolerable twisting at the heart
of things. He moved, fluid and sure even as part of him
struggled to open his fingers and halt his arm—

Crack.

There was an instant when they were looking at each
other eye to eye. His arm quivered, the muscle knotting,
and sweat ran down his face. The grip around his right
wrist was intolerable, but the pain as the bones ground
together had no bearing on what he was doing, what
whatever *it* was was doing.

Cole Salander was a passenger in his own head, like a
rich man riding the mail-coach except that he was beating
at the windows and trying to smash his way out and getting absolutely nowhere, but that distant part of him had
time to feel professional admiration. He'd never seen a
control-counter done that fast, and despite the awkward
cross-body position the strength that held him was unbe-
lievable. Cole knew he was exerting ten-tenths of his

body's capacities, almost enough that the hard muscles
tore loose from their anchors on his sturdy bones, but he
might as well have been pushing at something carved out
of seasoned maple-wood.

"No! Don't kill him!"

Rudi Mackenzie's voice rang out, the tone flat and
even though the point of the dirk was a half inch from his
belly. He snapped:

"Hale and alive, Edain!"

Something hit Cole across the backs of his lower
thighs with savage force. The pain alone wouldn't have
made any difference, but simple mechanical leverage
made the joints of his knees buckle and pitched him backward. Hands seized him in half a dozen places and began
to bend his arms behind him. A guttural sound escaped
his throat, as if he was trying to pronounce something
that *hurt* because it wasn't meant to be said.

Vision began to strobe, the firelit night interspersed
with somewhere else, somewhere that was black in a way
that negated the possibility of anything else.

He twisted against the strength that pulled him away
from what he *must* do. Flashes, a man's square face, a
blond woman's locked in a rictus of effort.

"Fáfnir's *bones* he's strong!" a soprano voice gasped.

Hands and arms gripped him, half a dozen strong warriors just enough to contain the quivering violence that
locked them all into a dynamic stasis. It took two to get
the knife out of his hand.

"I . . . see . . . you," rasped through his throat.

"And I you," the High King said grimly.

To the others: "Hold him fast, now."

His right hand stripped the Sword out of the sheath at

that hip, leaving it pommel-upright in his grasp. The world froze in a blaze that was light and darkness, a smile that was and wasn't his mother, a feeling of *completion*. Nothing more was necessary, but something that was/wasn't him shrieked. In the same movement Rudi pressed the antler-cradled crystal to Cole's forehead.

Click.

There was something like steel wire around his brain, straining and then *snapping*.

He didn't black out, but everything became irrelevant. The sudden rag-doll limpness of his body almost tore it out of the hands gripping it, where the previous instant's unnatural strength had been checkmated. They carried him back and plunked him down sitting on top of a barrel full of something heavy and solid, a posture that kept his feet off the ground and made it impossible for him to move even if he felt like it, which he didn't.

When his eyes fluttered open again he felt almost normal, except that he had no desire to do anything whatsoever except sit and there was a film of something like flexible glass between him and the world. Hands rested heavy on his shoulders and a Mackenzie short sword was close enough to his throat to make the little hairs crinkle a bit, but that was nothing he could care about.

"No."

The High King's voice, facing off against Bow-Captain Luag's anger and meeting it with a slight smile.

"He's foresworn!"

"That he is not, Luag. He had no more choice in the matter than a man hit on the head with a sledgehammer can choose not to fall."

A hand fell almost caressingly on the hilt of the Sword.

"I've met the like before. They must have foreseen that the line of his fate would be tangled with mine, so. And I can tell you with a great and certain certainty that it won't happen again. Not with this one. He's guarded against such now, for all his life to come."

"It would be just as certain if he were dead, but you're the High King," Luag said, but it was a grumble now and not hot rage.

"Indeed I am."

The bow-captain sheathed his own weapon and stepped back.

Cole felt enough life return to smile slightly at the shocked, uncertain faces of Alyssa and Talyn and Caillech. Rudi held out his hand.

"A bit of a pick-me-up, Edain."

The square-faced young man Cole remembered stepped forward, a flat silver flask in one hand. The other held an unstrung bowstave of impressive thickness.

That part of Cole's brain that handled logic was starting to work again, as were his nerves, and he suspected that was the thing that had whacked him across the backs of his knees in a way that was going to make him limp for days. All things considered, he didn't mind much.

"Waste of good brandy, sure and it's a crime, Chief," the archer said, but handed it over.

"Drink."

Cole did as the flask was held to his lips. The sweet fire coursed down his throat; he gasped, and things stuttered to life within him. For a moment he had a crazy sensation of *being* a grape, and feeling utter completion as he was picked and fermented and distilled, then it spun away and the world began to break through the film around his being.

"What—" his voice began to rise.

The High King stooped a little, one hand braced on his knee, which put their eyes on a level.

"Look at me, man." Cole did. "Now, you've met a High Seeker of the Church Universal and Triumphant at some time, have you not, the misfortune of the world?"

"I . . . yeah, of course, I—"

A gust of panic suddenly squeezed his throat shut. He knew he had, a red-robe priest of the weird cult that ruled beyond the Rockies. One had shown up to be chaplain, and . . . but he couldn't *remember* it.

"I . . . I can remember remembering that I did, but—"

"Easy, easy. Drink again. My guard-captain can refill his flask later."

Cole did, gulping and coughing. The light changeable eyes were steady on his in the firelight, but their presence was like a burning limelight, like looking into the sun for a moment.

"How can I remember remembering but not remember?"

"The Sword of the Lady healed your mind," Rudi—Artos—said. "A compulsion was laid upon you, like a seed . . . or a spring trap set for game. The Sword removed it, but that means a scar upon your memory. Count yourself lucky; the compulsion was subtle, and meant to be hidden. If it hadn't been, more of you would have been lost when the tainted part was burned away."

The flask was empty. Cole looked down at it—there was a wolf's face on it, thin black lines set into the silver—and wondered whether he should ask for more or just upchuck. A gust of wild laughter threatened to break free. Probably puking all over the High King would be blasphemy or *lèse-majesté* or something like that.

"Cole Salander, is it?"

"Yes," he said. Familiar ritual straightened him a little, as he rattled off his rank and serial number.

"And you've two brothers, Jack and Tanner?"

That startled him enough that his stomach subsided. "Yeah. They went missing—"

"At the Horse Heaven Hills last year, yes," the High King said. "There was more than a little chaos, just then."

His hand was on the Sword again, eyes slitted in thought for a moment before he went on:

"They're alive. Tanner I grieve to say lost his left foot at the ankle, a matter of a six-pounder round shot, but he's recovering and will be able to get about well enough to do a man's work yet. Jack has taken service with Frederick Thurston, the one of your first President's sons who yet lives, and the one who didn't betray and kill him and sell his country to the enemy of humankind. With which enemies you have just now had, I'd be thinking, a closer acquaintance than is comfortable. Not so?"

"I, uh. Yeah."

Rudi straightened and clapped a hand on his shoulder. When he spoke he raised his voice to carry among the onlookers; faces stretched back into darkness.

"This man did no wrong of his own will. He's now free of all taint, and I swear by the Sword of the Lady and She who chose me to bear it that he means to abide by his oath. He strove his utmost to resist the bane laid in his soul, and that may well have slowed the stroke just enough to spare me. And he's now under my protection and that of the Goddess through me, so heed the word of the Mother-of-All."

A babble broke out, as the late-comers were filled in. The square-faced man took his flask back and tucked it into his sporran.

"You'd think they'd have learned by now it wouldn't work, and they so full of eldritch knowledge," he said cheerfully.

Cole thought he was a little white around the gills, though.

"It didn't work *this time*," Rudi said grimly. "If we do well, we'll keep dodging and weaving long enough for me to accomplish what I must. There's a reason I was given the Sword. The Lady's protection does not sleep, but neither does the hatred of the Malevolent."

He turned his attention back to Cole. "You can see your brother Jack soon," he said. "And perhaps he can acquaint you better with the rights and wrongs of this miserable war."

The beautifully modulated voice rose again. "Are there those who'll care for this man?"

Three stepped forward. "Ah, cousin Alyssa. And Talyn and Caillech of Dun Tàirneanach. See that he sleeps, and that he's bundled warmly; shock's a possibility."

They helped him back, and got out his bedroll to wrap around him while they built up the fire a little and set rocks to heating; he did feel core-chilled.

After he stopped shaking Cole looked into the darkness where Rudi Mackenzie had vanished.

"He's . . . quite something, isn't he?" he said slowly. "He's got . . . impact. Whatever it is about a man that . . .

the old General had a lot, and my CO has some . . . but that guy, he's got all there is to get."

"*Baraka,*" Talyn said soberly. "The Mother marked him for Her own when he was yet a boy, in the *nemed*, the sacred wood above Dun Juniper. My own father saw it, the great Raven flying out of the setting sun . . . the mark of Her beak is between his brows, you saw it? That was put there by no human hand. Some say he's Lugh come again, the Sun Lord's self returned in His joy and wrath and splendor."

Cole nodded. It was weird, but somehow it made sense. Then he yawned enormously, and the world faded away. He scarcely felt hands moving him into the tent and laying him on the pine boughs, hot stones at his feet and back.

CHAPTER EIGHT

CASTLE TODENANGST, CROWN DEMESNE
PORTLAND PROTECTIVE ASSOCIATION
WILLAMETTE VALLEY NEAR NEWBURG
HIGH KINGDOM OF MONTIVAL
(FORMERLY WESTERN OREGON)
JUNE 15TH, CHANGE YEAR 26/2024 AD

"Órlaith!"

Mathilda ran. Vision came in jerky flickers, fast and at the same time unbearably slow. Sandra scooped her granddaughter up and rolled into the swept outdoor hearth, curling her body around the infant's, and the wet-nurse stood in front of them with a poker in her hands like a baseball bat. Signe spun out of her chair, the Bearkiller backsword snapping into her hand, a bright glint of steel in the flickering green gloom. The two Countesses swept up the skirts of their cotte-hardies in their left hands and each drew the dagger that marked them as Associates with their right; the weapons were ceremonial, but quite functional as well.

Delia de Stafford and Virginia Thurston started throwing things—teapots, for starters. One smashed right into the face of the Cutter assassin, boiling-hot water flying with shards of Sèvres porcelain that had come down two centuries to meet its end here. The de Stafford nanny took Heuradys in one arm and Yolande in the other, retreating behind her mistress.

Buy time, Mathilda knew. *The guards will be here in seconds.*

Then a clash of steel came from the inner rooms as she raised her sword. One of the magus-assassins turned to meet her.

Lioncel struggled to keep his breathing even; it wasn't the effort of the brief run, but the tension, and that ratcheted upward when they came out into the central space of the Queen Mother's level. There was a dead man lying on the stairs that led up to the Guard barracks, blood leaking out of his armor, and the clash of steel on steel and the dull beat of blades on shields from farther up. Two dozen men-at-arms in the black harness of the Protector's Guard waited in the great groin-vaulted chamber that lay outside the Queen Mother's private rooms, their visors down except for the man in front. The leader of the living was a young knight.

Lioncel recognized him, but vaguely, Sir Evroyn-something, from somewhere north of the Columbia, one of the valleys on the eastern slopes of the Cascades. His face was white and sweating—though to be fair, if Lioncel's liege was standing in front of him looking like that Lioncel would have sweated too. Some of the men-at-arms behind him were stirring slightly, not much, but not the statue-still immobility you expected from the Protector's Guard. Not all of them were in on this; the rest must have been fed some story.

"There's a conspiracy against the Crown. Stand aside," she said, not halting her forward stride and pitching her voice to carry to all the guardsmen.

And a conspiracy against my mother and sisters! Lioncel thought.

"My lady, I have orders that absolutely nobody should pass—" the knight began, clearing his throat.

"I am Baroness Tiphaine d'Ath, and I am Grand Constable of the Association," Lady Death said. "By my office I have right of immediate access to Her Majesty. *Get out of my way.* Last warning."

It was also the first, but this *was* Lady Death speaking. Not for the first time, he knew a deep comfort in the fact that Delia de Stafford was also Tiphaine d'Ath's Châtelaine. Then his ears twitched. Was that a scream from within? His mouth went dry.

"I have orders—" the knight began again.

Lioncel had been around his liege all his life, and seen her in battle. He had never seen her move so quickly; one instant she was walking, then next extended in a perfect long-lunge with the flat of her blade horizontal to the ground, right foot forward and arm and sword extending the line, shield reserved and tucked against her torso for balance.

Sir Evroyn reeled backward, and she recovered with the smooth precision of water running downhill, like an exercise in the *salle* rather than the desperate scramble that real fighting usually was. Red blossomed where his right eye had been, and on the last few inches of her longsword. He fell with a clatter of armor as if all the strings that held his body together had been severed at once . . . which was more or less what happened. The point had punched through the thin layer of bone at the back of the eye socket and into his brain, just far enough and no more lest the steel be trapped by the edges cutting into his skull.

What part of last warning *didn't he understand?* Lioncel thought, a little dazed. *Did he think* Tiphaine d'Ath *was just* bluffing?

"Throw down!" she barked, as the *menie* of Ath locked shields behind her and knocked down their visors. *"Now!"*

A few did, dropping their swords with a clatter and dropping to their knees with their hands on their heads. The rest started to close ranks, their big kite-shaped shields coming up to make a wall, but the kneeling men hindered the precision of the movement.

"Shoot!" the Grand Constable snapped.

Six crossbows fired, a dull multiple *tung* of vibrating steel and cord and right on top of it the hard ringing *tank* sound of the pile-shaped heads hitting steel, like a ripple of blows from a hydraulic punch in a mill. At point-blank range even the best armor didn't always stop a bolt from a military crossbow. Lioncel felt as if something in front of him was pulling his hands up, snuggling the butt into his shoulder, squeezing the trigger—

A man stumbled backward with the bolt sunk deep in his bevoir, the jointed piece that shielded throat and chin. Blood leaked around the short thick arrow, and sprayed from under the visor and even through the vision-slit. Steel gauntlets scrabbled at it for an instant and then the armored figure fell and lay twitching and gurgling. Tiphaine d'Ath went through the gap like a falcon stooping, with Rodard and his brother Armand behind to either side. A man in the black harness of the Guard tried to overrun the Grand Constable—tucking his shield into his left shoulder and charging, to ram her off her feet by sheer weight and impetus. The shields banged together with a lightning *crack*, but she was already pivoting as if they were dancing a volta. She ignored him as he staggered where she'd put him, into the stroke of Sir Armand's serrated mace. It smashed his visor with a sound like a boot heel stamping on a metal cup.

The sword flicked out again, its narrow point punching through the mail grommet covering an armpit and the edges breaking the links. . . .

Using the sword against opponents in armor requires absolute precision because of the limited number of targets. The armpit is a weak spot. Don't throw your arm back so it's exposed.

The voice in his mind was Tiphaine's in some *salle d'armes* sometime in his life, running like an inhumanly detached commentary.

I will now demonstrate why . . .

A minuscule sway, and a sword went past her. She reversed her own and thrust backward into the spot behind another man's knee without looking behind her, blocking a thrust with her shield while she did, moving with the leisurely certainty of someone who had all the time in the world to line things up. . . .

The knee is another vulnerable area, but rarely easy to reach. . . .

He'd been reloading the crossbow as he followed, dodging through the shouting clanging mass of armored forms, with the two household knights to either side. The initial lines of combatants had broken up into knots of steel-clad forms who shoved and hit and shouted and screamed. And increasingly threw themselves flat and called for quarter.

"Follow me who can!" his liege called, in a voice like a contralto war-trumpet.

Four of the Guard men-at-arms who *weren't* giving up retreated through the door into the Queen Mother's chambers, a boom and clatter and crash of metal utterly incongruous in the pale splendors. For a moment they stood in the door, and then one of the Ath spearmen—he was actually carrying a glaive—thrust his polearm past the edge of a shield and used the hook just below the blade to drag the shield forward with a double-handed heave. The man attached to the shield by the arm he had through its loop staggered, then screamed as the war hammer came down on his shoulder, denting the metal in and breaking the collarbone beneath. The Grand Constable and her two knights burst through into the great chamber, and there was a blurring flurry of motion and the surviving man in black armor was running away . . .

. . . not running away. That's out towards the balcony. He's running towards Mom and the girls and Her Majesty.

His liege and Rodard and Armand were after the man, but he dodged behind an old tattered-looking statue on a plinth. Lioncel brought the crossbow up with a steady concentration, as if he were watching someone else aim—someone perfectly calm, as if this were a shooting range.

Tung.

The bolt punched through the ancient bronze without slowing and hammered into the man's shoulder, twisting him around. Tiphaine d'Ath passed him with a sway of her torso, running with the liquid fluency of a leopard and ignoring the scrap-metal succession of blows from mace and war hammer that rang out behind as Armand and Rodard followed and finished the man in passing. Lioncel fumbled at the cocking lever of his crossbow as he dashed behind her; there was something dreamlike about it, his frantic speed not keeping up with her strides.

The dappled light of the balcony flashed into his vision like a tableau. A figure with a face dripping blood and boiling water and broken bones jutting through a servant's livery stood before the hearth, leaning forward as if straining at an invisible barrier with a curved knife in his hand. Juniper Mackenzie and his own mother were between the man and the Queen Mother and the child, their hands upraised in an odd hieratic gesture; they and their opponent were in total silence, utter immobility, but he could feel immense forces straining against each other, as if the air between them *rippled* somehow without anything really visible at all.

The Grand Constable threw her shield aside and took the sword in the two-handed grip and spun like a wheel, the blade a silver blur. There was a heavy *chunk-crack* sound, and the assassin's head leapt free. Juniper and his mother staggered and collapsed together clutching at each other, as if they had been pushing on a door that suddenly opened. The headless man fell . . . which was a relief, because some corner of Lioncel's mind hadn't been sure he *would*.

Signe Havel was fighting another broken man, one who slapped the strokes of her backsword aside with the flats of his hands. She screamed—as much frustration in the sound as rage—and lunged.

And the blade went through the man's ribs and grated

home in bone, a killing stroke in any sane fight. He lunged for *her*, grinning, his left hand reaching for her neck even as he laughed and coughed out bits of lung. She dove backward in a tuck-and-roll, just barely avoiding the slash of the curved knife in his right by sensibly not wasting time trying to pull the sword free. Huon Liu darted in, his own blade in the two-hand grip and flashing down.

"Huon!" Lioncel shouted at his friend.

The older boy's face was set. His light sword thudded down at the junction of neck and shoulder; then he spun away, clutching at his stomach with an *oooff* as the dead man's knife cut. Light mesh-mail showed through the rent cloth of his jacket, and then blood welled over his hands. Lioncel breathed out and forced calm on himself, and fired. The bolt transfixed the assassin at the pelvis, and he could *hear* the point crunch into bone, but the man—if he was one—just pivoted for a moment under the horse-kick impact, then lurched forward again.

The moment was enough. Tiphaine and Rodard and Armand were all on him at once, and blood spattered into the air behind a wall of armored shoulders and weapons rising and falling and harsh meaty sounds.

Lioncel shuddered, as if he'd been dropped into cold water when he was fevered. Or had suddenly woken from a *very* bad dream. A glance showed him his mother and sisters were all right, though Heuradys was frozen in shock and Yolande was sobbing; Lady Juniper had to help Delia de Stafford up before she clutched them to her. The Queen Mother was emerging from the hearth with her granddaughter, who was waving pink fists and making a wuh-wuh-wuh sound, less frightened than offended at not being in the center of the universe, which was where babies thought they belonged.

Sandra Arminger looked . . . alarmingly determined.

The High Queen was kneeling beside Huon, laying aside a long sword that looked a bit big for her, after a similar quick check. The blade and her right arm and side were heavily spattered.

"Where did you get that?" Tiphaine d'Ath said, as she knelt on the boy's other side, ripping the clothing aside. Then: "Rodard, Armand, get this cluster . . . fracas . . . under control. See that the staircase up is secured. And we need a medic."

"Two of the Guard knights leapt after the assassins," Mathilda said. "Neither of them survived, much less arrived in shape to fight, but one of them lived long enough to give me this. A good thing, because there were three of the assassins. I got one, but . . ."

"They operate in threes, yes." She looked up. "Brave of him."

Lioncel did too, and shuddered; the men had deserved that accolade, even from so exacting a source. He wasn't particularly afraid of heights, but the thought of deliberately hurling yourself off that drop, in armor, on the off-chance you'd survive long enough to be useful. . . .

He approached Huon himself. The Grand Constable gave him a slight approving nod, and he found that flushed a lot of the shakiness out of him; she held out her sword, and he started to clean it and check the edge for nicks. The High Queen was tending to the wound in his comrade's stomach, a long shallow slash from around the left hipbone slanting up to the navel, ignoring the blood with the matter-of-fact competence of long experience.

One of the songs the troubadours had made about the Quest was how the nine companions had dressed each other's wounds in the wilderness. Then she frowned.

"Wait a minute, this wound isn't deep enough to . . . he's in shock!"

He was; his pale-olive skin was gray, and the pupils in his eyes had shrunk to pinpricks. The breath rattled in his throat.

The medics Tiphaine had called for arrived; they didn't have far to come, since there were several clinics in the Silver Tower. One went to where Signe Havel lay clutching at her ribs and wheezing amid two countesses wielding smelling-salts and flasks of brandy, and the other to Huon. She was in the habit of the Sisters of Mercy, with a gold cross on the black leather of her doctor's satchel.

"He's dying," she said flatly after a moment's skilled investigation. "He shouldn't be, it's a superficial cut, but he is."

No, Lioncel thought helplessly, inconsequentially, his hands freezing in the middle of their familiar task. *Huon can't* die . . . *we were supposed to go hawking tomorrow.* . . .

"No!" Mathilda Arminger said; but there was no helplessness in her voice.

Then, very softly, with her eyes shut and her hands on the injured squire:

"Mary pierced with sorrows, Queen of Angels, you said that I should be as a mother to this land. This boy is flesh of its flesh and bone of its bone, wounded because he put his body between a child and evil. I ask . . . whatever grace is given me, let it pass to him."

Nothing dramatic happened, except that a pink flush returned to Huon's face; he sighed, began breathing more easily, and seemed to slide into a deep sleep. The Sister gave the High Queen a single sharp glance, and then began to swab and sew at what was now a perfectly ordinary mildly serious injury. Lioncel fought down a gasp.

Mathilda's eyes opened. "No need to make much of this," she said quietly, looking deliberately at the three of them in turn. "As the good Sister said, it's not a life-threatening wound."

Not now, Lioncel thought, and fought an impulse to fall to his knees in awe, or at least to cross himself.

He wasn't entirely surprised; he'd seen the Sword of the Lady, after all . . . and there was something beyond the human in an anointed monarch, everyone knew that from the stories.

In theory. It's a lot more alarming in practice. But I know keep your mouth shut about this from someone of high rank when I hear it, even if it's . . . tactfully put.

He and his liege stood, bowed deeply to Mathilda, and backed away. Lioncel met the Grand Constable's unreadable gray gaze and nodded very slightly: *I understand.* She almost-smiled in approval before she turned away. He was almost shaking with relief himself, now that there was time to appreciate just how bad the situation *had* been, but that helped to steady him.

Signe Havel was swearing mildly as the other medic—a layman—probed at her ribs and pronounced that several were probably cracked, but only slightly.

"I could have told you that without your sticking fingers into it," she snarled. "Do you think it's the first time I've had a sprung rib?"

He heard Virginia Thurston speaking in a similar tone to someone else, her Powder River accent much thicker than usual: "I'm pregnant, not sick, y' durned fool, and I didn't get hit. Leave me be and tend to them as needs it!"

Things were getting set to order; more of the d'Ath *menie* had shown up, and some of the Lord Chancellor's men, and attendants of the Countesses, who were giving crisp quiet directions of their own.

"Scrub down the blood from the assassins and then burn the rags and the instruments," Tiphaine d'Ath said. "Then wash yourselves and burn your clothes. Burn Her Majesty's dress once she's out of it. No, don't touch those knives with your bare hands, you idiot! Take them to Lord Chancellor Father Ignatius, in a box, he knows how to deal with them. The assassin's bodies will have to be burned. Prepare a pyre outside the castle walls . . . a big one. With no people downwind."

The servants gulped and paled and set to following her instructions with exaggerated care, and she went on to her household knights:

"Armand, get this troop of armored . . . people . . . out of the Queen Mother's chambers, get up there with enough men and see to disarming the Guard detachment. Obviously most of them weren't in on this but some of the ones who were may still be alive. Rodard, immediate message to Sir Tancred via the heliograph net and courier that he's to have the High King comb the ranks of the Guard in the field."

"Separate cells, preliminary interrogation, kid gloves, my lady?" Armand asked, clarifying.

"Right. Get going. Rodard, once that dispatch is off, go brief Conrad, he'll be having kittens. The last thing we need is him wheeling his chair through this mess waving his cane and roaring."

"Yes, my lady."

She made a small exhaling sound as the knights departed briskly, glanced around to see if there was something else time-critical that needed doing immediately, and decided there wasn't. The Queen Mother gave her an inclination of the head and mouthed: *well done*, which straightened Lioncel's spine even further.

I was right, my liege is *a strong right arm of the Crown*! he thought proudly. *And so will I be, one day*!

He remembered to sling his crossbow, and tossed the cleaning-cloth and the glove he'd been wearing onto a growing pile of to-be-burned with gingerly care before he followed her and slid her sword efficiently back into the scabbard. She'd headed straight for his mother, who was holding Heuradys and Yolande and sitting on a bench. When she saw Tiphaine d'Ath approaching and Lioncel obviously unharmed beside her something seemed to go out of her, a stiff tension in her very bones.

"Good job, sweetie," Tiphaine said quietly.

"You too, darling," Delia said, then shuddered. "May I have hysterics now?"

"You earned them."

His mother handed the infants to the nanny, hugged Lioncel hard enough to wind him through the mail shirt, then threw herself into the Grand Constable's arms, sobbing.

CHAPTER NINE

"Hello, love," Rudi Mackenzie said. "I'm back from the fields, ready to sit by the hearth and talk over the day's doings while you stir the stewpot."

Mathilda laughed and waved without taking her eye from the focusing piece of a telescope whose tripod stood on the rosewood of the room's main table. One wall of the tent had been rolled up, which gave her a view as far as the City of Boise itself.

The great striped canvas pavilion had started out life as one of Sandra Arminger's, of the type she used for tours and presiding at the tournaments that were such an important part of Association life.

And for intimidating the bedamned out of fractious noblemen, Rudi thought, handing his shield to Mathilda's squire Huon Liu de Gervais with a smile and a nod.

Huon was still moving carefully, but fit enough for light work, and had insisted on coming with the High

Queen with an exquisitely deferential stubbornness. It was hard to say *no* to a lad who'd thrown himself without hesitation between a walking dead man with a cursed knife and your daughter . . . and who was visibly determined to do the same again should the need arise.

Mathilda had taken Huon and his sister Yseult under wardship and into the Royal Household for their brother Odard's sake, and despite their mother's proved treason. That had turned out to be a *very* good idea.

I never entirely trusted Odard, for all that we'd fought and hunted and sung songs and drunk wine together for years, Rudi thought. *He was one of those men whose inwardness is always a secret, full of unexpected things like a forest at night. Until at the last . . . now, did I do him an injustice earlier, or did he grow on the Quest into the man he was when he died? For* that *man I miss, and badly.*

The Baron of Gervais had gone with them not quite all the way to Nantucket, and fell on the shores of the Atlantic like a knight from an old song, with a broken sword in his hand, a circle of dead foemen around him and a jest on his bloodied lips. Mathilda had promised the dying man that she'd look after his family, but his younger siblings had since more than justified the grace of her favor by their own deeds.

And Matti has squires old enough to fight as men-at-arms; it's not as if the boy will be overburdened.

The raised tent wall let in light—though the setting sun was behind them—and mildly warm air, along with some dust and the usual livery-stable-outhouse-and-sweat smells of an army camp, heavily seasoned with cook fire. They'd stripped out most of the comforts from the big tent to cut the weight for the transport train's sake, but the sheer space was useful since the High Kingdom's government had to be dragged around with it, as well as Montival's military headquarters.

That meant a lot of meetings and a fair number of clerks, cartographers, typewriters, adding machines, reference books and knock-down filing cabinets. And a lot of the original folding furniture was perfectly practical, light and strong and compact even if given to parquetry and mother-of-pearl inlay. The chair he chose did nothing more than creak a little at his armored weight; he was spending most of his days in harness, to help keep fit and to set a good example. Fortunately it wasn't really hot yet; if you had to fight, this sort of seventy-degree weather was the best for it. The main drawback of a suit of plate wasn't the weight, it was heat exhaustion.

Huon helpfully fished another crock of mild cider out of a bucket and placed it not far from Rudi's hand after he poured him a glass. The High King didn't have any squires himself, as yet. He'd been knighted by Association ritual before the Quest, but that had taken him away soon after and since his return he'd been too busy. And he had spent enough time in the Protectorate in his youth to take the obligations involved seriously; he wouldn't take a squire's oath if he didn't have time to fulfill them. The king hung the Sword over the back of his chair himself; he didn't like anyone else to touch it anyway except Mathilda . . . and generally speaking others liked touching it even less themselves.

"I know Órlaith will be safer with mother at Dun Juniper than anywhere else on the green breast of Earth," Rudi said to his queen.

He was continuing a conversation they'd been having

for some time. Even he could hear that there was a little fretfulness in his tone, not to mention downright fear. Edain's dog Garbh stopped her vigorous scratching and nibbling at recalcitrant parts of her shaggy fur to come over and put her gruesome head in his lap by way of comfort, rolling her eyes up at him and looking as meltingly sympathetic as a hundred and forty pounds of scarred gray-muzzled man-killing wolf-mastiff mixture could.

High Kings shouldn't be fretful, he told himself, ruffling the great beast's ears; the dog had walked all the way to Nantucket and back with them, and knew him well. *On the other hand, I'm a father too—and someone just tried to kill my child. I can't even declare war on those responsible, because I'm already fighting them. But possibly I can bash someone tonight with my own hands, the which will be an immense comfort.*

"She'd be just as safe at Mt. Angel," Mathilda said, sighing and sitting back from the telescope.

That had been her first choice, and it was indeed a mighty fortress in more senses of the word than one. They both knew she referred to the safety gained from what might be called sanctity more than physical protection; the threat to their daughter wasn't from armies, or even ordinary knife-men. He met her eyes for a moment and she shrugged ruefully.

"Agreed. But . . . well, I would say my mother is better at looking after children," he said. "Didn't she raise both of us?"

"That's a point. No insult to the good monks of your order, Father Ignatius," Mathilda went on hastily.

The warrior-monk, and now Chancellor of the High

Kingdom, looked up from his folding desk in one corner of the chamber for an instant and nodded, solemn but with a twinkle in his slanted dark eyes. He was a man of middle height, slim but broad-shouldered and with a swordsman's wrists, who looked graceful even sitting on a camp stool and dressed in the rather voluminous black Benedictine habit.

"None taken, my daughter," he said, carefully signing a document and blotting the ink before peeling the paper off one of a little stack of wax disks, applying it to the paper and stamping it with his seal. "The Shield of St. Benedict is not primarily a nursery order. When the Crown Princess is a little older, my brotherhood will be delighted to assist with her education at our university. I hope to delay my senile decline until then."

They all chuckled. Ignatius was a few years older than them, though a Changeling for all practical purposes, and he had a natural dignity that wasn't all incompatible with his dryly ironic sense of humor. Beneath her amusement Rudi could *feel* the underlying anguish in Mathilda at deciding to leave their daughter in the care of others. Even an *other* as beloved and competent as Juniper Mac-kenzie. It was the spiritual equivalent of a constant low-level toothache, stoically endured.

There were times when the Sword was a burden; sometimes even the link to each other and the land that had come with the Kingmaking was. He didn't know how much of that went with being a ruler in other times and places, but it was most assuredly true if you were High King of Montival—or High Queen. For that matter, he could sense a muted hint of Ignatius' longing to be back at the hilltop monastery of Mt. Angel, to lose himself in the ancient round of prayer and toil and meditation. He hadn't become a cleric to seek secular power.

The monk's sense of duty was like a blade of forged steel, though; he didn't have to give speeches to be an inspiration. Rudi sighed.

Time to be Artos, he thought, as he drew up his chair. *Or as the good Father would say, take up your cross.*

"Here, look at this," Mathilda said, pushing over the telescope. "We both need distracting. Come get a good *military* reason to be depressed."

He did, turning the focusing knob. Rudi had first seen Boise's fortifications a few years ago, on the Quest to Nantucket, and more recently from the observation balloons that now ringed it. Like many, the modern city had contracted to its original core, which here meant a rectangular block to the east on the far side of the river and a little back from it. Three bridges crossed the water, heavily fortified at both ends, virtual castles on the western shore surrounded by clear land worked as vegetable plots and running into massive complexes of towers on the wall.

Unlike most still-inhabited cities the sprawl of buildings around Boise's edges had been thoroughly torn down in old General Thurston's day. Many places left their suburbs to the attentions of time, vegetation, scavengers and fire, but around Boise even the foundation pads had mostly been broken up for reuse in the fortifications and cellars filled in for truck gardens—Lawrence Thurston had been a man with a very strong sense of order, among other things.

The walls he'd built reflected the other, bleakly pragmatic part of his nature. They were mass concrete reinforced with girders but they included some of the pre-Change high-rise buildings, themselves in-filled with cemented rubble, and it gave the fortification an odd mottled, angular look. They weren't as elegantly historic as Todenangst or the walls of Portland, or as brilliantly sited as Mt. Angel, and they didn't have the snarling cyclopean menace of Larsdalen's Bear Gate, but . . .

"We're not going to batter those down, or storm them," he said.

There was a click from the sentries as he spoke, the High King's Archers touching their bowstaves to the brow of their helmets in salute, and Frederick Thurston came in. He was in the hoop-armor of a Boise regular, with a red-white-and-blue crest running fanwise from ear to the ear of his helm. It gave his tall form an extra element of menace—which was one point of the gear, of course. He took it off and laid it down on the table, throwing his metal-backed gloves beside it and unbuckling his cavalry saber.

"Thor's mighty goats, no," Fred said, answering Rudi's last comment. "Can you imagine trying to land on that nice inviting strip of land between the east bank of the river and the walls, for example?"

Rudi could; he winced at the thought of the sudden rain of bolts and round shot and balls of flaming napalm among troops crowded into the narrow band—it was a deathtrap masquerading as an opportunity, even more than the moat-encircled remainder of the ramparts. It said something of Fred's father as a soldier that he'd done that, and not put the wall at the water's edge.

"No, you'd have to try it from the other side," he said. "Which we won't, but it's essential they think we'll try."

Fred nodded, family pride in his face for a moment. "That's why Dad put the wall as far back as West River Street."

Rudi turned the instrument from the city to his own siege lines, a ragged but substantial line of trenches and earthworks, some of them smoking faintly where stick-flame had landed. It was amazing how much dirt you could move in a week with fifty thousand sets of reasonably willing hands, spades, wheelbarrows, Fresno Scrapers, horses, mules, oxen and some well-trained field engineers. A crew in a pit a little behind the front were sweating at a trebuchet, grunting as they levered a four-hundred-pound block of stone into the throwing cup; the boulder had been shot at them by a similar machine on the walls and landed in the soft earth of the berm protecting them and was about to be sent home postpaid.

An officer barked a command, they all stood back, and the lanyard was pulled. A trebuchet was the simplest of siege engines in principle, if the strongest, just a great lever pivoting on an elevated axle about a fifth of the way from one end. You put weight—tons of weights—on the short end and a metal-mesh and cable sling arrangement on the long one, and you were in business apart from a few incidentals like the supporting frame to hold the axle high in the air and the winches to haul the long arm down and the general massiveness needed to withstand the stress. This one was about the height of a three-story house, the product of a foundry and machine shop in Corvallis, and in knocked-down form it took twelve eight-horse wagons to transport it.

The triangular block of weights in a steel frame box on the upper, shorter end of the arm began to fall as the

catch released the restraints. The long throwing-arm between the two giant steel upright A-frames started to
move, slowly for the first few instants then more quickly
as it whipped up, dragging the sling along the alignment
trough on the ground.

The loop of the sling swung skyward above the giant
beam and lifted free in a blur of speed; the free end came
loose from the carefully shaped hook at the top of the arc,
and the machine lofted the boulder at the city with the
casual ease of a boy shying an apple core at a crow in the
fields at sowing-time. It rocked back and forth with the cup
and sling dangled down as the crew hooted and jeered at
the defenders—probably variations on *eat this!*—and a few
ran up to the top of the berm before turning to bend over
and rhythmically slap their arses in derision.

Corvallans tended to be vain of their city-state's scien-
tific accomplishments and manufacturing prowess; the
university there ran the place, more or less, and had since
the Change. Its far-travelling merchants and skilled artisans and ingenious factory-owners were numerous, ener-
getic and shrewd too, shrewd enough to use that
accumulated knowledge well. A third of his artillerists
and half his engineers were Corvallans. Their bankers
were equally famous but far less liked, though Rudi had
reluctantly found them as indispensible as the troops.

The roughly shaped boulder tumbled away into the
distance, turning to a dot. Then there was a puff of dust
from the great ramparts above the blank steel surface of
a gate, and the hard *tock* sound of impact echoed back. At
this distance imagination had to fill in the way the wall
would shake underfoot, and the deadly whine of fragments of shattered rock and concrete like flying gutting-

knives. A rock that size packed a lot of energy into its travelling mass, and when you stopped it all at once . . .

Almost at once another sound came from the wall, a metallic chorus of catapult springs that had started their lives in the suspensions of heavy trucks releasing and sending paired levers slamming into their stops. Little thread-like blurs went streaking towards the trebuchet. The crew interrupted their celebrations to throw themselves flat as the four-foot darts from the springalds and scorpions came in; one struck the frame of the stone-thrower with a long *tannnnngggg* and flipped upward in pieces.

Nobody seemed to be hurt this time, but the artillery duel was producing a steady trickle of casualties . . . presumably inside the walls too. He was only slightly less unhappy about that. He wanted those men on his side, or at least going back to their farms and workshops and helping to repair the damage. Every one killed or crippled on either side was a loss to Montival as well as to themselves and their kin.

"Hurrah!" Rudi said sourly. "We could do *that* for fifty years and not knock down those walls. Not to mention I'm bombarding one of my own bloody cities, technically speaking so-to-speak."

"You could think of it as a *rebellious* city," Mathilda said helpfully.

"No, for then I'd have to wonder what I'd done to make folk supposedly my subjects willing to fight me," he said wryly. "Artos the First I may be—the Powers insist, it seems—but Artos the Tyrant I will not."

"Pass the cider, Tyrant," Fred said with a crooked grin; evidently he'd been watching the bombardment too. He went on:

"Both the pontoon bridges are finished, and we've got the east bank thoroughly invested. And the siege towers are coming along, for all the good it'll do us. We could lose twenty thousand men trying to storm the walls . . . and I'm not sure it would even *work*, at that. The Cutters have things sewn up tight in there, particularly the gates. What's left of the US Army troops aren't very enthusiastic, but . . ."

Rudi grunted thoughtfully and nodded; the *but* was that in an all-out assault the defenders were almost certainly going to die if the attackers succeeded in taking the wall, pushed off the inner edge if nothing else. Which was a powerful motivator for well-trained troops who knew the way things worked.

"Surrender at the last moment is always . . . problematic," Rudi agreed.

Problematic, he thought, *was a tactful way to put it. When warriors' blood is up and they're primed to kill, they tend to keep on doing it while anything alive is left before them. Turning your back is suicide, and those who've seen the elephant know it. So it's kill or be killed.*

They had excellent general intelligence about the state of things in the city. There was a trickle of deserters, men who let themselves down on ropes in the night, or just shed their armor and jumped into the river and swam for it. He'd interrogated some of them himself . . . and caught one or two with the CUT's taint on them. Forewarned, it was easy enough to spot.

"Then we'll have to chance the scheme we came up with," Rudi said. "We have the asset . . . and the asset is people, who I'd rather not sacrifice unless I must. But without me . . . and the Sword . . . it will not work."

Everyone looked unhappy at that; *he* was unhappy, though it made no difference. Mathilda looked positively mutinous. He raised his hands.

"No, my love and my Queen. There's nobody I'd rather have by my side for a venture like this . . . but it is a risk, and it would be a hard day for Órlaith if the dice came up snake eyes for both of us. Nor can we risk a long regency with her so young; and the kingdom so young itself. Though Father Ignatius would do a fine job as Regent, to be sure."

"I would rather juggle rabid skunks," the cleric said dryly, reaching for the next in the stack of State papers. "With respect. Your Majesty."

"That's one reason you *would* do it well, my friend, but I hope to spare you the nipping and the stench. So we'll go with Fred's plan."

"Hey, don't pin it on me! I just told you about the . . . secret."

Rudi nodded. "It needs the Sword, and only I can wield it."

Ignatius said nothing more; he'd argued against Rudi's scheme, then taken the High King's decision as final and switched stride without stumbling to bend all his efforts to make it work. Fred Thurston grinned, and poured himself a glass from the jug of cider that hung in a rope sling, sweating through the coarse pottery—it was fermented just enough to make it safe to drink without boiling or chlorine.

"It's *almost* worth missing the birth to have Virginia safe away from this and not able to argue with me," he said. "This way I get to go along without sweating blood every minute."

"Todenangst wasn't all that safe," Mathilda said soberly, then laid a hand on his arm when he winced. "Sorry, Fred. I know it must have been hard, hearing that Virginia was there and in danger, her and the baby, after you thought she was so well guarded."

He snorted. "Rudi and I had a cussing contest. He only won because the Sword lets him speak more languages. I learned how to say *motherfucking son of a BITCH* in eight or nine. It sounds really odd in Elvish." Then he looked towards the city. "I hope to hell this comes off for a whole raft of reasons."

"This Cole Salander is a good man, and has his wits about him," Rudi observed. "And a most powerful degree of motivation."

"Yeah, I thought so too. I'm going to bump him up a few grades. Provided we all live through this. And your cousin Alyssa is even sharper, I'd say. Between them they may be able to pull it off."

Rudi raised his glass; the cider cut the dust very satisfactorily, just sweetly acrid enough.

"I'll drink to that," he said. Then, overriding someone's throat-clearing: "And yes, there's enough for more. That's what you were about to say, wasn't it?"

Mathilda jerked in startlement; Ignatius kept writing; and Fred's head whipped around. Rudi's hand had already been going to the pitcher.

"No fair," two soprano voices said in a disturbing almost-chorus. "You've got the Sword."

The etiquette of the High Kingdom was quite flexible in the field—Rudi and Mathilda had made sure of that, having spent enough time in the Protectorate in their youth to see how you could get sewn up in ritual like a cross between plate armor and a cotte-hardie. Certain people had access without prior notice or challenge from the guards, first and foremost his companions on the Quest.

Some of those people could move *very* quietly, and liked to show off about it even now.

His half sisters Mary and Ritva were among both categories. Signe Havel's daughters weren't Bearkillers except by birth; in their teens they'd decided to live with their Aunt Astrid and uncle-by-marriage Alleyne Loring in Mithrilwood, what had once been Silver Falls State Park. That . . .

Eccentric lady, Rudi thought charitably as he waved them to the table.

. . . eccentric lady Astrid and Rudi's elder half sister Eilir Mackenzie had founded the Dúnedain Rangers a few years after the Change, inspired by a series of books that Astrid had insisted on calling *The Histories* and which she'd been obsessed with even before the Change. She was dead now, in the spectacularly successful rescue of Fred's mother and sisters and sister-in-law from Boise last year. The folk she'd founded were even more devoted to her martyred memory than they'd been to her charismatic person.

The Dúnedain specialized in what the ancient world had called special operations, well taught by experts in the early years. In peacetime they hunted bandits and man-killing beasts and escorted caravans and led expeditions to the dead cities. In time of war they were even more valuable, the more so as the High Kingdom fitted so neatly into their founding myths.

"Mae govannen, maethyr," he said: *Well-met, warriors.*

"Mae govannen, Aran Raud, i 'wanur vín," they replied, putting their right palms on their hearts and bowing before they sat: Well-met, High King, our kinsman.

Among the Dúnedain eccentricities was using a language from the books . . .

Pardon me, from The Histories, he thought.

. . . though that had its practical benefits since very
few outside that fellowship could understand it. One of
the many minor disturbing things about carrying the
Sword was that it had made him fluent in *that* tongue as
well . . . including immense amounts of grammar and vocabulary, which the long-dead Englishman *hadn't* in-
vented but which fitted perfectly with the rest and
included all the elements you'd expect in a living speech.
In fact, he spoke *two varieties* of it, one of which *felt* more
formal than the other; Ranger scribes had been pestering
him for details ever since he got home.

Mary had been identical to her twin Ritva until she
lost an eye and acquired an eye patch during the Quest.
The two tall fair young women still looked very much
alike in their mottled sage-green-brown Dúnedain field
gear, with three blue eyes between them and the white
Tree, seven stars and crown on the breasts of jerkins that
had light mesh-mail riveted between two layers of soft
leather.

"Help yourselves," Rudi said. Raising his voice slightly.
"And you two come in as well, so that I may punish you
suitably for allowing these depraved Rangers to attempt
a practical joke on the ineffable majesty of Artos the First,
the shame and sorrow of it."

The two women were accompanied by their
husbands—though Ritva and Ian Kovalevsky hadn't yet

found time to formalize their obvious bond. Ingolf Vogeler was a big battered brown-haired and vastly experienced man in his thirties, originally from a remote part of
the Midwest. Ian was younger, slighter, fair-haired, and
hailed from the Peace River country of northern Drumheller, which he'd left to become a member of a red-
coated band of mounted warriors who kept peace in the
Dominions. That had put him in Ritva's way as they all
returned to Montival, and they'd hit it off. Or Ritva had
decided she wanted him, which would amount to much
the same thing.

*The poor lad hadn't a chance once Ritva set her sights on
him; though to be sure he's able and clever as well as comely,
the which does not surprise me, she has high standards.*

She'd told him once that she and Mary had thrown
dice to see who got Ingolf, who Rudi considered one of
the better all-round warriors he'd met and a good friend
to boot. As well as the man who'd ridden into Sutterdown four very eventful years ago to tell Rudi that the
Sword of the Lady awaited him in Nantucket . . . and had
done so with the Prophet's killers on his trail.

*I'm rich in real comrades, something a King can't count
on, from all I've heard and read. Which reminds me . . .*

"Ignatius, do you have that letter from Drumheller
that came in with the morning courier?"

The cleric silently produced it. Ian's ears had pricked
up hopefully, and Rudi went on, sliding it over to him:

"Not from your family, Ian, but of interest still."

He handed it to the younger man. The northerner's
pale brows went up. "Well, well! *Indefinite detached duty
as liaison*, straight from the Deputy Commissioner Western District! That sort of . . . regularizes things."

From his looks, he'd been guilty about it too; they were a painfully law-abiding lot where he came from. Ian went on:

"I'd been worried about that. How did you manage it, Your Majesty? I wouldn't have thought the Force, ah . . ."

"Cared much what Artos the First desired? Yes, but they do care what the leaders of the Dominions want, and Drumheller may not wish to be part of the High Kingdom, but they do want good relations and they are our allies against the CUT. I merely wrote to Premier Mah politely asking a favor of her."

"Thanks!" he and Ritva said simultaneously.

"You're welcome. Just invite me to the handfasting. No need to inflict *Rudi* or *Artos* on any of the children. Now to business."

He unfolded the map, and they went over it as dinner arrived. Since the army was now stationary, and newly come in a rich irrigated countryside that trusted the Montivallan forces to pay for what they ate, the food was better than usual; skewers of peppered grilled beef and onions, steamed cauliflower, fresh risen wheat bread, butter and the luxury of a green salad. After a while in the field you lusted after greenstuff the way a drunkard did for whiskey, not to mention needing the fiber to keep your guts in order.

"Mmmm," Mary said, forking a piece of tomato. "Good thing we've been winning the battles—they didn't have time to strip the countryside before we besieged the city, and we're getting what the townies usually eat. I get *so* sick of trail mix and dog biscuit."

Rudi's fist slammed down on the table, making the plates jump. Everyone looked at him in surprise; he wasn't much given to displays of temper.

"I'm *tired* of winning battles!" he said, controlling the flush of anger. "I'm tired of killing brave men whose only fault was to be born in the wrong place and to get levied from the plow! I want to win this bloody *war*, and get back to my proper work and my family and let everyone else do the same!"

He cleared his throat, feeling their eyes on him and feeling a bit self-conscious too.

"Sorry."

Ingolf chuckled and spoke, a little unexpectedly—he was normally a little taciturn.

"No problem, Rudi. You're too God-damned self-controlled for your own good, sometimes. Anyway I agree."

Just then a snatch of marching song came through the open flap, in time to the tramp of boots:

"Dry your eyes—it's no cause to weep
The weather is fine and the road isn't steep
The world is still round, my compass is true
Each step is a step back to you
Each step is a step back to you."

"And so do the troops," he said.

Mary grinned and cocked her one eye at him with good-natured skepticism. "And what will you do, lover, when the reign of peace arrives?"

He shrugged. "Sleep a couple of years, and then try not to see anything more exciting than a field full of sheep eating grass and crapping where they please, ever again. You youngsters—"

"Hey, you're only eight years older than I am!"

"Nine, but it feels longer. You youngsters don't . . . look, guys, you take the dipper to the bucket long enough, the bucket's going to run dry. And you only get one bucketful per life. I've drunk a lot of dippers on a lot of hot days."

Most of the people around the table looked blank; Rudi suddenly realized he was the third-oldest there, which was a bit of a shock. He was used to thinking of himself when the word "youngster" was thrown about.

I'm still a young man, he thought. *But I'm not a heedless overgrown boy leaping into the blue anymore, that's true. Ingolf is sounding less and less cynical and more and more wise when he says something like that.*

He'd had warnings from the Powers, direct and blunt, that he wouldn't make old bones, too. Every year spent warmaking was a waste he couldn't afford.

I've been that boy, but now I'm a husband and a father . . . and a King, to be sure.

Ignatius nodded slightly over his spare dinner of salad and bread, catching his monarch's eyes and inclining his head towards Ingolf in silent agreement.

Rudi made a gesture of acknowledgment. "With luck, this will speed things up considerably. Now, here's how we're going to handle the timing. First the Rangers will—"

CHAPTER TEN

The streets of Boise were dark. Cole Salander was used to that where he grew up—night simply *was* dark, unless there was a full moon—but normally the capital of the United States had gaslights along the main avenues, burning the by-product of the sewage plant. The incandescent mantles had seemed almost painfully bright to Cole the last time he'd been here, about a year ago. Now they were closed down, the iron posts just another hazard along the streets. Here and there a glimmer of lamp or candlelight showed, usually from behind shutters. The air was still and smelled of the smoke confined by the walls, and somehow of fear. In the distance, off to the east, a flare of light showed as a ball of napalm came over the wall, and there was a faint clanging as the fire-wagons headed towards the spot.

"I am completely insane," Cole Salander said, *sotto voce*, striking along briskly with his right hand on the hilt of his short sword. "I volunteered for this. I rest my case."

"Absolutely no dispute," Alyssa answered in the same low tone, walking with a suitable humility, the (jiggered, non-locking) handcuffs on her wrists. "And I'm *twice* as absolutely insane as you are."

He could sympathize. He certainly wouldn't want to be a prisoner, particularly a woman, in this Cutter-controlled city. How *thoroughly* controlled had come as a bit of a shock to him—and, he thought, to Captain Wellman. Theoretically the Captain had come in to report to a general who was part of the Emergency Steering Committee about a possible intelligence asset; developing those was one of the things the Special Forces were *for*, after all. In point of fact there had been a red-robed High Seeker standing in the same room, arms crossed across his chest and shaven head gleaming. The general had slid his eyes in the man's direction every few seconds, and there had been sweat on his forehead even though the building was cool. And a rayed sun pendant on the breast of his uniform.

Wellman had been silent for a long time when they came out of that; not that you expected an officer to be chatty with the enlisted men, but the Special Forces were a lot less stiff than the Regulars. He hadn't doubted Cole's cover story of prolonged flight and hiding; why should he? It was exactly what *could* have happened if they hadn't run into that Mackenzie patrol, and he'd gotten a commendation and field-promotion to corporal out of it. Alyssa, complete with an excellent set of false papers prepared by her own side, had been his ticket into Boise; their story was that she'd talk to him and nobody else—it had produced a lot of embarrassing kidding. But the thought of how many things could have gone wrong along the way made him sweat even now.

Especially now. So close to pulling it off . . .

A hard multiple clatter of hooves made them halt. They didn't run—that would be ruin—but simply stood back against the grill of a shuttered store that sold *Planters, Reapers and Spreaders, made to order* according to its sign. Cole stood at parade rest, with his right hand on the hilt of the short sword sheathed high on that hip. You couldn't go far wrong by falling back on the drillbook.

About a hundred cavalry went by, heading eastward at a walk, and not in the neat ranks that even Boise's ranch-country reserve mounted troops used—more of a shapeless clot, kept off the sidewalks only by an instinct to avoid the unfamiliar loom of buildings. A hundred horsemen took up a lot of space even in strict column of fours, and these loomed like an endless horde in the dark. One had a lantern on a pole, from the light containing a tallow dip or two that cast a flickering yellow glow on the hard scarred faces and shaggy plainsman's horses.

Cutters. Ah, crap.

The light cavalry wore coarse homespun and leather and the gear that he'd seen before on the Rancher levies of the CUT. Mostly steerhide breastplates and arm-guards studded with nail-heads or eked out with strips of salvaged washers or wire—the far interior was poorer in metal than areas closer to the coasts, and more people had survived to use it up. They had steel helmets, though, slung at their saddlebows and leaving bare heads bristle-cropped or shaven or shaven save for a scalp-lock, beards shaggy-wild or braided or trimmed to a tuft on the chin.

Uh-oh, Cole thought. *Crap. Goat crap.*

That style of haircut was a sign that these men came from areas that had been under the Church Universal and

Triumphant's control for a long time; the Prophet's elite guardsmen out of Corwin shaved their heads, and they'd imitated it if not the regulars' discipline. So was the way some of them had the rayed sun that was the CUT's symbol tattooed on their foreheads. That meant they'd be harder-assed.

All of them had shetes at their belts or slung over their backs or strapped to the saddle—a heavy, slightly curved slashing-sword derived from the old agricultural tool, and common everywhere east of the Rockies. One of Cole's older unarmed combat instructors had said they looked more like a *liuyedao*, whatever the hell that was with its pants on. They had recurve horn-and-sinew bows in scabbards at their knees and quivers and round leather shields as well, and there were a few rawhide buckets of short javelins or light lances.

Some of them had strings of scalps dangling from their saddles, too. That and the way they smelled—rather rank even for troops who'd been in the field for a while—made him think they came from the Hi-Line, the high bleak plains of central Montana near the Lakota territories. He'd heard that there was nothing to burn on those dry treeless expanses but dried cowflops, and that between fuel shortages and scarce water and long brutal winters folk had mostly gotten out of the habit of washing regularly there.

He blew out a breath of relief when they passed with just some hard looks, and the glow of the lantern disappeared around an intersection.

"Those stinkers were too close for—" he began.

Hooves clattered again; just two of the horsemen this time, one carrying a newly kindled torch that dripped sparks and shed a flickering globe of red light. They reined in, and the one who wasn't carrying the torch turned his mount left-side-on to the two on foot. He had his bow in his hand with an arrow on the string and his drawing hand ready, though he carried the weapon point-down.

The archer was one of the shaven-headed ones, and wore a light mail shirt over broad bowman's shoulders. Mail represented wealth out on the high plains, like the silver studs in his saddle; he looked about thirty, though heavily weathered, with a face marked by dusty white healed cuts on the forehead and cheeks and jaw, narrow blue eyes and a yellow tuft of billy-goat-style beard on his chin bound with leather thongs. The chest of his armor had a symbol picked out in brass rivets, like a number eight lying on its side, which was probably the brand of his ranch—roughly equivalent to the coat of arms of an Associate, which group Cole still privately thought of as *those neobarb castle freaks* despite the recent change in his political allegiance.

They smelled better, though.

"You," the man said in the hard flat eastern accent. "Who are you, who's the abomination bitch, and where are you-two going?"

"Sir," Cole said—which was stretching a point; the man wasn't in *his* chain of command in any way, shape or form. "I'm escorting this prisoner to the Special Forces battalion HQ for questioning."

Actually my orders are to convey her to Boise garrison HQ at Fort Boise over on the east side, *and we aren't near either, which will look suspicious if this goat-raper knows the town at all. We are* pretty close to this place that

Fred Thurston heard about from his dad, and which nobody else alive probably knows . . . I really hate having my life depend on probability like that. . . .

It was hard to see the rider's expression in the dimness of the flickering pine-knot torch, but Cole thought he could see the eyes widen.

"All enemy prisoners are to be turned over to the Church Universal and Triumphant—the blessings of the Ascended Masters be upon Its Prophet and the Seekers," the plainsman said. "I'll take this one now."

Alyssa tensed. Cole saluted. "As you say, sir."

He reached for Alyssa's handcuffs as she backed away. "On three," he said very softly.

"One—"

He grabbed the chain and heaved, links biting into his palm; she pulled backward and kicked him realistically in the shins—which hurt.

"Oww Goddamn two—"

"Three."

He released the chain, staggering backward himself as if her tug and kick had shocked his grip free. Alyssa dropped flat and rolled under the torch-bearer's horse.

"Catch her, sir!" Cole shouted.

As he'd hoped, the bowman in the mail shirt took his eyes off Cole. What wasn't in the half-formed plan was that the other man dropped his torch and swept out his shete, the broad-tipped blade glinting along its honed edge as he leaned far over with a born rider's casual skill and prepared to swipe at the slight figure on the pavement. Those things could leave a drawing cut a yard long and inches deep on an unarmored body.

"Shit!" Cole cursed.

He'd been unlimbering his crossbow since the instant the horse-archer turned his attention to Alyssa, and contrary to regs he'd been carrying it cocked and with a bolt in the groove in town. Instead of shooting the man in the mail shirt, he whipped it up to aim at the swordsman.

"Shit!" he said again, a strangled scream this time.

Alyssa had rolled out the other side of the horse, and as she bounced back to her feet her hand went to her collar and then whipped down the horse's haunch. The animal gave an equine shriek of indignant hurt and went into a bucking, leaping twist; the punch dagger was razor-sharp, and had parted the beast's hide in a slash that was shallow but twenty inches long.

There was no time to readjust. The crossbow went *tung-snap* in the darkened street, and the bolt tore through the steerhide armor over the man's shoulder and gouged a groove through his deltoid. That was actually very good shooting even at pointblank, in the dark and at a twisting, jerking target. Unfortunately it was the *left* shoulder, and the man got his horse back under control almost immediately. He also didn't seem to be the sort of guy whose concentration could be broken by a little pain.

The first one was already turning his attention back to Cole, standing in the stirrups and drawing the arrow back against the resistance of the thick composite bow. That was exactly the right decision tactically, since Cole was obviously the real threat. It would have been much nicer if the man had been stupid.

Cole dropped the crossbow—which was a hell of a way to treat a fine weapon, but needs must—and flicked out his gladius. He bounded forward in the same movement, jumping side-to-side as he advanced, to get to close quarters and crowd the horseman too closely to let him shoot.

Or shout for his buddies, for Christ's sake, he thought desperately. *If I can land a cut on that horse—*

Unfortunately the man in the mail shirt was an even more superb horseman than his follower, and his horse was just as well trained; the pair operated like parts of the same organism. It skittered right back crabwise to a shift in the rider's balance, backing up about as fast as Cole was advancing, and the man drew his bow to the ear. The pile-shaped point caught a last flicker of red light from the torch guttering out on the patched asphalt.

The other one had his horse in hand too, though its ears were back and its eyes rolling in a bite-and-stomp fit of temper, and he was boring in on the dodging form of Alyssa with a yard of edged metal in his hand, as opposed to her three inches of holdout knife. Unfortunately he wasn't stupid enough to get in the archer's line of fire despite the way she immediately tried to draw him into it.

Shit, isn't this where I came in? Cole thought desperately as the horse-archer prepared to skewer his brisket. *Only I'd rather have Old Eph, there was only one of him and the big hairy fucker couldn't* shoot *me!*

I'm officially colonel of the First Readstown Volunteer Cavalry, and here I am sneaking around in the dark again, Ingolf Vogeler thought.

He'd always thought of himself as primarily a horse-soldier, which was how he'd spent the first four years after leaving Readstown at the age of nineteen. He'd joined the volunteers heading northwest from the Free Republic of Richland—what had once been southwestern Wisconsin—to

Marshal and Fargo for the Sioux War because he'd quarreled with his elder brother and it was an honorable way to run away from home. He'd stuck all through the miseries of the Red River campaign, and then ridden with Icepick Olson's band into the outright epic horrors of the Badlands Raid, mostly because he was too stubborn, or looking back on it too pig-ignorant, to quit. The learning curve had been steep, if you survived.

After the war petered out in mutual exhaustion he'd led what was left of the cavalry company he'd ended up commanding into salvage work, eventually into the high-return and insanely risky long-range branch, all the way to the dead cities of the Atlantic coast where the cannibal bands were only the *worst* danger.

But Icepick had been a scout-and-slash specialist, anyone doing that against the Lakota had to be good at it, and salvage work deep into the death zones didn't involve many boot-to-boot charges or even the formal minuet of a horse-archery duel. Hence he'd often ended up in this sort of situation, paddling across a river with slow strokes and a crawling awareness that someone might be about to hit him with anything from a handy rock in their hand to a twenty-four-pound glass globe shot from a catapult, full of napalm and wrapped in burning cord. Luckily it wasn't a very wide river, less than a quarter bowshot, about the size of the Kickapoo on whose banks he'd played as a boy.

It sure doesn't get any more fun, though, he thought mordantly.

Those long rustling barefoot summer evenings by the water seemed a very long time ago, listening to the bullfrogs and watching the first stars come out.

Christ, the things I do!

The rubber raft bumped softly into the mud of the eastern bank and stopped as they all pushed their paddles down into the muck for a moment; the city wall of Boise was about one bowshot away, a looming black presence against the bright stars. The man at the tip of the blunt wedge of the bows went overside with hardly a splash or sound of boots in wet soil, which was very respectable considering that John Hordle was a three-hundred-plus-pound slab of Anglo-Saxon beef halfway between six and seven feet tall, none of it fat despite a legendary consumption of food and beer.

Not slowing down any that I've noticed, either, Ingolf thought. *Despite the way that red mop's got some gray in it.*

The older man heaved the inflatable boat and its dozen occupants forward and held it steady with the casual grip of one great red-furred paw until he was certain they hadn't run into a welcoming committee. Which was all comforting to Ingolf, who was thirty-something and beginning to feel that while he could still do nearly everything he'd been able to do ten years ago, it took longer and cost more and sometimes he just plain didn't *want* to anymore. Hordle had to be around fifty; he'd been a young soldier over in England at the time of the Change, in something called the SAS, arriving in Montival-to-be years later by a series of wild accidents.

Though I wouldn't be one to talk about wild accidents, Ingolf thought.

He reached over his shoulder to make sure the thong holding his shete in its sheath down his back was still in place and that his arrows weren't going to rattle in their padded quiver. His strung recurve was thrust through a

set of carrying loops on the outside of the quiver, a Mackenzie trick the Dúnedain had modified for their shorter,
handier weapons. It was very useful after a little practice,
letting you switch weapons quickly without dropping
your bow. Checking stuff was so automatic he could do
it with about a tenth of his attention and it was obscurely
soothing somehow, like stroking a rabbit's foot.

*He and the Lorings came across the ocean, but I started
out in Wisconsin and ended up here after crossing the entire
continent nearly four God-damned times, no less—Iowa to
Nantucket, Nantucket to the Pacific, all the way to Nantucket again and back. With time out to be a prisoner in
Corwin, most of which I still don't remember and the rest I
wish I didn't. Christ, the things I do. . . .*

After an instant the one-time Englishman made a small
clicking sound with his tongue, lost in the usual humming and buzz of summer woodland—the strip along the
river had been a park before the Change, and largely left
alone since. The crew went up past Hordle in a smooth
silent stream, spreading out just inland of the water. Ingolf and four others gripped the rope loops along the side
and helped haul the boat out of the water and carry it
into the shelter of a willow tree's drooping branches.
That would keep the too-regular shape invisible from the
wall towers. There were observation balloons up in a circle around Boise, but the enemy didn't have any flying
after a couple of hair-raising episodes early in the siege.
Montivallan gliders had dragged barbed forks of burning
tow into their gasbags at the end of long ropes, and a
couple of the aircraft had even survived it.

*I'm not surprised that Alyssa Larsson volunteered to go in
there. She's a glider pilot, being crazy is a job qualification.*

The Rangers were all nearly invisible in the moonlit dark, everything dull-toned and non-reflective, their faces covered by the hoods of the war-cloaks, which included masks with a slit for the eyes. Ingolf was relying on his helmet-cover and the brown beard, which made his face less likely to glimmer in the dark. The brown acid-treated steel of his mail shirt was good enough camouflage too.

I haven't had time to get full Dúnedain kit . . . or maybe I'm afraid of feeling silly, and the First Readstown is here and I do lead them now and then, and they certainly think it's silly-looking, except for the ones like my nephew Mark who think it's unspeakably cool. Granted it all works well, but . . .

Hordle clicked again, and they all ghosted up the slope and into the brush and woods, fanning out in a semicircle around the place they'd landed. The big man came past all of them, checking. Ingolf nodded with sober respect as he eeled past, and caught a glimmer of a grin in return. Hordle's personal weapon was over his back too—what they called a greatsword around here, with a massive forty-inch blade broad as a palm and a hilt as long as a man's forearm. At nearly seven pounds he'd have thought it too heavy to use effectively even two-handed, if he hadn't seen the Dúnedain leader walk down a row of oak pells, leaving a row of stumps behind him.

The big man was married to Eilir Mackenzie, Rudi's elder half sister and co-founder of the Dúnedain; Ingolf suspected that he and his compatriot Alleyne Loring were responsible for a fair part of the Rangers' military side. Not that they hadn't had able pupils, and by all accounts the recently deceased Astrid Larsson-Loring had been a natural anyway. Ingolf had seldom met troops better at noise discipline on a night movement, even his own Vo-geler's Villains in the old days. After a moment the only solid proof he had that he wasn't alone in the woods feeling the damp gradually soak up through the padding under his mail shirt was the unmistakable mixed military odors; oiled metal gone a bit rancid and amalgamated human and horse sweat and wood smoke soaked into wool and leather. Even those were faint.

The undergrowth wasn't too thick; obviously the riv-erbanks were used as turn-out pasture in peacetime. A city needed a lot of working stock, horses and mules and oxen to do everything from pulling streetcars to rich men's carriages to hauling fodder in and manure out. According to the intel reports the enemy had cancelled night patrols here because they'd been losing too many deserters and needed their loyal troops to watch the oth-ers. It didn't really matter to them if the Montivallans landed men here, since they could be annihilated at dawn once the artillery on the walls could see their targets.

Or so they think.

The reports seemed to be accurate; at least they didn't run into anyone as they pushed out to establish a perim-eter. It was dense-dark, and he moved slowly, feeling his way with hands and the toes of his boots. The rest of the squad was an occasional rustle, not even a broken twig marking their passage.

Ingolf went down on his belly again not far from where Mary probably was—she was extremely good at being inconspicuous—and waited. Three more rafts grounded behind them, and more of the Rangers filtered through the brush. Alleyne Loring came up beside Hor-dle, and they conversed for an instant in Sign, holding their hands close to each other's faces in the darkness. Alleyne was about Ingolf's height, though slimmer; next to Hordle he looked like a teenager.

Of course, being with the Dúnedain means you have to learn two *God-damned new languages, one with your fingers.*

Sign was useful, he had to admit—though they'd made it compulsory originally because Eilir Mackenzie had been deaf from birth and just wanted it that way, and Astrid loved secret-rules-and-passwords stuff. The Rangers were core-practical enough now despite the elaborate stylishness, but he suspected that back in the very beginning there had been a substantial element of teenaged let's-pretend-in-our-tree-house to it all. A lot of them actually did live in tree houses, though the Ranger term was *flet*.

After that they all settled down and waited. Ingolf chewed on a couple of slices of dried apple to keep his blood sugar up, and did silent exercises to keep himself supple, setting muscle against muscle without moving. The inevitable bugs of summer woods near a river he just ignored; that went with the job, and he'd been doing it since he was seven and his father first took him out after deer.

An hour later he began to worry.

He could just see the North Star and the Dipper from here, between the leaves of two cottonwoods, and he lined them up and did the trick. Draw a line through from the North Star to the two top stars of the Dipper, treat that as the hand of a clock, add an hour for every thirty days after March 7, double the figure and subtract it from twenty-four. That gave you the time, and he made it oh three hundred hours give or take. Which was much later than the signal was supposed to come.

Something had gone wrong.

He was worried, but not very surprised. This was a big complex plan, and in his experience those never went off perfectly. You were ahead if they worked at all. The only reassuring thing about it was that if nothing happened, they could just go back the way they came and let the regular infantry and the engineers and artillerists get on with the siege while they drank a toast to the memories of Cole Salander and Alyssa Larsson.

As long as we get back before dawn, unless we want a catapult bolt up the ass on the way out. And dawn comes early this time of year.

CHAPTER ELEVEN

Cole Salander knew he was going to die. He supposed it was something to do it with your sword in your hand and facing the thing that killed you, though right now he'd have settled for "in bed, asleep, at seventy-five." Alyssa would have to look after herself, which was a damn—

"Break left!"

Cole went down on the pavement in an automatic dive, landing on his forearms with the sword laid on its flat so he wouldn't cut himself on it, which was appallingly easy to do.

Tung-snap!

The arrowhead started to follow him, then came back up, then released to arch out into the darkness over the rooftops as a crossbow bolt sprouted in the center of the archer's chest. Cole heard it strike very clearly, the metallic ping of the mail links breaking mingling with the hard crackle of bone as it sank to the fletching. It must have cut the spine as well, because he went over as limp as a sack of grain, thudded to the pavement and lay leaking from nose and mouth.

Two more crossbows snapped less than a second later, there was the crisp sound of steel hitting tallow-treated boiled leather, and the other Cutter horseman gave a hoarse grunt and fell. He was still sprattling and trying to choke out a shout despite having a couple of twenty-two-inch bolts crisscross through his torso; a man was surprisingly hard to kill quickly unless you got lucky. Alyssa darted in, her hand moved in the darkness, and the man gave a final jerk and lay still.

That little knife was *sharp*.

Cole rolled back to his feet. "Glad to see you, Captain Wellman, sir," he said to the officer, sheathing his sword—there was a trick to doing that without looking—and standing at parade rest again.

'Cause it would sort of sound odd to say that I'm glad you didn't trust me and followed me to see what the hell I was doing.

The camouflage jackets and pants were unmistakable Special Forces issue, plus he knew all the faces. Sergeant Halford was standing there too; he had a crossbow in his hands and his brown face was absolutely blank as he worked the cranking lever, *clack-clack-clack-clack-clack-clack*-click. The half-dozen troopers behind him were also . . .

Giving me the hairy eyeball. It's pretty obvious I was fibbing just a bit in my report at this point . . . lying like a rug made out of dead fish, actually . . . and these are all guys who've been with the Captain for a long time. I noticed that when he picked them to come in.

Wellman nodded. "Maybe you'll be glad," he said, which was a little ominous.

Garcia and Jones had already gone for the horses, slinging their weapons and getting the animals under control with practiced gentleness.

"You know where to take them?" Wellman asked.

"Sure, sir," Garcia said. "My uncle Larry's butcher shop is only a couple of blocks away and he won't ask any questions."

I'll bet he won't, Cole thought.

Politics aside, civilians in Boise were already down to a ration of a quarter-pound of meat every second day per adult. The city hadn't been properly provisioned before the Montivallan armies closed in, another symptom of the way things had broken down. And the High King's men had carefully herded every possible Boisean and Cutter soldier into the city, to put more strain on the supplies.

"He sells hamburgers as a sideline," Garcia went on.

"Can he handle the bodies, too? That won't cause questions?"

"Sure thing, sir. They're really terrible hamburgers even when the city's not cut off, so I don't think anyone will notice."

Halford made a grinding noise, and Garcia went on hastily:

"Sorry, sir. Yes, he can hide them under his manure heap. That was my job before I got called up—it was why I reenlisted for the Special Forces instead of going home. Believe me, nobody looks there until the compost guy comes with his wagon."

"Which with the city under siege isn't going to happen soon. See to it and rendezvous at the safe house soonest."

The squad extracted the bolts and found Cole's where it had stuck in a wall—that was essential because they were easy to identify. The two men detailed to the job took the blanket rolls strapped behind the saddles, wrapped the corpses so they wouldn't leak—cursing mildly when the wool cloth proved to be most certainly hopping with fleas and probably lousy—and heaved them over the horses' backs, and walked off looking official. Two other men had taken the dead Cutters' canteens, and emptied them to dilute the stains.

"I take it you're not actually named Maria Hernandez, or from Corvallis?" Wellman said to Alyssa while the cleanup went on.

"No, Captain, I'm not," she said coolly.

She'd wiped the holdout knife on the dead man's pants and slid it back into the leather sheath sewn into her collar, but there was a splash of blood down her right forearm. She was rubbing her left in the elastic bandage and flat splints.

"You OK?" Cole asked.

"No compound fracture. Yet," she said.

"Follow," Wellman said.

The rest of the squad grouped around Cole and Alyssa; he noted that they were bracketing the two without being obvious about it, and from the way she flicked her eyes so did she.

"Ah, sir, it's a long story but I have something time-critical to do—" Cole said.

"When we're out of view, corporal," Wellman said. "You can give me the condensed version of why you're trying to let someone else's army into Boise."

Well, that explains the maybe you'll be glad to see me

part, Cole thought. *On the other hand, he's obviously not just following orders himself, what with killing those two Cutters who were about to do us.*

He was sweating a little when they reached the safe house—which was a bunch of substantial three-story pre-Change buildings that had been knocked together, plus a former parking lot now surrounded by a twelve-foot wall of salvaged brick with broken glass cemented to the top, and sheet-metal gates. Part of it was a dwelling-place for the owner, and a little lamplight leaked out through shuttered windows. Wellman let them into the courtyard through a smaller door in the larger gates, using a key; the men relaxed—very slightly—when it closed behind them.

And a little more when they turned away from the dwelling-house into another section of the U-shaped complex. Inside they made sure the shutters were closed before Halford raised the glass chimney of a lantern, lit the wick from his lighter and turned the knob down. The yellow light showed shadowy glimpses of big open rooms with treadle-worked sewing machines and piles of cloth, in bolts or laid out over patterns on long cutting tables, and racks of spools of thread and sacks of buttons and pine boxes of finished product. From the olive-gray color and the shapes and the familiar slightly musky lanolin smell of coarse linsey-woolsey he guessed that in daytime they would be busy with seamstresses making uniforms on government contract.

Yeah, I heard the Captain's older brother lives in Boise and is something big in cloth, Cole recalled.

Buying raw materials from people who grew flax or kept flocks, spinning it all in a water-powered mill in some convenient location, supplying looms to folks on credit, then buying back the bolts from the weavers and dyeing and finishing the product at his home-place, the usual system. You could make a lot of money that way, certainly a hell of a lot more than a Captain's pay. Though he didn't know anyone except their kin who actually *liked* putting-out merchant clothiers. Well, except by contrast with bankers. And even their blood relatives . . .

There was supposed to be some sort of quarrel between them, but family is family and kinfolk stick together at a pinch.

Sergeant Halford set the lantern down on a table and stood at Wellman's right with his hand on his swordhilt as the officer seated himself.

"Henson, Malurski, Jens, you're on perimeter," he said.

Captain Wellman leaned back and looked at the two quasi-prisoners, sighing and rubbing a hand over his balding head; he was around forty, about Cole's height but whip-thin and wiry, with tired-looking green eyes. The other two Special Forces troopers weren't exactly pointing loaded crossbows at Cole and Alyssa. But then again they weren't exactly not pointing them, either.

"OK, let's hear it, corporal," he said. "As you said, time's a-wasting."

Cole exchanged a quick look with Alyssa and gave him the real story.

Well, no need to go into all *the details just yet,* he thought, skipping over the bit where the Mackenzie *fiosaiche* had sent him to sleep and simply saying they'd caught him.

There was no way around the part about his being turned into an involuntary assassin, though: his tongue stumbled at that, simply because words weren't adequate, and he still struggled with a flux of involuntary rage when he thought of it. Not to mention a deep-in-the-belly cold wash of fear. Halford made a skeptical sound, and Wellman stopped him with a gesture.

"Remember the one we . . . sent on, sergeant? That Seeker?"

From the noncom's grimace, he did, and not fondly.

"Yes, sir. I've seen a lot of men die but nobody that slowly when they should have been gone already."

"Had to hold him below the surface of that latrine with a pole for what was it, five God-damned minutes, as I recall."

"Seemed longer, sir. Particularly considering how hard I hit him to begin with."

"It eroded my natural skepticism a little. Not as much as seeing what Corporal Salander says he saw would, but a bit."

Wellman turned those tired, sharp eyes on Cole again.

"So you're going to let the enemy into the city?" he said a few minutes later, his face flatly unreadable.

"Captain, the *Cutters* are the enemy, and they're already in the city. And three-quarters of the army around Boise are our own people. The rest are Mackenzies and Bearkillers, mostly," he went on. "They're disciplined troops, they're not going to sack the place."

"Bearkillers are very well disciplined," Alyssa said. "That's what I am, by the way. There aren't any Associates within a day's march of Boise right now—Rudi . . . His Majesty . . . is keeping them out of the picture because he knows they're unpopular. Not that the Grand Constable would let them get out of hand. Basically Frederick Thurston is running the siege."

Cole went on: "I've met Fred Thurston, sir, and I trust him to keep his word, and he's promising strict order and a general amnesty except for specific crimes, and a free election."

"And what does *King Artos* say to that?"

There was an official poster not far away, showing a bad artist's conception of Rudi Mackenzie in plate armor, flogging emaciated serfs pulling a wagon. The way things had been since the old general died and Martin Thurston took over, you were well-advised to buy the latest and stick them up. You never knew if someone was reporting to the NatPols. . . .

"Well, he says that's exactly what he wants too, sir, and he's said it publicly. It's his policy that every member of the High Kingdom gets full internal autonomy. Boise won't be part of Montival unless we decide that on our own in a plebiscite, and we're to be completely self-governing with our own laws within our borders as of the old general's death if we vote yes. And I believe *him* too, sir. He's . . . well, he's . . . quite impressive. Sir."

Unexpectedly, Wellman smiled slightly. "That's what the old general said, too, about Rudi Mackenzie," he said. "He met the young man a couple of years ago, just before he died himself at the battle of Wendell. I wasn't there for that. Maybe if I'd been at Wendell I could have saved . . . never mind. Go ahead."

"I mean, hell, I intend to vote for Fred Thurston, *and* to vote for joining Montival," Cole said bluntly. "Assuming I live that long. The old general wanted to reunite the country, but he couldn't. Montival, the High Kingdom . . . well, it's not the way he wanted to do it, but it's going to be a great big chunk reunited, with some of the same stuff he was for. No more fighting our neighbors, for starters. Freedom of religion, and I sure as s . . . shoot know the Cutters don't have *that* in mind. And no slavery allowed—"

He jerked his head at the poster. "I mean, that's complete bullshit, sir. Everyone in Montival can move if they want to—it's one of the few laws that they have that applies everywhere. Which is also something the Cutters don't have in mind, they don't even *call* their slaves something different like they do in some places, they just outright call 'em *slaves*. Apart from all that thing about how half the human race are Spawn of the Nephilim stuff and it's abomination if women wear pants and who knows what else."

Wellman closed his eyes for a moment. "You know," he went on quietly, "I stayed in the Army because of Lawrence Thurston. I never did trust Martin or the men around him, but I didn't want to believe his own son would . . ."

"Captain Wellman, I talked to the First Lady . . . I mean the old General's wife . . . hell, I talked to *Martin's* wife. They agreed that Martin killed the old general in the confusion at Wendell to cover up his coup; and that he was . . . changed, somehow. After he met Sethaz, the Prophet. He went from being an ordinary evil son-of-a-bitch to . . . something else."

"Yeah, I noticed that," Wellman said dryly. Then he shook his head: "Witches, spells, prophecies, red-headed kings with magic swords . . . Christ. What's next, dragons? And I never even liked playing D&D."

Silence fell for about three minutes while Cole searched his memory for the obscure ancient reference to distract himself from the way the time stretched out. Then Wellman sighed again and looked at Sergeant Halford.

"Jack?" he said, startling everyone by using the man's first name.

That seemed to be some sort of signal; Halford's face lost its military stiffness for a moment.

"Kid's right," he said. "Time to get it over with."

"You've got a point," Wellman said, turning back to Cole. "There's only one way this war is going to end, anyway; let's get it done before the country gets ripped up any worse than it has. Where is this place?"

Cole exchanged another look with Alyssa, and she nodded slightly. They weren't supposed to tell anyone, but it was the only way to pull this off.

He gave the directions. Wellman grinned, this time a mirthless carnivore expression.

"Just in case you hadn't noticed, corporal, there's a Cutter observation post on the roof of that building."

Cole gulped; he hadn't.

Wellman went on: "But hey, sneaking around is supposed to be what Special Forces do, right? Let's go do it."

Mary got within six paces of Ingolf before he realized she was there. He didn't start, which must have disappointed her, but she silently touched his forearm and moved her fingers in front of his eyes:

Come.

He followed, slowly—there just wasn't any other way to move quietly in woods at night, especially unfamiliar woods. He *did* start when something the size of a medium dog scurried away noisily through the underbrush with a crackling and rustling; probably a raccoon. *It* didn't have to do anything but run like hell, a desire which he viewed with profound sympathy. Up from the edge of the river the trees were smaller and scrubby, grown up since the Change except for a few that had been planted in the old days for shade and ornament. The only thing left of buildings was a few snags of wall. . . .

And the Dúnedain leaders were grouped around one of those, unmistakable from the sketches at the briefing. Ingolf came up and went down on one knee; the others were too, or making like snakes on their bellies—this was only a hundred yards from the wall, although when you looked back you saw that there was artfully arranged dead ground most of the way to the river. Cole Salander was there, and Alyssa Larsson, neither of whom he'd expected to see alive again, deep down. And a man he didn't recognize, in Boise's Special Forces summer camouflage uniform. That *wasn't* part of the plan; the two were supposed to guide the assault force in by themselves.

As he came close he heard Alleyne Loring say something in Sindarin, his mellifluous aristo-English accent obvious even through the alien syllables. The only other one like it Ingolf had ever heard was Alleyne's elderly father, and it had made some old books he'd read make more sense. Alyssa answered abruptly and in English:

"Yes, of course they're trustworthy, Uncle Alleyne— that's why they sent both of us, to show that we're not under threat. Now, are we going to do this?"

"You're not, we are, Pilot Officer," Loring said. "Salander, you're with . . . Mary, Ritva, Ingolf, Ian. John, feed a link in after them."

"Lead it in, more like," the big man said imperturbably in his soft burring accent that rendered *more like* as *murr loik*.

Loring nodded. "Confirm that all's well on the other end and relay the code."

Alyssa didn't complain, though even in the darkness he thought he could see she'd like to.

In the soup again, Ingolf thought. *Christ, the things I do. . . .*

The hidden door was cleverly concealed; an aluminum slab had random pieces of rock and brick fixed to it, and enough soil to grow honest-to-goodness plants, all cunningly arranged to overlap the opening. A counterweighted lever system opened it from within.

Mary flashed Ingolf a thumbs-up as she followed her sister in; all he could see was an indistinct flash of one blue eye behind her mask. She made the same gesture to Alyssa, who was a cousin—daughter of her mother's brother—and got the purse-lipped glare and elevated middle finger of resentment as she passed. Alyssa mouthed something silently; no way of telling what, but something along the lines of *you big blond horse* wouldn't have surprised him.

Fred Thurston had described the tunnel concisely, and Ingolf's hands and feet found the metal rungs set into the concrete wall without trouble.

"Go," he said softly, as Ian landed beside him.

His voice fell into the void with the flatness of still enclosed air. The near-absolute dark grew worse still as the five went forward, each guiding themselves with a hand on the wall. The scent of damp concrete and old stagnant water was strong in the chilly air, and occasionally his boots made a *tack* sound in a shallow film of it as they slanted downward towards the bottom of the tunnel's curve. It was probably some sort of pre-Change engineering work mostly, and he could almost feel the monstrous weight of the city wall above. Perhaps it went by an old building's foundations that were taking the weight. He certainly hoped so.

There must be drainage, but it was far from perfect, and the film of water turned to a shallow puddle when they reached the bottom. He could feel it when the floor started to climb again, you always could, especially when you were in full gear—even a slope invisible to the eye was all too obvious to the legs. Everyone drew a weapon, mostly daggers; Ingolf thought of his bowie and decided on the tomahawk he kept tucked through a loop at the back of his belt. If it came to it, he wanted something handy in close quarters, and the light axe had stood him in good stead before.

Knife-fights in the dark, *in a* cave. *Wouldn't that be a treat, not knowing who you were hitting. Christ, the things I do. . . .*

The tunnel was fairly broad, enough for three men to move abreast and high enough that he could only just touch the top with the poll of his belt-axe when he put an arm up. In the darkness it was impossible to tell whether it was pre-Change, or something the elder Thurston had installed to have up his sleeve. Apparently the workmen hadn't talked, his elder son hadn't told anyone before he died, and the secret remained safe with the younger. That would end tonight, one way or another.

From what Fred said, his dad arranged this when his grip on Boise was still shaky and kept it close because it might turn out handy. It's doable for the numbers we have planned, but it's still going to be tight, he thought, as they came to a halt as much by instinct as anything else.

Cole Salander tapped out a sequence somewhere in the blackness ahead, softly, knuckle on solid-sounding metal. There was a breath of warmer air and . . . not exactly light, but not-quite-total darkness. Then a small glimpse of genuine light above them, a beam from a bull's-eye lantern, the dull gleam of roughened piping set in the wall for climbing, and a voice:

"Up here, and quick. There are Cutters on the roof three stories up, so keep it quiet."

Oh, joy, Ingolf thought. *We've got enemy ass right over our heads ready to dump on us. This night just gets better and better. Christ, the things I do. . . .*

Mary and Ritva went up first, climbing with the light silent grace of cats. Ian Kovalevsky followed, and then Ingolf, noting in passing that the trapdoor was a solid block of concrete with a square of worn old-style synthetic glued to its top. That would overlap onto the surface beyond, concealing any line, and the trap itself was beveled in all around the edge, fitting into a similar circuit in the floor. A counterweighted lever mechanism raised it; the thing was four feet on a side, and far too heavy to lift by hand. A splendid little asset, now being expended for its one and only use, fulfilling the purpose for which it had been made.

They were in a walk-in closet as they came out; that gave onto a smallish room that had probably been an office once, though probably not now since it had neither gaslights nor an exterior window. Beyond the frosted-glass cubicle was a sense of shadowy gloom around them, and concrete pillars; what had been something called a *parking garage* before the Change, and warehouse space since, the old openings in the walls bricked up to keep out weather. He'd seen the same done elsewhere, since the ramps between the floors were perfect for moving loads around.

"I'm Captain Wellman, Special Forces. This is it?" a man a bit older than Ingolf said, as the two women checked the situation outside and then turned to whisper a code word down the way they'd come; he had Captain's bars, the same sort as a lot of the National Guard insignia in the Midwest, likewise derived from the old American army.

"Ingolf Vogeler, Captain Wellman," Ingolf said softly, sketching a salute after he sheathed his weapon.

Carrying an axe to your first conversation was tactless. He could see that the Boisean officer recognized the name, if not his face. It was a little disconcerting how often that was happening these days. He'd been well known at home in Readstown, of course, but he'd been the Sheriff's son there. And anyway, Readstown was a very small puddle to be a bullfrog in, and over the wandering years since then he'd gotten used to being just another stranger to everyone except the people he was working with. In Montival he was one of the people who'd been on the Quest, Ingolf the Wanderer according to some bards he'd like to strangle. A certain degree of fame had its drawbacks, and he made a mental note to figure the likelihood of being known into his calculations.

"Pardon me if we're not being entirely trusting," he said. "Last-minute changes of plan in a major operation give me hives."

That got a smile, a slight unwilling twitch of the lips, and a nod as from one professional to another.

More of the Dúnedain came up through the opening in the floor, and then the unmistakable troll shape of John Hordle. He gave a gesture, holding up two fingers. Ingolf winced slightly. That meant both-of-you-know-who were on the way across the river along with the assault echelon, and that was so dangerous he didn't even say the names to himself.

It's amazing how much more protective I've gotten about Rudi than I was when it was just the nine of us out in the wildlands. Maybe there's something to the way he complains that being king is a lot less fun than becoming *king.*

They were committed now. Wellman nodded at Hordle too, evidently recognizing him on sight. That wasn't very surprising, particularly considering how distinctive the man was; the Dúnedain were Montival's equivalent of Wellman's outfit, after all. He seemed to know his job, which would include finding out all he could about his probable opposition.

A hard-looking dark man had a map spread out on the floor. Ingolf pegged him instantly for a long-service NCO. They knelt beside it, and Cole's former superior did too. This hadn't been part of the original plan, but you used what came to hand. A quick glance saw four other men keeping watch through narrow slits in bricked-up arches, with pairs of Ranger archers joining them and others spreading out through the space. The bull's-eye clicked on, opened just enough to show the details.

The map was of Boise, about the same as the ones Ingolf had been studying. The quality was very high, fine-line engraving on excellent paper waterproofed with wax. Ingolf heartily approved, remembering times when it had all gone down the three-holer because someone got lost or didn't know where something was . . . or worse still, where *they* were, or worst of all was convinced they were somewhere they really weren't.

"We're here," Wellman said, tapping the corner of South Capitol and West Myrtle. "Which I assume you knew before you came through."

South Capitol ran southwest from—logically enough— the old State Capitol building, ending in the main gate complex; Myrtle ran northwest to southeast, crossing it in a good sensible grid. The building he touched was a rectangular mass a block long and half a block wide. It never hurt to spend a little more effort getting a good grasp on the area you had to operate.

The Boisean pointed upward. "Three stories up. At that level, it's a flat roof for half the area, and then this section goes up another six."

He put a sketch down by the map. The higher section was L-shaped, with the bottom of the L facing Myrtle.

"The part we're in now was rental storage until trade went to hell. The upper section is government offices except for the last two floors, which are long-term records storage."

Everyone nodded; the higher parts of still-occupied ancient buildings tended to be used for purposes which didn't require climbing that many stairs multiple times a day. Dumping old tax records to be slowly nibbled into oblivion by mice was a typical one. There were ways to use the old elevator shafts, but they were all expensive, usually treated as luxuries for rulers and the very wealthy or employed for military necessities.

Wellman went on: "All deserted at this time of night, even the janitors have gone home."

Well, that's nice to know. There had been no way to check on little details like that from the outside, and the devil was in the details. *Maybe Wellman getting involved was a* good *thing.*

"The problem is that there's a Cutter detachment on the flat roof right above us, keeping an eye on things; they've got a perimeter like that around all the approach roads to the gates on the inside, I presume exactly to guard against an attempt from within the city to rush one and open it. They've got a signal fire ready to go, and cowhorn trumpets. They report by blowing a signal every hour. It's not as bad as a night heliograph, but it's workable. Nine men, three placed *so* and three mobile and three resting. They're relieved at sunset, midnight and dawn."

His finger traced South Capitol towards the gate, tapping to either side of the road. "These used to be parking lots. They're mixed-use row housing now, three stories, workshops and stores on the bottom and people living over. Nothing to worry about, the people will probably keep their heads down until they know what's happening."

Ingolf nodded. That sort of infilling was standard practice in modern walled towns. Space was always at a premium; the whole point of a wall was defense, but the number of men required to hold it went up geometrically as you increased the area enclosed by the perimeter. Fortified settlements were always as densely packed as water supply and hygiene allowed. Besides their sheer ludicrous size, pre-Change cities seemed to have come in two varieties: insanely overbuilt, or insanely dispersed and spread out. Or both. Usually both, in fact.

"The gate complex is here, two blocks. Street patrols are all Cutter light cavalry, though how they plan to feed that many horses during a siege is anyone's guess. There's definitely a High Seeker there—one at each of the major gates, in fact. I dealt with one of the junior Seekers once, and it was a memorable experience. I wouldn't go near a *High* Seeker if I was on fire and he had the only water in miles. You have some way of handing this one?"

"Yes," John Hordle said, glancing at the way they'd come. "Oi've done it, taking off their 'eads works foine." He tapped the greatsword's hilt. "Or burning them or chopping them to bits. They *do* stop moving in the end. But loikely we won't 'ave to do it the 'ard way because we've zommat special coming. Good thing there aren't more of them, innit?"

"The problem is going to be getting to the gate," Wellman said. "The bastards can . . . *see* things. See them coming before they're visible."

"The *first* problem is the sentries," the hitherto silent noncom said.

"Sentry removal?" Ingolf said. "*That's* not a problem."

Ian Kovalevsky chuckled. "Not if you've got the love of a good woman," he said.

Hordle grinned, which made his face look like a boiled ham in a good mood. He got the joke, but the Boiseans looked baffled.

"We'll 'andle it," he said, and glanced at the tunnel entrance again.

The last of the Dúnedain were up, about fifty in all, with Alleyne Loring bringing up the rear. A man in the gear of a Boisean regular came next out of the office, with the traverse side-to-side red crest of an officer on his helmet. More followed him, not too noisy for men wearing armor of articulated lames and hoops of steel, but a lot more so than the Rangers. The second wave of the assault group had made it, or at least the lead element had. Though how many more could before someone on the wall noticed was anyone's guess. The regulars filed off to quiet commands, taking knee in ordered rows with the points of their *pila* like a growing thicket of steel points in the gloom.

"Got a job of work to do," Hordle said. "Won't go away by itself."

CHAPTER TWELVE

CITY OF BOISE
(FORMERLY SOUTHERN IDAHO)
HIGH KINGDOM OF MONTIVAL
(FORMERLY WESTERN NORTH AMERICA)
JUNE 26TH, CHANGE YEAR 26/2024 AD

Fifteen minutes later, Ingolf was remembering a story he had run across while he was dickering over a salvage contract for the Bossman of Iowa back about five . . .

No, six. Damn, goes faster all the time. I thought I knew how things worked even if I didn't like it, I got the contract for the run to the east coast, and that was when this really strange stuff all started, six years ago.

. . . six years ago. Just about the only good thing he'd ever heard about the CUT was that it disapproved of burning coal; mining it was among the very limited set of jobs that made soldiering look good. Iowans dug up a lot of the filthy stuff around Des Moines, not having near enough wood for such a huge city, and the air there always smelled of it.

When the dicker was over and while they sat and twiddled their thumbs and waited for the young Bossman to come in and OK the deal—he hadn't been the most reliable of men, having been raised without hearing the word "no" very much—one of the ministers had told him that cages of small birds were taken down into coal mines in Iowa. To test for poison gasses that sometimes accumulated underground and either choked the miners or swept through the tunnels in walls of flame that burned them alive.

Yeah, there are *worse ways of making a living than fighting cannibals to salvage artwork for rich assholes.*

The little critters keeled over and went toes-up behind the bars before the gasses reached dangerous levels for humans, which sometimes gave the workers time to throw down their picks and run. It was a neat trick when it worked, and Ingolf had been raised among matter-of-fact farming folk who were prosperous enough but couldn't afford much sentimentality. He would have been sorry to use a dog that way, but he'd have done it if he had to and birds came in only three categories: edible ones, nonedible ones, and ones which were pretty before you decided whether they were edible or not. And at a pinch, they were all edible.

The thing was that the *birds* probably thought the miners kept them around and fed them and cleaned out their cages because they loved them.

Likewise, the Cutters on the rooftop probably didn't think of their role as making plenty of noise while getting killed so their main force would know what was coming, but that was about what it amounted to. That was why officers who knew their business tried to get someone else's men assigned this sort of duty, and rotated it when they couldn't. Or saw that the ones they could spare most got it.

I pulled a lot of outpost duty when I was young and stupid, he thought as they padded forward through darkness as black as the ink of the bureaucrats who laired here in the daytime. *So the whole point here is to kill this bunch* without *making a lot of noise. Don't think it's necessarily going to be easy just because you've done it before, Ingolf old son. Nobody ever managed it with* you, *though that was partly dumb luck at first.*

The inside of the office part of the building was very nearly as inky-black as the tunnel had been; there just wasn't much ambient light to come through the windows with the moon down and the sun not up yet, and the Cutters outside were sensible enough not to eliminate their night vision by keeping a fire going. The downside was that they were concentrating on the streets and relying on the access door alerting them if anyone tried to break through that way because it was thickly fastened with chains and padlocked. Or on hearing the sound of windows breaking. It was a double-type door, windowless pre-Change metal and still strong.

"Saw," Hordle said softly.

He gripped a section of the chain, pulling and twisting to hold it rigid. Ian pulled the flexible wire saw out of a pouch; the Force used them too, and the Dúnedain had good gear. Unlike their models in *The Histories* in peacetime they charged heavily for their services when the clients could afford it, with a bank in Corvallis as their business agents, and *nobody* tried to stiff them. Not twice. A bunch of pissed-off Rangers *and* a Corvallan debt-collector . . . that was like a grizzly bear with a catapult mounted on its head.

Ian looped the flexible blade around the chain and began to work the handles, going slowly to keep it quiet and prevent heat buildup that might ruin the tool's temper. The miniature chips of diamond set into the wire carved at the soft steel, a quiet *ruhh . . . ruhh* sound.

"Stop."

Ingolf had been around the man Mary and her sister called *Uncle John* a fair bit since they got back from the Quest. Sprawled by a fire with a mug at his elbow, cracking walnuts between thumb and forefinger, bellowing some off-key and usually off-color song, you'd think him a genially boisterous bruiser and not too bright. Unless you looked closely at the little piggy russet eyes in the massive face. Right now his actions were as precise as a surgeon's.

Hordle's fingers explored the cut in the darkness. "Enough."

Ian withdrew the saw, coiled the loop and put it back in the pouch. Hordle's monstrous hands clamped and twisted, straining for a moment. There was a soft *ping* as the weakened steel yielded. Then an occasional slight *clack* as he threaded the chain cautiously through until the doors were ready to open. The hinges were on this side, and the doors swung inward too.

Hordle worked the catch with infinite care, and applied his eye to the crack. Then he tapped two fingers towards his eyes and made the signs that meant: *One man close. Ready.*

Hordle set himself like a sprinter. Ian nodded, got out his bow, put an arrow on the string and held the weapon in his left hand. Ingolf drew his tomahawk again; he needed only one hand to pull his side of the double doors open. Cole Salander waited behind them, crouched slightly with his crossbow already at the shoulder.

It was a pleasure to work with people who really knew what they were doing. . . .

The third finger came up. Ingolf gripped the old metal handle and pulled, fast and not trying particularly to be quiet, but without any unnecessary jerk. Ian did the same, like the motions of a country-dance. Hordle lunged through in the same instant, his shoulders clearing the opening doors with not a hair to spare. There was a Cutter trooper about six feet from the door, looking at it curiously; probably he'd been wondering at the small sounds.

He started to leap back, started to draw his shete, started to open his mouth and yell. Hordle took one long scissoring stride, and his hands closed on the man—one over his face, one behind his head. His size did *not* mean he was slow. A single wrench, and the Cutter's face was pointing out between his shoulder blades; there was a crackle like a green branch breaking when you twisted it, a stink of human waste.

One down, eight to go.

Hordle threw the body aside like a broken doll as he charged and drew his two-handed blade. A human grizzly with a sword, silent in the night.

Ingolf went through on his heels, Ian beside him already drawing his bow and loosing. The arrow struck a man at the edge of the roof high in the chest. He staggered back three steps, hit the balustrade with his buttocks and pitched overside. Three stories down and he hit concrete with a clattering, very final crunch. Imagination

filled in the figures who darted out and grabbed his ankles to drag him out of sight.

Seven left.

After the ink-pot inside, the rooftop looked almost
bright. Two more Cutters were at either corner of the
rooftop, squatting on their heels with the ease of men
who'd grown up without chairs, looking out over South
Capitol. They turned and rose snake-swift at the flurry of
motion, one reaching for an arrow and the other drawing
his blade, a quick glimmer of metal.

Cloaked shadows rose behind them, flipping up like
gymnasts from where they'd clung to the brick, hidden
by the overhang and their war-cloaks. Mary hit the cop-
ing with her soft soundless elf-boots, crouched with the
motion and sprang. Suddenly the two Cutter sentinels
seemed to be dancing, dropping their weapons and putting hands to their throats. Mary's fell, with her riding
him down with her hands straining back, like a bad horseman sawing at the reins, and Ritva's was down too.

Mary bounced up to her feet, leaving the *rumal*
around the dead man's throat where she'd flicked it with
a backhand cast—a long silk handkerchief with a gold
coin knotted into one end. Ritva used a piano-wire garrote, but Mary was a traditionalist, in her way. . . .

Five . . .

Cole's crossbow spoke as soon as he was clear of the
door, and a man threw up his arms, took two more steps,
and fell.

Four.

Ingolf had his own target. One Cutter had very sensibly ignored everything else, and even more sensibly ignored the long trumpet hanging from a tripod of

poles—standing and blowing in the middle of a fight wasn't likely to be conducive to long life or prolonged music either, more like a single strangled blat followed by a dull thud. Instead he snatched up a covered lantern and ran towards the fire signal, a big steel trash bucket heaped with straw and splintery pinewood. There would be no hiding *that* if he pitched in the flame and the alcohol in the glass reservoir too.

Ingolf halted, took stance, flipped the two-foot hickory handle of the tomahawk to get the balance perfect as it smacked back into his callused palm and threw in the same motion. Less than twelve seconds had passed from the moment the door opened to that when the wood left his hand.

Thousands of hours of old Pete's patient coaching when he was a child and a teenager went into it, more in camps since when there was nothing else to do but practice or drink. God help him, times when he'd taken turns throwing and standing in front of a tree as a mark, and done the whole thing while a whiskey jug was going the rounds after dark and the deceptive flickering of firelight shone in his eyes. A dozen times for real. You didn't need a tomahawk as often as you did a bow or a shete, but when you needed it nothing else would really do.

The throw had the sweet surprise of something perfect. The blackened steel of the head flickered through the night and went into the back of the Cutter's thigh, splitting the tendon just above the knee; he hadn't dared try for the torso, armored with a leather coat covered in steel washers. The man went down with a thud and the lantern clattered ahead of him away from his outstretched fingers, rolling to the foot of the trash bucket.

An arrow—Ian's—went through the space he'd just vacated a fraction of a second after he fell, a flicker of half-seen motion in the night.

Ingolf was already charging the instant his follow-through finished. He didn't pause when he came to where the man lay, just starting to push at the pebbled asphalt with his hands and reach for the lantern again and making a breathless squealing sound. Instead he leapt up when he was two paces away, as high as he could, and came down boot heels-first with all the momentum of his more than two hundred pounds of bone, muscle, weapons and armor.

The impact jarred him all the way up to his teeth and he stumbled to his knees and one hand. He could hear bones crack as he landed and an agonized wheeze as the man's breath was driven out of his collapsing lungs. Then he wrenched the tomahawk free from where it had sliced through tendon and muscle and into bone and struck twice at the base of the man's skull—with the blunt poll, not the blade, which might stick in bone.

Damn, but this gets a little more disgusting every time, he thought as the crunching feeling vibrated up the handle, like hitting a teapot full of jelly.

Three . . .

When he got back to his feet everything was over, as he'd expected; surprise was the greatest force multiplier, and when you got total surprise and threw in guys like John Hordle, there was only one possible outcome. Ambushing beat the hell out of a stand-up fight. He'd been aware of the greatsword's blackened blade moving in a pivoting figure-eight, and a couple of meaty thudding, cracking sounds.

And then there were none. Forty-five seconds, max.

It wasn't even very startling that they'd all come through with nothing but bruises, though he still had a slight unacknowledged sweat of relief break out when Mary came up grinning. It wasn't that she actually enjoyed killing men, even Cutters, but she did like the rush of a successful action, that crazed sensation of godlike immortality. He knew the feeling. It was like telling yourself that you could always put the corncob back in the mouth of the jug after one more swallow. . . .

Or possibly hitting yourself on the head with a hammer because it feels so good when you stop.

"Ready for that meadow full of sheep?" she said cheerfully.

"Ready and eager."

"Too bad. How can a girl compete with ewes? Maybe if I started wearing a fleece to bed . . . that might be fun. . . ."

Hordle was wiping down the blade of his greatsword with a swatch of linsey-woolsey, as they all cocked an ear to check if the noise had carried. There hadn't been much, but it hadn't been absolutely quiet either. Ingolf looked at the bodies Hordle had left and blinked, altering course to avoid getting his boots wet. The first one was beheaded, which was more common than you'd think, and he'd taken the leg off another just below the hip with the backstroke. The other . . . it must have been a straight overarm cut landing on the base of the man's shoulder.

Ingolf had seen at lot of battlefields, but nothing much like the results of that appalling blow.

No, I lie, he thought. *When that Refugee, what was his name, Jesse something . . . Hanks . . . tripped and fell into the circular saw at the timber mill back home, when I was around ten. Just after Dad got that waterwheel running right.*

Hanks had been stumbling-drunk that afternoon and every other time he could cadge or steal enough booze, but possibly he'd just let himself fall. The man had been like many who'd made it out of the cities after Change Day; he'd never really recovered from what he'd seen and done and suffered, so that only raw kill-devil corn liquor could make his brain stop squirming like a toad in a bone cage. Ingolf's ten-year-old self had been hustled out of the building, but he hadn't forgotten.

You can always add something to your memories, he thought as they dragged the bodies over to lie at the base of the higher section of the building.

It wouldn't hide them, exactly, but neither would it have the distinctive sprawl of dead men left where they fell to catch eyes at a distance. Hordle's victims required two trips each. Ritva's was a bit messier than her sister's, since piano-wire cut deep when used for what her folk called SSR . . . or Silent Sentry Removal.

Cole pursed his lips and nodded thoughtfully, eyeing the twins out of the corner of his eye.

"You ever think we're insane?" Ingolf murmured to Ian Kovalevsky as they followed the Dúnedain back down the stairwell to the top of the ramp. "Or maybe too dedicated to finding women who really *understand* our work?"

"Eh?" the ex-Mountie said. "We just like really active blondes with forceful personalities, I guess. You never met my mother, but let me tell you . . ."

"Oh, you betcha. But most husbands, when the wife

says *I could just strangle him!* they don't have to wonder whether to take it literally."

Ian chuckled. "Hey, if they were absolutely perfect, would they still have been single when we met 'em?"

"I heard that!" came from below.

"Oh, *shit*."

Rudi Mackenzie followed Fred Thurston up the ladder and into the room. He was just in time to see John Hordle and a group of followers trotting back down the ramp from the next level; it was too dark for the blood to show on dark clothing, but the smell was rank.

"All taken care of," the big man said, jerking a thumb upward. "Until someone notices."

"No trouble?"

"Routine, just routine."

Fred walked over to a man in a mottled camouflage uniform with Captain's insignia.

"Wellman, I know you're thinking *have I done the right thing?*" he said quietly. "That's something I can only demonstrate by actions, not promises."

"Sir," the man said, saluting in Boise's fashion.

Fred returned the gesture and stepped aside. Captain Wellman's eyes went wider than the darkness would account for. Rudi was in plain gear, a brigandine with the rivet-heads dulled to the same green color as the outer leather, a visored sallet and vambraces of browned steel, boots and leather pants; just enough battle armor to let him fight in a melee while leaving him maximum agility. Evidently Wellman recognized him anyway . . . or the Sword.

"I understand that I owe you my thanks, Captain Wellman," Rudi said soberly.

"For what?"

"For deciding I'm the least bad choice of a short and unpleasant list, wouldn't it be?"

The older man met his eyes steadily. "I didn't do it for you," he said, his voice flat. "I did it for my country and my people, and to save the city my family lives in."

"Good reasons, and all the better to hear them from an honest man," Rudi said, equally matter-of-fact.

The Boisean's words had rung with truth like a bronze bell. He went on:

"Having, as you might expect, to deal with a good many of the other sort. You have my thanks anyway, if you'll take them. And as a reward, Fred here will be giving you more work."

They shook hands. "You're . . . ah . . . not quite what I expected," Wellman said.

Rudi inclined his head to the poster; it wasn't the first he'd seen since they crossed into former Boisean territory.

"Ah, well, the serfs absconded with my glass carriage, and took the gilded armor and second-best crown of ruby and massy gold with them as they danced away clicking their heels and snapping their fingers. And stole the very last bag of honeyed filberts in the pantry to boot, the spalpeens," he said lightly, startling a smile out of the other man.

"Ah . . . Your Majesty?"

Rudi raised an eyebrow, and the Boisean continued: "Why are you here? Personally, I mean."

"Ah. Well, fair enough. Two reasons. First, I don't like to send men into danger I haven't shared. Mind, I'll do it, needs must, for I've found my likings have little to do with this job. And second . . ."

He drew the Sword. Here was a slight hiss from the assembled troops, and for an instant everything about them seemed washed-out, as if there was a light so bright, so *real*, that the world faded next to it . . . yet the room was still shadowed-dark. Wellman blinked openmouthed for an instant, and Rudi judged him a man who wasn't used to being disconcerted. The hard-faced noncom next to him swore softly.

"And there is this, which I alone among men can bear," Rudi said gently.

Matti can, among women, but she doesn't like to and I don't blame her, he thought to himself. *As I told the man, likings have little to do with necessity.*

Wellman swallowed, visibly forced his mind to work, and then began to smile in a considering fashion, which said volumes about the man.

"The High Seeker?"

Rudi nodded. "Locked within this is a power against which their demon lords cannot stand, and which blinds their seekings and the harm they can do the minds of humankind."

Wellman winced slightly. "I'd rather there wasn't any of this sort of stuff around. But if there has to be, it's nice to have some that doesn't actively creep me out even when it scares me shitless."

"I can see your point," Rudi said. "The Sword can even free such men as the Seekers from their dominion, though sometimes there's little enough left. Mind, it won't stop an arrow. But just as a *sword*—"

Rudi flicked the Sword against a concrete pillar, a hard swift cut from the wrist. Wellman cried out involuntarily in alarm—that would wreck the edge of any common weapon. The Sword of the Lady was different even simply taken as a blade with a handle; it had an edge better than the finest razor could take, fit to part a drifting hair and therefore far sharper than any battle sword was ever honed. Normally the thinner the edge the more fragile, but as far as he could tell it was utterly impervious to any harm. It never needed to be oiled, or wiped down . . . or taken to a sharpening stone.

He suspected that it could be dropped into the hottest furnace, or the heart of the Sun for that matter, and not even grow warm to the touch. He wasn't altogether sure it was physical matter at all as humankind understood the term, perhaps instead an embodied *concept*, a thought that could be touched. Most of the time he treated it with the same care as he would any fine weapon, from reverence and lifelong habit, but the demonstration was a legitimate use.

The edge struck the pillar with a *crack*, and a fist-sized divot of the stone-hard material came free with a puff of dust.

For the Triple One has given it into my hands not least to hearten my folk.

Wellman leaned forward, peering. Within the shattered concrete a piece of rebar gleamed, severed clean and smooth. A full swing of a heavy axe in the hands of a very strong man—John Hordle, say—might have done nearly as much . . . once . . . nearly, but not so neatly. His eyes went back to the supernal blade. Even the shower of dust left the Sword unmarked, sliding off the surface in a little stream.

"This is not just a war of men," Rudi said. "So the Powers who gifted me with this, and Who are well-wishers to humankind, have told me."

"Jesus," Wellman said softly.

"Jesus too, though Him I've never met. For They wear many faces, all true and none complete. It's an hour to dawn, the hour when dreams grow brighter and winds blow colder. We'd best be about it."

CHAPTER THIRTEEN

West River Street still existed; along the section facing the river it was the *pomerium*, the interior cleared strip just within the city wall where no buildings were allowed. It was even called by that name, since Boise under the Thurston family's rule had always had a weakness for things Roman. Where it met South Capitol a triangular fortress rose sixty feet to cover the gates and the two bridges; the core of it had been, oddly enough, a library building and the whole had an angular, lumpy, improvised but highly functional appearance even now. The ramparts were black against the western sky, though the stars had begun to fade behind them where the mountains a few miles away eastward were outlined against the first gleams of sunlight.

Two hundred hobnailed boots crashed down in unison with each regulation thirty-inch stride, a harsh martial sound echoing back from the walls on either side of the road. Every forty paces the trumpeter up at the maniple standard in the lead blew a short blast on his curled *tubae*, a signal to make way—unnecessary now just before dawn, but standard procedure and something everyone would be used to. The company—century—guidons swayed at the head of each unit, each a gilt upright hand on an eight-foot pole, garlanded with the actions the unit had fought.

Rudi strode along beside Fred Thurston, about three-quarters of the way along the column of Boisean troops in his friend's service; the Dúnedain and the detachment of the High King's Archers brought up the rear amid the baggage carts, giving a fair imitation of the varied auxiliaries that accompanied the Boisean army's heavy infantry, at least with the streets so dark.

"This is the loudest clandestine approach I've ever made, that it is," Rudi observed.

"Yeah, it's not every day you try to sneak up on someone with most of a battalion in close order, while blowing a trumpet," Fred agreed.

Rudi breathed deeply; they were both being elaborately casual, not least to fool themselves into dismissing the possibility of dying in the next few minutes, which was a useful trick. Courage in combat was mostly training and sheer animal reflex. It was much harder to walk towards a fight than it was to fight it, because that required a continuous effort of the soul.

Be as you wish to seem, an ancient had said. It was good advice. *Because* acting *brave and* being *so are very much the same thing*.

Two long blocks wasn't very far, though they'd mustered on West Myrtle so that they could do a right wheel onto South Capitol and not look as if they'd popped up from under the earth . . . which of course they *had* done. It was working well so far. Who could imagine so many men appearing within walls so strong and closely guarded?

Unless someone detected the movement when we came over the river . . . in which case we'd all be dead because they would have fired up the searchlights and catapults. So far, so good.

"Wellman is going to be very useful here," the last of the Thurston sons said. "It's a hell of a lot better than fighting our way up the escalade stairs of some random section of the riverwall, and we'll lose a hell of a lot less men in the assault force if they can come through a gate. Not as much time under fire on the approach."

"That's if this works as smoothly as Wellman hopes, of course."

"He has the password of the day, and the gate commander will recognize him."

"Sure, and he'd recognize *you*, Fred," Rudi observed.

"Oh, go ahead, joke about it."

Fred wasn't at the head essentially because of his appearance. Every second street corner still had ragged posters of his father Lawrence and elder brother Martin side by side in armor, both holding their helmets in the crook of an arm as they stared heroically into a space occupied by a shining, waving flag, with the elder's hand on the younger's shoulder as if to push him forward into that radiant future. The family resemblance was striking; they were all three handsome men, in a commanding sort of fashion different from Rudi's own sharp-cut features.

Martin Thurston had started the poster campaign as

soon as he took power, trading on his sire's popularity in a way his father had never tolerated; the first time Rudi had been through Boise there had been plenty of posters, but they'd all been of personified abstractions—symbols of Work or Patriotism or whatever. And apart from Fred's individual looks, his part-African coloring and cast of features were a little uncommon in Boise, enough to attract a fatal second glance even with the cheekpieces and overhanging brow-ridge of the Boisean helmet hiding most of his face.

In this city that shade of skin would scream *exiled prince*.

The inner gate didn't have a drawbridge or portcullis; the original builders hadn't been too worried about attack from within. It did have sheer massiveness, a rectangle of welded steel girders as wide as the street and three times a man's height mounted on dozens of old railroad-car wheels built into its lower edge and running on a strip set into the pavement. It didn't swing in or out, but slid instead into or out of the solid bulk of the flanking towers. The road to the bridges ran through the gate, through the thickness of the fort in a passageway like an arched tunnel, and into another slab of metal just as huge at the eastern wall; that *did* have a drawbridge just beyond it. The tunnel had murder-holes in the upper curve to give anyone who somehow got through the solid metal a very hot greeting—literally so, since they could pump streams of burning napalm down. The granite-faced concrete meant that nothing within could catch fire.

Except the flesh of an attacker, and blackened brass

spouts above the portals showed where more flame could be pumped down onto the road outside the gate too. The gate was blazoned across its width with the stylized eagle that Boise used as its main symbol, and the raptor eye seemed to regard them with a ferocious watchfulness.

Peace between us, Eagle Spirit, Rudi thought. *I come as Your friend, to aid Your people.*

Even with good high-geared winches, moving the main gate wasn't something you'd want to do more often than you must. A more human-scaled door stood to one side in the right-hand tower; it was small only by comparison to the gate, being wide enough for two men to pass abreast when it was open. Like the gate it slid sideways rather than swinging on hinges, locking snugly into a matching slot on the left side, which made it immensely strong; it would be easier to knock a hole through the concrete than beat it in.

Wellman's voice barked an order and the century commanders and noncoms repeated it:

"Vexillia—"

"Century—"

The warning command rang out, combined with a two-note call from the trumpet.

"—halt!"

A crash and stamp as the troops slammed down their right heels and the steel-shot butts of the pilae. They were as still as so many statues afterwards, to a degree that had always seemed a bit unnatural to Rudi—he approved of discipline, of course, but there was something a little inhuman when you took it to this level. He'd once seen a housefly walk over the eyeball of a Boisean soldier, on guard outside Fred's tent, and the man had only blinked, slowly.

A slit window beside the postern door opened and someone looked out.

"Who goes there?" a sharp voice asked. "Advance and be recognized."

"Vexillia of the Fourth, reporting to carry out relief," Wellman's voice said. "Cap . . . Centurion Wellman, commanding."

Lawrence Thurston had modeled much of Boise's rebuilt military on that of Rome, but he'd kept the old American Army ranks. His parricide son had started replacing them before he died at Rudi's hand in the Horse Heaven Hills, but intelligence said the change was still superficial. Fred, of course, had restored the old terms in *his* forces. As he said, *he* didn't have a man-crush on Julius Caesar and the traditional system was just better than calling everyone a centurion.

The voices dropped as they exchanged the sign and countersign, then the man inside almost yelped:

"We didn't get any orders about that!" the voice said, sounding a bit more natural in its startlement.

"Well, *I* did," Wellman snarled. "Look, is Major . . . Goddammit, Senior Centurion Betjeman there?"

"Yes, sir," the voice said. "But he's asleep. . . ."

"Well, then, wake him up! Or open the God-damned postern so I can deliver this detachment and get back to work! Tell him Cap . . . Centurion Wellman is here. Move it, straight-leg!"

There was a tense wait, and then the postern rumbled open, showing the serrated edge on one side that locked into saw-shaped holes when closed. An officer stood there, impeccably turned out except that the morning's stubble was still on his cheeks, and Wellman saluted and handed over a packet of documents. They'd been modified from ones already in Wellman's possession, by a Dúnedain who was an artist in such matters. They wouldn't take close scrutiny, but then they probably wouldn't have to.

"Wellman, what the hell's going on? Where's Gianelli? You're not in the Fourth's chain of command. Hell, you're not even a Regular."

"Sir, don't I know it, and I haven't the faintest. *I* just got the order by runner to show up at Fort Boise and march this detachment here—something about enemy movement on the west bank of the river."

The other officer rubbed at his eyes; Rudi's experience of war was that you went through most of it with your brain fogged from inadequate or interrupted sleep, or both. Particularly at those moments you most needed to be keenly alert.

"Yeah, we have been seeing some of that, but I hoped it was the usual feinting, marching men back and forth in view to keep us guessing," the man said. "What's going on over east?"

"Some incendiaries from their trebuchets aimed at the fort, and they're pushing zigzag saps forward to get cat-apults closer to the wall. Straight-out Vauban. And they're building more wheeled siege towers. I didn't have time to observe much. You know how it is right now—"

"Screwed," Betjeman said. "All right, it's irregular, but I'm glad to see the troops. It doesn't *feel* right here. They're going to try something, I can smell it, but we've got no air reconnaissance at all."

I hope we don't have to kill this one, Rudi thought.

It was illogical, but somehow you minded more if a man was good at his trade. War was a filthy business, but the qualities someone needed to do it really well were fine ones. The man seemed to be brave, stubborn, and to have an animal nose for trouble.

This Betjeman could be a pillar of the realm, him and his children and children's children.

He and Fred made a smart right face and marched to the side of the road, as if in response to some order. Other commands were being barked out; file after eight-man file of men began trotting forward, through the postern and up the spiral stairs towards the ramparts. Rudi closed his eyes for a moment and concentrated. He could *feel* the men, in a way—they were part of Montival, part of the great living organism that stretched from the single-celled things that dwelt in the deep crevasses of Earth and fed on its heat to the golden eagles balancing the wind high above. Himself and Mathilda not the heads of it exactly . . . not so much the rulers as a . . . focus, or an embodiment.

But of the High Seeker, nothing. Perhaps a coldness, an absence, but even that was weirdly nonspecific. As if the man's presence—and the things that somehow used him as a portal into the world of matter they hated—was simply not inscribed in the story of existence as everything else was.

For this war is but a single chapter in the story of how the universe is to unfold. Two rival versions of that, each seeking to overwrite the other, throughout all the cycles of the world, to make the other as if it had never been . . . never even been imagined *to be.*

He and Fred were most of the way to the postern when the gate officer's voice rose:

"Wait a minute, I know that man! He was in the Third Brigade, they all got taken at the Horse Heaven Hills, their Eagle and all! You, soldier—*guard, guard turn out the—*"

There was the sound of a blow and a grunt, but even for an expert it was very difficult to quickly disable a man in armor with your hands if you hadn't taken him by surprise. They sprinted through the door, the moving column crowding over to make room. The tubae snarled and blatted again: *at the double-quick* and the entire snake of troops stepped up to two strides a second, a steady jog trot, without missing a beat.

The door through the thickness of the wall opened into a wide space, the walls bare concrete with square beams inset and the ceiling twelve feet up. The walls held racks for spears where they weren't staircases, the throwing *pilae* that Boise's infantry used, and between them the big curved oval shields. Wellman was shaking his hand and cursing; Betjeman had his own blade out and was backing away with a group of half a dozen around him. Fred's soldiers continued their controlled rush up into the interior of the fortress, moving like a single multi-legged iron centipede to seize the key points—the gate hydraulics, the napalm system, the heliograph station on the tallest tower, and the interior doors that could cut the fort off from the walls on either side.

Formal discipline was a wonderful thing; they were all doing the job they'd been detailed to do, and leaving anything else to the people who were presumably tasked with it. It was an attitude that made them like a single weapon moving to its commander's will on a battlefield. Sometimes there were drawbacks.

"Sergeant Dawkins, fall out three files!" Fred barked. "Envelop!"

The noncom pivoted as if the command had played directly on his nervous system. Twenty-four men followed him, their shields snapping up until they were held just below the eyes. The files slid past each other like sheets of oiled steel in a machine, one facing the little knot of men directly, the two on the flanks angling forward slightly to flank them.

"Pilae—ready!"

Two dozen heavy man-high ironshod javelins cocked back on brawny arms, moving like the bristling feathers on the crest of a bird. They weren't long-distance weapons, but they didn't have to be here. It was a big room, but only a room. Rudi cast a glance backward. The eyes visible over the shield-rims differed—shades of blue, mostly, or hazel or black—but they were each as impersonal as a stamping-mill or the long narrow pyramid-points of the spears themselves, waiting for the word of command. It was as frightening as any physical threat he'd ever seen, in a short but eventful life.

Betjeman glared defiance. Rudi drew the Sword. Cool fire flooded him, as it always did when he wielded the gift of the Powers in battle; as if he were a God himself, some thing that commanded sky and sea and the flicker of the lightning and strode laughing through the storm.

"Leave this to me," he said, stepping forward, drawing his dirk with his right hand, the one he used for his shield at other times.

The Boisean officer glared at him. Then something *changed* in his face. First dawning recognition, a silent movement of the lips in a *holy shit*. Then the pupils of his eyes flared wide, until the greenish iris shrank to a thread hardly dividing black and white. The man vanished, leaving an alien and incarnate Purpose. He gave a guttural roar, a shocking sound, and charged.

Rudi pivoted as he did. The Sword licked out, and the point touched the side of the man's leg just above the knee. The wound was trifling, and so cleanly cut that it took an instant before the blood welled. The man went down as if poleaxed; then he curled around himself and buried his face in his hands, weeping. After a moment he raised his face.

"I don't . . . I don't remember . . . where *am* I?" His eyes darted around, his own now but bewildered. "This is West Gate Main . . . what day is it?"

"He's been keeping bad company, whether he knew it or not," Rudi said grimly to Fred.

Then to the subordinates still clustered with their weapons up: "Throw down! Throw down, and I promise you your lives. Tend to this man, he's had a bit of a shock."

Steel clattered on the concrete pavement, and the three files moved forward. There was no unnecessary roughness in the way they disarmed the men and put them under guard; they *were* countrymen and essentially in the same army, with accidents of location mostly determining who was on what side. He saw relief on their faces, the expression of men who'd been prepared to die for honor's sake but realized they didn't need to.

One of Betjeman's men went down to a knee beside him, taking him gently by the shoulder: "Sir? Sir, do you recognize me?"

"Of course I bloody—what's going *on*?"

Edain and the High King's Archers poured into the room as the last of the Boiseans climbed upward; he was sweating and swearing under his breath at being separated from his charge. Most of the Dúnedain followed.

"Let's be about it," Rudi said.

Alleyne Loring nodded. "I'll go for the emergency trip controls."

The gates were usually opened by high-geared winches, and that took a modest number of hands but a fair amount of time. They could be opened or slammed shut much more quickly by a system of hydraulic cylinders and dropping weights, though resetting them was a long process.

Hordle jerked a thumb at a device of levers and springs two of his followers were carrying by the handles set into its square base, with a finned dart the length of a man's forearm standing up from its center.

"I'll get this to a parapet." A beaming grin. "Won't they be gobsmacked when it goes off from the gate'ouse!"

The dart contained a color-coded flare and a spring-deployed parachute; it would loft up several hundred feet and signal where they'd achieved a foothold. They'd *expected* to take a stretch of wall, drop climbing ropes, and hold long enough for storming parties to get through the killing ground and come up to reinforce them. This was much better. . . .

If it works, Rudi thought.

Aloud: "And I'll go for the High Seeker, who's their last hope of stopping us now."

*   *   *

They found him twenty minutes later, on the crest of a high rampart, just as the dawn-light cleared the mountains to the east and spilled across the world in a tide of fresh wind and clarity. The flare floated in a speck of eye-hurting brightness, trailing smoke red and white as it sank towards the river.

"Back, back . . . oh, God*dammit*!" Fred shouted as they pounded up the last flight of stairs and rounded the crouching shape of a turntable-mounted catapult.

A man sprawled dead over a pyramid-shaped pile of cast-steel round shot. Knots of combat sprawled over the top of the square tower, Boisean scutum and short sword against the long curved shetes of a few remaining easterners. *That* fight was ending quickly.

But two of his troopers had thrown their pilae and then rushed the man in the red robe, uncovered as the last of his followers fell. He flicked the weapons out of the air with two slapping motions of his hands. One of the Boiseans came in crouched, shield up and blade lunging in the economical gutting upstroke. The red-robe's hand slapped down and bone broke in the man's wrist with a crackle audible ten feet away. His shriek of unbelieving pain mingled with his partner's bark of:

"USA! USA!"

The point of the gladius crunched into the High Seeker's ribs. The skull-like shaven head pivoted to stare into the soldier's eyes. For a moment the two stood immobile, and then the Boisean threw aside shield and blade and turned, screaming as he ran over the edge of the ramparts. The scream trailed away all the way down and cut off abruptly.

Bows snapped behind Rudi, and the High Seeker's body staggered under the impacts of the longbow shafts. Some passed completely through him in double splashes of red; others hammered into bone. The red-robe flexed and recovered and advanced, grinning as strings of blood and spittle drooled down from his lips.

"No farther," Rudi said quietly, advancing with the Sword of the Lady poised. "You end here."

The man—or the thing that had once been a man—tittered. One soldier dropped his weapons and started hitting himself on the ears, trying to block the sound of it.

"Oh, hardly a beginning," it wheezed. **"Not this plan, bungled into wreck . . . by fools . . . only a beginning of eternity . . ."**

Behind him, someone was retching, and others clapped their hands to their ears and whimpered. The Sword of the Lady protected him, but he could feel that shielding flexing like steel armor under the pressure of heavy blows.

Finish it, he thought. *Let the man who was at least die free of that.*

"I . . . see . . . you . . . forever," the thing said, and turned and leapt from the parapet before his lunge could begin.

The sleeves of the red robe fluttered all the way to the earth beneath, where he sprawled to lie beside his victim with his brains leaking out of his burst skull.

There was a rumbling that made the stone quiver beneath his feet. The great steel gates were sliding into their grooves, opening the way. Below on the banks of the river barges were being shoved into the water and lashed together, and moments later the first century of troops marched across at the double-quick, shields overhead and to the sides to make a tortoise. A few catapult bolts flicked out from the walls to either side, but the assault party was fanning out on them, and the column was an endless stream with a standard at its head—a starry flag topped with a wreathed eagle.

Roaring, the soldiers of the Republic crashed through the gates and into their city.

Well, there's a good deal to be said for Boisean discipline, Rudi thought at the end of the day.

He looked down at the hollow; the smell was fairly strong, with that many men crowded together. They glared back at him, some afraid, more defiant, most simply blankly impassive. He was in full plate now and mounted; Edain had insisted, and it was a useful touch as well. Gentler means would come later; right now he had to talk to them in the language they'd been taught to respect.

Several thousand of the Prophet's riders had survived the day, though many of them had improvised bandages. The folk of the city had gone for them with a concentrated rage that meant *torn to pieces* was far more than a metaphor. Fred's men had used the butts of their spears and their shield-bosses to protect those who surrendered, and they'd been ready to use the points too—which was why they hadn't had to. The fact that they hated these men just as much as the civilians did hadn't mattered a damn, nor the fact that some of the civilians were their own families. So far as he could tell, not one unit had lingered accidentally-on-purpose or gotten "lost" to arrive too late when a knot of easterners was in danger of being mobbed.

Old General Thurston built well, and Martin didn't have enough time to wreck it. There's a strength here in Boise that will strengthen us all.

"You men have served the enemies of humankind," he said, pitching his voice to carry—a trick his mother had taught him. "But that's mostly an accident of where you were born. Since you've asked for quarter, you will have it. You'll be kept under guard until this war is over; you'll have food enough, if no more—we're short ourselves, thanks to your ravaging—and no more work than is needful to earn your keep. When the Prophet and all his works are gone, you can return to your families and your herds and your steadings and take up your lives, provided you give oath to live in peace . . . and believe me when I say that I can tell a man false to his word, for I can. Or you can go elsewhere in Montival, to any community that will take you in."

One of them shouted: "The Prophet will never fall! The Ascended Masters will bear him up!"

Rudi grinned, a hard expression though not cruel. "Then you'll be in a prisoner-of-war camp a very long time," he said.

A couple of the men's neighbors nudged him; from the way he staggered and cursed booted feet had been in use as well. One snatched off his fur cap and beat him on the head with it by way of encouraging tact. Their captor suppressed a grin.

These are men too. It wasn't their fault that they've been corrupted by the world's enemy.

Then Rudi went on, bleakly: "Do as you're told and you'll be treated well. If you try to escape or fight or injure my folk further, my men will hunt you down like rabbits, and there will be no mercy then. For mercy to the guilty is cruelty to the innocent."

He drew the Sword and held it high. The setting sun gleamed on it, a fire in the crystal pommel, and the prisoners swayed back; a moan ran through them.

"You've been given another chance at life, and to live as men should. Don't waste it. Do some thinking, for you'll have time for it."

CHAPTER FOURTEEN

HIGH KING'S HOST
NEAR ASHTON
LIBERATED NEW DESERET
(FORMERLY EASTERN IDAHO)
HIGH KINGDOM OF MONTIVAL
(FORMERLY WESTERN NORTH AMERICA)
AUGUST 15TH, CHANGE YEAR 26/2024 AD

The map had originally been from a publication called *National Geographic*, often a source of useful knowledge. The older collections particularly were eagerly sought after. Rudi's cartographers—a mixture of Boiseans, Corvallans and obscure clerks from the PPA's Chancellery—had done up an excellent large-scale transcription of one covering the core territories of the Church Universal and Triumphant and its marchlands, pyrographed on bleached deerhide, with a few modern additions like puff-cheeked faces blowing from the four quarters.

Now it was tacked to a piece of ancient plywood, itself set on an easel for easy reference. Rudi stood beside it, waiting with his left hand tucked through his sword belt and his right resting on the pommel of the Sword. The wall of the tent was rolled up, to delay the necessity of lighting the lamps. It wasn't *very* hot even at the tail end of a summer's day, since the easternmost part of the Snake River plain here was a mile above sea level, but the High King thought the view of the smoking ruins of the town were instructive as well for the assembled contingent commanders and their aides. The CUT's forces were retreating, but doing as much damage as they could—not that this area hadn't been badly wrecked anyway, in the long CUT-Deseret war that had been going on for most of the last decade before the greater struggle started.

In a way it's weirdly comforting that they're doing it, so. The Powers behind the CUT are trying to weaken Montival in every way they can, which means we're a threat to them in the long term. At least I think so; I'm dealing with beings I cannot understand, any more than a coyote can understand a man. But try as they might, even with the tools of the ancients, men have never been able to kill all the coyotes . . . and we have Those who help us as well as those who hunt us, that we do.

The air held a fair bit of dust as well as the smell of the camp and the reek of things not meant to burn, but this area got more rain than most of the Snake River valley, which was one reason he was pausing to regroup here. The grazing was better, which helped when you had so many horses to feed. The more he spread out, though, the more he was vulnerable to the swift slashing counterattacks the enemy specialized in. They were retreating, but they weren't going willingly and they weren't running witless.

More's the pity; I want this war over, he thought, and began:

"As usual, it's the logistics that are the problem—the

more so as we're far from home," he said when everyone had settled and the orderlies had handed around cups of chicory to those who wished it.

"*We* aren't, Your Majesty," Donald Nystrup said.

He was technically a Brigadier in the army of New Deseret, and in fact had been the leader of the guerillas who'd been making the CUT's occupation of the eastern Snake River country less than a delightful experience. The riders who'd been under his command were still trickling in from their hidden lairs in canyon and side-valley and badland, in groups from companies to little handfuls of men and women as desperate and lethal as so many starved wolves. Rudi had met their leader going east on the Quest, and he looked much older now than those few years would account for, with streaks of gray in his cropped brown beard and new scars, and hammered-out dents and nicks in his breastplate. He also looked like a man who'd had a pile of rocks taken off his back recently; relief mingled with an awareness of pain long suppressed and harder to bear for that.

"Yes, Brigadier," Rudi said gently. "This is your home, and now truly yours again."

What was that word Ingolf used, in his ancestors' tongue? he thought. *Heimat, yes. This is Nystrup's heimat, his little homeland of the heart, what some call the* patria chica. *Where his ancestors are buried, a landscape rich and alive with their woven memories and stories, where his blood and sweat and theirs have watered and made sacred the soil that fed them. As the dùthchas of the Clan is to me. And it's badly hurt. He must bleed with its wounds. Best be careful of his pride.*

He met the eyes of the soldier of Deseret, his hand on

the pommel of the Sword. There was an odd inner flash as he did, of something that was there but not to the unaided eyes of the flesh.

As if another man stood behind the seated Nystrup, slender work-battered hands resting on his shoulders. A big man in a blue uniform, high-collared and fancifully ornate with gold braid and buttons and epaulettes in the manner of the middle nineteenth century. The figure had a shock of unruly fair hair and bright humorous blue eyes shaded by long thick lashes, and a smile showing a chipped front tooth. It was a Yankee farmboy's face, oval and long-nosed. At first glance a yokel out of an original America long generations gone even at the Change, save for a sense of a glowing golden charm that could bring the birds out of the trees. Full of shrewdness and good nature . . . and yet a touch of something *other* about it, a power and a wisdom and a deep sadness.

He blinked the moment aside. Nystrup looked startled for just an instant, then squared his shoulders as if new power had flowed into him from a familiar reservoir.

Rudi went on: "But it's a badly ravaged part of your home. Can you provide much in the way of fodder and provender?"

"Well . . . not until we get the rail line to the south repaired, from down by the old Utah border. Our farm-lands there are still productive, but . . . and we've lost a *lot* of our working stock."

"Not this campaigning season, then," Rudi said.

"My troops don't need much. We've gotten used to doing with very little, and we're not going to stop until the enemy is utterly cast down."

"And it's a great help your lads and lasses have been

and will be, but we have a large force here, and it limits our options."

He stood to one side and tapped the eastern part of the map so that they could all see where his finger fell. "The armies of the League of Des Moines reached Casper in old Wyoming a month ago, and took it from the CUT garrison by storm after a brief siege, though with some loss."

Sober nods from everyone. Storming a fortified position . . . the antiseptic phrase covered a multitude of sins. Men falling off ladders screaming as boiling canola oil splashed into their faces and ran under their armor, for starters.

"The Bossman of Fargo will fill us in on the details."

The League powers had a liaison officer here, who'd come over the mountains to the southward as a small party could do in summer; a high-ranking one, the Bossman of Fargo no less, one Daniel Rasmussen.

He strode confidently up to the map, a tall lean man in his forties in plain leather and linen and wool, an equally plain shete at his belt, with two fingers missing from his left hand and gray in his cropped yellow beard. He'd been notably cool when the alliance called the League of Des Moines was formed as Rudi went through Iowa on his way back west. Not least because he enjoyed being entirely sovereign in his family's Red River bailiwick—he'd seized power from his elder brother in a coup, originally, and ruled as an iron-fisted though competent and reasonably popular dictator. The thought of mighty Iowa awakening from its inward-looking sleep wasn't one he found delightful.

A concern for which Artos the First has an underwhelming sympathy, I will not say aloud.

His eyes were gray and very cold, with the wary bitterness you often saw in those who'd come to adulthood in the terrible years right after the Change, those damaged in their souls but not outright mad. Though they'd had a considering respect in them since he rode into the Montivallan camp and seen the size of it, and the good order and fine weapons and most of all the tough veteran faces of the troops. He hadn't altogether believed in the High Kingdom as anything real, until then, but he was a man who believed in armies if nothing else and knew a good one when he saw it. He was casting the occasional considering look at young Rick Three Bears, the head of Rudi's token Lakota contingent—a useful token, though most of their forces were out east of the mountains.

Rasmussen lost those fingers fighting the folk of the Seven Council Fires as a young man. And unlike Ingolf, he hasn't let the fire of his anger die; he's a man of cold enduring hatreds, I think. Here I thought things were complicated two months ago! Rudi mused. *The Iowans are keeping that kettle off the boil, Lady bless them and the Lord guide their hands, but once the war is over I'm going to have to spend some time out east, settling things with the Lakota and their neighbors, if we're to have real peace there and not just a truce until a new generation gets an itch in its collective sword-hand.*

The number of contingents in his army had increased once again now that the US of Boise territories were secured. There was even a Nez Perce battalion; very likely and useful light horse they were, but touchy about the increased degree of autonomy Fred had given in their new charter, suspicious of Boise under *anyone's* rule and needing a fair bit of stroking. It hadn't helped when he'd thoughtlessly spoken to their commander in the Nez Perce language, and found that the man had only a few phrases of it himself; evidently only a few score people still knew it, most of them elderly. That had put him in a sulk for days, convinced it had been done to embarrass him before his followers.

Sure, and it's like juggling porcupines! Wiggling ones intent on nibbling each other!

His blood brother and guest-friend King Bjarni of Norrheim winked at him. The burly redbeard with the axe was the least troublesome member of the war-council; all he was interested in was hacking his way through the CUT to get back to his distant realm. And absorbing every useful bit of information he could along the way; his baggage-train contained mostly crates of books and diagrams and models, not to mention a careful selection of experts in a dozen skills enticed to make the trek with offers of rank and reward. Norrheim was a bit backward now, but he suspected it would be much less so by the time Bjarni's son was hailed on the Thingstone.

Bossman Rasmussen stepped up to the easel and spoke as Rudi moved politely aside:

"Casper's where we started running into hard trouble. We came west up the North Platte valley as soon as the ground was dry enough and the grass was up this spring, eighty thousand strong, horse, foot and catapults, not counting the screening forces we'd had securing the approaches since last fall, or the Sioux."

Respectful nods; that was a great many fighting-men.

A great many to muster and equip, and a very great many to feed away from the farms producing the grain and meat. Eighty thousand men meant tens of thousands of draught-horses, rail and road wagons, teamsters and roustabouts, crates of boots and harness, barrels of salt pork and sacks of flour and cornmeal and beans and oats and bale after bale of blankets and socks . . .

Armies ate wealth like drought or locusts.

"That was fairly straightforward; Nebraska's forces joined us and they had everything organized, supply dumps and plenty of fodder and replacement horses. After that we had to re-lay some of the rails as we came, sending scrap back east to the rolling mills in Des Moines. We've been doing that all summer, because there certainly wasn't enough on hand once we were out of the settled zone, and every mile of track we fixed was another one we had to guard against Cutter raiding parties. We sent a secondary force along here to the south—"

His finger traced a line through Cheyenne and then far westward and north into the Powder River basin.

"And the people all joined in, the ones still free were scared stiff of the Cutters and happy to see us, the independent Ranchers and the tribes both. And the occupied zone rose against the CUT as soon as our scouts arrived, and the, ah—"

"Chenrezi Monastery," Master Hao said.

His voice was still strongly accented despite twenty-eight years in what had become the Valley of the Sun when the Change stranded a convention of Buddhist monks at an off-season tourist hotel there. Fortunately for the other inhabitants, since most of the monks had started their lives as mountain peasants and remembered those skills.

"The Monastery of the Most Compassionate Bodhisattva. And those in the Valley who accept our advice."

"Yeah, I'd heard you guys ran the place."

Hao was a stringy man in some indeterminate place between middle aged and elderly, apparently naturally hairless and assembled out of rawhide and sticks, the sort of old man who looked as if he'd never die or had some time ago and didn't let it slow him down to speak of. He was dressed in a set of lamellar armor, lozenges of metal laced together, with a *dao* at his side. In the Valley's position, Rudi would have hesitated to refuse any *advice* he gave; from his time there he knew that was in fact the attitude of most. Not that Hao was a bad or violent man, and the Monastery's rule had been almost comically tolerant and benevolent from all he had seen. But the High King remembered his tutelage during the winter he'd spent there, recovering from wounds. Even old Sam Aylward had never worked him harder.

"Chenrezi Monastery helped get things organized," Rasmussen said. "The Powder River people all jumped when they said *frog*."

The particular order Hao had represented at the conference so long ago emphasized the Way of the Warrior. How exactly they reconciled that with Greater Vehicle Buddhism was a matter of theological complication Rudi wasn't much interested in, but Hao had been in charge of the training and leading of the Valley's hosts since the beginning. The Valley had not been protected by its geography alone.

"There is much respect for the holy Rimpoche Tse-

wang Dorje," the old Han said a little severely, naming
the abbot of Chenrezi.

"As there should be," Rudi said, quite sincerely.

In an entirely different way the Tibetan abbot was even
more formidable than his warrior subordinate. The *Rimpoche* had sworn him fealty in impeccable style; then
winked, and they'd both shared a chuckle as the old
bonze's face turned into a network of wrinkles like an ancient merry child. You got that sense that most of life was
a game he played punctiliously out of an innate courtesy. . . .

Tiphaine d'Ath had been standing like a gray-steel
statue of a warrior Goddess, Lioncel de Stafford behind
her with a stack of documents. Now she used her silver
baton of office to sweep from east to west along the lower
edge of the map.

"That's all very well, Bossman, but going that way is
like running your little finger up your own nose; limited
possibilities of advance and you're not likely to reach anything useful. Unless you're going to fight your way over
the Tetons, where it can snow any damned month of the
year, July included."

"They'll have to guard the passes, but yeah," Rasmussen said, nodding. "Thing is, the supply situation was
even worse than we thought it would be, and we realized
we had more troops than we could feed on the axis of
main effort, so we might as well have them do *something*
instead of just going home. Whoever we picked to turn
around and march back, the rest of the troops wouldn't
like that, to put it mildly. A lot of the League's army . . .
the Iowans particularly . . . well, they were drilled troops
and well equipped and ready enough to *fight*, but a lot of
them hadn't realized how much time in the field you

spend being so bored and miserable that fighting's a relief."

That brought some chuckles; everyone here had been fighting for years, and not a single summer campaign each year on someone else's fields, either. Whatever else you might say about him, Rasmussen had *been* there. Someone murmured *poor babies*! Nystrup looked angry rather than mocking; what his people had been through was beyond conception.

"And once we got the CUT out of the area, the Ranchers there could spare stock to be driven north, we got some from as far south into old Colorado as the San Luis valley. Gratitude, gold and fifteen thousand men with shetes can produce a big herd. That helped a lot with our transport bottleneck. Horses too, and war eats 'em fast."

A bad man is Bossman Rasmussen, in my opinion, but a fair sound general, and a realist, Rudi thought. *Hmmm. I must see to that area in old Colorado after the war . . . another bit of work to add to the plate!*

The Midwesterner went on: "Our main force turned north at Casper. There's more support for the CUT there as you head north, more people who actually buy that loony line of goods they peddle, and we started getting serious harassment. God tailor-made the Bighorn country for a cavalry guerilla. Horse-archers are a pain in the ass that way to an infantry army. I *told* them in Des Moines to take more light cavalry, but . . ."

There were mutters from the ranked commanders, along the lines of *tell me about it*. The CUT's armies were mostly plainsmen with recurves, and with a string of several ponies for each man they could *move*. Trying to force them to give battle when they didn't want to fight was like trying to punch smoke with your fist, too; even a little carelessness and they'd ride around you and burn the country behind you while you stood scratching your head, or arse, or both, and wondering where they were.

Though there were answers to that. Rudi grinned like a wolf. "We're approaching things that they must stand and fight for," he said. "For all that they put their capital in a land so remote, they still have one."

Rasmussen nodded, with an identical expression, and went on:

"The Lakota—"

This time his nod to Rick Three Bears was genuinely polite instead of hostility masked by a politic pretense of courtesy. He also gave them their own name for themselves, too, which best translated as *friends* or *allies*. The name *Sioux* more commonly used among outsiders to name those tribes was derived from what their bitter rivals the Anishinabe-Ojibwa people had called them long ago, filtered through French and then English, and had originally meant something like *little snakes*.

That hadn't been intended as a compliment or taken as one.

"—have been invaluable keeping them off our backs."

Rick shrugged and drew on his cigarette, the cheeks of his narrow hook-nosed face pulling in for a moment and his braids swinging.

"We have lots of practice with the Cutters," he said in a not-quite-insolent manner, blowing the smoke upward.

And with your gang, white-eyes, went unspoken; his father John Red Leaf had been a leader in the Sioux War, when the resurgent Lakota *tunwan* had tried to take back their ancestral lands in the Red River valley. It hadn't worked, but they had ended up once again dominating what had been the western Dakotas.

Though I've met his mother as well, and she's suspiciously red-haired, Rudi thought whimsically. *Our tribes and clans and nations are stories we tell—though none the less real for that. But real because we believe in them, not because they're written in natural law . . . and as we Changelings know, even natural law isn't as unchanging as our parents thought.*

Mathilda coughed at the tobacco smoke with resigned disgust, where she sat with a stack of reports from the staff and Huon Liu de Gervais at her elbow. The Midwesterner lit one of his own, the habit being much more common where he came from than in Montival, ignored the High Queen's glare and several others, and went on:

"But the harassment slowed us down—we kept having to deploy from march column to line of battle, and occasionally fight a set-piece engagement. We shoved 'em back every time, but the Cutters always broke off before we could really wreck them."

More moderately sympathetic nods. Montival *had* wrecked the CUT and Martin Thurston at the Horse Heaven Hills, but mainly because the enemy had stood and fought there beyond the point of reason in an attempt to win the war at one throw.

"It would have been fu . . . frankly impossible if there had been twice as many of them, I grant that, so you and us hitting them at the same time was crucial. But while that went on they had labor-gangs ripping up the rail, piling it up over heaps of ties, and setting those on fire—we could see the flames against the sky for weeks and smell the burning creosote. That meant we had to re-lay *everything* as we advanced into the Bighorn Basin and went west, except the actual grading, and some of that's washed out since the Change so we had to shove the *dirt* back. Not to mention bridges. Plus they set grass fires wherever they could, and drove every head of livestock out of our path. Right now we're here—"

He tapped the map south of Billings, the old Montana capital and mostly ruins now. "Only a few hundred miles left to go. Damn bad miles, though, and the Cutters are thick as grass. Infantry, not just their ranch and Rover levies, and the Sword of the Prophet, what's left of it. I understand you guys wiped out most of that crowd of maniacs in the red armor last year, for which many thanks."

Tiphaine gave a small chilly smile. The Grand Constable had brought the Association's chivalry down on Corwin's elite troops like a war hammer on a skull, with hideously perfect timing. Rudi gave her a small crisp inclination of the head. He'd spent most of that long and ghastly day setting the move up, but she'd carried it out faultlessly and deserved to be proud of it.

"Thank you for the summation, Bossman," Rudi said, and tapped the map himself. "And the Dominions, Drumheller and Moose Jaw and Minnedosa"—the old Canadian prairie provinces, which had come through the Change with *only* the loss of their larger cities, like the Upper Midwest—"are here, around Great Falls."

"Hurrah," Tiphaine said dryly, holding up a fist, extending her index finger and moving it in a very small circle of celebration.

Rasmussen gave her a look and then an unwilling grin

as he resumed his seat. Mathilda snorted in agreement; Great Falls wasn't so very far south of the Dominion of Drumheller's prewar border. And the Dominions were rich and populous, by the standards of this continent in the twenty-sixth year of the Change, and they didn't have as far to go as the other combatants.

"It's mountains there," Rudi said mildly.

Ian was bristling back where he stood in the Dúnedain contingent, but far too junior and too polite to say anything at the aspersion on his native land.

"Also they didn't *have* to intervene in this war at all. We'd have beaten the CUT eventually anyway if they hadn't, and they'd have gotten all the benefits of victory without any of the costs."

"Every Cutter they engage is one we don't have to," Mathilda put in judiciously; when she thought politics, you could hear her mother in her voice. "Corwin was a bad neighbor, but they'd never taken any territory they considered their own. The Association took the old Canuk territory west of the Rockies, which is now part of Montival. It was really quite forethoughtful of the Dominions to come in on our side."

"So, how are we going to get at Corwin, Your Majesty?" Tiphaine asked. "And do it before snow closes the passes, and get the bulk of our troops back in time? So that all our neighbors can go home for Yule?"

"That *is* the question," Rudi agreed.

You're the High King, you're the man with the magic sword, so you tell us what to do . . . and you'd better be right, he thought sardonically.

In the end you had to decide; you never had enough

information and what you did have might be wrong. That, and the sheer work involved, were among the reasons he'd always found it surprising that so many *wanted* power. He'd read the philosophers, Plato and Aristotle and Jefferson and the others, and there was something to be said for republics; but the great asset of a monarchy was that you could put men in office who *weren't* obsessed with a ruler's power, wanting it so much so that they twisted their whole lives into a search for it.

Who knows, Bossman Rasmussen's grandson may be a fine fellow.

"We're going to follow the old Highway 20 route, east over the Yellowstone Plateau and north then up Highway 89," he said after a moment's echoing silence; he saw shoulders relax as the dice were cast for good or ill. "Then down from the old park territories and into Paradise Valley. We have to take Corwin within the next month, and then get the bulk of the troops out to somewhere we can feed them through the snow season. The number who we can overwinter there without producing a famine, or even in the Bitterroot country as a whole, is strictly limited. Even in what passes for lowlands hereabouts."

Tiphaine pursed her lips. "It's direct, and it doesn't give them the chance to get off their back foot," she acknowledged. "Given the time constraints . . ."

"Least bad," Rudi replied. "The western part outside the old park was cut over about thirty years ago, and the remainder burned hard just before and then just after the Change; it's grassland and shrub now for the most part, good grazing—and heavy with game, buffalo and elk, deer and boar and feral cattle. That will help a fair bit; we'd send light cavalry and scouts first anyway, and they can shoot as much as possible and rough-gralloch it. The troops can eat roast meat and save the iron rations for later."

Everyone looked at the map. That route meant hauling everything they couldn't forage with wagons on roads that had spent a generation getting worse, repairing where essential as they went. And even on a *good* road a horse or ox could pull less than a tenth of what it could on rails, and more slowly too.

He tapped the map again. "We have to guard our line of communication here, at Henrys Lake and up to the ruins of West Yellowstone town; there's a possible approach from Corwin to the north, where they could flank us. I want the bulk of the remaining Association foot there, Grand Constable, to patrol and block the possible approaches from the north. Delegate the command as you see fit. You'll keep . . . two thousand of your lancers with the main field force advancing on Corwin. We'll take the light horse, fifteen thousand of the pike-and-crossbow infantry from Corvallis and the Free Cities, three brigades of Boiseans—Fred, you pick which ones—the Bearkillers, the Mackenzies, and field artillery in proportion. Most of the siege train we can leave west of here, and all the heavy pieces; Corwin isn't heavily fortified, much less so than Boise, though there are forts, especially to the north."

The staff at their tables began frantically scribbling, to translate that into the movement orders.

"It's doable," Tiphaine said. "But only just. And that's provided we don't get locked up skirmishing and breaking ambushes on our way through the Park. That's mainly still forests, according to the reports. I've fought in similar country before, and it's dead easy to end up chasing each other around in circles for weeks while your main column sits and eats. Or starves."

Rudi smiled. "I have . . . contacts there. They'll deal with it."

Hopefully, he added to himself.

CHAPTER FIFTEEN

The glider blazoned with the crimson bear's-head whispered by overhead. Sunlight blinked from the canopy as the wings waggled, once and twice and thrice; then it banked off, caught an updraft, and spiraled up into the sky.

"OK, cousin Alyssa, message received," Mary Vogeler said, waving broadly with her sword in one hand for emphasis and to catch the light as well. "Company's coming."

Then she repeated it aloud and in Battle Sign, and the word was passed on from mouth to mouth, quietly and without visible stir. The Dúnedain Rangers were out in force for the great hunt, along with the other scouts and light troops. The day was only just warm even in high summer, for this rolling volcanic plateau rose seven thousand feet above the level of the sea; nights would make bedrolls and fires very welcome, though actual hard frost was unlikely for another month.

Somewhere a work party was singing at their labors, in the Noble Tongue:

"East and west of the Misty Mountains
North and south of the sea—"

Mary smiled; it was good to be back among her own folk for a while. She'd been travelling and adventuring among strangers for a long time by the time they got back from the Quest, and even since. Spending some time in Mithrilwood would be even better, badly though Aunt Astrid's absence was felt there . . . though she had to admit that this part of Montival was just as comely. Mountaintops winked eastward, icy teeth stretching towards a sky aching blue and streaked with high white mare's-tail cloud.

The rolling ground around was mostly grass tall and lush and green, starred with yellow sand lily and thick drifts of crimson Indian paintbrush, yard-high purple bunches of fringed gentian and more. There were occasional stumps or the remnants of logs in the grassland, charred and rotting; this land had a natural burn cycle that pushed it from forest to prairie and back. Already there were clumps of aspen and tall slender lodgepole pine up to forty feet high on the most favorable locations on south-facing ridges. They'd cut some of those and erected tripods to hoist up the carcasses of the bison and elk and black-tail deer; if gutted and drained they would keep acceptably for days in this climate.

There were dozens of the tripods in use within sight, and teams of horses dragging in more bodies. This was strictly killing for meat, just methodical hard work like farming. Very much like slaughtering season in the fall, in fact, down to the collective thanks-and-apology prayer. They'd used screens of beaters to drive the herds onto the waiting spears and bows. Even upwind the smell of blood was strong, though clean enough, mingled with the smell of grilling kidney and liver, the strong-tasting organ meats that went off so quickly and were the rights of the hunter. They'd dug trenches for the guts, once the dogs had gorged themselves into a stupor, and the hides were stacking up, to be used to wrap around butchered, quartered carcasses for easy transport.

Mary still felt slightly guilty, since they'd be wasting so much valuable sausage casing, horn and fat and leather and sinew and bone, not to mention the brains that could be used for tanning. The Valar recognized that humankind had a right to eat just as the other carnivores did, but they disapproved of wantonness with the gifts of Arda and Eru the Creator.

This is rich land and we're not taking the calves or young females, she thought a bit defensively. *The herds will bounce back quickly. For that matter, the way the herds are composed shows that* someone *is cropping the wildlife here, and someone who knows what they're doing, too. You see the same thing in Mithrilwood or our other steadings. I think I know by whom, too.*

The Lakota had been most impressed; they lived by ranching as much as anything these days with a little gardening here and there and some crafts, but they managed the swelling buffalo herds of the *makol*, the high plains, very carefully.

Nobody was alarmed at the message from the glider;

she wasn't the only one tasked with waiting for it, and anyway they had a perimeter of guards out and everyone was on the alert. If nothing else, the killing had brought every opportunistic predator in the area out hotfoot, and when wolf-packs and grizzlies and tigers got the scent of blood, you had to be cautious.

Oh, wolves usually didn't attack adult human beings, unless they were cornered or mad-hungry or had some other good reason . . . but *usually* was the operative word and it was *their* idea of a good reason that counted. Not to mention what would happen if they caught you alone with a broken leg. Grizzlies were another matter. Oldsters said it was amazing how fast they'd realized that guns weren't a problem anymore. And all tigers were either man-eaters or their descendants, since that was the game they'd survived on right after the Change, the easily caught meat that tided them over while they gradually learned how to live in the wild once more and then bred and spread explosively.

It was difficult to imagine the landscape she'd grown up in without tigers. That would be like seeing it without dandelions or tumbleweed or sparrows, but apparently the ancients had just liked keeping big cats around in pens for some reason and be damned to the risk to their descendants' children and dairy cows.

They were . . . strange back then. Very strange.

Ingolf came up, naked and still running with water. He'd stripped as most did while working his turn on the butchering and then he'd gone for a dip in the nearby pond to clean off. That was much easier than getting blood out of cloth or, even worse, leather.

"Oh, now you're tempting me to neglect my duty,"

she said, giving her husband's hairy, muscular, glistening six-two a long look; *just* the right height for a woman who was five-ten herself. "It's not the time to drag you into the bushes, more's the pity. The Expected Guests are on their way."

He was carrying his clothes and gear strapped up into a bundle in one hand, but he put them aside while he dried in the mild warmth. He also had a bunch of smoking skewers in his other hand, and juggled things to hand her one.

"And here I thought you were reading the life-story inscribed into my tattered hide," he grinned, with that boyish look she'd always liked.

He *did* have a remarkable collection of scars; you could tell he'd been flogged once, knotted white tracks that told of a barbed whip. That had been the Cutters. And the thick white mark across his shoulder had been them too, a triad of assassins pursuing him into Sutterdown. If you knew wounds that one told you how tough he was, to have lived and healed. He'd gotten that the night she first saw him, in Brannigan's Inn. There had been something about him, even then.

She touched the patch over the socket where her left eye had been. It gave them something in common.

"The scars just show you're a survivor type, lover, fit to make excellent babies," she said, and stood hipshot for a moment, looking out at him from under a fall of yellow hair and putting a hand behind her head. "It was your manly charms I was thinking of."

"Good thing that water was *cold*," he grinned.

"Oh, we've managed. Remember that little waterfall?"

"My back hurt for days, but it was worth it. Here, keep your strength up."

She took the skewer, blowing and biting off a chunk. "Mmmm!"

There was nothing quite so good as fresh buffalo liver taken right out of the beast and onto the coals with no seasoning but a little coarse salt; richly meaty, but with a very slight tang of musky bitterness. Even buffalo-hump and kidney pie wasn't quite as tasty.

"Remember that time we were with the Lakota for their summer hunt, on the Quest? Around the time they did that adoption thing with the tent and the sweet-grass?" she said.

"I'm not going to forget that, *Yellow Bird*."

"*Iron Bear*, backatcha," she grinned.

In fact they'd both taken that ceremony quite seriously. They ate in companionable silence. After a few minutes there was a coded whistle and five figures came trotting towards them from the westward through the waist-high grass, where a dark green line marked the beginning of the thick forest. Two wore Mackenzie kilts with a pair of enormous dogs loping at their heels, two were her sister Ritva and Ian in Dúnedain field gear, and the last was a young man in Boisean Special Forces camouflage outfit.

"Cole," Mary called with a grin and a wink and a raised index finger: "Cousin Alyssa just paid a call. That girl chases you in aircraft."

"She gave us the heads-up first," Cole said, stolidly ignoring the teasing; Boiseans could be annoyingly businesslike at times.

But then, so can Bearkillers, so maybe they deserve each other. Manwë and Elbereth witness we were right to move in with Aunt Astrid.

Ingolf handed out more of the skewers; Talyn gave a sharp *no* when Artan and Flan looked interested, whereupon the dogs completed their sniff-and-greet and flopped down with sighs. As far as they were concerned it was a wonderful day to do nothing in particular but enjoy a well-fed nap in good company. There were times she thought that dogs were more sensible than human beings.

"Company?" Ingolf asked.

"Yeah," Cole said. "*Sneaky* company."

Ritva rolled her eyes and nodded with her mouth full, and Ian spoke:

"If we hadn't had warning, we wouldn't have known a damned thing. As it was, we *just* had time to make it look like we'd seen them a mile off. I think they were pretty disappointed. Anyway, they said their Council emissaries would be showing up soon and then faded away again."

Cole frowned thoughtfully: "I don't think they know about aerial reconnaissance at all. Apart from that . . . perfect technique."

Talyn rolled his eyes and juggled one of the sticks of hot meat. "*Ochone*, the black pity of a Mackenzie hunter and First Levy warrior being surprised! Still, this is their home ground, and doubtless the spirits of place—"

He made a gesture of propitiation and tossed aside a fragment of the liver.

"—help them. They'd not do so well about Dun Tàirneanach, that they would not."

"Not unless you were drunk," Caillech said dryly.

"Like that time you swore you missed a deer with two heads by an inch and saw it run off north *and* south. That was *just* before the Lady Flidais bore you off to her bower of love, I do not think."

Ritva nodded. "Only guy I've ever met who successfully snuck up on me came from around here. He was working for the Prophet at the time . . . but I don't think it was a love-match. I kicked his ass in the fight, and he did tell me about sis being in trouble so I could save her life *again*—"

"Which *just* made us even," Mary said. Lightly, but she shivered a little inwardly. The man who'd cut the eye out of her head had been technically dead at the time, and if Ritva hadn't known—

"—but it was close. Far too close for comfort," Ritva said soberly.

Ingolf grunted. "Now we find out how they're going to jump. I do resent that he tried to carry my sister-in-law off."

"Well, *you* carried *me* off," Mary pointed out.

"The hell you say," Ingolf replied. "As I recall, you won me from Ritva at dice."

"She cheated—"

"*I* cheated?"

"—one or both of us cheated, so we did rock-paper-scissors," Ritva said helpfully. "Nobody can cheat at that . . . well, maybe Rudi could, but he wouldn't." Virtuously: "And we were really deciding who got a *chance* at you. I mean, twin sisters should share, but there are limits. Combs and pads yes, men no."

"Sure, you were deciding who got a chance. And how much chance did I have?"

"None at all," Mary said cheerfully. "I mean, we're the *Havel twins*? What man could resist us?"

"Rigobert de Stafford aside," Ritva added, which Mary had to admit was true.

"All right," she said. "No man who likes women."

She saw a dangerous glint in her twin's eyes; hair-splitting was a favorite sport of theirs, and Rigobert *did* like women. The baron of Forest Grove was delightful company, in fact, not to mention gorgeous in a rugged manly middle-aged way. He just didn't consider women to be sexy.

"Correction: no man who *desires* women can resist us. But I got dibs, so there."

"Hey, what does that make me?" Ian said. "The alternative menu selection?"

"It makes you younger and prettier," Ritva said, giving his arm a squeeze.

"But mine has more *character*," Mary said.

"Character? You mean he's grumpier in the morning and makes bad puns," Ritva said.

"Honey-smooth skin and chiseled jaws aren't everything."

"Hey!" both men said, antiphonally.

Ingolf started dressing. He'd just finished cinching his sword belt over his mail shirt when two parties of mounted Dúnedain closed in from the north and south; one included John Hordle on his usual warmblood destrier and the other Alleyne on a more conventional dappled part-Arab. Alleyne was tall, around six feet, but if you put Uncle John on an ordinary horse . . .

He looks like a man trying to ride a big dog.

Mary put her monocular to her good eye and looked

eastward. The people she saw weren't making any attempt to hide, but they ran through the tall grass with a smooth economy that made them look just at home there as the lobo packs.

"Here they are, three of them," she said. Then: "Oh. It *is* our old friend with the badges, right? Not just the bunch he runs with?"

"Right," Ritva confirmed when her sister passed her the optic.

The party of the *Hír Dúnedain*, the Lord of the Rangers, pulled up and dismounted. The standard-bearers thrust the butt-spikes of their flagpoles into the ground—the silver-and-black tree, stars and crown of her people, and the green-and-silver Crowned Mountain of Montival.

Mary and Ritva stepped forward to greet the three emissaries; presumably they weren't their people's sovereigns, which meant proper etiquette would be for them to meet someone of rank, but not one of the lords of the Dúnedain. She recognized the tall lean redhead from her sister's description; he looked a lot neater and cleaner now than in that tale, but then he was on his home territory and not leading a fast pursuit on the trail of nine Questers. And *she* wasn't dazed with pain and horror, in a way that still gave her bad dreams occasionally. With him were a medium-tall man in his thirties with dark brown skin—several shades darker than Fred Thurston—and a pale freckled woman of around her age with braided black hair.

The two men both wore broad-brimmed hats with wings of eagle feathers attached; the woman had similar headgear, but sporting falcon feathers. All three had loose well-tanned leather britches that ended above the knee, moccasins, and long belted tunic-shirts sewn over with round badges bearing stylized symbols—bows and arrows, tents, knapsacks, various tools. There were kerchiefs around their necks, too, run through carved bone rings. They had knives at the belts, and tomahawks a lot like Ingolf's; her old acquaintance and the woman had recurve bows and quivers over their backs, and the dark man had a broad-bladed spear taller than he was.

"Good G— . . . by Manwë and Varda," Alleyne Loring said quietly from behind her. "I thought you were exaggerating, Ritva."

"Not in a *report*, Lord," she said. "But they're a bit . . . fancier than the one I saw three years ago. I suppose because it's a diplomatic mission."

"I was one myself once," he murmured. "Before the Change. I wonder if I should mention it or not? It seems another world."

The three halted. The redhead smiled at Ritva. "We meet again, woman worthy of badges," he said, then gave a broader smile and nod to Ian's scowl.

The man with the spear frowned himself and stepped forward and grounded the weapon with a formal gesture, raising his right hand shoulder-high, three fingers up, thumb crooked and holding the little finger. The other two copied the movement and the spearman spoke:

"I am Andrew, called Swift, a Scout of thirty-one badges, a bearer of the Eagle, of the Keen Spear Patrol of the Snow Tiger Troop, and I speak for the Council of Troops of the Morrowland Pack," he said.

"I am Sheila, called Dauntless, a Scout of twenty-eight badges, a bearer of the Falcon, of the Thrown Hatchet Patrol of the Otter Troop, and I speak for the House of

Girls and the Council of Troops of the Morrowland Pack," the freckled woman said.

"I am George, called Tracker, a Scout of thirty badges, a bearer of the Eagle, of the Bright Lightning Patrol of the Wolverine Troop, and I speak for the Council of Troops of the Morrowland Pack," Ritva's old acquaintance said.

The spearman went on: "You have come on the Pack's land and hunted our game without our consent, game that we need to feed our cubs in the cold months. Who are you, to make free with what is ours?"

Alleyne bowed slightly, with hand over heart; the other Rangers copied the gesture, and the rest made salute in their own fashions.

"Mae l'ovannen," he said, in the formal mode. "Well-met, Scouts of the Morrowland Pack. I am Alleyne Loring-Larsson, Lord of the Dúnedain Rangers, vassal and kin to Artos the First, High King of Montival. We have come onto your land as part of the Host of the High Kingdom, for we are enemies of the false Prophet of Corwin. High King Artos needs this meat for his army, and passage to the north . . . and you have served the Prophet. Are you our enemies? Or our allies? Or will you stand aside and take no part in this war?"

The Morrowlanders . . . whatever that meant . . . looked at each other. Mary would have been very surprised indeed if they hadn't been following events outside their bailiwick, and even more surprised than that if they didn't know the approaching Montivallan army down to the nearest battalion.

"We have heard of your war and we have scouted your great army," the spearman named Andrew said, confirming her guess. "But the Prophet's men . . . the red-robes . . . can find us in the forests. Find our cubs and our dens. There are not enough of us to fight their soldiers, if the woods cannot hide us. Nor can we live entirely without trade; we need metal for tools, and salt and cloth. But we could hurt them badly, so they leave us be in return for Scout service."

"We come to cast the Prophet down, destroy his city of Corwin, and free all his slaves," Alleyne said. "Then this will be part of Montival, and under the High King's peace none will trouble you in your own land if you keep his law."

The three looked at each other again. "We must test your words," their spokesman said. "Send us emissaries, and we will see if they are worthy to speak with the Last Eagle."

The woman spoke: "Send us emissaries, and your she-wolves among them. We see that you are not as the Prophet's men, who seek to turn Girls—"

I can hear the capital letter there, Mary thought.

"—into sheep."

Well, good for you, Scout of twenty-eight badges! I know everyone's entitled to their own customs, but some are just plain creepy about that. At least we can beat some sense into the Cutters.

The dark spearman frowned; he seemed to be the senior here, but *primus inter pares* rather than commander.

"We must see that you are worthy of badges, folk of merit," he said.

Alleyne raised his brows. "You want us to send our people among you without guarantee of their safety?"

"If you wish us as allies, there must be trust," the woman said.

"And I will stay as hostage," the spearman said proudly. "A Scout is trustworthy!"

The redhead grinned. "And you hold our best hunting-ground hostage, too," he said irreverently, looking at the parties of horsemen and butchering-camps scattered for miles to the westward.

I think this one has gotten out of the woods more, Mary thought. Then to Alleyne, in the Noble Tongue:

"Lord, I think this is a time for . . . for the sort of gesture Lady Astrid would have made."

He looked at her quickly, his sky-blue eyes blinking thoughtfully. Ritva made a small private sign: *Good call, sis!*

Uncle Alleyne had always been affectionately respectful of the founder of the Rangers, but while he was the husband of the living woman he'd been a mixture of chief-of-staff and Reality Anchor. He'd always loved *The Histories*, that was how he and Astrid had first come together, but he hadn't had the *fire* she did. Since she'd died, though . . . since then, he'd lived her dream for her, meticulously.

"You're right, woman of Westernesse," he said quietly. Then he replied to the Morrowlanders, with the air of a man quoting from a sacred book, the way bards did from *The Histories* around a winter hearth in Mithrilwood:

> *"For the strength of the Pack is the Wolf,*
> *And the strength of the Wolf is the Pack."*

They looked at him sharply, obviously recognizing it.

"I need no hostage, Andrew, called Swift," he said. "For a Scout is, indeed, trustworthy."

"Well, thanks," Ingolf muttered. "For this glorious heart-warming display of trust and so forth your Uncle Alleyne made. *He's* back there, I note."

"We need to take chances," Mary said back, quietly. "We're in a hurry."

She'd seen hints some of their . . . guardians was a more tactful way of putting it than *guards* . . . knew Sign. If they really needed to be secret they could use the No-ble Tongue, but Ingolf wasn't really fluent yet, and Ian could follow simple sentences but not really talk it at all, beyond stock phrases. Cole had none at all, and Talyn and Caillech only a few words. So far everyone had been impeccably polite to them anyway.

In the meantime the seven of them followed the trail at a wolf-pace, which was what the Morrowlanders called it too: a hundred yards at a jog, a hundred at a fast walk, a hundred at a normal walking pace, then repeat, with a ten-minute rest every hour. You could really cover terri-tory that way. If you could keep it up, which they all could without much trouble. The Morrowlanders seemed slightly surprised, which they might well be if their stan-dard of comparison was Cutter cowboys who thought they lost caste if they got out of the saddle. The Dúne-dain didn't think that way, nor Mackenzies, nor Cole's service, and Ingolf was just plain versatile.

The game trail wound as their boots made a dull thud-ding on the soft pine duff. It took the easiest way through the hilly woods with the unerring skill animals had for a slope and for the least-effort way between two points.

The land it led through varied, from open flower-meadow to dense pine forest and Engelmann spruce and pockets of aspen, and there were almost always mountains in view. The thin air was crisp in the mouth and lungs, like a dry white wine, scented with sap and meadowsweet and an intense green savor. Once she stopped for a moment with a gasp as they turned a corner and came into the open.

A river lay well below the hillside trail, winding in S-curves through a meadow intensely green and starred with blue and crimson and gold like one of Sandra Arminger's neo-Persian carpets, only at this distance the color was more of an is-it-there mist flowing over the velvet, teasing the edge of vision. Beyond was the darker green of forest, turning to blue distance rising to the white teeth of the Absaroka Mountains.

It wasn't a painting, though: it was full of life. A bison bull shook his bearded head and snorted as red-and-white mustangs swept by with their tails raised like plumes. A pack of lobos had started the horses moving, but they skirted the bison warily as they followed, their heads held high to keep them over the level of the grass. From a twisted spruce below the hillside trail two golden eagles launched themselves into the cool limpid air, banking out over the murmuring white water with the feathers splayed like fingertips on their yard-long wings. Waterfowl rose up in a cataract from a quiet stretch surrounded by willows where a bear nosed through the shallows, climbing like a twisting spire of smoke.

"Now that's pretty," Ian said, and everyone nodded agreement; several whistled softly.

Nearby tiny hummingbirds with iridescent orange-red throats circled each other in a buzzing blossom-war.

"Even compared to the Drumheller Rockies, that's pretty," he went on. "Even compared to *Banff*, that's pretty."

"Damn, yes," Ingolf agreed. "I bet the winters here are something to behold, though, even compared to where I grew up."

"*Oh* yeah," Cole said. "Lucky to get two months without a frost around here, probably, up this high."

He was a native of the interior, if considerably south of this, drier and at a lower altitude. Ian nodded too, looking around at the vegetation. He had a right to be a connoisseur of winters, since the Peace River country lay a thousand miles to the north. The two Mackenzies and the Dúnedain winced a little. They were from the Willamette, off west of the Cascades. Where winter meant chilly and rainy and muddy, not howling weeks of freezing blizzard that could snatch you dead. Campaigning and travel had shown them the difference.

"I've done winter training, ski and mountain stuff, in country a lot like this," Cole said. "And it's no joke. But it's pretty then, too. Sort of . . . pure."

They all took a moment to absorb the quiet. The two Mackenzies drew their pentagrams and nodded, then opened their water-bottles and poured libations. Mary put her hand to her heart and bowed. It was actually difficult to say what part of what she saw was prettiest, like a complex piece of music; she'd heard that people came from far away just to walk these woods before the Change, and she could believe it.

The three representatives of the Morrowland Council halted too; they didn't say anything directly, but they did make that salute gesture again.

"A Scout is reverent," one of them added.

The whole group—less the unseen but definite escorts who were pacing them out of sight of the trail—stopped at a shelter built into the side of a hill for the night. It wasn't elaborately camouflaged, but it was fairly inconspicuous anyway, being three-quarters sunk into the slope. There was a bark-shingled roof extending a bit outward over walls of notched logs; a trickle of spring had been turned into a rock pool. A corral stood not far away with stone posts and wooden rails, and a lean-to packed with hay—baled hay tied with straw twists, which was an oddly advanced touch for the backwoods.

Aha, they do use horses, at least sometimes, she thought. *Those horse apples are about a day old. This run is a test, too.*

The interior of the shelter was interesting, when they spread their bedrolls; neatly folded robes of tanned wolverine fur tied to the bottom of the bunks, mattresses of fresh spruce boughs, clean polished wood table and benches, and a puncheon floor. The stove was an ingenious little affair of stone and metal sheets at the rear with a water heater of salvaged aluminum around the flue, and the food-store was built into the wall where the natural temperature-control of the earth would help it, lined with more aluminum to keep the vermin out.

There was also an arrangement for a block of ice to be inserted above and a water-drain below, and within Ian found a dozen two-foot cutthroat trout, neatly gutted, and bundles of greens and roots. He looked at the contents, at what in the way of herbs and ground roots was racked beside the stove in the usual miscellany of salvaged glass and some rather attractive glazed modern pottery, and rubbed his hands.

"Nothing like running all day to work up an appetite," he said. "Anyone else volunteering for dinner detail?"

"Caillech is a monstrous fine hand with trout," Talyn said helpfully, peering over his shoulder and smacking his lips.

"Volunteer *yourself*, man!" she said, taking his bonnet off for a moment and whapping him with it playfully.

"Well, if it were duck or grouse, I would," he replied reasonably, adjusting the headgear. "I'm better at those. It's respectful to make the most of the Mother's bounty, isn't it, now? If it's my part to enjoy eating it, then that I'll do, as my duty."

"I hereby volunteer *you* to go fetch the wood, I do," she said, then went with him.

"Nobody else?" Ian said, stripping off his jacket, rolling up his sleeves and beginning to scrub his hands. "All *right*, then."

"I'll take first watch," Ingolf added.

Mary had seen any number of small groups stranded in the wilds by the Change, though most had headed in to more civilized climes as soon as they could; apart from the Eater bands of the death zones, of course. But . . .

"A Scout apparently knows what the hell they're doing," Ingolf said to her as she sat beside him on a rock. "I've seen plenty of wild men but not many who knew their way around the woods as well. Old Pete's folks, yeah, though they weren't as . . . as tidy. Remember the Southsiders that Rudi picked up east of the Mississippi, Jake sunna Jake's crew? They didn't know *anything*."

"You took the words out of my mouth; they barely knew what made babies. Or the London Bunch, north of the lakes? They were *pathetic*. At a guess, the Morrowlanders have a lot of these little places as bases for hunters and people working the woods for foods and medicinals and whatnot," she said. "We have something similar in the Ranger *staths*, though the climate's a lot nicer in the Willamette."

"Yeah, I wouldn't like to go through February here in a *flet*. This dugout thing would be comfy enough even in winter . . . even in the winters they're supposed to get around here . . . but you'd go crazy after a while if you couldn't get out. Notice the ski-racks, and the second entrance up on the roof section? Back in Richland we do a lot of our heavy hauling in winter—frozen rivers are best of all. Maybe that's how they *keep* from going crazy, spend all their spare time studying for Badges and such."

She nodded. He'd picked a good spot to overlook the little way station; from the tracks he wasn't the first to do so.

"You took the words out of my mouth again, lover," she said. "When he was chasing us for the Cutters, George called the Tracker . . ."

"Followed us over ground where you'd swear an eight-hitch yoke of plow oxen wouldn't leave a trace," Ingolf agreed.

"They'd make valuable allies," Mary said, her enthusiasm growing. "Not just getting out of our way, I mean."

Her husband nodded, but frowned as well. "Hmmm. There's a drawback there."

"What?"

"We're supposed to be impressing *them*. I think these folks make knowing how to do stuff a real big part of their opinion of someone."

"Doesn't everybody?"

"Yah, but they're more . . . more formal about it."

The three Council members were at least impressed with Ian's pinion-nut crusted trout, accompanied by twice-boiled burdock and roasted arrowroot and bannocks of sweet camas flour studded with dried huckleberries, with a side of Miner's Lettuce salad with wild onions. The representative of the House of Girls shooed the men out after the meal; evidently a Scout was *clean*, too, and women got first crack at the hot water and essence of soaproot.

Much later, Mary murmured to Ingolf in the darkness:

"And a Scout likes *privacy*. Or at least this Ranger does."

He sighed.

Ingolf looked down on the Scout headquarters not long after dawn; the air was still chill and a little damp.

"Well, that explains how they got here," he said.

It was on the shores of a great lake, so broad that the water stretched north almost beyond sight even from this elevation, with occasional small islands and a few sails visible on fishing boats and a landing-stage for big birchbark canoes. There had been some buildings on the rocky edge before the Change, but it was obvious they'd burned that very night. Mostly because the midsection and tail of the great flying machine still stood, with the scorched and crumpled ruins of the nose stuck into the green scrub that covered the ruins. Bits and snags stood up, and most of a stone chimney. Parts of the aircraft were skeletal where the sheathing had been torn off; aluminum was easy to work and had dozens of uses.

Ian frowned. "That's a . . . 747," he said. "I think.

You can still see the sort of hump thing at the front, it's not all burned."

"What?" Talyn said. "Those numbers would mean what, precisely?"

"A type of big flying machine. They could carry hundreds of people."

They all looked at him; it wasn't the sort of remark you expected of a Changeling like themselves.

"We had a recognition course for recruits to the Force," he said, a little defensively. "I don't know why. Nobody ever thought to change it, eh?"

Talyn snapped his fingers. "Yes, in the 'Song of Fire and Grief.' The Chief, the Mackenzie Herself, she saw one such fall and burn in Corvallis on the night of the Change! And made the song about it later."

Cole whistled softly. "Alyssa goes on about what a great pilot the Bear Lord was, to get a *little* plane with six people in it down safely. And he landed in a river. Whoever was flying that thing must have been . . . something. I'd have expected it to fall like a brick."

They all nodded somberly. They all *knew* that the ancients had been able to make huge things fly, but suddenly seeing this—as big as a northern baron's hall—made you *feel* it all of a sudden.

The modern buildings became clearer as they approached. From a few remarks their close-mouthed hosts had made Ingolf had gathered that there just weren't all that many Morrowlanders, less than a thousand and possibly much less, and that this was their winter HQ. Certainly there was plenty of space in the building they were shown to; a room for each couple and one for Cole, and a big dining chamber with only a few other people to share the camas griddle cakes with spicy caramel-tasting birch syrup and—what seemed to be a special treat for guests—French fries, followed by wild blueberries and—another treat—cream. They were courteously shown to a bathhouse afterwards too, before strong hints brought them out again.

Now in summertime most of the Morrowlanders were probably spread out through this vast stretch of wilderness, laying in the food and other goods they'd need in the long deep-snow winters. That made what they'd done here all the more impressive, not least the inconspicuous but substantial storage cellars and icehouses, recognizable mainly by the doors set into what looked like low mounds.

The buildings scattered amid raised-bed gardens and pruned bushes and corrals and many trees were deepnotched logs on fieldstone, carefully set into the southfacing sides of the low hills. The largest reared like a whale among minnows, and from the color of the carved and varnished wood it was the newest, but like the others it had a steep-pitched roof covered in sod. That gave them an intensely green look, like great plants, colored with flowers that must be carefully cultivated despite their wild exuberance.

"Looks just a wee bit homelike," Talyn said in fascination. "But more spread out than one of our Duns. No wall. And no grain fields and not much in the way of herds, either, just these little bits of garden. They must live mostly from the hunt and what they gather."

The carving was less ornate and less colorful than, say, Dun Juniper, though there was plenty of it, mostly themed on animals and plants, and including inlays of different woods and colored stones. There were totem-pole-like erections in front of a collection of smaller but still big buildings surrounding the main one.

"What are those?" Ingolf asked.

"Those are the Houses of the Troops, and each Patrol has its Den," George Tracker said; they seemed to use their epithets as surnames, more or less. "They stand around the House of the Eagle."

Then, taking over the role of tour guide for a moment, he went on:

"That is the Hall of Boys, and that the Hall of Girls, where they meet for special ceremonies. There are the smithies, and the woodworking shop, and the library. That log flume brings springwater for drinking and washing and to turn wheels; it was finished the year I became a Bearer of the Eagle. That long building is—"

Nice composting toilets, too, Ingolf thought; that had impressed him most of all. *Same system we used back in Richland.*

The first Bossman of the Free Republic of Richland had been a gadget enthusiast, always pulling a new notion out of his books or someone's memory or from some traveller. He had sent artisans around to show people how to build the composting thunderboxes a couple of years after the Change, and met warm agreement among a people no longer living in fear of starvation and ready for something better than smelly, dangerous makeshifts. The Bossman had been a self-important fussbudget and easy to mock—Ingolf and some friends had gotten a memorable whaling with a hickory-switch from Ingolf's father the Sheriff for carving a roadside stump into a caricature of him just before a visit to Readstown—but he'd had some good ideas. And he'd been a much harder man than you'd think to look at him or listen to him burbling about how to rig a side-delivery hay rake or a silage chopper, though he'd used others to do the bone-breaking and head-knocking parts of the job.

Ingolf wouldn't have expected something so sophisticated in a place so rustic as this, though. The settlement smelled clean, too, with less stink and flies than nearly any warm-season farming community. To be sure, they didn't have much livestock, which were inescapably messy no matter how careful you were. The water and forest were the strongest odors; there was wood smoke, of course, and cooking, and the scorched metal, glue, leather and sawdust of crafts. His nose didn't detect the unmistakable reek of a tannery, either, which meant they must have put it elsewhere.

The people were out to see the newcomers when they emerged from getting settled, outsiders obviously not being something that were seen very often here. They were all dressed pretty much like the three representatives of the Council, though less elaborately. Apparently everyone wore knee-length pants in warm weather, roughly the way Mackenzies all wore kilts; many of the young children had nothing on *but* the shorts. There was a lot less jostling, pointing or exclaiming than he'd have expected from backwoods villagers—probably less than there would have been in Readstown, and certainly than in some other parts of Richland he could name. The hunting dogs that were fairly numerous were well-mannered too, hardly any barking and most staying close to their people even while their noses followed the stiff-legged strut Artan and Flan put on in a strange pack's territory.

Speaking of children and older people . . .

"Notice something about these folks?" he said to Mary.

"Lots," she said. "What in particular?"

"There are plenty of kids, but the adults are all my age or a bit older, and the Changelings, the born Changelings—"

Strictly speaking, Changelings *were* people born since the Change, of course. More loosely the term included people like Ingolf who'd been young children at the time; he'd been six going on seven. If you used both senses together Changelings were a majority of the population now nearly everywhere, or would be soon. Here they were apparently everybody.

"—just coming full-grown, only a few with babies of their own."

She blinked and he could sense her focusing, counting and averaging—numbers were something you had to be able to do well on reconnaissance.

"You're right," she said. "Like a clump, and their kids, and only a few people in between. It's a bit odd. And you don't expect a lot of really old people but there aren't *any*. Nobody even as old as Uncle John and Uncle Alleyne, who were about my age at the Change. I've never seen anything exactly like it, and we've been from the Atlantic to the Pacific and back. Odd."

"No it ain't," he said. "Scouts, before the Change that is, they were kids and youngsters."

In Readstown these days you were *a baby* up until you could get around, use the outhouse on your own and do simple chores, then *a kid* until puberty, and then *a young-ster* until you grew enough and learned enough to do the things a grown man or woman did. After that you sort of slid into being a full adult over the next few years, capping it off when you got your own house and a job or farm or workshop or whatever and started your own family.

Most places were roughly the same, though he was vaguely aware that they'd seen things differently before the Change when being *a kid* had lasted a lot longer. That Scouting business had been part of the way they stretched things out back then. It must have been irritating, since as he remembered it he'd been eager to grow up.

"My dad was a . . . what did they call it . . . Scoutmaster. And my older brother was a Scout, and they talked about it a little now and then. And they had some books about it that were real useful, practical stuff. Nobody kept it up after the Change where I come from, though. Too busy."

"No need, either, I imagine," Mary said thoughtfully.

"Yah. You learn that stuff from your folks or uncles or whatever, like farming or hunting or smithing. Or at school."

From their sixth year to around twelve kids in Richland went to school, at least between fall and spring, which was when they could best be spared from chores. Enough to get their letters and how to do sums and a bit of this and that; children of Farmers and Sheriffs usually stuck with it a little longer so they could keep account books and deal with the outside world, especially merchants and tax-collectors. That was about the way most civilized, advanced places worked, with arrangements running downhill from that to wildmen bands in the death zones who'd forgotten that there ever *had* been such a thing as writing. Modern life just didn't demand much book learning for most.

He went on slowly, marshaling his thoughts: "But say there were a couple of hundred of these . . . Scouts . . . flying through the air on that thing over there, and most of them lived through the crash. They'd mostly be . . . oh, teens or a little younger."

"Ah, I knew I didn't marry you just for your looks. So they wouldn't have started having children until a bit later, would they? That's why the born Changelings are all younger than me, nobody Rudi's age, or even Ian's."

"Right, and no grown-ups to raise them, probably. None still around, at least. And you know how kids get notions and run with them."

"And they'd be isolated from the outside world. By the Cutters, and by distance. Who'd come here if it weren't for the war?"

"Oh, afterwards they'll get a trader and some mules every year. Or every two or three, fur traders maybe. Or hunters. It's nice country if you like the woods."

"Yup, but there's plenty of places with pretty scenery and good hunting somewhere closer to somewhere, if you know what I mean. They haven't got anything anyone outside would want, they're not on the best road between anywhere and anywhere, and they're the only people at all in ten or twenty thousand square miles. I can see how they've turned out strange," Mary said solemnly.

What's that saying Edain likes? My, how grimy and sooty is your arse, said the kettle to the pot? Ingolf thought behind a poker face.

The Dúnedain had been started by a couple of teenagers, and look how *they'd* ended up. Though in his private opinion the PPA and the Mackenzies were just as weird, and adults had been responsible for that. Not adults who'd have ended up running countries before the Change, granted. You saw a lot of that if you travelled far, places where some charismatic lunatic or small bunch with some set of bees in their bonnets had ended up on top in the chaos and then shaped everything like a trellis under a vine. Most people had been ready to grab anything that looked as if it worked with the desperate zeal of a drowning man clutching at a log.

Like the Church Universal and Triumphant, he thought with a shiver. *The way it turned out after the Change. Of course, something . . . else . . . is at work there.*

The three Council representatives came to meet them. They were back in full formal fig, and there were a dozen more behind them in the same, with carved staffs if they didn't have spears. After a solemn exchange of greetings— the Morrowlanders were a ceremonious folk—one of them handed over a document written on something he recognized as a sort of paper made from birch bark.

"We didn't want to tire you excessively," the member of the Council said.

Ingolf looked down the list of Badges they were supposed to earn and wondered what it would have been like if they *had* wanted to tire them out.

"I'll take the *Tomahawk Throwing*," he said, briefly remembering that night in Boise. "And *Wrestling.*"

You never knew when keeping up a skill would save you grief. Mary and Ritva were looking over his shoulder.

"Dibs on *Storytelling*!" Mary said.

"We can do that together," Ritva said. "We'll do *Rid-*

dles in the Dark and *Conversations with the Dragon,* and switch off the speaking roles, how's that? And then one of us can do *Shelob's Lair.* Those all come across pretty well in the Common Tongue."

"OK, I'm cool with *Identifying Plants and Their Uses,*" Cole said thoughtfully. "I aced that part of Special Forces training and it shouldn't be too different around here. And *Field Shelters.*"

"I'm for *Snowshoes and Skis,*" Ian said decisively. "My dad taught me that, my family had a sideline in making them and swapped them for our blacksmith work back on the farm. And *Camp Cooking.*"

Everyone looked at the Mackenzies. "Well, *Folk Song,* and *Musical Instruments,*" Mary said. "What else?"

Talyn grinned and slid the longbow out of the loops beside his quiver and made a flourish with it. Caillech just strung hers with a step-through and a wrench.

"Need y' ask?" the young man said. "For let me tell you—"

"You talk too much," Caillech said, grinning herself. "Let's show instead."

It took a while to get to the archery, but the reception was all that could be asked when they did. A cheer went up as Talyn and Caillech straightened and leaned on their bows, panting and their faces running with sweat. The shooting range was overlooked by informal bleachers made by cutting seats into the hillside and cultivating turf. The cheering came mostly from the younger element—what the Scouts called *cubs.* The older spectators were enthusiastic too, but a lot of them were looking rather thoughtful.

I would be too, Ingolf thought.

The range included pop-up targets of various sorts and even some rigged to move, but the final test had been straight speed-and-accuracy shooting at a hundred yards. Both the round wood targets bristled with gray-fletched cloth-yard shafts. Many had punched their heads right through the four-inch thickness of pine. The ground below was littered with the ones that had been broken by more recent arrivals simply because there wasn't any more room in the bull's-eye. The Clan warriors had emptied their big forty-eight-arrow war quivers in less than five minutes of concentrated effort, and not a single shaft had missed the targets; most were tightly grouped in the centers, though admittedly there wasn't any wind to complicate matters.

I couldn't have matched that, Ingolf thought. *Oh, accuracy, sure, but not the speed.*

Cole Salander smiled as he fingered the new badge sewn to his camouflage jacket; it turned out to be made of beautifully tanned and colored deerskin, and sported a red leaf against a green background.

"Makes me ever more glad I wasn't at the Horse Heaven Hills with you guys shooting at me," he said. "But I'd have figured these guys here for good shots, too. That was some impressive, yeah, but should they be *this* impressed?"

"I know why they're startled," Ingolf murmured. "They're hunters, not war-archery specialists like our Clan friends."

Mary nodded, though Cole still looked a little puzzled; his folk mostly used crossbows for distance work, at least when fighting on foot.

Hunting . . . particularly hunting on foot in woodland . . . you very rarely shot more than once or twice at any particular animal. After that you'd either hit it or it had run away, so there wasn't much point in carrying more than half a dozen arrows. And you got just as close as you could; Ingolf would have bet the Scouts were good enough stalkers that they ended up shooting from point-blank more often than not. They were fine archers with their light handy recurves within that envelope, and he certainly wouldn't want to try and force his way through this rugged, forested country with them stalking him from ambush.

Mackenzies did a lot of hunting too; you had to in the Willamette, as in most places, if only to protect your crops from animals breeding fast in a world where humans were scarce. But the Mackenzie longbow was a battlefield weapon first and foremost. On a battlefield you were shooting for your life, not your supper, and your steel-clad targets came at you, screaming and waving sharp pointy things with ill intent. The training regime that old Sam Aylward had instituted right from their beginnings was aimed at shooting very fast with very powerful bows from the maximum possible distance, not taking your time.

To get into the Clan's First Levy, you had to be able to shoot twelve arrows in sixty measured seconds, and hit a man-sized target at a hundred yards with eight of them; that was the minimum standard, not the average. With a bow of at least seventy pounds pull as measured on the tillering frame; Talyn's drew a hundred-odd, and Caillech's a *mere* eighty. Both of them were well above the entry level in speed and accuracy, too.

When they were serious, Mackenzie archery contests *started* at a hundred yards.

The badges were presented; the Dun Tàirneanach pair got carried around the bleachers shoulder-high, too. Then everyone stood before the Council.

Andrew, called Swift, came forward again. "You have proven to be people of skill and merit, worthy of badges," he said. "You are worthy to speak with the Last Eagle, our Akela. So will your King be, when he can come here."

The Montivallans looked at each other. "Well, about that, Andrew of the Council." Mary said. "We didn't want to presume before you'd decided, but there *is* a bit of a hurry . . ."

The glider banked out over the water and turned in towards the shore; the pennant on a tall pole showed the wind to be directly out of the south. The long slender wings on either side of the tadpole shape flexed visibly, and the speed slowed. Suddenly it turned from a bird-sized dot out over the sun-glinting chop of the waters into something of visibly human make. It slowed, slowed, dropped . . . and then it was trundling over the grass, stopping, dropping one wing to the ground.

A long *ahhhhhhh* came from the Morrowlanders. Flying wasn't something they'd ever seen in their own lives; they didn't travel much, and the Cutters who were their neighbors regarded balloons and gliders as abomination. But flying was important in their founding myth.

Ingolf and the others walked forward. The transparent upper front of the fuselage tilted to one side; the glider was a two-seater model. Alyssa Larsson hopped out, and a second later Rudi Mackenzie did likewise and stood with the wind from the lake ruffling his plaid and long

sunset-colored hair and the spray of raven-feathers in his
bonnet.

"Hail, Artos! *Artos and Montival!*"

The cry was sincere enough, though Ingolf could see
a glint of humor in Rudi's blue-green eyes. They all saluted, and he walked forward. Mary and Ritva fell in on
either side of him, giving him a rapid précis in the Noble
Tongue; Ingolf caught about half of it. Behind him he
could hear:

"Cole, we're going to have to stop meeting this way."

"Well, at least you didn't crash-land upside down on
top of a *bear*."

"That was only *once* . . ."

Rudi nodded to his half sisters and looked at Ingolf.

"Yeah, he's . . . strange, the Last Eagle," the Rich-
lander said. "Not exactly wandered in his wits, but
strange. And he's not a well man. I got the feeling he's
hanging on with his fingernails because he thinks he has
to get a job done first."

Rudi's smile was crooked; not for the first time Ingolf
reflected that he seemed older than his face would indi-
cate, sometimes.

"I suspect I know how he feels, and will the more so
as time goes on," the High King said quietly.

A drum was thuttering in the background as the party
paced towards the Council; there were flutes too, and
flags. Rudi halted for a moment, went to one knee, and
raised a clod of the dirt to his lips before he stood again.

"I greet the Morrowland Pack in the name of the
High Kingdom of Montival and all its peoples and the
kindreds of earth and sea and sky," he said, his beautiful

almost-bass carrying clearly through the still cool air. "I step upon the Pack's territory by its leave, obedient to its Law, making no claim without the free consent of its folk."

The Council formed up on either side of them, and they not-quite-marched into the House of the Council. The big interior room was a little dim, but comfortably warm despite the lingering chill of the night, from the stoves in the corners more than the crackling fire on the big hearth at the north end. The figure in the fur cloak sitting waiting for them struggled to his feet, helped by the anxious hands of a young man and woman on either side of him. They put a staff whose head was carved in the form of a wolf's head in his hand and he leaned on it, breathing a little harshly.

The Morrowlanders all stopped and called: *"Akela!"* They added a chillingly realistic collective wolf-howl. The Montivallans saluted in their various fashions, and Rudi Mackenzie inclined his head briefly.

And yeah, this is a man to respect, Ingolf thought.

Ingolf Vogeler had never seen anyone burned so badly who'd lived to heal—heal after a fashion. One blue eye looked out of the ruined face, and it was obvious that the Aklela's left knee hadn't bent properly for a very long time.

Twenty-six years, to be precise, Ingolf thought. *I've seen a lot of people hurt in the Change, but usually they're not only a little more than my own age. Children mostly either made it or they didn't.*

The High King and the Last Eagle Scout stood for a quiet time, meeting each other's gaze. Then the single eye closed for an instant, with a long sigh.

"Sit," he said when he looked up again. "Sit, everyone . . . I have waited so long. . . ."

. They did, and then the Last Eagle spoke to the king, as if they were alone. "Captain Morrow got us down, but he died the next day, he was all broken inside, and burned so bad. I went forward with Scoutmaster Wilks to get him out, it was all burning . . . that's why we're the Morrowland Pack. When the ground thawed we buried him up on the high place, and every year on that day we go there and sing for him."

Rudi nodded. "Fitting indeed," he said quietly. "A great honor, but well earned. There are far worse ways to die."

"It was so cold, and we got so hungry . . . Scoutmaster Wilks was hurt too, but he got us through. We chopped holes in the ice to fish, and we dug pine nuts, and made bread from whitebark, and found animals in their dens, and then we got a buffalo, we were so happy about it . . . I could help by then . . . And Ms. Delacroix knew so much, she was like our mom . . . Mr. Androwski left to get us help in the spring, but he never came back, he went north and I think . . . I think he met the Prophet, the first Prophet, in Corwin, and . . . and then three years later Scoutmaster Wilks was killed by a bear. And Ms. Delacroix had this cough, it got worse and worse, after a while the herbs didn't help anymore. She said I'd have to be brave for the little ones, be a real Eagle Scout. We buried her next to Scoutmaster Wilks and the Captain on the high place, that was the year we saw the first tiger."

A long silence and then: "Sometimes I dream about them, dream they're back and then I wake up. . . ."

The story rambled on. Ingolf had heard much of it yesterday, and it gave him an odd lost feeling anyway, as if he was one of those children alone in the dark as the plane fell and broke open to the cold and the fire. Or the hurt boy ignoring his constant pain, working and teaching, holding himself and them to a dream. Instead he looked at the rack of books on the wall behind the hunched figure: *The Boy Scout Handbook*, *Best of Ernest Thompson Seton*, *The Jungle Book*, books on crafts and ecology and some he didn't recognize at all. Most of those would have been on the 747, though there were a few modern leather bindings that must have trickled in from the outside world.

"Did I do the right things?" the Last Eagle said finally to the King. "I tried, but sometimes I just had to make things up . . . I hated to help the Prophet, I bargained as hard as I could, I never let them send their priests here, said we'd die first, but . . ."

"You saved your people," Rudi said, leaning forward for a moment and putting a hand on the older man's shoulder. "More than once, you saved them, from perils to body and to soul. You did what you could, and what you knew you must do, and you fought the good fight, Scout."

He nodded to the books. "What those men dreamed in the ancient times, you have become in truth. Now we will free your people."

He raised his voice slightly: "We will throw down Corwin together, and then all this land will be the Morrowlander Pack's, forever; to hold in trust for all the kindreds of fur and feather and scale, for the very grass and trees and the rock beneath, as guardians and helpers. None of humankind shall come on it without your permission, nor harm it, while the line of my blood lasts."

The cheer rose to the carved rafters of the House. The Last Eagle rose to cheer with the rest of them, then staggered. Rudi frowned in concern, and the two young attendants stepped forward.

"Our father is tired. Akela should rest. He's worked so hard."

Rudi nodded. "Indeed he has," he said softly. "Hard and well, and well he has earned rest from the Powers. Rest and blessing, in the land where no evil comes and all hurts are healed."

CHAPTER SIXTEEN

"**H**old them off, by Our Lady of the Citadel!" Rudi heard Tiphaine d'Ath mutter. "*Don't* chase them, just hold them and look like it's killing you with the effort."

"They'll do it long enough, Grand Constable, long enough," he said. "And the effort *is* killing some, to be sure."

Mathilda swept the horizon northward. "Nothing that the gliders missed. Everyone's here, and the Volta can begin."

They sat their horses on a slight rise about long catapult shot from the action, surrounded by the usual staff and couriers and guardsmen; and they were out of the woods, literally if not metaphorically. Well behind them lay the arched stone gate that had *For the Benefit and Enjoyment of the People* on it—another of the old American ruler Roosevelt's works, like Timberline Lodge on

Mt. Hood; the man had certainly left his mark on the world and usually in a way Rudi admired.

The Valley of Paradise opened out before them. As far as looks went, it lived up to its heavenly name. To the west were the Gallatin Mountains, to the east the Absarokas, blue in the distance and tipped with white. The lowland ran north-south, opening out in a broad diamond shape with the Yellowstone river running through it in a broad swath of gallery forest, aspen and willow and big cottonwoods. Up from the valley flats rose buffalohump foothills, dark where tongues of spruce and fir and pine thickened amid the grass, fading into the endless mountain forests. Even with the heights upon every hand it felt . . .

Big, somehow, he thought. *As if the sky were larger, somehow. And yet—is that sense of some menace just things working below the surface of what my waking mind thinks, or am I really feeling it?*

"The League and the Dominions are on the other side of Bozeman Pass," Rudi said aloud.

"The League's siege-train was most impressive, what we saw in Iowa," Mathilda said, her voice carefully neutral. "Now they'll get a chance to use it."

"Lucky it is that the CUT put their major forts there when they were thinking how to protect Corwin, is it not?" Rudi said, with just a little sarcasm.

"Because nobody would be crazy enough to come through Yellowstone," d'Ath said dryly. "Always better to fight nature than men, when you can. They're earning their corn, our gallant allies . . . at last."

Mathilda made a slight chiding sound; she'd never say

anything so impolitic in public. Ruling folk were seldom really alone, and their words travelled. You had to remember that what you said casually could hit like a club.

Rudi glanced upward; sunlight flashed off his reconnaissance fliers, wheeling thousands of feet above. The High King's host had direct communication with the League and Dominion forces now, by very daring glider pilots, which cut about a week off the closest land route. Coming through Yellowstone had been nerve-wracking, mainly because he had to cover both banks of the river, giving the enemy the chance to cut one half of the army off from the other and destroy it . . . or it would have given them the chance, if the Scouts hadn't given him a better grasp of the Cutters' movements than their own commanders had.

Sure, and it's the Threefold Law in operation.

"Not long now," Mathilda put in. "A month or two, and we'll be seeing Órlaith again."

Rudi nodded agreement, putting aside a stab of longing that felt like a wound to speak judiciously:

"There's no doubt about the outcome. Their last chance to preserve anything was to keep us from crossing into this valley . . . and they failed at that, thanks to our Scout friends. We're just seeing to the details the now."

The *details* would mean an arrow through the gut for some, which would be unpleasantly final whether you were winning or losing. No point in mentioning that; it was a cost of doing business.

"About now, I think," he said aloud instead.

The surface of the valley was open, with few buildings and those clustered inside palisades or earth berms. Much of it was tilled in big square fields colored brown or

shades of green, planted with buckwheat and rye and potatoes and other hardy crops that could grow in a climate
that consisted of an eight-month winter briefly interrupted by two months each of spring and autumn. Most
of the harvest had been gathered, except for some rye
that was cut but still standing with the sheaves in stooks.
The rest was pasture and hay-meadow, and there was
rarely anything tall enough to be much obstacle to a
horse.

He leveled his binoculars. The skirmish—it would
have been counted a battle in any war less huge—involved
several thousand fighters on either side. There was a
block in the reddish-brown armor of the Sword of the
Prophet, about a regiment's worth, six or seven hundred,
hanging back to the north, waiting to punch at the right
moment. That was more than he'd seen of them since the
Horse Heaven Hills last year, and he hadn't missed them
at all; the Prophet's guardsmen were as disciplined as any
of his own troops, too disciplined by far, and fanatically
dedicated to their cause and leader. They waited quietly
with the thread-thin shafts of their lances standing upright topped by the bright slivers of the heads.

The main action was between the light horse on both
sides, armed with bow and round shield and curved
sword, few with more armor than a helmet and mail shirt.
His CORA levies and some of the PPA's eastern cavalry
and the Boisean equivalents, along with the Richland volunteers under his brother-in-law Ingolf, and Rick Three
Bear's Lakota and the Dúnedain.

The Grand Constable was using her own binoculars,
below the raised shelf of her visor. "Now, the question is,
will the CORA-boys obey the signal to get the hell out of

the way? They've got lots of motivation, but not much discipline."

"Oh, I think so," Rudi said. "We've all been working together for some time now. You have Baron Tucannon . . . Lord Maugis de Grimmond . . . in charge of your first detachment of men-at-arms, correct?"

She nodded. "I've been giving him more work, now that a lot of the Counts are out of the picture. He's very able, and well-born enough he doesn't have to kill anyone to get the others to pay attention. And he's mentally flexible as well as intelligent."

Which was not something you could say for every Associate baron; they were all brave, but many had about as much subtlety as a war hammer in the face. Maugis was a vassal of the Counts of Walla Walla, a smallish wiry young man with frizzy red hair and jug ears, and he was very clever indeed. Also . . .

"Also the enemy burned his manor house and villages and those of his vassals, and chased him and his men like a wolf before hounds through the Blue Mountains for months while his lady held their castle against the besiegers."

Motivation like that could turn a man into a berserker; or if combined with intelligence and self-control into someone very useful to his King.

"Let's bring it all together and sample the taste of the stewpot," Rudi said. "Now, Grand Constable."

D'Ath nodded and raised her gauntleted hand and the wand of office, chopping it downward. A signal team nearby worked the lever of their heliograph, flashing the sun through an angle. Instants later trumpets blew below, half a dozen different varieties.

The Montivallan light horse had been busy at the

deadly swirl of a horse-archery engagement, small parties sweeping past each other, rising in the saddles to shoot as they passed, advancing or retreating with eyeblink agility. Only occasionally would two bands clash hand to hand when one or the other miscalculated. A brief melee of shetes and sabers, the clash of steel on steel or the cracking thud of blades against the varnished leather of shields, a scream of war cries or just animal shrieks of rage and pain, then the combatants exploding outward with riderless horses galloping and bodies lying in the green grass.

At the sound of trumpets the Montivallans all turned tail and ran for the shelter of the woods as fast as their horses could carry them, turning in the saddle to shoot behind. The Cutters pursued, but cautiously—feigned retreats to draw an enemy in were the favorite tactic of all the vast interior lands of mountain and steppe and desert. The Cutters would be afraid of artillery, too, field catapults that outranged even the powerful composite bows. They didn't make the machines themselves, and now that Boise was part of Montival they didn't have allies to supply the lack. What they wouldn't be afraid of, hopefully, was what was really waiting for them. Down there Oak Barstow Mackenzie, the First Armsman of the Clan, would be judging distances and preparing to give the signal.

About . . .

"Now," Rudi said crisply; it was the moment he'd have chosen.

Three thousand Mackenzies stood and threw off their disguising war-cloaks, trotting forward out of the final screen of trees. They were in open order, and they drew as they came, halting only when they needed to pull that last few inches. The savage snarl of the war-pipes sounded, raw and hoarse, and the inhuman roar of the Lambeg drums.

"Let the gray geese fly!" Rudi murmured to himself, what the bow-captains would be shouting down there. "Wholly together—shoot!"

The arrows flew upward at forty-five degrees for maximum range, two more flights in the air before the first came slanting down out of the sky and struck like steel-tipped rain. The loose mass of horse-archers wavered, men dropping clawing at the iron in their flesh, horses running in bucking frenzies.

"They're really going to have to stop underestimating infantry," d'Ath said thoughtfully, in a detached professional tone. "Particularly longbowmen. Everybody understands a pike when it's pointed at them, but it's taking them a while to realize foot-archers have three times as many bows per unit of front than mounted ones. Horses take up a lot of space."

"It's a bit late for them to learn. Now let's see how desperate they are to knock back our vanguard."

The cowhorns the Cutters used sounded in a series of snarling blats. The whole mass came forward after an instant's wavering, and the contingent of the Sword of the Prophet moved up in support . . . or to take advantage of the arrow-absorbing capacity of their light cavalry, depending on how you wanted to look at it. The Mackenzies were spread out, and they hadn't planted their swine-feathers—the knock-down double-ended spears they carried to jam into the dirt and hold off horsemen with a hedge of points while they shot.

It would look like a tempting bit of arrogance by an

overconfident invader, a chance to get in close with the shete and cut down footmen.

"There they go, taking the bait. Sure, and when something's too good to be true, it usually isn't true," Rudi said. "But you'll also seldom go wrong encouraging men to believe what they strongly want to be so."

"Let's see how Lord Maugis is at timing," d'Ath said meditatively, raising a brow for permission to wait. He nodded; that *was* something you needed to know.

They waited a few moments more; Mathilda was looking a bit unhappy at the length of it by the end. She was a good competent field commander but a little more conservative in her style than Rudi. Or the Grand Constable— the gauntlet was just going up again when the Portlander oliphants sounded down below, long and shrill, a sound that somehow gleamed like polished metal in the sun, fit to raise the hair on the back of your neck.

"He's *good*," the Grand Constable said. "Waited until the last minute but no longer."

"Or we're all three wrong in the same way," Rudi said dryly.

He wished he were down there, ready to charge with the rest, but that would have been self-indulgent under the circumstances.

There was a concerted flicker from among the underbrush, as the knights walked their destriers forward. They'd had time to add the horse-barding for their mounts as well, or rather their varlets had; armor of articulated steel plates riveted to padded leather, covering for head and neck, shoulders and breast. It made the great beasts look like dragons uncoiling as they emerged into the sunlight, the more so for the touches of fancy, plumes nodding, rondels and silvered unicorn-horns on the chamfrons, spikes or brass inlay. There were five hundred of them, their formation a block of two staggered lines, a mass of muscle and hoof and steel that would make ground quiver hundreds of yards away once they got moving. The clatter and ring of the harness of men and horses carried clearly to where he waited.

More metal glittered as the low-held lances went up to the *rest* position, hand on the grip behind the bowl-shaped guard and the butt resting on the thigh. The trumpets screamed again, and the mass of horsemen began to move, first a walk, then a canter, the colorful pennants on the lances beginning to flutter, blazoned with the arms of knight and baron and count like the big kite-shaped shields. Then the fast pulsing call for the charge *à l'outrance*.

The horses were as well-trained as the men, and they rocked up to a controlled hand-gallop as the lancepoints fell in a rippling wave amid a crashing bark of:

"Haro, Portland! *Artos and Montival!*"

"Go for it, ironheads," d'Ath said. "Another chance to die with honor."

The words were cool, but there was undertone of affection; Rudi reflected that the Grand Constable had mellowed somewhat over the last few years.

The Cutter horse-archers had learned enough not to try to play at handstrokes with Associate men-at-arms or their Bearkiller equivalents. With enough room to run and sting like an elusive cloud of wasps they could be very dangerous, but here they were caught between the onrushing lancepoints and the Sword of the Prophet frantically deploying and countercharging behind them; their only option was to slide away eastward, and that put them in the killing ground where the Mackenzie arrows still rained down. The men-at-arms slammed through the ones who remained without slowing, spearing men out of the saddle or just letting their chargers bowl the light cow ponies aside with their armored shoulders. The tall long-legged destriers were fast once they got going, if not as nimble as the quarter-horses, and they built up massive momentum.

The Sword of the Prophet answered with a charge of their own, but they'd never done well against the heavy metal of the western knights in this sort of stand-up fight. Twenty minutes later the whole Cutter force was in flight north, with half the Montivallan light cavalry ant-tiny figures in pursuit. A brigade of Fred's Boiseans came swinging down the cracked, potholed pavement of the old US Highway 89 and out into the valley, with a regiment of Bearkiller cataphracts deploying into the open on their flanks; their leader Eric Larsson had argued furiously that they be allowed to launch the charge, and had still been grumbling about it when Rudi left him.

Behind them came blocks of sixteen-foot pikes, like rectangular walking forests topped with a glitter of honed steel; the levies of the Free Cities, with the banners of their towns before and their batteries of field catapults rumbling along between. A crash of boots and squeal of fifes, and a deep chorus paced to the marching stride:

> "O'er the hills and o'er the main
> Through mountain snows and burning plain
> Our King commands and we obey
> Over the hills and far away—"

Rudi nodded to the Grand Constable; he and Mathilda turned the noses of their coursers and trotted down to the main body. Their escorts followed, the High King's Archers and the lancers and mounted crossbowmen of the Protector's Guard bristling slightly at each other. Huon turned and gave a friendly salute good-bye to Lioncel de Stafford where he stood by the Grand Constable's stirrup, handing up a leather map folder.

"D'you think they'll be a book, someday, *Songs of the Prophet's War*?" Rudi said. "There are enough to fill a mort of pages. Mind, there's been a fair deal of marching and waiting in camp, and singing does make that go faster."

Matti grinned. "If there is a book . . . maybe *Marching to Corwin* . . . your little sister Fiorbhinn will write it. And make up half the songs, and change the rest to make them more lively, and nothing anyone but an expert could sing or play."

"And claim the credit for the whole, the scamp," Rudi chuckled. "Mind, she does have the talent; to be just, for simple things as well as the high art. Odd that she and Maude are so unalike, in looks and nature both."

Rudi's two younger half sisters had both been sired by his mother Juniper's second husband, Sir Nigel Loring. Maude was tanist of the Clan now—hailed as his mother's successor-in-training by the *Óenach Mór*, the Great Assembly—and she was brown of hair and eye, steady and calm by inclination and very clever; Fiorbhinn was fair and slim and had the music and magic running through her soul strong and wild. Along with a good deal of wildness in other directions.

"If there's one thing I always envied you it was having siblings," Mathilda said.

Rudi raised a brow at her. "Ah, but I was lucky in mine, or at least the most of them. Your friends and your lover you can choose, most often: your blood kin you're stuck with. And it's . . . how did Ingolf put it . . . a crap-shoot."

She nodded. Their friend had spent a long time quarreling with his elder brother, or in exile; and then there was Fred and Martin Thurston to consider. Being born to power magnified the usual rivalries and gave them a malignant importance that ordinary folk didn't have to take into reckoning.

Their path took them past the First Richland coming back to fill their quivers and head out again to sweep the western side of the valley. Ingolf saluted from their head. The volunteers were still young men—the war hadn't lasted *that* long since they joined in as the Quest returned through the Midwest—but their gear was battered and their faces had an indefinable something that hadn't been there when they were just gentry sprigs riding off heedless to seek adventure in distant lands, the sons and brothers of Farmers and Sheriffs back there on the Kickapoo.

They'd had the adventure and no mistake, and taken the measure of it. He'd be sorry to see them go when the High King's Host met the army of the League and they headed home. No doubt Ingolf would be too; the older man was committed to Montival, and he'd left home as a youngster anyway, but his heartstrings would always be there. Having seen it, Rudi didn't blame him; it was a fine fair land, fairer to his eyes with its rolling forested hills and winding river valleys than the endless flat, fat black earth of Iowa or the Red River. He'd liked the hardy, stoic, plainspoken folk who dwelt there as well.

"They'll have a tale to tell, back on the Kickapoo," Rudi said. "For the rest of their lives. Of mountains and battles and strange folk and stranger Gods."

"Mostly lies," Mathilda said, but with a smile. *"And then sixteen Cutters and a grizzly bear had me cornered in a gulch! With my leg broken and nothing but a roast turkey drumstick to fight them off!"*

"Whereupon I died," Rudi finished for the hypothetical storyteller sitting before a winter hearth waving a mug of mulled cider while his grandchildren gaped. "The which is why I'm not here drinking this and telling the story!"

The easterners gave him and the High Queen a cheer, which was gracious in foreigners fighting for the sake of the thing, and went back to the jaunty marching song they favored, roaring it out loud if not particularly tunefully as they trotted along in an orderly column of fours:

"Instead of water we'll drink ale
And pay no reckoning on the nail
No man for debt shall go to jail
While he can Garryowen hail!
We'll break windows, we'll break doors
The watch knock down by threes and fours—"

They passed Oak among the Mackenzies retrieving their arrows; the big blond man was laughing and exchanging a fist-bump with Lord Maugis, who leaned over with a gruesomely spattered war hammer held across his saddlebow. They both waved to him, well pleased with how the stratagem had worked, and he returned the gesture; now the Montivallan army could deploy unhindered in the broad open valley. Tomorrow would end the war,

bar the mopping up and reconstruction . . . which unfortunately might occupy the rest of his life.

*And isn't that a sight, to be sure, the two of them thick as
thieves, when Oak marched in the War of the Eye against
the Protectorate, and his first arrow sent in anger perhaps
aimed right at the breastplate of Maugis' father? And isn't
it a hopeful thing to see?*

Mathilda caught his eye, and she knew that she shared
the thought. It was natural enough, since their own parents had been bitter enemies once and their sires had
killed each other in single combat.

"To work," she said.

The first chore was visiting the wounded, those who
weren't actually still on the operating tables; a painful
task, but something those willing to risk maiming and
death for them and the kingdom had a right to expect.
Mathilda did the same, and they went from one form to
the next while the hospital tents were going up.

When he'd finished, Ingolf Vogeler was waiting outside, pacing and slapping his leather gauntlets into his
palm. His nephew-cum-trumpeter Mark stood nearby
holding the horses, a youth who looked much like his
father's brother, though lankier with hair of light sun-
faded tow rather than brown. Right now he was looking
a bit pale despite summer's tan, as well. Ingolf was merely
grim, but something in his eyes brought Rudi up.

"Couple of things you need to look at, bossman," the
Midwesterner said.

Rudi nodded. He trusted Ingolf's judgment as to
what was important. And the High King had a good staff,
which freed him from administrative detail, as long as he
remained reasonably available. Part of commanding was

standing aside and letting your subordinates do their jobs; his was to concentrate on the big picture.

"You too, bosslady," Ingolf said to Mathilda.

The enemy dead mostly lay where they'd fallen once the Montivallan medics had—carefully—checked for living men to be carried off; bitter experience had shown that some of Cutter wounded were given to pretending helplessness and then lashing out with hidden weapons at any who approached them. Policing up weapons and gear wasn't the maximum priority, and burial could wait. Followers of the CUT usually cremated their dead, in any case. Rudi's brows went up a little when he saw a dozen of the Sword of the Prophet laid out in rows, the lacquered leather and steel of their harness oddly bright in the midmorning sun. The smell of blood and opened bodies was fairly heavy, as it always was, though it was cool enough that they were spared the quick bloat and stink. He brushed aside flies; overhead the buzzards and crows and ravens were hanging, waiting, or descending to tear at the dead horses who'd been given quick mercy-strokes.

Oak and the Baron of Tucannon waited for them. The Mackenzie nodded casually, and the nobleman gave a Protectorate military salute, fist to chest in a clash of steel gauntlet on articulated breastplate.

"Take a look at their faces, your Majesties," he said grimly.

The pleasure of doing a difficult job well seemed to have fled, and neither was a man to be easily upset by the miserable aftermath of battle.

"Aye, *Ard Rí*," Oak said. "This is just a sample, mind, but it's the same with most in the red armor. Save for

some officers. It wasn't until we went over the field looking for the wounded that we noticed the pattern."

Rudi did too. At first glance along the row of battered,
bloodied bodies he thought some were women. Which
was vanishingly unlikely, since the CUT regarded females
as a lesser creation and had strict rules restricting them to
domestic tasks. Far more so than even Associates, and
unlike them with no provision for exceptions for those
too stubbornly bloody-minded to accept or work around
customs they found grated on them. Then he realized . . .

"Young, First Armsman Oak, my lord Maugis," he
said. "Very young indeed—too young to raise a beard,
every one."

"Yah," Ingolf said. "They take them young from their
parents, six or so, but I've never heard of them putting
the cadets in the line before they're full grown. That's
eating the seed corn with a vengeance, wasting all that
training."

"*Tuili,*" Rudi said flatly. "Bastards. They're desperate,
but even so."

There were battlefield chores youngsters did; junior
squires among Associates, *eòghann* in the Clan, military
apprentices among Bearkillers. Some of those tasks involved danger, because there was no absolute safety in an
environment full of flying metal and human beings in the
mildly insane state of savage focus required for naked extreme violence at arm's length. Tasks like pulling back the
wounded, bringing up arrows or a fresh lance, carrying
messages. Riding in the ranks to meet a charge of knights
was *not* among the things that youths just learning their
trade were fit for.

"There wasn't anything we could do," Maugis de Grimond said. "It's unchivalrous, but there *wasn't* anything we could do but cut them down."

He seemed to be trying to convince himself, which spoke well for him. Rudi knew plenty, and not necessarily wicked men, who'd simply shrug and move on.

"Not if they were serious, no, there *wasn't* anything you could do but strike," Rudi said. "My lord, I slew my first man in battle when I was barely ten. It would have been fair enough if he'd killed me instead. Since I'd a blade and I intended to see his blood."

That had been when a Protectorate deep-penetration squad led by one Tiphaine Rutherton kidnapped him and rescued Mathilda, who the Clan had in turn captured in an earlier raid, all part of the build up to the War of the Eye. Or the Protector's War, as they called it in the north-realm. That was the feat that had won the future Grand Constable knighthood and the barony of Ath, though it wouldn't be very tactful to mention the details right now.

The knight nodded, his eyes still haunted. "We . . . we just thought it was one or two exceptions, some squire getting a rush of spirits, a boy pushing into a man's work, that happens. They were out to kill, and for squires that junior they were very well trained. And they wouldn't give up. Then just now we rode back over the battlefield and saw how *many* . . ."

Mathilda put a hand on his shoulder. "Duty is hard, my lord," she said. "And facing mere danger is not the hardest part of war, sometimes."

The baron nodded, his face relaxing a little.

Rudi gestured agreement. "After years each in the House of the Prophet, I'm not surprised they wouldn't give up. And a lad of fourteen can kill you dead as dead, if he's determined enough and you don't fight back with all your force. Weight of arm isn't the only thing that matters."

He turned back to Ingolf. "There was something else?"

"Yah, you betcha," he said, the sing-song guttural of his native speech a bit stronger than usual in his voice. "The Dúnedain overran one of these farm things."

"Temple-farms, I think they call them."

"Yah." Ingolf glanced at Maugis; they were good friends, if not particularly close ones. "You ought to come too, Maugis, if you can. I think you might feel better about this"—he indicated the enemy dead—"if you did."

"What is it?" Mathilda asked.

"Better just to show you, and I wish I didn't have to know it myself, Matti," he said.

They cantered in his wake, a squad of Ingolf's Rich-landers added to the party leading the way. The path turned off the old highway and onto a narrower road, dirt but well maintained and covered in rolled gravel. Ingolf was closemouthed.

"I'd have planted trees on the roadsides," Mathilda said, to fill the silence—something unusual for her.

"The Cutters don't do anything just for nice," Rudi said.

The headquarters of the temple-farm was a set of plain log buildings surrounded by an earth berm twelve feet tall, the wooden plank gate sagging open. Within were barns and grain-stores and the usual workshops essential to cropping and grazing, though there was far less machinery than in most places; the corrals outside were empty, which was logical—nobody left livestock to be swept up by an enemy. Storehouses trailed sacks of grain and potatoes, evidence of a hasty attempt to move the just-completed harvest as well, and a rather crude wagon lay with a broken wooden axle and crates and boxes spilling out of it. The traces lay before it, sliced and loose where someone had cut the team out of its rig rather than bothering to unharness.

Rudi's lips tightened in a snarl. A pile of scrap wood and straw had been piled against one long low-set building that looked like a cross between a bunkhouse and a fort and set alight, with parts of it still smoldering and reeking. From the look of the shattered door someone inside had broken open the barred portal and then pushed through the flames.

"The Cutters killed the male slaves and pushed the rest inside that building, it's only got one door, and then lit the fire," Ingolf said, confirming his guess. "They busted out—which took some presence of mind."

"Not something the Cutters would expect of women," Mathilda said, a little white around the lips.

"Yah, well, *stupid* evil shits, fortunately. The Dúnedain came along about then, and signaled for us. Though damned if I know what they expected us to do that they couldn't, just at a loss, I guess."

There were other signs of haste as well. An X of stout timbers held the body of a man; his throat had been cut recently enough that the blood pooled at his feet wasn't completely dry, but from the look of his body he'd been on the cross for some time. Several other bodies lay about, all men with lash-marks, sprawled naked where they'd been shot or cut down. They had arrow-stubs in their bodies, or just the wounds, and slash-marks from shetes.

So much is bad, but I've seen as bad or worse, in war, Rudi thought.

That wasn't what made his escort swear until their officers' barked commands for silence, or make signs against ill luck, or cross themselves if they were Catholics. Nor even the fact that all the dead men-slaves had been gelded, and had their right eyes burned out.

One whole man in a rag loincloth crouched beside a cage of poles lashed together with twists of iron-hard rawhide, a short but muscular fellow with bewildered eyes roaming about and his face slack. Two Dúnedain with spear and shield were in front of him, protecting him from a crowd of women. Most of them were naked too, and many were pregnant, had burns on their legs and hands, or both. A round dozen were trying to get towards the man, some of them with billets of firewood or rocks in hand. Others wandered about, or sat and wept, or stared vacantly, several score in all. One dangled from an improvised noose that ran out of a window, and he didn't think that the Cutters had done it. A team of medics, Rangers and from Ingolf's volunteers, was tending to the burns and other injuries of some of the women.

The sound the women-slaves all made was a thick gobbling, stammering through tears and moans. You could see why there weren't any words when one suddenly screamed; her tongue had been trimmed and split. There was a hard stink in the air, manure and dried human waste.

Huon Liu started forward with a shocked exclamation, reaching for a flask from his saddlebags. Mathilda restrained him with a gentle gesture, her eyes the only things moving in a stony face.

"Slave-breeding farm," Ingolf said grimly. "That guy the Rangers are guarding—look, you two, stop standing there with your thumbs up your asses and get that moron *out* of here before you have to hurt someone to stop them lynching him! Edain, get a detail to give them a hand, would you?"

Ingolf took a deep breath as a squad of the High King's Archers attended to it, and went on to the monarchs:

"He's the stud. Not really his fault, poor bastard, he's just smart enough to know what to put where. They were breeding for stupid, for people just barely smart enough to do basic work and feed themselves."

Rudi nodded soberly. He'd heard of this. Once you'd looked into the eyes of a High Seeker, it didn't even seem very . . . unexpected. Seeing it in person was different, though.

"I know," he said. "And"—he touched the hilt of the Sword—"I've seen what this would end in, left unchecked. By themselves humans couldn't do such a thing, if only because we can't maintain a set purpose long enough."

Though that vision of a possible future was so alien it didn't have as much . . . impact . . . as this.

Mathilda crossed herself; for once she seemed at a loss. He could see *where do we start?* in her eyes. Lord Maugis was staring, blinking, looking away and then looking back. His area had been occupied for a while, but mostly by Boiseans in Martin Thurston's service; the war there had been savage enough, but comprehensible. Young Mark Vogeler abruptly rode his horse around a wall and dismounted. They could hear him vomiting, then washing his mouth out from his canteen.

"What are your orders, Your Majesty?" Ingolf said formally.

He tactfully ignored his young kinsman when he returned, though a signaler wasn't supposed to leave his commander's side.

"We'll have to care for these people," Rudi said, taking out his dispatch pad. "Messenger! To Brigadier Nystrup, and would he please report here; and this to Lord Chancellor Ignatius, would he have the quartermasters attend to the matter of clothing and basic gear. Many of these ladies will be Nystrup's people; he'll want to see to identifying as many as he can. For the rest . . . well, the Clan will take in any who wish, I think. Certainly if my mother has anything to do with it, and she will. There may be others who are willing."

"The Sisters of Mercy," Mathilda said. "I'll . . . I'll talk to Father Ignatius. The Superior of their Mother House . . . they have a unit with the medical train. . . ."

"See to it, please, Matti," Rudi said. "We'll do what we can, but the first matter is to overthrow the ones who planned . . . this."

"Where are the children?" she said suddenly; there weren't many, beyond some babes at the breast.

"You really don't want to know, Matti," Ingolf said softly. "Creches, most of them, but . . . you don't want to know."

"By God . . ." Maugis said, crossing himself with a hand that shook. "By God, I'd heard that the Cutters kept slaves, but . . . is it all going to be like *this*, lord King?"

Rudi shook his head. "No. We're close to their center, here. Elsewhere it's bad, but on a more . . . more human scale of wickedness. But it would have been all like this, in time."

The baron's face worked. "They're . . . they're not *human* at all."

Rudi felt his mouth twist wryly. There was a certain innocent vanity in that viewpoint, but he had to prevent it from spreading. The former Cutters would be his subjects too. He intended to see the headsman's axe had some work, but a little of that went a long way. The Cutters . . . former Cutters, they'd have to find a different term . . . had to learn to live in peace with others. However, that implied just as much willingness in the other direction.

I cannot have a disgust with the folk of these lands persisting down the generations. That way would lay the groundwork for other wars—of less import to the Powers, perhaps, but just as deadly to humankind and our hopes and our homes.

He spoke carefully: "Alas, would that were so. The Power behind all this, yes, in a sense. But its instruments are all too human. At least most of them, and all of them to start with; and they are what they are because they've been mistaught, not because there's any corruption in their blood, which is as ours. Do you understand me, Lord Maugis? For your own confessor will tell you the same—in somewhat different terms, but the same in the essence of it."

The other man reluctantly nodded. "Yes. We're all subject to Original Sin, that lets Satan whisper in our ears."

Mathilda spoke: "Original Sin, as a wise man once said, is among the few dogmas which can be proven from experience."

Rudi sighed agreement; occasionally Christians just had good points. Then he reined around.

"And now . . . let's go. Thank you, Ingolf . . . Colonel Vogeler. I *did* need to see this, and not myself alone. I suggest men from each battalion be brought here. It's a good thing to know why you're far from home amongst angry strangers."

"Yah." Ingolf's face lost a little of its pinched look, as if he was withdrawing his memory from a very bad place. "That's a good idea. I'll look up Oak, and Eric Larsson, and see to it."

Another courier rode up as they cantered off. "Your Majesty!"

Rudi opened the dispatch. "Ah. Our blocking force caught the Cutters as they attempted to withdraw. Several thousand surrendered."

Everyone looked baffled. "What blocking force would that be?" Lord Maugis asked, transparently glad to have something else to think about. "I didn't think we could get troops much farther north."

"It's a case of . . . how do you Christians put it . . . *bread upon the waters.*"

"Major Graber," Rudi said.

The former officer of the Sword of the Prophet dismounted and came forward with a brisk stride, a medium-tall man in his early middle years dressed in rough plainsman's garb, looking as if rawhide had been wrapped around his bones and covered in weathered skin. The meeting was informal, but it still amounted to pacing between two rows of the High King's Archers with the commanders and contingent leaders from the High

King's Host standing thickly behind them. Everyone who could had come flocking at the news.

There was a rattle and a small instinctive growl from the ranked Montivallan officers as he approached. Rudi smiled at it; just so did dogs growl at a stranger in their territory. Though Rick Three Bears was stone-faced and silent; Graber had personally threatened his clan when they sheltered the Questers. The silence itself was a concession, since it wasn't in his people's customs to forget such a thing.

The small group of Graber's followers who followed behind him had a stiffness that spoke of nervousness.

Though in fact this is Graber's territory, in a sense. And though Nystrup is looking pure murderous hate. Not that I blame him, but the needs of the Kingdom take precedence. Not to mention those of humankind, in the long run.

He turned his head slightly and murmured to the Mormon commander: "Why am I angry because of mine enemy? Awake, my soul! No longer droop in sin. Rejoice, O my heart, and give place no more for the enemy of my soul. Do not anger again because of mine enemies."

Nystrup glanced at him startled—that was from his people's holy book—and angry. Then he nodded slightly.

The last sunlight was dying on the Gallatin peaks to the westward. Rudi stepped forward, pitching his voice to carry.

"This man was my enemy and hunted me and my comrades across the continent on the Quest. He was like a burr on our tail, never giving up, faithful unto death to his pledged word and his lords. Only when they betrayed him and he was shown that they were unworthy of a brave man's loyalty did he renounce them."

He put the palm of his right hand on the pommel of

the Sword for a moment, reminding everyone present that he could detect any deceit.

"And when he did turn on them, he did so honestly and with a whole heart, for right's sake and not for advantage. He risked death by torture and worse to oppose them here on their own ranges, when he might have returned to Montival with me and had a post of honor, because these are his folk and he wished to set them free to live as humankind should once more. Has any man or woman here done more?"

Silence, and the High King went on: "Not to mention he just removed . . . what, twenty-two hundred riders from the enemy's order of battle. Men we will not have to fight again tomorrow, and some of *our* warriors will live, or see their homes again whole of limb because of it."

The almost-grumbling died away. Graber's face was a thing of slabs and angles. He might have renounced his allegiance, but twelve years as cadet in the House of the Prophet had effects he would never shed entirely, not to mention the years as a warrior in Sethaz' army afterwards. It wasn't an accident that the Prophet had assigned him the task of foiling the Quest. Despite that masklike impassiveness there was relief and gratitude in the cold blue eyes. Graber showed unexpected tact when he reached arm's length from Rudi; he gave a military salute, and then sank down on both knees with his hands held forward, palms together.

It didn't surprise Rudi that the man had learned the etiquette used nearer the Pacific, but it was a graceful gesture. The subordinates behind him, his company commanders and staff, went to their knees as well; that meant they gave their assent through their leader.

The High King drew the Sword and planted it in the earth between them. Graber took the hilt between his palms, and Rudi enfolded the other man's hands between his own; that was a *new* custom, the way the High King took fealty, and a guarantee of sincerity on both sides.

Graber's eyes widened a little; touching the Sword of the Lady was never easy, though he had before when Rudi freed him from the bonds laid on his mind. His voice was steady as he spoke, a little harsh but confident:

"I, Justin Graber, pledge my faith and honor to the High King of Montival and to the heirs of his blood; I will be his sworn man in peace and war, with goods and with counsel, with aid and with arms, taking his foes and friends as mine, though my life be the price of this oath. This I swear on my honor as a fighting-man, and by whatever Powers watch over me."

The which he will find, I think. This is a man of faith, and he will hunger for one to replace that which was broken.

"I, Artos, the first of that name, High King in Montival, Son of Raven, Son of Bear, accept your oath, Justin Graber. From this day forth I am your liege-lord. In peace you may hold secure all that is your own under my hand; in need you may appeal to me for aid; in war we shall be comrades of the blade, and I shall ward your family and children at need should you fall in my service. As you keep faith with me, so I will with you: I promise good lordship and fair justice, to you and to those who follow you—"

He added that deliberately, just to drive the point home that Graber's folk—and all the dwellers here not in arms against them—were his subjects now too. He didn't think there was anyone in the Host who still doubted that he meant what he said about things like that. Out of the corner of his eye he could see Mathilda nodding approval, which was reassuring; he had the most profound respect for his wife's political judgment.

"—and I will hold your honor as precious as my own. This oath I will defend at need against all men, and any who do you wrong do also so to me, and at their peril. So I swear by the Lady of Stars and by the Lord Her Consort, and by all the Gods of my people; by Earth, by Sky; and so I bind the line of my blood and yours until the sky fall and crush us, or the sea overwhelm the land, or the world end."

Most of the officers made formal greeting and left; a few came forward to shake Graber's hand. All of the ones who'd been on the Quest did so, and Rudi led them to the open flap of his tent, with a quiet word to have the needs of Graber's subordinates seen to.

"How many in your band?" Rudi asked, when they'd been seated and the plain stew and flatbread brought.

Graber ate with wolfish intensity; he and his were well equipped for the sort of war they practiced in these parts, as far as Rudi had been able to tell, but evidently they hadn't been eating high off the hog. Or the rangeland steer, in this country.

Mind, with years of war levies and now fighting on their own territory, it's going to be touch and go to keep famine out of this land as it is.

"Fifteen hundred, not counting about five hundred women and kids brought along because there wasn't anyplace safe to put them."

Out of the corner of his eye Rudi noted Ignatius making a note and handing it off to a staff messenger who stepped forward at his crooked finger. The quartermasters would be attending to feeding the newcomers by morning.

"Including both my wives and my children; friends helped to get them out before the hunt started. My wives are women of excellent character and acted quickly," Graber added. "The . . . High Seekers seemed curiously blind about what I was doing."

"They would, my friend, after you were touched by the Sword; and they've grown careless about using ordinary means. It's good that you rescued your little ones and their mothers. There are some prices that are steep even for honor; I'm glad you weren't forced to pay so high."

Graber nodded. That had been another risk he'd taken. "And about three times as many have taken up arms against the CUT here and there on their own, once I showed it wasn't just suicide," he said. "I'm in contact with their leaders; that's not counting areas we . . . the Prophet, that is . . . overran in the last few years, they've just gone back to how they were before."

"Not entirely," Father—or in this context, Lord Chancellor—Ignatius said. "The CUT's occupation has left many grudges, many feuds. And the reprisals going on right now against collaborators, or people who their personal rivals and enemies can paint as collaborators, will make for more. We'll be long years settling them."

Graber shrugged; those lands weren't his affair. "A lot more of the Prophet's levies have just gone home—or gone home to defend their ranches and neighborhoods—as they were driven back into the lands they came from. Not to defend from the invading . . . liberating . . . armies, so much, as from bandits and deserters and each other. And, ah—"

"From the Lakota, the ones who aren't riding with the armies," Rudi said ruefully.

He liked and respected the folk of the Seven Council Fires, but they had their own grudges to pay off—and raiding for horses was an ancient tradition with them, one they'd revived gleefully after the Change. Nor did what passed for their central government have all that much control over the individual tribes and clans or for that matter individuals. It operated by consensus, or not at all.

"I'll tend to that, but there're other things must be done first, and I'm afraid some damage will be done."

Graber spread his hands in acknowledgment; it was a cost of finishing the job, and you did what was necessary for that.

Consideringly, Rudi went on: "Fifteen hundred riders . . . that's more than I expected."

Graber gave a rare smile: "For a while I was hiding in the woods with about four men, two of them brothers of my eldest wife, while the Prophet's hunters beat the bush for us and we put our hands over the children's mouths to keep them from giving us away," he said.

"You wouldn't be the first to win back to power and fortune and victory from such a state," Rudi observed. "When we've more time, I'll tell you of a man named Temüjin . . . it means The Iron One . . . in a land far away, but not unlike this in some respects. Cold mountains and vast plains, at least."

Graber looked interested, then returned to business: "But it's been obvious for a while now the Prophet is going to lose the war, especially after news got back of the Horse Heaven Hills, and the Midwesterners started heading our way. The Church, the Church United and Triumphant, that is, got a lot of credit for the way they reestablished order right after the Change, but that ran out some years ago. What they had left was fear."

"And fear alone is a chancy basis for a realm," Rudi said; leaving unsaid that Graber and his ilk had been among the main instruments to instill that terror.

Mathilda nodded decisively. "Fear leaves you with nothing to fall back on when the bad times come," she said, echoing things Rudi had long heard her mother say.

Graber inclined his head; apparently he'd overcome any feeling of shock at a woman speaking in a council. Or wearing breeks and boots, which Matti was.

"True, your Majesty. And I had some other good arguments. Not least, that if we wanted to have any say in how things are arranged here after the war, we'd better show we're willing to fight for the High Kingdom now."

"Good," Rudi said. "A most cogent point. I'm going to need a commander here to keep order, and eventually to rule as my vassal. I've no desire to import battalions of unpopular alien bureaucrats, and more battalions of soldiers to enforce their writ at the sword's edge, and then spend the rest of my days reading and annotating the reports of both. Montival isn't that sort of realm. After things settle down here, the form of rule must arise from the folk themselves, as the years since the Change have shaped them in their hearts. For that I need a man born of these lands who also has a record the rest of Montival will respect, and I think I've found him."

Graber looked blank for a second, and then astonished

when Rudi leveled a finger at him; so did some of the others. Rudi chuckled.

"I'll have to spend more time here than I wish, Major . . . hmmm. We'll come up with some title . . . Range Boss, perhaps? Lord of the Eastern Mark? I'll be wanting a man who understands the land and the folk, for I'll have other calls upon my time, even though this will be Crown land. It's not an easy job I'm offering. The lands long under the CUT have been badly harmed, not least in the minds and souls of those dwelling here. It'll be a lifetime's work to even begin to repair the damage. Will you take it?"

Graber hesitated for a second or two, then nodded decisively. "Yes," he said. "It's necessary."

Then, shrewdly: "And having a local man in charge will make a lot more Ranchers likely to come over willingly—it'll be a sign that bygones are to be bygones and that they won't be excluded from power and office as long as they renounce the CUT."

"Exactly," Mathilda said. "And I don't think anyone will doubt you mean what you say . . . my lord. We found you a very determined man when you were chasing *us*!"

Rudi covered a yawn as the Questers all nodded. "First we must take Corwin. After that . . . more work. But building is more enjoyable than tearing down, even when that's necessary. Even when the building involves cracking a few heads!"

CHAPTER SEVENTEEN

Corwin was falling.

The Earthly House of the Ascended Hierarchy was falling in fire, falling in blood. Everyone who felt like defecting or just absenting themselves had done so, or been killed trying; those who remained were mind-bound or more often the core of real believers who were simply determined to die in the last ditch for their faith. The Montivallan forces were in no more forgiving a mood, after what they'd seen on the way or in the Prophet's capital itself and what had happened to those of their comrades unlucky enough to fall into the enemy's hands.

I would of course prefer that the beithacheen *had a change of heart and surrendered,* Rudi thought, coughing to clear his lungs, leaning back against a broken table and working his left hand where it ached from clenching on the hilt. *But if they won't, I would very much prefer that the irreconcilables die fighting here, rather than taking to the hills.*

The city was smallish and had no wall, but the buildings

were stout and mostly stone-built, windowless on their first floors, and all interlinked both by tunnels and enclosed overhead bridges. Many had nothing but slit windows, no other entrance save the tunnels, and every house had to be reduced and then held lest enemies emerge from hidden exits and attack the assault parties from the rear.

Edain turned, cursed and shot in one movement. A figure above them dropped the rock he'd been hefting to shatter on the granite-block pavement and then followed an instant later, breaking himself and lying limp. The narrow spike of the bodkin head stood up from between his shoulder blades, driven through rear plate of the leather armor by the fall. His helmet clattered away and rolled

"This is like me mother goin' after cockroaches," he said. "Cursing and splashing boiling water to get the last of the little boogers. Wish we could have just stood off and shot at the place with artillery."

"If it wouldn't take forever and a day," Rudi grunted agreement.

He swigged from his canteen and passed it to the master-bowman. They had their backs resting against a barricade of broken furniture, with the bodies of its Cutter defenders still sprawled around them. The troops with them were a mixture—Boisean regulars, dismounted men-at-arms and crossbowmen from the Protector's Guard and Bearkiller A-listers, the High King's Archers and even some of Graber's Montanans. Under their varied gear the faces were much the same, filthy and streaked with soot and sweat and blood and lined with strain and exhaustion. Stretcher-parties had taken the last of the wounded to the rear a few moments ago.

"Water," Matti croaked.

He handed her the container, and she splashed a little on her alarmingly red face before she drank, coughed, drank some more. Huon trotted up from somewhere with a collapsible leather bucket that had probably started its life watering horses, and she plunged her head into it for a long moment to emerge blowing.

"If you're too tired to fight, don't try," he snapped. "I need you alive, not to mention Órlaith. We've enough troops to rotate."

"I'll be fine," she wheezed. "Just needed to cool down for a bit. Mother of *God* but that felt good. Thank you, Huon; hand it around."

It wasn't very hot, even with the soot and flames from a few structures that had caught fire, though that caught at the throat. He was in full plate as well, though—there was nothing like it for close-quarter work—and he could feel how the heat buildup inside dragged at your strength. Even the very fit just tired faster with this carapace strapped all over the body.

"At least I'm getting back in shape," she said, in a more normal voice. "Sort of a drastic exercise program!"

"Let's go," he said, nodding grudging agreement. "Not much farther now."

There was a groan and clank and rustle as everyone levered themselves to their feet. Rudi pushed himself up with the point of his shield—he hadn't bothered to take his right arm out of the loop on the inside of the big teardrop construct of plywood and bullhide and metal when they paused to catch their breath. It was a twenty-pound nuisance, but you only had to look at the stubs of arrows in its surface to see why even full-armored men carried them.

They turned a corner. Corwin was almost all built post-Change, laid out in a manner that Rudi found rather attractive in its way, buildings grouped around small squares. Broader avenues divided the squares in turn; in the central zone they were lined with larger buildings, three or even four stories. Everyone kept a wary eye on them, but apparently the assault groups tasked with it were keeping the inmates busy. This street they'd just entered gave into the central, grander open space where the half-finished ziggurat bulk of the Temple rose in a mass of dark stone and scaffolding.

And it never will be finished, Rudi thought grimly.

They'd managed to overrun the labor camps before all of the slaves who'd been building it could be killed. He wasn't altogether sure how much of a mercy that had been. Many of them were quite mad.

Gliders circled overhead, occasionally darting down to drop message containers with colorful pennants attached; there were a pair of tethered balloons north and south of the city with heliographs, and messengers on foot or horseback or on bicycles dashed about. Mostly it was a matter of small bands hammering their way forward, or even worse of men fighting and dying in the closed spaces of the underground warren, daggers and short-gripped spears and fists and feet and teeth in the dark.

Ahead was one last barricade, this one apparently mainly made of rough sacks filled with something lumpy—he guessed that it was potatoes, from the size. Hooves clattered behind him, and he looked around: it was a battery of three Bearkiller scorpions, medium fieldpieces each drawn by three pair of horses, with the snarling red bear's head on the shields.

More surprisingly, Eric Larsson was with them at the head of a squad of Bearkiller A-listers in their plain good armor, a big blond man with a steel prosthetic where his left hand had been until a few years ago. The Bearkiller war-leader reined his horse in and looked at the barricade; an arrow shot from behind it sparked on the stone blocks of the road's pavement not far in front. Knights of the Protector's guard formed up before the leaders, one line kneeling and the other standing with their shields raised to form a wall of overlapping protection.

"It's not a cataphract's battle," Eric said at Rudi's raised eyebrows as he dismounted and his troops followed.

He turned reins bridle over to his military apprentice, who was also his son William, a tall youth of nearly eighteen with an arresting combination of skin on the cusp between light brown and very dark olive, midnight blue eyes and curling brown hair. Rudi nodded to the young man, who responded with a slight crisp inclination of the head and then stood in silent, focused readiness in the Bearkiller manner. His father went on:

"Hell, it's more of a giant brawl, most of our A-listers are fighting dismounted. Good practice in being flexible. The Norrheimers are coming up, I pulled them out of reserve before they mutinied at being left out. Gotta be careful with those Asatruar types. They tend to start baying at the moon if you keep 'em from a fight. Something about the Nine Impulsive Vices or something like that. I just tune Signe out when she gets on about it."

Rudi nodded; the words were only slightly in jest. Eric and his son both had crucifixes around their necks—he had become a Catholic when he married his half-Tejano wife Luanne just after the Change—but Signe's branch of the family followed those Gods.

"Ah, excellent," he said. "Bjarni and his band are good at this."

"Yeah, he's hell on wheels in a close-in fight, and no mistake, and so are all his merry band," Eric said with complete seriousness.

Then he grinned; it made his face look younger than his forty-four years. When he leaned forward he whispered a little:

"As my sister could testify, especially about Bjarni."

Rudi looked a question and he went on:

"Signe's expecting and refuses to say who's the other party . . . to the very few who dare to ask, of which I was one. Only by letter, though. But just between me and thee, I strongly suspect . . ."

Rudi chuckled; he wouldn't have expected it, but he supposed she was still beneath the Moon . . . his own mother had been older when she bore Fiorbhinn. Motherhood had never mellowed Signe before—she was as fierce as a she-wolf with her cubs—but one could hope.

The crews had been putting the scorpions into operation as they spoke, lifting the trails off the limbers and swiveling them around before splaying them open. Sledgehammers rang as they hammered spikes into the cracks between paving blocks to anchor it—the usual method of digging in the hinged spades at the ends of the trails wouldn't do for absorbing the recoil here. A clanking tramp sounded behind, and the Norrheimers were there, with their standard at their head.

That banner had been that of Bjarni's father, Eric the Strong. The flag had a stiffener jutting out from the top of the pole at right angles, and a curved outer edge bore bullion tassels. The rim of the cloth was black, the center white, and on it a stylized black raven—for the birds Thought and Memory who sat on the shoulders of Odhinn Father of Victories and whispered wisdom in his ears. On the bird's breast was a double letter A, the outer strokes curved and the inner straight and parallel. The flag commemorated a band of pre-Change warriors Eric had fought with as well as his faith; he had borne it north with his followers and friends into what had once been Maine right after the Change, from which much had followed.

The redbeard had his four-foot axe over his shoulder; the outer edge had been hastily wiped so that a nick could be ground out and the edge redone, but the rest of it was thickly clotted. His followers came up behind him in a bristle of spears and swords and eyes glaring beneath nose-guarded conical helms, their big round shields making a wall. Their byrnies of chain or scale mail clinked as they moved.

"Awkward as hogs on ice are these Cutters, when they fight on foot," the king of Norrheim said cheerfully. "Still, warm work."

Rudi held out a hand, and he clasped wrists in the fashion of the folk of that far bleak land, and then both did the same with Eric.

"This may be our last battle together, blood brother," Rudi said to Bjarni.

"Good. We've been doing a man's work, but it's time for us to go home."

He looked admiringly as the Bearkiller crew worked the levers of the hydraulic pump that cocked their weapon and loaded a globe of cast steel into the trough. His shrewd blue eyes took in the barricade. Rudi could guess why he grinned; if there was one thing someone from Norrheim— what had once been northern Maine—was going to recognize at first glance, it was a sack of a certain root vegetable. He called over his shoulder to his followers:

"They want us to peel their potatoes for them! Then we'll have meat with the mashed, boiled and fried!"

A roar of hoarse laughter went up; that was just the sort of jest to tickle a Norrheimer funny bone. Rudi glanced around, nodded crisply, and spoke:

"Now!"

Whung-whap!

The catapults spoke one after another, the wheels coming up a little and then thumping down again. Long bowshot to the west top of the barricade fountained up in a shower of burlap and fragments of root vegetable . . . and men. They waited while the throwing-machines worked their way along the parapet, knocking it down into a slumped chaos in a steady rhythm of one shot every four seconds, and then the bowmen trotted forward.

"Let the gray geese fly!" Edain barked. "Wholly together—*shoot!*"

A hundred bows snapped, and the arrows sleeted down. For once, Rudi felt little of the grim urgency of impending battle, only a smoldering anger at the necessity of it.

I've done this too often for too long, he thought. *I'm . . . not quite bored with it, but nearly. It's time to finish it. This isn't the climax of my life, it's something I have to get out of the way before I get on with my life.*

One thing the bards usually didn't talk about was the

essential *sameness* of battle; there was more variety to farming. He judged, knocked down his visor, glared through the vision slit at a world like a bright distant painting. . . .

"*Morrigú!*" he shouted, and charged.

"*Ho la*, Odhinn!" Bjarni roared.

"Haro, Portland! Holy Mary for Portland!" Mathilda shrieked, not a step behind.

"*Haakaa päälle!*"

"*Artos and Montival!*"

The catapults and the longbowmen kept shooting as long as they could—beside Rudi a knight swore and ducked as a cloth-yard shaft zipped by and clipped the last ostrich plume from the rather ragged assembly on his helmet. The Bearkiller artillerists had all the self-confidence that common wisdom said their folk showed—some called it arrogance—and the last ball thumped home in the tumbled arrow-studded sacks when the front rank of the Montivallans was only thirty yards from their goal.

It was good to keep the enemy's heads down; bad to have yours smacked right off your shoulders by a six-pounder ball fired from behind you. That last one left a Boisean white-faced and sweating as it went overhead so fast that it was a mere blurred streak and so close that the wind of its passage made him stagger. Then Frederick Thurston's men threw their heavy javelins and drew their short swords.

The surviving Cutters popped up again, but they had time for only one volley of arrows from their powerful horn-backed bows as the Montivallans stormed up the obstacle in a roaring wave of shields and blades. One whistled by Rudi, another went *thwack* into his shield with a hard sound and a feeling like a blow from a club. The High King sprang up the remains of the barricade, agile as a great hunting tiger in the sixty pounds of steel despite the shifting footing. A shete tried to stop the Sword of the Lady, and the tough spring steel was shorn straight through. The man beneath spun away clutching at his severed throat . . .

When he fought with his own hands, there was a . . . going away, since the Sword came, a madness that was completely lucid. Black wings bore him up, amid a storm of buffetings. More of the guardsmen crowded ahead as the fight tumbled down the inner side of the barricade. Their shields came up to protect the monarchs and Rudi shoved his visor up again as he came back to himself and stood on a sack to give himself a better view. Across the square a snarling scrimmage of fighting at the entrance to an avenue broke apart, and a walking wall of leveled pike-points came through, marching to a hammer of drums and a wordless chant of *ha*-ba-da, *ha*-ba-da . . .

A flick of his glance right and left, and only the details were different; the Cutters had been pushed back into the open space at last, where the westerners' numbers and drill could take effect.

"Let's go," he said.

He'd been afraid they'd have to dig the Prophet out of some underground lair, or wall him in and never be completely sure there hadn't been some path of escape. Instead Sethaz stood at the last step below the platform where scaffolding and scattered blocks of stone told of decades of labor. His shete was in his hand; he was protected by two men with great round shields, but every now and then the steel would flick out and come back red.

This high up the pyramidal structure the artillery couldn't be elevated enough to fire, but archers could. Carts were carrying bundles of shafts in a ceaseless stream from the reserves, and sighing clouds of gray-feathered cloth-yard arrows and stubby crossbow bolts went by overhead, sweeping the upper steps, their impact like the sound of hail on tile roofs. The dead were thick despite shields and what armor they had, and blood ran down the granite and made it slippery beneath the foot. The stink of it was thick, iron and copper and salt, the butcher's smell of battlefields redoubled—this was a huge building, but still more packed and smaller than any open field could be. The noise was stunning, individual voices and even the hammering pulse of the Mackenzie Lambegs lost in an all-consuming white roar.

The heavy-armed troops of the High King's Host fought their way upward, shields up against spears and blades stabbing and beating from above—the steps of the structure were around three feet tall, just enough to make the business as difficult as possible, like always fighting against mounted men in the perfect position to strike downward.

"Ready—*now!*" Rudi called. *"Follow me!"*

Pikes slanted forward from behind, jabbing over their shoulders. He turned a spearhead with his shield—the fourth he'd had that day—and chopped. A young man in red armor blocked desperately with his shield, bringing it awkwardly across to face the left-handed attack; the Sword cut through a section of the bullhide and wicker and into his leg above the knee and through the bone.

Rudi snarled, *"Morrigú!"*, crouched and leapt.

The dark wings of the Crow Goddess indeed seemed to bear him up. He landed, buffeted one man aside with his shield, took off a hand at the wrist and shoved his way into the gap made when that man turned shrieking and sprayed blood into the eyes of his comrades. Blades hammered at him, thudding on his shield and cracking off the smooth steel of his armor.

"Jesu-Maria," Ignatius wheezed, somehow beside him.

An arrow flashed *between* them and into the face of a spearman, Edain shooting from recklessly close. Matti was back at the base of the Temple, directing operations and feeding in reserves with a wrenched knee—some distant walled-off part of him was glad of it. One more step, and the Cutters would be forced back onto the flat unfinished top, where there was no protection.

Moving with a unison like one man monarch and monk hacked down the shieldmen protecting the Prophet and went in to kill.

Sethaz blocked a Bearkiller backsword hacking for his leg, kicked out and sent Eric Larsson tumbling backward with a yell and a dented breastplate, killed a Boisean with a slash that laid his arm open from elbow to wrist, launched a flurry of strikes at Ignatius that sent the warrior Benedictine down on one knee, guarding frantically.

Rudi lunged. The Sword slid along the Prophet's shete, the counter cunningly sloped to keep the supernal edge from chopping through mere steel. Sethaz' other hand snapped out and took him by the throat like a grab made of steel and gears. The metal of his bevoir began to grate and crumple.

"I . . . see . . . you . . ." he grated, in a voice like the death of stars.

And the world vanished.

Too big, Rudi thought.

He was nowhere, and everywhere. It was dark and utterly cold and all that was material had vanished so long ago that even the memory of it was gone, but there was order here, complexity, a structure that vibrated at a level next to which atoms were coarse and chaotic as a lump of horse-dung. There was a beauty that he could not grasp, that left him weak with longing, and thoughts rushed by like huge glowing matrixes of the pure sublime. He could not grasp them, but if he could, even the least of them, he knew he would be utterly transformed, lost and yet fulfilled beyond all reckoning. . . .

They vanished, and he was Rudi Mackenzie once again, crying out with grief and loss for an instant.

Then he gained command of himself; what he had . . . not seen, there was nothing for light to reflect off in that place, but somehow apprehended, fled like a dream. It was too *big* to remember.

Instead he was in a forest. A real forest, as far as he could tell, though not of trees he was very familiar with; he could see the great trunks rising around him like reddish pillars upholding the sky, smell a green spiciness, hear the trickle of falling water. Light speared down between the needled boughs so far above, and smaller plants reached for it. Birds whistled and chirped, and insects buzzed; a hummingbird circled him in blue iridescence and then departed. He turned and walked along the creek that tumbled over lustrous brown stream-polished stones, conscious that he was no longer wearing the battered, blood-spattered armor or the sweat-stinking arming doublet below; instead he was in kilt and knee-hose and schoon, saffron-dyed linen shirt and plaid pinned over his shoulder.

The sun was slanting to the westward, and the air grew a little colder. The light was golden—somehow, more real than a nugget of the metal itself, be it polished never so bright. He walked in a dream, but it was more *real* than the waking world. Suddenly he dropped his hand to the pommel of the Sword of the Lady at his right hip. It was thee, but . . .

It feels . . . at home. Without that sense that the world might rip around it. Here, the world itself is like that. More real, more itself. *Myself it is that feels fragile and not-quite-real.*

A fire flickered through the gathering dusk. He walked into the circle of its light, his feet soft on the duff and fallen ferns.

"Ladies," he said, with a deep bow.

As once before on Nantucket, there were Three. This time he knew all the faces. The youngest was his sister Fiorbhinn, a maiden of a little more than twelve summers; slender but strong, breasts just beginning to bud beneath her pale gown, white-blond hair torrenting down on her shoulders, and a small harp on her knee. The huge pale blue eyes met his, depths within depths. . . .

He took a deep breath and looked at the others; Mathilda, her slightly irregular face beautiful as she looked down at the swaddled form of Órlaith on her knee, and his mother Juniper—but not the hale, graying figure of eight-and-fifty that he knew in this twenty-

eighth year of the Change. This woman in tunic and ar-
said was Juniper Mackenzie as she might be in the years
of her deep age, hair snowy, face deeply lined, a little
stooped as she leaned on the carved rowan staff of a High
Priestess topped by the silver moon waxing and full and
waning. The leaf-green eyes were nearly the same, warm
and kind.

"Are—" he began, then stopped. *Maiden, Mother,
Crone,* he thought. *Of course. How otherwise?*

Fiorbhinn laughed. "Of course we are who we seem.
All our seemings. And not. Time is different here."

"And there are no words for it all," Rudi said patiently.
"I'm no longer angry at that. Irritated, perhaps."

All three of the Ladies smiled. The youngest spoke
again:

"If we could explain—"

"You would, yes." A thought occurred to him. "Was that
place . . . that place I was . . . was that how this really is?"

His nod took in the forest, and the frosted glory of
stars that was showing overhead, brighter and more colorful than any he had ever seen, even in glimpses beneath
the black swaying shapes of the treetops.

His mother spoke. "No. That was the . . . heaven, you
might say . . . the dream of the Powers behind the CUT.
Behind many another dream of men. Dreams of order
and of knowledge . . . in the beginning."

He blinked, shocked. Mathilda spoke: "You've been
told before, that *here* this is not a war between good and
evil."

"It most certainly is in the world of common day!"
Rudi said, and they all looked at him with fondness clear
in their eyes.

"Yes, it is," Juniper said. "That is the shadow it throws there, and those in the cave see it upon the wall. And it is true, what they see. But . . . let me ask you: which is better, the utterly particular, or the absolutely infinite? Immanence or transcendence?"

"I'm tired of shadows!" Rudi said. "And—with respect—tired of moving amid forces the which I cannot understand!"

"You may understand if you will, brother," Fiorbhinn . . . possibly Fiorbhinn said, her voice as her name, *truesweet*. "That is why you are here, to make that choice."

He looked up again, and the stars *spoke*; if only he could read that vast slow dance it would be *everything*. Rest that was high adventure, infinite knowledge that was just a beginning, home and a journey without end . . .

Mathilda spoke. "You have done everything you were born to do, my beloved," she said. "Thus is the will of God fulfilled."

"You have sung a good song," Fiorbhinn added. "One that echoes even here."

"You have earned homecoming, if you choose it," his mother said, and there were tears in her eyes. "Homecoming beyond all sorrow, beyond all loss."

Slowly, Rudi bowed his head in thought. "What is a man, if he should leave those he loves?" he said at last.

"I *am* here," Mathilda said. "We all are. Time is different here, and choices."

Rudi raised his eyes to the stars again, feeling himself begin to fall out among them. As one himself, a star in glory . . . but that was only a symbol, a thing his mind clutched to give him words for something beyond words.

Then he lowered his eyes again, his smile crooked. "What is a man, if he puts aside his work?" he said. "I don't ask you, Ladies, if it is finished. Just that I be given the time to do it, needed or no."

Silently they rose and passed him, each pausing to press her lips to his forehead.

Sethaz staggered back, snarling. The Sword moved once more, and he gasped as the not-steel transfixed him, then half fell backward off it and dropped his shete as he went to one knee. A hand pressed to the blood welling out through the slit in his armor.

"I . . ." he began.

Then the rage left his face, and he looked at the blood on his hand. "So . . . pure. I wanted it to be . . . pure."

And he fell, features slack against the bloody stone, years seeming to melt from them. Until he was merely a man, dead among so many.

Rudi raised his eyes to the blue of the sky, and let the tears well past his closed lids.

PART TWO

THE SPRING QUEEN

CHAPTER EIGHTEEN

BARONY HARFANG
COUNTY OF CAMPSCAPELL
(FORMERLY EASTERN WASHINGTON STATE)
HIGH KINGDOM OF MONTIVAL
(FORMERLY WESTERN NORTH AMERICA)
AUGUST 28TH, CHANGE YEAR 32/2030 AD

Órlaith Arminger Mackenzie wasn't bored with the train ride, though they'd been travelling for days. There were too many interesting things to watch outside the windows. Besides, she was with her mother, and her father, and they were the most fun people in the world. And Butterball, her new pony, was in a car of his very own at the end of the train, and she could go and visit him any time she wanted, and ride him when they stopped to change teams or visit.

Also her puppy Maccon was back there. Maccon meant *Son of a Wolf*, but Maccon's grandmother was Garbh. Garbh had been Uncle Edain's dog on the Quest, and bards had made *songs* about her, which hardly ever happened with dogs, though it had with Da's famous horse Epona. Maccon would be just as brave and loyal and fierce as Garbh had been, when he was big, and go on adventures with her. He was already brave for a puppy, and smart, too—he already knew her and licked her face whenever she came. Uncle Edain had said that he'd train them both up, and teach Maccon not to chew her shoes, which he'd done with her *best* shiny red silk ones.

She folded up her book, which was about Dorothy of Oz with pictures, put it neatly away in the bookshelf with the strap as Dame Emelina had taught her; Dame Emelina was wonderful, but strict. Then she knelt on the seat and looked out of the window with her elbows on the sill; the leather cushion made a sort of sighing sound. She liked the story, and she could read now.

Well, read a bit, she thought, with stubborn honesty. *Some of the words are still too hard.*

But after a while she wanted to *move*. The window was pushed up, so she could put her head out and let her long yellow hair fly in the breeze of their passage, and the air was hot with summer and smelled like dust and dry hay and a little like thunder somehow—she was glad she was in a kilt and shirt, though they were here in the north. The new girl's kirtle she'd gotten for her birthday was very pretty, with little birds around the hems in silver and gold thread that sparkled, but it could be too warm for anything but sitting around. She had to sit around sometimes, but she didn't like it.

There were hills outside, odd smooth-looking ones, this was a place called the *Palouse* that was all hills but no rocks, and the railroad wound like a snake through them, staying on the tops of the ridges mostly. A little while ago she'd seen a herd of Appaloosa horses running across them, with their manes flying in the bright sunshine and their coats all spotted against the brown of the summer pastures. Da had taken her up the ladder onto the roof of the car, where a couple of the archers rode, and stood with her on his shoulders so she could watch and wave and whoop. Now the ground was sort of a dark yellow where the wheat had been, and there were rows and rows of sheaves piled up together in tripods curving across the hills, brighter yellow than the stubble, looking like . . .

"Tipis!" she said. "They look like tipis! Like the *La-ko-tah* had when they came on the visit. Chief Three Bears said I could sleep in a tipi sometime!"

Her father looked up and smiled, his blue-green eyes crinkling. He was the handsomest man in the world, and the bravest knight, and he was King. It was wonderful that he was King, though it meant he was busy a lot of the time. Now he put down the paper he'd been reading and came across and knelt down on the floor by the seat so that their eyes were level as he looked out the window.

"Well, by the Powers, so they do!" he said.

"Can I really sleep in a tipi?"

He nodded solemnly. "That you can, if Rick promised you could, for he is a great warrior and a wise chief and a man of honor; also he has little girls your age and knows their ways and how important a promise is."

"Can I sleep in a *Lakota* tipi?" she said, thinking of the stories about the lords of the high plains. "Chief Three Bears fought with you in the great battles, didn't he?"

"Not only that, he aided me on the Quest, when we used a stampeding buffalo herd to hide us from the Cutters who pursued us."

"I remember that story!" she said, eyes shining. "That must have been the most fun ever!"

There was something a little odd in his laugh. "It was . . . exciting, that it was in truth. And so the Seven

Council Fires are also among our peoples. In a few years you'll come with your mother and I when we go east for the summer buffalo hunt. You can see the Sun Festival where the camps of the Lakota carpet the prairie, and the dancers, and the great stone faces carved by the old Americans into the Black Hills, the kings of the ancient world. They'll give you a Lakota name, and perhaps you will become one of the girls who apprentice to the White Buffalo Woman's Society or the Sacred Shawls, and you will indeed sleep in a tipi. Though the Lakota themselves sleep in ger, most of the time now—tents on wheels with round tops. Tipis are for ceremony, to respect their ancestors."

She laughed and clapped her hands at the thought of the tipis and the gers, and put an arm around his neck; his hair was redder than hers and had less yellow, and smelled like summer.

"That sounds like a lot of fun!"

"It will be." He turned and kissed her cheek, his mustache tickling a little so that she giggled. "But it will be important too, for these are sacred things. You understand?"

She nodded solemnly. Then something occurred to her.

"Da," she said. "I was wondering. The horses make the train go, don't they? Walking on that treadmill thing up at the front."

"Indeed they do."

"But how can we go so fast? This is like a gallop. Horses can't go this fast for long. Horsemaster Raoul told me so, that it would hurt them if you made them go fast for too long."

"Very true, and when he speaks on horses Sir Raoul is

a man to listen to most carefully. It's the gearing that lets them do it, so that they walk at their best pace and the wheels are made to go faster."

He held up a hand. "I'll show you later, and you can help grease the gears, but don't expect to understand it right away. 'Tis a mystery of the mechanics, and requires mathematics to really know."

"Oh."

She pouted a little. She wanted to understand it *now*, and usually her father and mother would explain things to her, though the greasing part sounded like fun. Math was . . . OK, she supposed. She could already add some numbers, but the times table was too difficult for now. Then something else occurred to her.

"Why does the train go more clackety-clack now than it did yesterday?"

"Ah, well, that I can explain. In the ancient times, the trains were much bigger and heavier than they are now, and they needed rails of solid steel, which we still use where they remain and which are very smooth. But now in modern times, when we lay more track we make wooden rails and then fasten a strip of steel on top. That's fine for our trains, and takes less of the metal, which has many uses. The rails here were torn up during the war, and now we've fixed them . . . the Lady Tiphaine and the Lord Rigobert have, their folk . . . and that's why the noise is different."

She nodded happily; she liked knowing why things were the way they were. Her father sat back in the seat, and she sat back in his lap; he put an arm around her. His arms were long, and you could feel how strong they were, almost the way you did when you touched a horse; when he threw her up in the air it was fun-scary, like being a bird and flying until she swooped down and he caught her. When she watched him practicing at arms with the guards, it was almost really scary sometimes, but when he held her like this it made her feel very safe, like pulling up the covers in winter when a storm was lashing against the windows and draughts made the candles flicker.

Her mother was in the seats across from them, which were like a big sofa; she was in a travelling habit, brown hakama divided skirt and a green jacket with pretty jade buttons over a blouse, not the High Queen's court dresses that shimmered. But the little golden spurs on her boots showed she was a knight too, who'd ridden with Da on the Quest and his adventures.

Her little brother John was curled up with his head in their mother's lap, snoring a little. John was only four, and still napped a lot; he had brown hair like their mother and looked more like Mom, when he wasn't just looking like a baby. But he could *sing* already, better than her at least; the court troubadour said he had perfect pitch, which meant he could listen to a note and make the same one.

Sometimes that drove her crazy, because he'd pick two or three and do them over and over and laugh. She loved him but he could be a jerk and of course he was still so *young*.

Mom was dozing too. There was going to be a new sister around Yule, and that made her sleepy a lot; Órlaith couldn't remember much about when John came, she'd been just a two-year-old herself then. The High Queen opened her eyes and smiled at Órlaith and then closed them again, letting her head fall back against the cushion.

Her round hat with the trailing veils was hung from the back of it, the peacock feathers standing up.

The railcar swayed and clacked. It was just like a nice room on wheels, there were chairs and sofas, rugs with flowers and vines, and a table where they'd had lunch, and where she sat with picture books and coloring books and did her lessons with Dame Emelina. There were ten more cars in the train, including the one with the little beds that folded down, which she liked.

"Will Heuradys and Yolande be there when we get to Lady Tiphaine's manor?"

"Yes, they will; and their father, and their mother."

"Oh, good," Órlaith said.

She could feel her father's deep chuckle through his tunic—he was wearing shirt and jerkin and breeks and a T-tunic, the way people did up here, rather than a kilt the way he did down in the Mackenzie lands.

"Indeed, and it's good for you to have some your own age to play with."

"They're nice, but they're not my age. Well, Heuradys isn't. She's older."

"Not so much."

"Two whole *years* older," she said. "And don't say it isn't important. It is, and Heuradys thinks so too."

He laughed, his beard tickling her neck. "To be sure, darlin' girl, that's the third of a lifetime, isn't it? I was forgetting."

"I like their Mom, though. Tell me a story. Tell me how you snuck into Boise and opened the gate!"

"I and some others. Well, if you must, though you've heard it before."

"I want to know all the stories! I need to hear it a lot so I'll remember all the parts. You have the best stories, anyway."

"It's my life, darlin' girl, but I suspect it's your story the now."

She wasn't sure exactly what that meant, but she settled back to hear his voice.

"There we were, sitting outside Boise, and no way of getting through the walls. Well, now, if you can't go through, you must go around; but there's no way around a city wall, for the wall itself goes around. And if you can't go through, and you can't go around, you must go over or under. Men holding a wall watch for you to try *over*—so, we thought, what about under? Now, Fred's father—"

Rudi set Órlaith down and sent her to Dame Emelina as the whine of the locomotive's gearing died, more conspicuous by its absence for a moment. Mathilda's lady-in-waiting and tirewoman appeared as if by magic to tidy her up as the train coasted into the village of St. Athena—theoretically named for a virgin martyr who'd died in Thrace about seventeen hundred years ago, though Rudi had his doubts; the other train of the Royal party was already there, having put on a sprint, and the two-score of the High King's Archers were already double-timing over to line up before he got down and stand in ranks with their longbows in their arms. Through the window he heard Edain say:

"Now, let's show these haughty northern lords that we know how to . . . Talyn, for Lugh of the Long Hand's own sake, try to look like you didn't spend the afternoon muckin' out a byre, man!"

Mathilda yawned a little as she checked that her habit was tidy and let the tirewoman redo her braids and put them up under the broad-brimmed hat and scarf.

"How are you feeling, my love?" he said.

"Worn out, but no worse." She crossed herself and made a gesture of steepling her hands. "But thanking *God* and the Virgin that the morning sickness is over," she said; she was pious, but not sanctimonious. "Though why they call it *morning* sickness . . ."

"A wishful hope, perhaps," he said, making the sign of the Horns.

He was thankful to the Mother as Brigid, she Who watched over childbirth, and as Matti's blue-mantled patron too that her births had all been—relatively—easy, with no complications. Hopefully this one would be too, and he had reason to so hope . . . but no certainty.

Dame Emelina had the children in hand; literally, with a hand to each. He gave her a friendly nod. She had dark freckles across skin a few shades lighter, handsome full features and keen black eyes; she'd been Órlaith's wet-nurse, having lost her own babe about the time Mathilda was brought to bed, but she'd also been a scholar of sorts before her husband—a belted knight and an Associate, but the third-son-of-a-second-son variety—was killed at the Horse Heaven Hills.

Between her own good birth and years of being Órlaith's wet-nurse it had been possible to appoint her to the governess position without offending any of the great houses in the old Protectorate who'd have schemed to get the job for protégés or daughters unlikely to do it with half her skill or devotion. They'd put out that Matti was deeply attached to her, which was simply true. Sandra had arranged the whole thing to start with, and that triple-play was like her.

"There will probably be a chorus of children and a bouquet," he said.

"I'll bear up," Mathilda said as she took his arm. "Let's not disappoint the audience."

"And my mother says a travelling bard's job was hard back before the Change," he said. "Always putting on a show. At least nobody gave her a second glance when she was driving her wagon around the Willamette between performances!"

He'd sent instructions for minimal ceremony, and he knew the Grand Constable shared his sentiments on that sort of thing most exactly. Her Châtelaine . . . not necessarily so much, but she would do her best.

A cheer went up as they descended from the train; varlets were bustling about, unloading gear down to Órlaith's pony, and Maccon in a basket—quite a substantial one, for the young beast had huge ears and paws already. A bright eye and pulsing black nose were visible through the wicker, wiggling with the desire to get out and smell and taste and acquire new admirers. This was an informal visit—up here in the Protectorate he generally used the full fig of a Crown visitation only on nobles he didn't trust, that being a polite way to use up resources they might otherwise put to mischief. They couldn't even complain, since it was an honor.

D'Ath was there, leaning on a stick, and Lady Delia with a lacy parasol protecting her creamy skin. Rigobert de Stafford was too, his bowl-cut blond hair and short dense beard showing a little more nearly invisible gray as he doffed his chaperon hat. So was his current partner, Sir Julio Alvarez de Soto, a slim handsome swarthy man in his thirties, quiet and dangerous-looking in dark country-gentry clothes that contrasted with Rigobert's peacock fashionability of blue velvet, black satin and crimson linings on the sleeves of his houppelande. He still had the lean erect broad-shouldered build to carry it off, though, and Rudi hadn't the slightest doubt that when he didn't he'd switch to something more appropriate.

That's six years they've been together, since the tag end of the war, so perhaps Rigobert is settling down in middle-age.

He hoped so; he liked the Baron of Forest Grove, both as a man and a valuable servant of the Crown, and had sensed a loneliness under his good humor and active social life.

Lord Maugis de Grimmond, Baron of Tucannon, was there too, and his wife Lady Helissent, and their son Aleaume, now a likely-looking lad of twelve just home for a holiday from page service in Walla Walla to Lord Maugis' overlord Count Felipe.

And taking after his mother, save for that rusty-nail hair—which is to the good because Maugis is, frankly, a homely man. It's also a very good thing they haven't far to come from Grimmond-on-the-Wold, which keeps this all looking completely casual and social, which it is, only not totally.

Mathilda made a gesture—hand palm-down and then turned up, which was Associate court etiquette for *don't kneel*. The noblemen and women responded with deep sweeping bows and curtsies respectively, except for the

Grand Constable who bowed as well. The assembled commons behind the gentlefolk knelt anyway, several hundred of them in their best Sunday-go-to-Church outfits, splashes of embroidery on hems and necks, bright printed wimples for the women. The village priest signed the air.

"Rise, my friends," Rudi said; they did, and cheered, waving straw hats and holding up children to see.

Pleasant to be popular; and to be sure, they get a party at their baron's expense out of it, he thought.

Yearling steers and pigs were roasting over open pits in the town square, filling the air with a pleasant savor as cooks basted them with paintbrush-sized brushes on the end of long sticks, and trestle tables had been set up with wheels of cheese and bowls and dishes of each household's prize contribution, and barrels were waiting in the shade along with tall baskets of new loaves. Another carried the lutes and hauteboys, drums and accordion that would provide music for the dancing later.

He and Mathilda extended their hands for the kiss of homage. The Grand Constable was limping and using her stick as she came forward.

"How is the leg, Tiph?" Mathilda asked.

"Healing, but damned slowly," d'Ath said. "He shouldn't have been able to touch me. I was careless."

"He was *twenty-five* and you're *forty-six*!" Lady Delia said sharply. "You're not getting those awful *lettres de cachet* from Sandra anymore, you don't have to *do* this."

A small chilly reminiscent smile from Tiphaine: "*The bearer has done what has been done by my authority, and for the good of the State.* Sandra always absolutely *loved* writing those. That was back before she got religion, of course."

Mathilda winced. Baron Tucannon looked up briefly as if considering the weather, unconsciously disassociating himself from the display of high-level dirty linen, while his son looked bewildered at the byplay and his wife carefully blank-faced. Rigobert simply laughed. Delia cleared her throat and went on:

"And you shouldn't be fighting duels at your age anyway! I spent far too much time sending you off to the wars; now that you're home I expect you to *live* for a while."

Her eyes flashed; she was in her thirties herself, and one of the most beautiful women Rudi had ever seen in a sweetly curved way, with translucent eyes the color of camas flowers in a cloud-shaded mountain meadow and hair of iridescent black, glimpsed in braids beneath her tall headdress. She had a reputation as an arbiter of fashion, which she showed now by the elegant variation on what she had christened *afternoon dress*. August in the Palouse was hot to people used to the Willamette. Lady Delia's red linen shift came to a daring two inches above her ankles, trimmed with a ruching of darker red and a scatter of pink ribbon roses. It was sleeveless and the light silk half-dress over it was a pale pink that took the warm tone below. From the waist to the knee it descended in long thin daggers of cloth, each neatly bordered with cream and crimson. The sort-of-sleeves were also dags of the translucent silk, dangling to her elbows and more thickly embroidered. Her wimple was more of the pink silk, held in place by a light ribbon braid in graduated pinks and reds, cascading down her back.

Rudi caught Helissent and Mathilda's tire-women both eyeing it intently, clearly memorizing details for later. Lady d'Ath's irritated answer brought him back from contemplation of feminine frivolities, though he'd always found Delia's skills in that regard seriously impressive.

"I'm alive and getting older, and he isn't, like that uncle of his I killed back in the old days," d'Ath pointed out. "And *he* challenged *me*, not vice versa."

"And forbye, for that very reason if he were alive, he'd be in very bad trouble," Rudi said grimly.

"I'm Grand Constable, for what it's worth these days," d'Ath said. "That's a Protectorate appointment, covering the Association, not one by the High King. You couldn't have touched him, legally."

"*I* could," Matti said flatly. "I'm Lady Protector. And I *would*."

There were two carriages drawn up with the d'Ath arms on the doors; sable, a delta Or over a V argent. They managed to disengage themselves, after the inevitable bouquet and chorus of children, singing quite nicely under the direction of a young and nervous priest, and after a sharp glare from the Baroness of Ath and a quiet word from Delia dissuaded the bailiff of the estate from proceeding from an introduction to a plan for a tour of the newly installed and state-of-the-art dam, well, hydraulic ram, windmill and solar-heated waterworks that he obviously had his heart set upon.

Rudi grinned to himself. He'd just received an anguished howl in the form of a petition from some Corvallan manufacturers complaining that workshops in Portland and Walla Walla had stolen the thermosiphon design. He'd replied politely, pointing out that the Faculty Senate had refused to include a patent law in the Great Charter and that they might want to take it up with them . . .

Tiphaine grumbled as she levered herself up into one of the coaches, and the High King's Archers deployed their bicycles; there were a dozen men-at-arms on coursers and mounted archers on quarter-horses, their look of grim efficiency marking them as much as the d'Ath arms, and smaller detachments from the *menies* of the other nobles. Rudi sympathized with the injured Grand Constable as he handed Mathilda up and seated himself; he would vastly have preferred riding horseback, after days of sitting in a train. There had been times he was tempted to go walk the treadmill with the horses, not being a man used to inactivity. Órlaith was on her Butterball, to the unspeakable envy of all the other noble children.

The whole settlement was on the south-facing slope of a declivity in the hills. The carriages jounced across the stone-paved central square with its church, tavern, smithy and workshops, school, bakery, bathhouse-laundry. There was rather more than the average, since this was to be the home-manor of the whole estate, and had a railway to boot. A long low building with large windows was a weaving-shed, where households with a loom could use it and store their yarn and gear without cluttering up the house; behind the whole ensemble was the tall skeletal shape of the village windmill on the ridgetop, its three airfoil-shaped vanes rotating with majestic deliberation.

The village was raw and new, the trees and plantings still small and struggling, but looked prosperous; the tile-roofed rammed-earth cottages of the peasants and craftsmen were on lanes lined with young trees, each in its rectangular fenced toft with sheds and gardens at the rear. Even the small dwellings of the cottar laborers had three rooms and a loft and an acre of allotment ground attached. A few excited peasant youngsters ran after them waving as they drove up the winding road to the manor between rows of fir saplings; Órlaith waved back with a broad smile, and various mothers and elder siblings dragged the youngsters back, often by one ear.

The manor sat on its own gentle south-facing slope some distance away, beyond the demesne farm complex with its squat circular grainaries and boxy wool-stores and a bit higher up for the view, behind a wall that enclosed its lawns and ambitious but rather tentative terraced gardens. The Great House and outbuildings were rammed earth too, the more expensive variety with some cement mixed in and covered in a warm cream stucco with just a hint of reddish gold. The composition was so charming that you took a minute to discern the dry moat disguised by a ha-ha and the fact that all the exterior windows were narrow and could be slammed closed in moments by steel shutters. It wasn't a castle but it was definitely defensible against anything short of a formal attack with artillery, and while certainly big it was by no means excessive for a moderately prominent baron.

Just a wing on that thing in the Venetian style the Renfrews are building in Odell, Rudi thought. *Though to be sure, Conrad is a Duke nowadays.*

The roofs were bright unfaded red tile and fairly steeply pitched; most Palouse winters had more rain than snow, but you couldn't count on it. It was newer even than the village, so new that there was still roofer's scaffolding on the top of the four-story square tower at one corner. When they'd been shown to their quarters—which from the battered gray suit of plate on a stand in one corner he guessed were the Grand Constable's ordinarily—there was still a faint damp scent of curing *pisé de terre* and plaster.

"This is lovely," Mathilda said once their bags had been unpacked and the staff left.

She looked around the bedchamber's expanse of smooth pale mosaic tile and the French doors opening onto balconies with their decorative wrought-iron balustrades overlooking the fountain, walkways and gardens in the courtyard below. Like many modern manor houses, it made up with interior inner-facing windows and glass doors for the light excluded by solid exterior walls. There was a big fireplace with a carved stone surround of owls and olive wreaths, swept and garnished with dried wildflowers for summer, but discreet bronze grill vents showed a central heating system.

"Handsome work," Rudi agreed.

"Beautifully proportioned, and I love the coffered cypress-wood ceiling . . . I like that arched-passageway Romanesque style too . . . though the murals and the tapestries aren't up yet, of course. It'll be even prettier than the Montinore manor house back on Barony Ath. Delia has exquisite taste and she got to start from scratch with modern methods here."

Órlaith came barreling through side by side with Yolande de Stafford, a dark-haired girl of her own age who resembled a younger version of her mother, and her elder sister Heuradys, who had a mop of dark-auburn curls and resembled neither of her parents. Maccon was at her heels skidding on the smooth floors in a rattle of claws and just ahead of the determined-looking Prince John, whose shorter legs were pumping to keep up with the older girls; Órlaith paused to give them both a hug while Yolande and Heuradys bobbed a preoccupied curtsy. Then she dashed on dragging her brother by one hand. Dame Emelina followed a moment later, with a half-apologetic glance, then went in pursuit with the folds of her riding habit swishing.

"If we could bottle that energy and commission the Guild Merchant to sell it, the Crown would have no financial problems at all, at all," Rudi said.

"Right now I'll settle for a nice long soak. That sunken tub looks attractive."

"Not nearly as attractive as you, in it."

"Why, whatever could you mean, good sir?" she said, batting her eyes and giving him a smoldering smile.

The hall of the manor was a little more finished, when they descended to dinner several hours later in formal garb, an hour before the summer sunset. The building itself was essentially an E-shape; the hall occupied most of the central arm with archways on either side filled with French doors, now open to the cooling evening breeze. Normally the whole household from baron to garden-boys and laundresses would dine in the hall; that was old Association custom, with the ceremonial golden salt cellar marking the transition from the gentry on the dais at the upper table to the commons below. Tonight it was a more intimate affair, since most of the staff and garrison had been given leave to join the celebrations in the village; at the upper table were the nobles, and the gentlefolk among their retainers, and Edain as commander of the High King's Archers. He kept a pawky eye on the detail standing against the walls.

Delia resolutely steered the conversation away from Tiphaine's wound, duels or anything connected to them; evidently she was embarrassed at her lapse by the train station. The closest she came to the subject was after the salmon bisque had been replaced by a salad of summer greens and cherry tomatoes garnished with slices of melon wrapped in paper-thin envelopes of cured ham.

"And Heuradys wants to be a knight," she went on, rolling her eyes.

"I don't see why she shouldn't," Tiphaine observed. "Lioncel and Diomede are both well above average for their ages and they're going to be very dangerous as adults. And don't give me that *but she's a girl*. I'm a knight. Her Majesty is a knight. Yeah, it's harder for us, but it can be done. It involves beating the crap out of a lot of assh . . . contumacious persons, but that's a perk, not a drawback."

"I think Órlaith will be a warrior," Rudi observed thoughtfully. "She's got the doggedness, she's naturally active, she's worked hard at the basics this last little while as much as we've let her, and from her hands and feet she'll have the heft—she'll be taller for a woman than I am for a man, or I miss my guess, which means that she'll have more reach than most men, and as much weight or nearly."

And to be sure there's that vision I had at Lost Lake, at the Kingmaking, but let's not put a chill on the occasion. It bothers me, and others understandably more so.

Aloud he finished: "And her balance and reflexes and situational awareness are excellent for her age. As good as mine were, folk who knew me then say. But if Lady Tiphaine says Heuradys has the potential—"

"She does," d'Ath said decisively.

"Then there's no better judge."

Delia frowned slightly. "Well, Órlaith's a princess. Crown Princess, at that. And Your Majesties spend a lot of time elsewhere in Montival, outside the Protectorate where customs are, ah, different from those of Associates. It *will* be . . . hard for Heuradys if she takes that road. I mean . . . you know."

Tiphaine grinned sharklike as she broke open a roll and buttered it. "Sweetie, I *do* know. Abundantly." To Rudi and the rest: "Heuradys is eight, and it's obvious she's going to take after her father—"

She inclined her head to Rigobert.

"—as far as her build goes."

Delia nodded. "Her coloring's more like my mother's."

"Or my father's," Rigobert said. "She has his eyes."

"I think she's serious, too, and she'll have the talent," Lady Tiphaine went on. "Whether she wants it badly enough to take the crap involved is another question. Time will tell, but I don't think we should discourage her. Just make it plain how difficult it's going to be."

Mathilda frowned. "Well, there's no actual religious prohibition, I mean, look at me. Or legal ones; there were some women knights even in my father's time."

Maugis put in: "Weren't you knighted by the first Lord Protector, Lady Tiphaine?"

"No, by Sandra; but Norman was right there and he'd have done it if she hadn't claimed the right as my patron. Just as well; when he gave the *colée*, Norman always hit hard enough to draw blood."

"That's right," Mathilda said. "I was there, I remember, I think. It's just custom that knights are largely men."

"That and it's hard to combine with small children," Lady Helissent said.

"Oh, *tell* me!" Mathilda said, and they all chuckled. "Heuradys is eight . . . how's this, Delia? If she still wants it in two or three years, she can come to the Royal Household as a page. That'll give her the best possible tutors, she can train with Órlaith, and we can keep an eye on her to make sure there's no absolutely outrageous bullying. I know what kids can be like at that age."

"Thanks," said Tiphaine. "And I can train her until then, and when she's home after."

"And I," Rigobert said.

"No better examples," Rudi said sincerely; Tiphaine had trained *him*, and if de Stafford wasn't quite at her level he was still very good indeed.

Delia sighed. "We'll see in a few years, then."

The salads were removed, and followed by roast suckling pig with honey chipotle glaze, florets of baked potato with flecks of caramelized onion, steamed colored beets with a delicate cream sauce, and new asparagus. . . .

Let's let everyone get comfortably full and into what the Dúnedain call the filling-up-the-corners stage before we get on to the more dramatic part, for all love, Rudi thought.

"Did you hear that, Herry?" Órlaith whispered. "You can be a knight!"

She whispered *very carefully*, because the gallery around the hall hadn't been furnished yet, not even with rugs, and it echoed. They lay on their stomachs side by side, only their eyes over the marble lip, below the carved screens of some pale hard wood that made up the waist-high balustrade. It was densely shadowed now, since the chandeliers hanging from the hammerbeam rafters overhead weren't lit, only the lamps on the table.

"I knew it," Heuradys whispered back, or lied. "I'm going to work *twice* as hard now! I'll be *your* liege-knight, Órry, and fight by your side and everything!"

Órlaith nodded solemnly. "Like Da's companions were, on the Quest," she said.

Heuradys put a hand on her shoulder for a moment, then said: "Shhh, I want to hear the rest, too. We're *scouting*. And it's funny . . . Dad never *talks* about his parents."

Órlaith put her finger to her lips; she wanted to hear everything.

"Your harvest looked good," Órlaith's father said; the hall was built so that sound travelled well, for during feasts musicians would play up here.

"Thankfully," Tiphaine said. "Developing this place has been swallowing money, fencing alone costs the earth. About time we got some return."

Delia nodded. "Sixty bushels of wheat to the acre on the demesne land this season and nearly as well on the tenant strips in the Five Fields, and very well on the barley and lentils. That's better than we do on Barony Ath out west, though of course there we have the vineyards and orchards and we're closer to the market in Portland. Fruit trees grow reasonably well here with some watering but there just *weren't* any, they didn't do anything but wheat here apparently in the old days, so we have to start from scratch and you need to find the right varieties just to begin with. I *think* we can have vines if we select the ground carefully for aspect and frost drainage."

"We manage in Tucannon, and it's only a little south of here," Maugis said. "The Boiseans didn't damage the vines at St. Grimmond-on-the-Wold, thanks be to St. Urban, though the winery was a wreck."

"Vines will take a while," Delia said. "Sheep are much faster and we're getting twelve pounds per fleece. The bunchgrass here is just fabulous for livestock in general and flocks in particular. It's a pleasure to watch them eat."

"Merino?" Mathilda asked.

"Corriedales. The wool fetches nearly as much and the yield is better and they make better mutton carcasses," Delia said.

"The sheep actually make most of the returns so far— don't judge the rest of this estate by St. Athena manor, we started here," Tiphaine added. "Most of the land is still native grazing."

"I resemble that remark," Rigobert said. "We're running six thousand head in our flocks on Barony Pomeroy this year."

The silent Sir Julio spoke for virtually the first time: "You haven't worked as hard at your grant as Lady Delia has on this."

"I'm leaving something for Lioncel to do, now that he's a belted knight and his father can put him to work," Rigobert said. "When he gets back from visiting Huon Liu at Gervais. He's there to attend his friend's knighting vigil."

"When he gets back from mooning over Huon's sister Yseult, you mean, *Rigoberto mio*," Julio said dryly.

"She's a nice girl, well-dowered, and beautiful. Smart, too," Rigobert said.

"She is. She is also too old for him, she has an ac-knowledged lover who carries her favor in the tournies and whom she will almost certainly marry soon, and she does not squash his tender young heart like a bug beneath her shapely foot solely for her brother's sake because Huon is Lioncel's brother-in-arms."

"Hopeless passion is good for a knight's soul. They say," Helissent de Grimmond said.

The adults all found that funny, for some reason.

"Lioncel and Huon both did very well in the war as squires," Mathilda said, and Lady Tiphaine nodded. "And afterwards in the San Luis expedition—that was more diplomacy than fighting, of course. It's a pity about Yseult in a way, but there you are."

Maugis de Grimmond spoke: "I'm surprised at how much both of you have gotten done, starting from nothing with land mostly abandoned since the Change or at least since the Foundation Wars or the border skirmishes with Boise back in the old days. We're only now getting back to where we were before the Prophet's War on Barony Tucannon, and we brought nearly all the people through, which is the important thing."

"We moved some younger peasant families in from our manors in the west," Delia said briskly. "One's not in line to inherit holdings if we didn't assart land from the waste or common, which we're not doing there for obvious reasons."

"And there were broken men, refugees from the interior, looking for a place where someone would lend them the price of the tools and seed. That's drying up, now," Rigobert added. "Lioncel really *will* still be working on this when he's my age, particularly since we can't neglect Forest Grove."

"And Diomede will be working here," Delia said. "At least when Yolande and Heuradys come of age they'll have manors on the estates. That will make it easier for them whatever they decide to do. A girl who's heir to three manors is in a different position from one with an annuity."

Órlaith's father leaned back and cleared his throat as the desserts were brought out; she wiggled a little and nudged Heuradys with her elbow, knowing that was something he did before he surprised people.

There was an ice-cream cake carved into the shape of a ship, which she knew was deliciously studded with hazelnuts and fruits; a smaller but identical one had been served at the children's dinner earlier. She had gotten an extra two servings to bribe Yolande to watch John while they were supposed to be *playing quietly* in the nursery— Yolande was nice, but she didn't like sneaking around as much as Órlaith or her own older sister did.

"You're both of you"—the King nodded towards Lady Tiphaine and Lord Rigobert—"doing the Protectorate and the High Kingdom well here. Still, this County is mostly a wasteland."

"Tell me," Tiphaine said.

"There are still bandits, too," Rigobert said. "I think some of them may even be deserters from the Cutter army still at large, at least the core of them. There aren't enough people living here to keep eyes on all the likely pockets where the scum can hide. And you can tell Fred Thurston from me that his patrols *don't* do enough in the hill country east of here over the old border. There are jurisdictional bunfights over hot pursuit *both* ways all the time, and there have been what, four Crown castellans at Campscapell since the war? As soon as one learns his business and the country here he gets reassigned. I've lost livestock, and we had a shepherd killed last year."

Rudi nodded gravely. "It's a puzzlement to find a Crown castellan who's both able and not needed more urgently elsewhere. Which is why, Rigobert, you're going to spend your old age working harder than you want. Here."

He slid a parchment he took from the wide trailing sleeve of his houppelande across the table. Rigobert glanced at it and choked on his sip of brandy.

"Congratulations, Sir Rigobert de Stafford, Baron of Forest Grove . . . Baron of Pomeroy . . . and Count Campscapell. We'll have the ceremonial investiture later in Portland—Matti will be appointing you, strictly speaking."

There was a lot of noise for a moment, and Lord Rigobert stopped gaping and coughing; his friend Sir Julio pounded him on the back.

"And as for a Castellan and second-in-command, well, that will be your responsibility. I've heard good things of a certain Julio Alvarez de Soto, though."

Wow, Órlaith thought. *Campscapell is a big castle.*

There was a murmur of congratulations from below. Heuradys sighed very slightly, getting a bit bored, but Órlaith loved to watch her parents being King and Queen, even if she didn't understand it all yet.

Delia stopped with a snifter halfway to her lips. "And Lioncel . . . Lioncel will be a Count!"

"Only when I'm *dead*, Delia," Rigobert grinned, and

she blushed. "I might point out that you are now a Countess. Don't be alarmed, I think I can handle it without demanding Baroness d'Ath give up her Châtelaine."

"You'll do a good job of it, Rigobert," Tiphaine said. "Better than I would. You're better at getting people to cooperate, especially in peacetime, but you've got an excellent record in the Prophet's War too."

"And in my fifties, people have different expectations. I can delegate . . . certain matters."

Sir Julio laughed, a low sound that made Órlaith feel a bit shivery, and flexed his sword-hand.

"Speaking of jobs," Rudi said. "Lord Maugis, you did say most of the war damage has been repaired on your Barony of Tucannon?"

"Yes, Your Majesty. The basics; only time will cure some things. My vassals and everyone down to the very cottars worked like heroes, just as they fought during the war."

"Good. Then I won't be taking you away from your folk in their hour of greatest need."

He produced two more parchments, and slid one to Lady Tiphaine and one to Baron Tucannon. Maugis read his, frowning and then blurting:

"Grand Constable of the Association?"

Tiphaine spoke simultaneously: *"Marshal-Commander of the High King's Hosts?"*

Her father threw back his head and laughed. "That's squeal-of-complaint followed by *Your Majesty*, if you please, my lord, my lady."

Maugis rose from his chair and went down on one knee, bending his head. Aleaume was fighting to keep an incredulous grin off his face.

"Your Majesty, I am not worthy of this honor."

"That is for your sovereigns to decide, and we have," Mathilda said. "Do you accept the office, my lord?"

That's me-and-Da *'we,' not the other type of* 'we,' Órlaith decided.

Maugis sighed, and looked at his wife. She nodded . . . after an instant's hesitation. "Yes, your Majesty," he said.

"You needn't look as if I'd sent you to the mines, Lord Maugis," Órlaith's father said. "Get back up and enjoy your cake, for all love."

Mathilda spoke: "I wanted an able man for this, one with a good war record in independent commands, administrative talents . . . and one who was *not* heir to a Duke, which is why Érard Renfrew Viscount of Odell isn't getting it, to be blunt. Also I trust your liege Count Felipe to be sensible about it, given that you're not a tenant-in-chief."

Maugis sat back down slowly, and Lady Helissent gripped his hand. "I . . . I will do my best to fulfill the trust you have shown me, Your Majesties. Though it will be hard, following such a Grand Constable as the one who led the Association through the war."

Tiphaine had been frowning. When she spoke it was slow and considering, her voice even more cool than usual. "Your Majesty, you're appointing me commander-in-chief for Montival as a whole? Creating a new ministry and me to head it?"

"Exactly. You're fit for the job, and you're also the only Associate most of the rest of the realm would accept. Being, as it were . . . unconventional."

"But you don't *have* a Host in peacetime for a Marshal-Commander to command. All you have is a Royal guard regiment and some people the provinces send in rotation.

You need a general the way a bull needs a mandolin! It would be like calling me a Lord High Admiral because you gave me a rubber duckie for my bathtub. If you and Matti don't want me as Grand Constable anymore, fine—the job's routine now anyway and I'm tired of it and the Gray-Eyed knows I've got enough other things to do. But this is make-work. I don't need my feelings soothed."

Órlaith's father raised a hand. "The job's organizational, not operational, yes, but none the less real for that. I need a staff structure that will be there and ready if . . . when, alas . . . it's needed and I call up contingents."

Tiphaine started to nod, then glanced sharply at her Châtelaine's carefully concealed delight.

"Wait a minute," she said. "This is an appointment by the High King."

"And High Queen," Mathilda put in.

"Both of you, yes. That *does* mean you could punish anyone who challenged me, have their head and forbid the encounter; the High King's ministers are immune, extraterritorial, even if they're Associates."

"That's in the Great Charter, yes, Marshal-Commander."

"I don't need protection—" she began sharply.

"Shut up!"

Órlaith blinked; that was her mother, and she'd accompanied it by a cracking slap of her palm on the table, and she was using the High Queen's voice.

She wasn't the only one surprised; she could see that all the grown-ups were too, except maybe Lady Delia. Mathilda pointed a finger at the silent face of Lady Tiphaine:

"Look, d'Ath, you've been carrying water for House

Arminger since you were fourteen years old. You rescued me when I was ten. You saved Rudi's life not long after. You held the Prophet out of most of Montival until the Quest got back. You only killed what's-his-name's uncle—"

"Sir Vladimir. Minor Stavarov connection. The late young idiot who just bit it trying to avenge his uncle was Sir Bogdan."

"Sir Vladimir in the first place because it was politically convenient for my mother to deliver a *pointed message* after the Protector's War. Do you think that we—that *I*—am going to let Lady Delia and the children be left alone because of blowback you earned serving *us*?"

"I'm not asking—"

"I'm not asking *you*. I'm *telling* you, Tiph. It's good lordship to protect a vassal, and you're going to get our good lordship *whether you like it or not*."

Tiphaine opened her mouth. Rigobert leaned forward. "Tiph, don't be an ass," he drawled. "And if you think either of us has anything to prove at this late date, that would be exactly the case. With gray fur and long ears yet."

"Darling, *please*," Delia added.

Slowly, Tiphaine subsided back into her chair and sipped her brandy. "All right," she said grudgingly. Then to Rudi and Mathilda: "I'll do it. Your Majesties."

Rudi sighed. "Thank you. And now, friends, why don't we have another drink, and perhaps some songs? And tomorrow . . . I understand the partridge are plump and plentiful hereabouts this time of year, by the kisses of Angus Og MacDagda. And that Marshall d'Ath has most excellent falcons."

"Wow," Heuradys whispered to Órlaith. "Your mom

is *something*. I've never seen anyone tell Lady Tiph off like that!"

"Mom and Dad *are* really something!" Órlaith said.

A voice whispered not far behind her in a Mackenzie lilt: "And the pair of *you* are little monkeys."

The horn tip of a bowstave rapped her behind the ear, just enough to sting a little. Heuradys gave a small squeak, hastily stifled with a hand. Órlaith slowly turned her head. Edain Aylward Mackenzie was standing there, scowling; she hadn't even noticed him slipping away from the table. Behind him was Dame Emelina, with her arms crossed and a foot beginning to tap.

"Ooops," Heuradys said.

CHAPTER NINETEEN

"**D**ang, what a bargain!" Ingolf Vogeler said, looking out over the tall grass, brush and trees of the grant. "To think we got all this for *free*. Well, for free and a few years' . . . twelve years' . . . work."

About a hundred yards away a wild gobbler stuck its head out of a berry thicket, a bit longer-legged and a bit more buff-colored than the variety he'd grown up around but with the same look of idiot turkey indignation. It cocked a suspicious eye at the tents and horses and people and then dashed back into cover. Birds were tweeting away in the giant oak overhead . . . and a tiger-skin was tacked to it for scraping and drying preparatory to tanning. There were about a dozen arrow-holes in the skin, which detracted from its value as a rug or coat, but had made acquiring it a lot less nerve-wracking when kittie had tried to get into their horse-corral last night. They'd turned a lantern on the green eyes and then cut loose.

Some people liked hunting tigers with spears; but then some people thought the sound of bolts and roundshot going by their ears an inch away was invigorating. If he'd had a catapult handy he'd have used *that*. In a ravine not far from here some coyotes were probably happy, and he wished them a satisfying dinner.

"Ingolf, my esteemed brother-in-law, back where I was born there would still be *snow* this time of year," Ian Kovalevsky said. "Whereas this land is green and pleasant and, pardon the expression, fucking *green* already. There are *pomegranates* growing here, and grapes and figs and apricots and olives. I think there are oranges around someplace. Stuff I've never seen before except in pictures. Some guys would complain if you hung them with a golden rope."

Ingolf put his thumbs in his sword belt and chewed meditatively on a long stem of grass, enjoying the warm spring air and smells of wood smoke and horse and wilderness and the blue arch of the sky. They'd landed at Sausalito Marina from the *Ark*, a Corvallan merchantman out of Newport, one that usually worked the Hawaii run but came here occasionally. That had been more than enough room for the two-score Rangers and their equipment and stock, and though the horses had been no happier about ocean travel than usual they hadn't lost any to equine hissy-fit hysterics during the week's cruise.

They'd hurried the wagons and livestock north through the zone of ruins as fast as possible—there were Eaters there, though not many, the collapse in urban California had been very swift—and made tracks northward. It wasn't his first glimpse of the grant, of course; the Dúnedain had been reconnoitering now for years, mostly in long overland treks. And with his salvage experience before the war, he'd been a natural to lead several of those expeditions. Those preparatory outings had updated the maps and cleared some of the obstacles, so the wagons could get straight through with a little effort. But this time they'd come to stay.

He had to admit it was a pretty spot . . . one of the reasons he'd picked it for the Ranger station that would send out patrols to guard the road to the salvage fields around the Bay and help with resettling this area. There was actually a civilized holding a couple of days' travel away, closer to the coast around Cape Mendocino, one of the very few that had managed to pull through the Change Year. It was tucked behind some low mountains and hard to get to, which helped account for its survival.

As far as he could tell from the signs, everyone had simply left this place in the hills east of the Sonoma valley within the first few months. If bands of savage wildmen had passed through since, they hadn't left much trace.

"I've got to admit you picked it right, and not just for looks," Ian said with farmboy practicality; his family were well-to-do yeomen up in their fertile but frigid homeland. "This stuff is going to save us a *lot* of work."

Sonoma Mountain and the Mayacamas were behind them, with a few last wisps of sea-fog dissolving as the morning warmed up. The rolling land about was a mixture of flower-starred green-gold grass with scattered oaks and oak-groves—tanbark oak, live oak, black oak—and ancient overgrown vineyards and orchards, and dense woods on the steeper bits of everything from fir to eucalyptus to millennia-old redwoods in the west-facing ravines. Things wild and those run wild tumbled together in a happy mélange, including all the usual animals and some weird-looking African ones as well, beasts that had run from zoos and parks and survived in this mild climate. The flowers were dense, everything from California poppy to feral rosebushes that rioted over some thick ruined walls nearby to leave them just a shape beneath green leaf and crimson blossom.

Besides the vines and fruit-trees—the surviving ones could be reconditioned a lot faster than planting from scratch, and some were in flower now—the big plus had been the buildings. There was a fair-sized H-shaped house built of lava boulders cemented together, solid as the hills and even defensible against anything short of artillery, with a long portico running out from the front on arches at right angles to the main building. The roof was good baked tile, and had mostly held despite the years and storms; fortunately someone had boarded up the windows before the house was abandoned. The water damage inside was serious but not structural, and could be repaired before fall.

"The house is almost modern," Ingolf said.

"Yeah, but I'd say it was probably built seventy, a hundred years before the Change," Ian replied. "That was before they forgot how to do things properly. It's a pity that other one burned down, from the looks it was even better built and *huge*. This one will do for now, though, until Ritva and I can put up something and stop crowding you. She's talking about a multilevel *flet* in a redwood. Around a redwood, whatever."

"That'll keep you skinny in your old age!"

Whoever had built the stone house had liked books, too; unfortunately they'd all been ruined one way or another, mostly critters tearing them up for nests and bugs eating them. Whoever it had been that held this land had been called Jack and had probably been English, because the word *London* regularly appeared around the place, and he knew that city had been the capital of the British Empire before it perished in the Change. The King-Emperors of Greater Britain reigned from Winchester these days, which was supposed to be quite the town.

Which I have no desire to go see. Ingolf the Wanderer has wandered far enough, thanks very much. From now on I stay here and grow roots like a turnip, and leave only for visits to places I've already been. My kids can go on adventures, the poor ignorant little tykes.

Almost as much of a prize were the stone barns, of similar construction, and what Ingolf's Kickapoo childhood had convinced him was what was left of an elaborate circular piggery with two tall concrete-block silos not far away. His father might have been a Sheriff, lord of broad acres with Farmers and their Refugees at his command, but he hadn't believed in letting his sons loll around without chores.

That experience was the reason Ingolf didn't particularly like pigs, as animals, though he was fond of dogs and horses, tolerated cats, and had nothing against cattle or sheep in their place. Feeding and slopping them and cleaning out pens had convinced him porkers were probably smart enough to know why people kept them around, unlike sheep and cattle who thought you loved them, and left him absolutely dead certain they were dangerous if you weren't careful. But he *did* like ham and bacon and chitterlings and bratwurst and headcheese.

Which was fair, because pigs were certainly ready to

kill and eat people if they got the chance; he'd lost his cookies as a teenager after running across what they'd left of a Refugee farmhand who'd passed out drunk where they could get at him, and that *had* put him off pork for a while. The great black bristly wild boar common in Montival's forests and marshes were far worse, like pigs in plate armor with swords in their snouts. They swarmed like giant destructive rabbits around here, with nothing but lions, tigers, bears or people willing to take them on. Good hunting and good eating, though . . .

"That little lake is best of all. It gets really dry here in the summers, from what the books say," Ian said with satisfaction.

Someone long ago had made an earth and stone dam in the hills to the east, and it stayed filled all year long. Rundown and a bit silted now, but with a little work it would be full of catfish and perfect for a dip on a hot day with willows and redwoods for shade. The kids already loved it, and they'd been here only ten days. There were channels to bring the water to where it was needed and they were repairable, especially with easy salvage for PVC piping and similar workaday stuff in the towns just to the west.

"Yah, when we've gotten it into shape this place is going to make us all rich," Ingolf said with satisfaction. "Particularly when more settlers trickle in to the valleys east and west. What with the wine, the fruit, good grazing and timber. And best of all those dead cities on the Bay haven't been worked over at all, hardly, and we've got that nice juicy concession."

"We're a bit far away from anywhere to sell most salvage," Ian observed. "Lot of big ruins closer to the center of things, eh?"

"Oh, not bulk metals," Ingolf said.

The economics of the salvage trade were something he knew inside out, but they were different up in Drumheller where there were only two lost cities to be mined and both had been thoroughly worked over under tight government supervision already.

He explained: "Sure, Seattle alone has enough rebar and girders to keep Montival in swordblades and plowshares and horseshoes for a thousand years, but those places south of us are stuffed with *real* salvage, stuff that repays long-distance transport. Optics, machine tools that can be rigged to work on waterpower, rare metals, bearings, gears, not to mention artwork and gold and silver and jewelry. There were a couple of things in San Francisco I spotted on the second trip that are so pretty I'm going to keep 'em for myself."

"And it'll provide a nice non-blizzards-and-freezing place to spend our declining years in comfort, surrounded by attentive grandchildren," Ian agreed.

The Dúnedain were organized as something like an army, something like a feudal lordship, and something like what lawyers called a cooperative employee-owned corporation: Dúnedain Enterprises, Ltd., if you preferred English, or *Gwaith-i-Dúnedain, Herth*, which was what was printed on the checks from the First National Bank of Corvallis. The business part was more important in peacetime. Everyone who was born into or accepted as a candidate to the Rangers got at least one share, and there were ways to get more. Being one of the Questers had proved to be worth a big chunk of common stock, for example, not to mention other accomplishments like getting this grant from the Crown for the Rangers. Theoretically all the Dúnedain lands belonged to the *Gwaith*, but they were leased out on a sort of franchise arrangement to the *stath*, which was Ranger-speak for stations and steadings.

It doesn't hurt to be married to Lady Astrid's sister's daughter, either, he thought a little complacently; he'd never come across a place where important relatives didn't count.

His eldest son and daughter ran up and started using him as an obstacle in a game of tag; they were nine now, tow-haired Malfind and his black-haired sister Morfind respectively as their names indicated. He'd learned to accept the names, after Mary had sternly vetoed his suggestion of Harry and Ethel. Her family was prone to twins on both sides, and they had two sets of fraternals now, boy-girl and two girls for the second, Eledhwen and Finduilas, who both looked as if they were going to take after Dad. Ian and Ritva hadn't had twins, much to her disappointment—as she said, it meant she'd had a third more work for two-thirds as many children so far—but their boy Faramir made up for it in energy.

He danced around, darting and lunging at Ingolf's twins while the adults raised their arms and laughed, until Malfind said:

"Up!"

Her brother braced himself behind Ingolf, grabbing at the back of his sword belt for an instant. Malfind ran up him and then up her father like a squirrel, leapt into the lowest branches of the oak, and gave her brother a hand when he followed. Judging by the speed and smoothness of the maneuver, they had a great future ahead of them as special operations types . . . or possibly as burglars.

"No fair!" Faramir shouted up. "Dad, give me a boost so I can catch these *cheaters*!"

Ian was grinning as he looked up and shook his head. "I don't need to. Take a look at what's above those two—and looking a lot like 'em."

Ingolf looked up along with the others. This area also had monkeys, gray-brown critters with naked pink faces and tails. One of the books called them *rhesus macaques*, and while they were funny as hell to watch they liked to throw things, their own dung when nothing else was to hand. Quite literally to hand. Along with Ian and his son he moved aside quickly, and laughed at the squeals of disgust as it suddenly started to rain young Vogelers, along with twigs and monkey by-products.

"Look before you leap," he called. "Pond's thataway and get it all out of your hair, both of you."

They trudged away muttering variations on *euuuw*. Faramir followed, dancing in glee.

"Crappy-heads!" he called. "Cheaters *and* crappy-heads!"

He stopped with the second repetition; he was a good-hearted kid, though a bit thoughtless, even by nine-year-old standards. A minute later Elvellon came by, a solid if rather slow woman in her thirties, a former Cutter slave who'd settled among the Rangers not least because being tongueless was less of a disadvantage in a group where everyone knew Sign. She worked for Mary and Ritva as a handyperson, and seemed devoted to the kids without the least desire for any of her own. Nobody asked about her past.

They OK? Her fingers asked.

Just a bit smelly, Ingolf said, and explained.

She laughed without opening her teeth and walked after them, casting:

I get them ready for dinner. Mothers back soon, over her shoulder.

Ingolf eyed the tree, where fifteen or twenty of the monkeys were chattering and leaping around to celebrate their triumph.

"Acting a bit like my boy, eh?" Ian said.

"We're definitely going to have to do something about *them.*"

"Bobcats?" Ian mused. "Falcons? Baited traps?"

"Arrows," Ingolf said. "It's the only way to be sure."

Then their heads turned. The fluting whistle of the sentries' call came through the afternoon air, only distinguishable from birds if you knew, and they relaxed as it said *our people come.*

Mary and Ritva had taken a half dozen of the younger Rangers out, not simply hunting for the pot but to start the familiarization process; really knowing every inch of your territory went with the job. All the hunters had returned, and over the packhorses were . . .

"Venison," Ian said hollowly. "Oh, boy, what a treat. On days in which the sun rises in the east, we Dúnedain Rangers shall have venison for dinner. I'm going to grow antlers this year, I can feel the buds itching."

"Looks like they got a yearling porker, too, and some turkeys . . . and *hel*-lo, there are visitors."

A dozen more riders came behind the Ranger party.

"Edain, by Eru! That's six of the High King's Archers and—"

Órlaith threw herself off the horse and into his arms, a solid weight of fast-growing teenager.

"Uncle Ingolf!"

"Sorry the house isn't fit for company, but we're doing spring-cleaning," Ingolf said.

Órlaith laughed as he jerked a thumb at a huge pile of slightly musty-smelling planks and laths that lay not far from the ancient stone building; not far from that was a pile of broken tile, ready to be ground for tempering powder in the new ones that would be made as soon as the kiln was built. The round Dúnedain tents were grouped around their hearth-fires, and they'd pitched their own set—the High King's Archers had three domed Clan-style bells, and she and Herry had a slightly larger rectangular model. For this trip she'd managed to escape the train of Court servants, all except for a couple of groom-roustabouts and the bowmen.

It had helped that things at Todenangst had been so frantic. Her father had been quietly and wisely sympathetic to her desire to escape, which had been wonderful but less comfort than she'd expected.

Even if your Da is wise and strong and King, he can't make everything better. I must be getting older, she thought.

There hadn't been much time to talk with the Rangers, apart from the *Alyssa and Cole send their greetings and the youngest is doing fine* level. She didn't know whether to be happy or depressed about that.

They all lay sprawled about the fire, with sparks drifting upward towards the shimmering roof of the oak's new leaves. Skewers of boar loin dressed with wild garlic were sizzling, and iron Dutch ovens of biscuits stood in a raked-down section of the coals, and a pot of wild greens was bubbling—amole leaves, with another of mashed dock. The smell made her mouth water despite it all; there was nothing like a long day in the saddle to work up an appetite.

Da said that getting tired and using my body would help. Hard work keeps sorrow at bay until you're strong enough to deal with it. *He was right . . . again.*

Maccon laid his huge gruesome head in her lap and rolled his eyes up at her, and she rubbed his graying chops. He was getting old . . . she had that on the brain right now.

"Yes, you'll all get *even more*," she said, leaning back against her saddle; two of his latest crop of puppies were a little farther from the fire, tall lanky shaggy young beasts named the MacMaccons. "Like you haven't been gorging on guts."

She was in a kilt and plaid again, which was a relief—the long deathbed wait in Castle Todenangst had all been in Associate formal women's dress, for which at thirteen she was now just old enough. She hadn't complained under the circumstances, but enough was enough.

She sighed. You could travel a thousand miles, but you couldn't run away from your thoughts; her father had told her that, too. She turned to Ingolf instead.

"It's good to see you again, Unc'," she said. Then, peering closer: "Are you going bald? I can see firelight on your *scalp*."

There was a roar of laughter around the fire, which surprised her; Mary Vogeler was laughing harder than any. Ingolf ran one big battered hand over his head, which was indeed getting a bit thinly thatched, though there wasn't much gray in it.

"Male-pattern baldness runs in my family," he said ruefully. "Dad, my older brother . . . damned if I'm going to grow a middle-aged Vogeler beer gut, though."

Heuradys nudged her with the toe of her boot; she was looking quite dashing in her squire's hunting outfit, with a Montero hat sporting a peacock feather tilted back on her bobbed mahogany hair; she had the knack of doing that even after hard travel through the wilderness. Unfairly, she'd shot up and filled out over the last couple of years, while Órlaith still had the build of a tall gawky plank. The two years between them *still* made a lot of difference.

"Ah, the comfort there's to be had in the voices of the young!" Edain said, grinning and taking a swig from a jug covered in straw that was doing the rounds. "Fair makes a man spring about like a goat, his youth renewed, it does not."

"Edain, you're ten years younger than me," Ingolf said, and smiled himself in a mock-nasty way. "Just you *wait*."

"What brings you down this way?" Ian said.

"Oh . . . I wanted to get out of . . . of the places I'm usually in," she said. Then she blurted: "Nona died. My . . . the Queen Mother," she said in a rush.

There were exclamations, but nobody among the Dúnedain knew her Nona Sandra the way she did. Sandra Arminger had been feared, and hated, and widely respected; she'd also been loved, but that mainly by people she was closer to.

"We'd heard that she was ill, of course," Ritva said.

A slightly awkward silence fell, and Órlaith continued doggedly. "We . . . there was some warning, but it came on fast and the end. I was there. . . ."

Memory took her back. The smell of incense, the murmur of chanted prayer in the background. John crying silently, tears trickling down his face from still brown eyes; Maria and Lorcan had said their good-byes and then been ushered out, they were too young yet to understand. Sandra had smiled and managed to squeeze Órlaith's hand. They were all waiting as the gaslamps flickered, watching the slow rise and fall of the sheet over her breast, and the glisten of the holy oil on her eyelids.

Then her eyes fluttered open. They seemed to be seeing *something*. When she spoke, her voice was very quiet but clear, perfectly ordinary:

"Norman, we have to talk."

Órlaith squeezed her eyes shut on the memory: "And then she died," she whispered. "She was just gone, and I realized how *alive* she'd always been. There was always this crackle around her. Like somewhere thoughts were coming out like sparks from a burning pine log."

When she opened her eyes again, the others were looking at her a little oddly: it was not the time you'd expect her to leave the family to go on a ramble. All those close to the fire were kin to her or the next thing to it, and old companions of her father on the Quest who'd helped raise her on and off.

"I wouldn't go attend the funeral mass," she blurted. "I mean, I wouldn't take Communion at it. I won't, anymore, I should never have been confirmed. I've decided I'm of the Old Religion. I know we're allowed to see it as . . . as you know, another form of the same thing, so we can do the ceremonies if we need to, but I *won't*. I won't deceive Mom. John's a good Catholic, but I'll never be. We had a big fight about it—mostly me yelling and her being so *quiet*. So I had to, to get away."

Edain reached over and put a hand on her back for a moment. "That's hard, my Golden Princess. Matti your mother I've known all my life, and she's a good Queen and an even better friend and a true comrade, but at seventh and last she's cowan, and . . . that means there are things she does not ken."

Órlaith nodded, scrubbing at her eyes.

"Oh, I don't know, Órry," Heuradys said, putting her arm around her shoulders. "My lady mother's a witch and I've had some *really* awkward moments with her, too."

"You have?" Órlaith asked.

"Yes, by the Gray-Eyed! Just a few months ago I had to sit her down and tell her something she *really* didn't want to hear. She wasn't happy about it, either, any more than your mother was."

"You *did*?" Órlaith said; she couldn't imagine the calmly cheerful Lady Delia de Stafford getting all coldly miserable the way her own mother had. "Why didn't you tell me?"

"Sort of embarrassing, really. It was a family council at Montinore Manor back on Barony Ath, when I was back for the Twelve Days . . . Yule . . . and it was just me and her and Auntie Tiph—"

She stopped and glared at Ian, who was chortling. "What exactly is funny? I haven't got to that part yet, unless you think my whole family is funny, Lord Ian?"

"Anyone calling *Lady Death* her *auntie*, that's funny. Sorry, sorry."

"Well, *I* don't call her Lady Death, you know. And my lord my father Count Rigobert was there, he spends that season with us mostly," she went on quellingly. "You see, my lady mother had been throwing nice girls from her coven my way since I turned fifteen, and I just had to tell her *Mom, I don't want to hurt anyone's feelings, but I really like boys better*."

"What did she say?" Órlaith asked, startled into intense interest.

"She sort of *looked* at me . . . you know how mothers do, like you're still about four . . . and put her hand on mine and said in this amazingly irritating calm voice: *'Darling, isn't it possible this is just a phase you're going through?'*"

Heuradys smiled ruefully at the ring of grins. "And my lord my father and Auntie Tiph didn't help."

"Did they get upset too?" Órlaith asked.

"No, they laughed. I mean, really laughed—I thought my lord my father was going to hurt himself. So Mom and I *both* got mad at them, which made them laugh even harder. I've never seen Auntie Tiph break up that way, not even when she heard about Sir Boleslav trying to drink a whole bottle of vodka standing in a castle window and the moat had been drained, and my lord my father was staggering when he got up and left. I think he told Sir Julio because then I could hear *him* laughing after a while."

Ingolf shook his head and grinned and seemed to be searching his memory.

Ritva frowned a little. "It's sort of funny . . . I mean, most Associates are such strong Catholics and they're really odd about things like that, so I can see, you know, some other mother doing things just like that if it were the other way 'round, or screaming and fainting . . . but why was it *that* funny?"

"I asked my lord my father and he just said I was far too young to understand—and so was my mother, a little too young. So it must be some pre-Change thing. You forget he's not a Changeling sometimes because he's so . . . not a fuddy-duddy. Even Auntie Tiph isn't a Changeling, not all the way—she was as old at the Change as you are now, Órry. But my lady mother was just a kid, younger than my sister Yolande."

The story seemed to break the awkwardness, and everyone pitched into dinner. Órlaith found her appetite was right back, and when you were sharp-set wild boar was absolutely scrumptious, rich but stronger-tasting than domestic pork. There wasn't any butter for the biscuits, but the drippings did fine, and then her aunts Mary and Ritva got out their mandolin and flute.

Much later in the tent, she reached across to the other cot and squeezed Heuradys' hand in the darkness, the calluses matching her own.

"Thanks, Herry. You've been a real brick."

"Hey, I'm going to be your liege-sworn knight someday, Órry."

"I know. But it's even better to have a friend. 'night."

CHAPTER TWENTY

Órlaith almost missed her step in the dance as she checked the bower she'd built out of the corner of her eye.

The *nemed* of Dun Juniper was a place whose name woke awe across the High Kingdom, the Sacred Wood. A circle of ancient oaks stood on a knee of land on the side of the mountain, many planted long ago with their successors in all stages of growth, a ring of smooth brown trunks like hundred-foot pillars and a continuous band of intermingled branches above bright-with-the-green new leaves. The path upward to the plateau was steep, winding back and forth through the dense green fir-woods, but it was filled tonight—not only with visitors from all over the Clan's dùthchas, but others from across Montival and even a few from beyond it.

For this was the center of the Old Faith in the world the Change had made, and its mistress was Goddess-on-Earth.

Tonight the great trees of the circle were bound together with chains of woven flowers, budding roses, wood hyacinths and lilies of the valley, pansies and impatiens and larkspur. Torches burned in the wrought-iron holders at the four Quarters, and fire flickered before the shaped boulder that was the altar. They beckoned and glittered through the cool dampness and the thickness of the hillside firs. It was a gathering, a party really . . . but there was something of *otherness* about this place, even on a quiet day alone. Tonight that feeling was raw and strong, the focused belief of the multitude like a weight stretching thin the walls of the world.

Órlaith shivered a little in spite of the thick white wool robe she wore, feeling goose bumps against the fabric.

Old Sybil Leek said it: Let those who would dance through the woods skyclad. I have too much respect for my own skin!

Her feet swayed and moved to the rhythm that turned the dancers' torches in the long line down the hillside. The ancient dancing style the Mackenzies practiced had various and sundry purposes; keeping you warm while on the trail to the *nemed* was certainly one of them. Another was the way the rhythm took you beyond yourself, until it seemed to settle into bone and breath and heartbeat.

Fiorbhinn Mackenzie was May Queen. She sang greeting to flute and bohdrán as she danced, her silver and crystal-embroidered robe like a glitter on dew-starred grass between the two balefires at the entrance to the plateau; the only other sound was the rippling of the fire as it ate the fir-wood, and the wind soughing in the tops of the trees. Her hands were upraised, and her great pale eyes full of the moonlight; long blond hair swept down past the shoulders of her robe mingled with wreaths of white meadowsweet and blue hyacinth.

The procession whirled by on either side, each dancer like notes of the song:

> *"Moon rise and star fall*
> *Fire burn and night wind call*
> *Drum beat the wild song*
> *That heart sings at summer's dawn!"*

The robed procession wound its way into the clearing, a spiral around the great circle of the *nemed*. Juniper Mackenzie was present with her consort Nigel Loring, seated in a pair of carved chairs whose backs echoed the twin ravens at the top of her staff and the corvine beak of his mask, each wrapped in a thick cloak. Her lined face was smiling, but this time for the first Beltane since the Change she was not presiding over the celebrations. That was for her daughter and successor Maude who now had the Triple Moon on her brow, no longer tanist but the Mackenzie Herself. She'd said she didn't intend to dodder into her grave as Chief, the time had come when the Clan needed a Changeling at its head, and Maude could always come to her parents for advice. . . .

> *"Sown are the new fields*
> *With bright seed of harvest's yield*
> *Far down the roots bind*
> *The heart's joy to summer's time!"*

That glance aside at her bower meant she nearly tripped over Aunt Maude. The Chief laughed gently as she caught her spinning niece and righted her, her usually rather gravely handsome features alight with the festival. Nobody was drunk before the ceremony, but wine and the whirling ecstasy of the dance and drums were in many veins. Órlaith gripped Maude tightly for one short instant before a quick, light push sent her dancing up the path to rejoin the rest of the May Queen's maidens, all dressed in white.

> *"Leave the fire and come with me*
> *We'll lie beneath the flowering tree*
> *And feel the breathing of the earth*
> *Rise and fall!"*

As one of the Maidens, Órlaith had set many of the stitches in the May Queen's robe, and the more hidden white ones on her own, matching the white rhododendron flowers confining her hair. Five maidens attended the Queen, for the Elements and the Quarters and the hidden thing that united them all.

Earth and Air and Fire and Water! And Spirit!

She was Air, a belt of pale blue sapphires and cloudy white opals set in silver around her waist to symbolize it. Fire was the daughter of *fiosaiche* Meadhbh Beauregard Mackenzie, all dark skin and tossing plaited hair, her white robes belted with ruby and carnelian and gold. Earth and Water were both younger, Earth the granddaughter of Cynthia Carson, Water Diana Trethgar's eldest boy's youngest daughter. Spirit was Heuradys d'Ath, grinning at her companions with an imp's light in her amber eyes.

> *"The green time sings its song again*
> *To wake the hill, to wake the glen*

And raise in every living thing
An answering call!"

Órlaith smiled widely at Delia de Stafford as she danced by, her daughter Yolande laughing behind her, their black tossing hair the same shade of night with the white blossom in it like stars. Órlaith's stitching had improved enormously in five weeks of tutoring Delia had given her and her robe reflected it. A Beltane robe was something you made with your own hands, as an offering.

"Leap o'er the May fire
Hold close your sweet desire
For life's Wheel will grant soon
The heart's wish for summer's bloom!"

Which is what I want! Órlaith thought.

Suddenly she was breathing quickly at the sound of horns lowing and dunting through the wood, as if the sound snatched her breath away. There was a music in that call too, low and hoarse and . . . *hot* somehow, like the sound of the bull elk's call echoing across a mountainside.

And as Fiorbhinn danced through the ancient oaks' arch, the men from Cernunnos' court entered the sacred grove from all points, a leaping torrent of torches and wildness, bare skin and paint and tossing fire. Raghnall McClintock of Clan McClintock was the Horned One tonight. Years back his father had sent him to Dun Juniper to learn the trade of chief, for the head of a clan was intermediary with the Powers as much as ruler and battle-leader, his folk's link to the land and ancestors. Now he returned from his southern hills to do honor to its mis-

420 S. M. STIRLING

tress. He was a tall man, strong through the shoulders
and with long brown hair drawn back in the McClintock
queue through carved bone rings, his face half-hidden
behind the tanned deer mask.

And his Fire Squire was Diarmuid Tinnart McClintock, whom she'd met days ago in the preparations for
the ceremony. Their glances had crossed. . . .

> *"Green shoot and pale flower*
> *Garland the Beltane bower*
> *Circle with joined hands*
> *For heart shines with summer's dance!"*

Órlaith felt the movement of her blood, from face and
heart and loins out to the tips of fingers and toes, an un-
folding like flowers beneath the sun, like waves beating
on a beach, a sweet inevitable rightness. Diarmuid was
wearing the horns and deer breechclout, his feet bare on
the flowered turf and the muscles of a runner and bowman moving clear as liquid metal beneath white skin that
glowed taut and clear. Though he was too young for a
McClintock warrior's tattoos, swirling blue patterns in
woad showed where they would run on back and shoulders, legs and arms. From behind the bright red paint on
his face, she could see his dark blue eyes cast about, seeking her among the maidens.

Generally I pay more attention to ritual, she thought,
halting in her dance in Earth's place. *But ritual is symbol
and this is the truth it speaks.*

> *"Leave the fire and come with me*
> *To walk beside the dreaming sea*

And watch the fading of the stars
As the new day dawns!"

Cynthia Carson giggled and pushed her back to Air's proper place.

"Your ribbon is *blue*!" she whispered and exploded into giggles again.

Órlaith felt herself flush to the roots of her hair, trying to keep her place in the circle.

Panpipes sounded, weaving themselves into the hymn. She skipped forward to the maypole set in the center. Fiorbhinn and Raghnall seized the silver and gold ribbons. Each pair of Maiden and Squire took the colored ribbon of their Attribute and backed away, turning the long ribbons into a net of colored tracery in the fire-shot darkness.

"We'll try to catch time in our hands
To hold the wave against the sand
And watch this glow upon the land
That soon will be gone!"

The drums beat and Órlaith felt a shiver stroke her backbone, like the touch of a feather drawn from the base of her spine to the nape of her neck.

This year, she prayed. *Mother-of-All, this year, when we are both together, please let him . . .*

She hesitated, not sure what she wanted from Diarmuid this year. There was a sense of eyes opening at the back of existence. A presence . . . a Presence . . . fond and amused, gone before she could be sure it was anything but her own yearning. Like a warm breeze carrying with it a scent of cinnamon and musk.

The circle had danced forward and back, now pulling on the orange and purple ribbons. And the beat came and Órlaith danced, weaving in and out, over and over, hand touching each passing dancer, men *tuathal*, women *deosil*, invoking and evoking the spring, the growth, the green, the rain. And each time Diarmuid went past, he stroked her palm rather than swing her hand.

> *"So drum beat and flute sound*
> *Once more we'll circle 'round*
> *For the world turns and the Wheel spins*
> *And all ends that once begins!*
> *This green hour, the heart knows,*
> *Is brief as the budding rose*
> *Though Wheel turn and bloom fade*
> *The heart sings the birth of May!"*

The ribbons tightened down as they danced and circled, binding the May Queen and May King in place, against the pole and each other, then the purple and orange ribbons closed upon her and the other Maidens and Squires, they were pressed forward, into the center, bound to the pole by the rest. The dancers halted and flung their hands up in a roar of laughter.

Órlaith heard the great shout and whispered, "Merry meet and merry part . . ."

"And merry get these ribbons gone!" she heard Raghnall grumble.

Delia came and tied the maypole ribbons tightly to the top above the heads of the May Queen and King and laughed, mischievous joy in her voice.

"So, Horned Lord, King of the Wood? Can you free yourself and take your prize?"

Maude stood beside Delia, laughing too.

"And free the Maidens and Squires that they may chase one another through the bowers!"

From the cocoon of ribbons Raghnall began to saw at the tangle of tough smooth fabric with the flint blade tucked into his breechclout, the cloth parting to the touch of the keen stone. By custom he should have taken the May Queen by the hand and led her to the Queen's Bower. Instead he caught her up in his arms and dashed headlong away, flourishing his antlers and giving a startlingly realistic bull-elk call, while Fiorbhinn laughed and threw up her arms in a theatrical gesture of helplessness. Maude paused thunderstruck. Out at the edge of darkness Juniper thumped her staff on the ground and laughed as well.

Órlaith was falling back when a feather touch on her shoulder brought her head around and her lips into a kiss.

"Diarmuid!" she gasped and then her hand darted forward, grasping and pulling at the wreath that encircled the gilded spikes of his antlers.

It broke and came away in her hand. By the law of the rite he must follow now; she darted away, hearing his sudden laugh, and knew him to be behind her. She ran, darting through the many people who cheered as she passed, calling luck-bringing—and bawdy—encouragement. Her legs kicked high, the skirts of the robe flying. As she ran, sweet heat gathered in her chest, and curled out, like a leaf uncurling in May indeed.

Diarmuid sprang ahead, spread his arms and she fled down another path, doubled back.

"By Flidais!" she invoked, trying to dodge under his arms and back to the main path. He caught her by the waist, spinning her around and up, and up and up, his horns falling off, her flower wreaths disintegrating into showers of petals. His lips sought hers, questing at first and then as her body took fire, becoming more insistent, more demanding. She gasped as he lifted his face and looked around.

"Where . . ." he asked, distractedly. Órlaith blinked and cast a quick glance at the woods.

"Here!" she said. "I was with the crew that prepared this stretch."

"A pity," murmured Diarmuid, "a pity. I set up a bower I hoped to bring you to."

Órlaith giggled, "But so did I! It's a little farther up!"

There was another bower, just behind them, with an oiled tarp, strewn with petals, a hay mattress, two quilts, one old, one new, one blue, one green, pillows and at the far end, a small box that would have wine and nibblements for later.

"They do say that it's bad luck to use the one you set up."

Órlaith hiked her skirts to get at the boots and squeaked when Diarmuid let himself fall like a tree next to her on the hay tick.

She yanked them off and he laughed. . . .

"Something borrowed!" he said holding up a pair of socks.

She was laughing, but it seemed to catch in her throat as Diarmuid leaned over her. "Shall I put them on you?"

She blushed furiously. "Not, not, not now. Diarmuid!"

He was bending for another kiss, but pulled back: "Yes, Golden Girl?"

"Bah!" she said, her embarrassed mood breaking, "You would tease on that! Diarmuid, have you? I mean, I, ah . . ."

He sat up abruptly. "Haven't," he said shortly.

Órlaith opened her mouth, looked at the tense back and flopped back. "Oh, thank goodness."

He turned swiftly, "Thank goodness?"

"Thank Goddess. It seems right to learn with somebody. All my tutors *teach* me, but this, this should be different and special."

His dark blue eyes lightened and he stroked a hand down her cheek. "Can I kiss every inch of your body?"

"Well, you can, but from all I've heard, it's not going to last very long."

"Yes, that's what Da told me, and all the older boys say the same."

"And the girls to me!"

"So if we can't make one time last, let's see how many times we can do! And that will take us to the dawn!"

CHAPTER TWENTY-ONE

"Speak to me, they speak to me
Of sky and wind, of sea and stone
Of moss and fern and cedar tree
Of cliffs where wild arbutus grow!"

Hooves beat through the mild spring warmth beneath the song as the Royal party and its escort of lancers and longbowmen and train of pack-beasts and varlets made their way south. It was as small a group as the High King of Montival and his heir could get away with on such a long trip to the wild frontier and not have Lord Chancellor Ignatius make yet another attempt to retire to his monastery in protest. The air was thick with birdsong, and swirls of Tortoiseshell butterflies rose before the hooves of the mounted party.

"Speak to me, they speak to me
Of orcas gliding through the deep

Of eagles balancing the wind
Above the waves where salmon leap . . ."

Threescore voices and a troubadour's mandolin across Heuradys d'Ath's saddlebow carried the swooping melody, everybody in the party who could sing and wasn't too self-conscious to do so in the High King's presence. Crown Princess Órlaith Arminger Mackenzie carried the tune effortlessly; she had a fine and well-trained contralto. There was the slightest tinge of envy in her enjoyment of the song; it was one of her Aunt Fiorbhinn's, her father's youngest half-sister and commonly thought to be the finest Mackenzie bard of her generation, if not the best in all Montival.

Órlaith had tried her own hand at *composing* songs and decided she was never going to be better than middling at it. That there were people who'd praise anything she did made it worse. Fiorbhinn was the daughter of one Mackenzie chieftain and the sister of another, but those weren't positions that made you the target of would-be flatterers.

"Speak to me, they speak to me
Of deer that browse the twilight fields
Of stony heron keeping watch
For what the silver sea might yield."

She couldn't even feel *very* envious; she'd always regarded Fiorbhinn as more of an elder sister—something she didn't have, being the oldest of five herself. John was the closest to her in age, and they were close in other ways, shared a lot of interests . . . he actually *was* a talented troubadour . . . but he *was* male. And a Christian at that. There were things you just didn't discuss with a brother, or a sister in her early teens. And having the said sisters confide in *you* just wasn't quite the same, glad though she usually was to serve as sounding board and wailing wall.

Thank the Lord and Lady for Herry, she thought, not for the first time. *We're near enough the same age—two years don't matter anymore—and we're both of the Old Religion, but she's an Associate not a Mackenzie. She really understands.*

> *"Speak to me, they speak to me*
> *Of what has been and what endures*
> *Of summer's bloom and autumn's fade*
> *In the circling of the years."*

The valley was a flattish plain on either side of the south-flowing river, bounded by low mountains to the west and lower ones to the east, opening out irregularly like a funnel southward towards the great Bay. She looked about as she sang, their voices startling flights of birds out of the brush and long grass, sometimes dense enough that they looked like climbing, twining skeins of air and smoke.

> *"Speak to me, they speak to me*
> *In voices humming in my bone*
> *In whispers rising on my breath*
> *In languages that tell of home!"*

The inland hills of the Vaca Range were distant; you

could just see how they were covered in rippling grass just turning from deep green to gold with tongues of woodland stretching up the ravines that scored them and clumps of blue oak and chaparral. Closer and westward the heights of the Mayacamas were dense-shaggy with forest, fir and pine and more. The air was warm and scented with smells stronger and spicier than the northern lands of her birth, arbutus and thyme and fennel. The broken remains of terraces showed here and there under the foothill brush.

"What do you think of Fiorbhinn's latest?" the High King asked her, as they finished.

"Wonderful, and spreading like a grass fire in the Palouse," she said. "Of course!"

"Your mother has told me for years that we need . . . what did they call it in the old days . . . a national anthem. A song everyone in Montival can like, that speaks to our love for the land itself. I think this may be it, and I'll talk to Fiorbhinn about that . . . hmmm . . . perhaps a few more verses about mountains and deserts . . ."

"And a *proud castle with banners* or two, Your Majesty," Heuradys said with an irrepressible grin. "For the north-realm."

"That too, Herry," he laughed.

Her fingers strayed to another tune, then to an occasional plucked note and to silence. They rode quietly for a while, to enjoy a land strange and foreign to them all; he was an easy man to be quiet with.

"Go n-ithe an cat thú," Órlaith cursed mildly as her horse stumbled, bringing the animal up with light hands and a firm grip of thigh and knee. "May the cat eat you, Dancer, and keep your mind to what you're about!"

Her black courser had caught a hoof on what was left of an old dead grape-vine, one of the innumerable thousands hidden by hock-high wild mustard. The main north-south road down the Napa Valley had suffered generations of summer wind and sun, winter flood and frost before the first Montivallan settlers arrived a few years ago, and they'd not yet done more than patch a few of the more manageable holes with dirt and gravel. Where the gaps in the ancient sun-faded asphalt were too wide traffic simply swerved westward away from the river, leaving ruts and trampled patches.

"That's harsh, *a stór*," her father chuckled. "Mind, my treasure, it's not Dancer's fault."

They were speaking *Gaeilge*, for practice sake; there weren't many people in Montival who could, though Heuradys had learned it for friendship's sake. Her father's mother Juniper, the founder and first Chief of the Clan Mackenzie, had learned it from *her* mother, who'd been born across the eastern sea, and taught it to her son and granddaughter both. It was a family tradition, and many clansfolk took the odd word or phrase from it, just as they'd copied her way of speaking in the early years and taken up the faith she and her core of early followers practiced. Over the generations the origins of customs and speech both had evolved from memory to legend for most.

Which is fair enough, Órlaith thought, remembering things her grandmother Juniper had said to her. *For what is the world of humankind, if not a story we tell each other so that we may live in it together?*

"This is a difficult patch, for horses," he went on.

"The ancients must all have been drunk as Dáithí's pig

seven days of the week and blind drunk the whole of Beltane month," she said, stroking the mare's neck. "I like a glass of wine as well as the next, but this is ridiculous! The whole valley must have been solid vineyards from east to west and north to south!"

"Now there's an *elevating* thought!" Heuradys said.

The High King laughed. "You just might think so," he said, with a wave of his arm. "Still, it's a bonny stretch of land, and at least they didn't cover the fields with buildings."

Some of the innumerable vines on the flat were still alive, monstrous house-sized tangled ground-hugging networks of shoots green with leaves or bone-hard and bare, sometimes climbing over a tree or snag of old building like a cresting vegetable wave caught in midmotion. More were dead gnarled knotted stumps, lurking among the tall grass and wild mustard and dense drifts of flaming gold California poppies, the brush and eucalyptus and oak and spreading feral olives. Even dead they lasted like iron.

A sound came from the southward, a deep rhythmic moaning coughing grunt, building to a shattering roar, loud even miles distant. The horses all shied a little. The humans frowned or grinned according to their natures. Something deep down in you whispered what that call meant: *man-eater*.

"And perhaps that was just a wee bit of an unfortunate way to swear," Órlaith's father chuckled. "Seeing as cats with a voracious and unreasonable appetite for horseflesh swarm upon the earth hereabouts."

Órlaith had been well tutored in ecology—which she'd enjoyed far more than the rest of the Classical curriculum inflicted on her, since that science still worked as it had before the Change. Tigers were common in most parts of Montival that weren't too dry and open, descended from zoo and park and private specimens sentimental owners had turned loose as the ancient world went down in wreck. Lions were not, being less common before the Change and much less able to adapt to cold winters after it. Down here in what had been California you met them more and more often as you went south, since they *did* like warm, dry open landscapes.

"Now, that would make an interesting rug," Heuradys said speculatively. "You up for a lion-hunt, Órry?"

"Now it is not as lion-food I have raised the Princess," her father said, then raised a hand: "But if lions were to try for our horses, of course, that would be another matter."

They'd seen mule deer, tule elk, feral horses and cattle, a troop of baboons, wild boar and flocks of emu and ostrich since they left the half-built castle at Rutherford, as well as scat and prints of tiger and wolf and distant glimpses of grizzly. A herd of lyre-horned antelope with tan coats and pale bellies had been grazing in the middle distance but giving the humans alertly nervous looks now and then. They took flight when the lion's roar added an extra dose of fear and white tails flashed as they bounced away like rubber balls in astonishing near-vertical leaps that she'd read were called *pronking*, ultimately derived from the same distant land as the lions via curious institutions the ancients had called *safari parks*.

Órlaith smiled at the sight, and Heuradys strummed the mandolin in time to the leaps, as if giving them musical accompaniment. The springboks lifted your heart to watch, and they looked as thoroughly at home as the flocks of yellow-breasted chats that rose like handfuls of flung gold coins as they passed, going wheet-wheet-wheet in protest.

More soberly, her father added: "And there were so many of the ancients. More in just one of the cities on the Bay south of here than in all our Montival even today. More than enough to drink the fruit of all these vines."

She nodded. She knew that, and unlike some of the tales she believed it down in her gut. Anyone did who'd seen the ruins and thought a little rather than just treating them as part of the landscape, though her generation was less haunted by it than their parents, and infinitely less than those who'd survived the great dying. That was why this land was empty. When the machines stopped hordes had eaten the countryside bare everywhere close enough to reach, then turned on each other amid plague and fire and horror. A few of their savage descendants still haunted the land, but only a handful of tiny civilized settlements tucked away in remoteness had greeted the explorers from the north. Mostly they'd been touchingly joyful to rejoin humankind.

"I'm glad we're not so crowded today," she said. "Portland and Boise are bad enough; you start to itch after a week or so."

He made a sound of agreement and Heuradys nodded emphatically; they were all countryfolk by raising and preference, which was something they shared with the overwhelming majority of their people. She'd gone far east once years ago, on a diplomatic visit to the Republic of Iowa with her parents, where mighty Des Moines had more than a hundred and fifty *thousand* folk within its walls. It had been a marvel and she was glad to have seen it, the largest city on this continent in this age but . . .

But once was enough, she thought. *And to think of towns ten or twenty times that size . . . brrr!* Aloud she went on:

"Bad for human folk to live as the ancients did, and worse for the land and the other kindreds."

"Truth," her father said, then dropped back into English. "Or at least that's *my* truth, and yours."

Órlaith began to nod, then gave her father a sharp glance, suppressing an impulse to scratch under her flat bonnet with its spray of Golden Eagle feathers in the clasp.

"It's a little disconcerting you can be at times, Da," she said in the same language; her voice held the musical Mackenzie lilt, though less strongly than her father's.

"What, and didn't I just agree with you?" he said blandly, then winked. "Most sincerely, too."

"Mother says you can be more aggravating by agreeing with her than any other dozen men can by arguing."

"Sure, and I have *no* idea what you might be on about. And you'll note she laughs when she says that."

Around a corner of the road, and a broad stretch of the renascent wilderness had been cleared save for some scattered valley oaks; winter wheat rippled waist-high across it, only a month or so from harvest and already showing heads. About the field young pencil cypress had been planted in a border. Beyond it southward the settlers were working on getting more land ready for plow and pasture, with a team of six big oxen leaning into their yokes.

A chain ran from them to a pit dug around a vine-root. Half a dozen folk were prying at the stump with long iron bars, and two men in kilts and little else leapt out of the hole, tossing before them the axes they'd used to chop roots halfway through. The teenaged girl in charge of the team yelled shrill encouragement and cracked her long whip, and the beasts leaned forward, pulling until their hooves sank deep and the muscles stood out beneath their red hides like cast bronze. The humans sang a working chant as they strained at their levers, and she could catch a bit of it, a hymn to the Maiden of Spring and Her consort:

> *"Far down the roots bind*
> *The heart's joy to summer's tide—"*

Then the oxen staggered forward as the grip of the dead vine parted with thunderous rippling *brack-kak-kak* sounds. The heavy knotted black form of the stump was dragged to join a windrow of other thigh-thick shapes amid laughter and cheers.

Several dogs had been lying in a patch of shade, of the big shaggy breed Mackenzies kept as companions and guards of hearth, hunt and war. They sprang to their feet and barked as the mounted column came in view, a deep baying that carried through the spring air like a bugle. Several padding along with the travellers answered in kind. The workers threw down their tools and turned towards the nearby spots where their longbows and quivers and sword belts rested, then relaxed as they saw men-at-arms and archers, not a skulking gang of wildmen. Glances turned to smiles and waves as they saw who it was; Órlaith and her father both wore plaids in the Mackenzie tartan pinned across their torsos over their saffron-dyed shirts.

"Oak, you're looking hale!" the High King called as he drew rein and raised a hand. "Merry meet!"

"Merry meet, and merry part, and merry meet again, *Ard Rí*," Oak Barstow Mackenzie replied. "Your scouts told us you'd be by, but not when."

"We're not in any haste. It's hard you're working, and that on the holy eve."

Oak was nearly sixty now, a tall man gone stringy and tanned to the color of his namesake tree's wood but still knotted with strong muscle moving under the sweat-wet skin. A long queue of graying blond hair hung down his back wrapped with an old bowstring, warrior-fashion; he'd been First Armsman of the Clan Mackenzie for long years before leading a party south to found a new settlement. A grin split his bearded face:

"We set ourselves a goal to be met before the festival, and when it looked like we wouldn't meet it our High Priestess—"

"That would be your daughter Rowan?" her father the High King said.

"So it is, her own self. She lost her temper, just a wee bit, and made it *gess* to stop before it was done, feast or no. This was the last stump we were scrambling at, cursing it to a Christian Hell the while, and your coming at its demise a good omen."

There was a little teasing in his voice as he went on:

"And doubly so since you brought our Golden Princess, and her so grown-up and lovely now, a fair young maiden like a vision of the Maiden of Spring herself!"

Órlaith blushed a little; that was what her name *meant*, but it sounded a bit embarrassing in common English. Also she hadn't been a maiden, technically speaking, for some time now; four Beltane Eves to the day, to be precise.

Ah, Diarmuid, she thought reminiscently.

Heuradys caught her eye and winked, obviously reading the thought—natural enough, she'd teased Órlaith about it at the time. Also, she'd renewed the acquaintance as they passed through the McClintock territories and guested with their Chief. His current leman hadn't minded—though as she'd said bluntly, that was not least because the Royal party *was* just passing through. In a way it was a pity he'd settled down, she was going to need a consort someday . . . no need to think of that right now, though.

It's a good friend you've been, Diarmuid, and a more than pleasant companion. I wish we saw each other more often.

"Merry met, Uncle Oak," she said, trying for a casual dignity; they weren't related by blood, but younger Mackenzies usually addressed the older generation that way, unless they were unfriends or the occasion formal. "How does Dun Barstow fare this fine day?"

"We're doing well, with Her blessing and the Lord's favor."

He made the Invoking sign. High King Artos—who was also Rudi Mackenzie—echoed it, and so did Órlaith and the others of the Old Religion behind them; some of the Christians crossed themselves politely.

Some of the clansfolk raised a brow in surprise when Heuradys echoed their gesture. Even apart from the arms of the Ath embroidered in a heraldic shield on the breast of her rust-colored T-tunic with a crescent of cadency, the rest of her garb left no doubt of what she was. She wore a teal-blue chaperon hat on her braided brown-red hair with the liripipe over her shoulder and a golden High Crown livery badge on it, sapphires on the buckle of her sword belt, tight leather breeks and folded thigh-boots, flared gauntlets and the small golden prick spurs of knighthood. Catholicism wasn't technically required by law among Associates these days—hadn't been since shortly after Órlaith's grandfather Lord Protector Norman Arminger died at the Field of the Cloth of Gold, in fact—but it was overwhelmingly the most common faith there, especially among the nobility.

Oak tossed a leather drinking-skin to her father, who uncorked it, spilled a drop in libation and took a swig before he handed it around; it was water cut with wine or possibly vice versa, and made them all formally guests on the Dun's land. The old clansman went on:

"We've got the watermill's Pelton wheel and the hydraulic ram working; the Dúnedain from Stath Ingolf just over the hills have been most helpful. The last harvest was good and the next looks to be even better—"

He spat aside and made the Horns with his left hand to show that he wasn't tempting the Fates.

"—this is fine land and we're learning its ways and how to please the spirits of place, who're happy to have humankind about once more. What brings you and your Da here, so far from Dun Juniper and so near Beltane?"

Rudi answered: "Seeing the land, and introducing Órlaith to it. And to mark out what we of the two-footed kindred and the animals who live with us may use in this valley, and what's rightly the domain of Lady Flidais and Her especial children."

Oak and his people nodded solemnly; so did Órlaith

and Heuradys. Flidais was the Goddess in Her aspect as Mistress of the Beasts; She drove a chariot pulled by sacred white deer, and Her very name meant *doe*; the wildwood and its dwellers belonged to Her and Her consort, the Horned Lord most often hailed as Cernunnos.

Órlaith knew that in other parts of Montival her father would have used different terms—in the United States of Boise he'd have talked of National Parks, and in the Association fiefs of the old north-realm about the rights of the Crown and Counts and baronage under Forest Law. In Corvallis, where the Faculty Senate of the University ruled, they'd speak confidently of the biodiversity of riparian wetlands and watershed maintenance; in the territory of Mt. Angel the learned warrior-monks of the Order of the Shield of St. Benedict would say the same, but also cite God's command that the sons of Adam exercise wise stewardship. The Lakota said White Buffalo Woman had told them what men might rightly take, and there were so many other stories. . . .

It all meant more or less the same thing, and she preferred the Clan's way of describing it. Besides, she'd seen Flidais in dreams herself, though not to speak to, and had a proper awe of Her power after a single glance from those moon-pale eyes. Wise folk asked Her permission to enter the unpeopled lands and walked lightly there, just as they thanked Cernunnos for luck in the hunt, and showed respect to the prey itself for its gift of life. You never knew when the Hour of the Hunter would come for you yourself—except that soon or late, it *would* come.

"It will be Órlaith's business soon enough," her father went on. "And—"

His blue-gray-green eyes narrowed. The High King

was just as old as the Change, born near Yule of that terrible year as darkness turned towards light, a tall handsome man with close-cropped red-gold beard and shoulder-length hair of the same sunset color; it suddenly shocked her a little to see how the wrinkles at the corners of his eyes were deeper than she remembered. Your parents seemed to go along changeless while you were small, but she was getting beyond that stage now.

Allowing for gender and age they were much alike, something more obvious now that she'd reached her full growth, save that her eyes were cornflower-blue and her hair wheat-blond with only a slight tinge of copper; she was about three fingers shorter than his six-foot-two, taller for a woman than he was for a man, with a similar long-limbed build.

"—and . . ."

His hand fell to the pommel of the sword by his right side, a sphere of milky crystal gripped by antlers. He wore it on that hip because his right arm had been injured long ago, on the great Quest to the eastern sea that brought the Sword of the Lady back from the fabled magic isle of Nantucket. The wound still pained him sometimes, and it had leached a very little strength and speed from the limb.

Everyone looked grave for a moment; the Sword of the Lady was *far* more than a weapon. Far more than merely a symbol of sovereignty, even, though it was that in truth. The bearer never talked much about it, but common knowledge was that it conferred powers, only the first of them being the gift—or curse—of telling truth from falsehood.

". . . and a feeling that I should be here, somehow."

"You'll guest with us?" Oak asked, plainly assuming they would.

"If it's not an imposition to feed four-score. We've supplies with us."

"There's plenty for the Beltane feast, and we're glad to share it. The lions and leopards and catamounts and tigers and wolves are a troublement to our herds, not to mention the grizzlies, but the hunting here . . . ah, you'd have to be blind and have no string-fingers to go short of meat. We've wild beef and fine yearling buck and a sounder of pig hanging in the icehouse right now, thanks be to Cernunnos, and everyone who isn't here pulling this last Annwyn's-Hounds-devour-it stump is cooking or baking or making ready to do so. Or rolling out barrels, the which requires a liberal testing of samples to make sure they've not gone off. Forbye we're also making trial of roasting a whole young ostrich overnight in a pit with hot stones. Halfway between chicken and veal, the taste is."

"Now you're making me drool. Offer accepted! You know Sir Aleaume?" the High King went on, indicating the commander of the men-at-arms. "He's come to the Guard since you hung up your bow."

The knight was a man in his twenties with bowl-cut reddish-brown hair, regular high-cheeked features only slightly marred by somewhat juglike ears, and slanted blue eyes.

Órlaith had known him off-and-on for years and thought him toothsomely handsome as well as brave and able and a fine singer and with a pawky sense of humor when you could get him to unbend a little. Unfortunately he was paralyzingly conscious of the gap in their ranks, or too much given to the troubadours' wilder flights of chivalry. The ones about true knights pining chastely over a fair maid from afar. Or both.

Particularly with her father about; Associates just thought differently about such things, and Christians were plain-and-simple strange. She understood, being half of that stock herself, but it could be a hindrance.

It's a fine thing to journey with Da, but it has its drawbacks. Not to mention that it took me and Herry falling about laughing at his painful discretion to convince Aleume that we're not lovers. Mother-of-All, but men can be idiots sometimes.

Oak gave a nod, friendly but not particularly deferential to the heir to the Barony of Tucannon; Mackenzies didn't pay much attention to rank.

"Aye, we've met," he said, to the knight's evident surprise. "Your father Baron Maugis and I worked together a good deal in the Prophet's War, young lord. I saw you once back then, but you'd not remember it, most likely. As I recall you were tugging at your mother's skirt and asking for a honey-tart. I hung up my bow about the time he became Grand Constable, and that in time of peace."

"I've heard the stories about what you and my father did at the battles around Corwin, good Clansman," the knight said in the clipped formal tones of a north-country noble minding his manners, leaning over to shake hands. "You and he and the others of your generation had all the grand adventures!"

Oak snorted, but declined to comment directly; a similar sound came faintly from Edain Aylward Mackenzie, the commander of the High King's Archers, who was riding just behind them. Órlaith could read the minds of both the old soldiers:

Adventure? You'd be welcome to my share, that you would, boyo.

She caught Heuradys' amber-colored eyes, and her liege-knight gave an almost imperceptible shrug. In theory she dutifully agreed with all the scarred middle-aged veterans who'd helped raise her; a ruler responsible for the homes and safety of her folk couldn't wish the wild times and deadly deeds back for their own sake . . . but they both understood young Sir Aleaume de Grimmond as well.

They'd both grown up in the shadow of those thunderous stories, much more immediate and more *real* than the tales of the ancient world. Then all their own lifetimes had seen a steadily spreading peace and prosperity in the broad lands of Montival and among the many peoples who hailed her father as liege, paid his scot and kept his laws. What the bards had taken to calling the Age of Gold, when a child with a full purse could walk from the western sea to the Lakota plains unmolested, and old feuds and hatreds receded into song and epic . . . or at least into nothing more serious than the odd brawl in a tavern.

It could get a little boring.

She suspected that was why many came south to this new province. It wasn't crowding, since there was still plenty of good land unplowed even in the Willamette Valley, the heartland of the realm.

Órlaith herself had taken to worrying a little about the hopefully distant day when *she* had to do the job and maintain what his father had built.

Da at least didn't have to start with being the beloved father-to-the-land. He got to be a wild youngster first, har-

*ing off into the back of beyond with his friends! I'll be ex-
pected to rule like him from the first day, but without the
Baraka his deeds brought with them. Lord and Lady pity
me . . . hopefully I'll be middle-aged by then. I know he
plans to give me more and more of the work, that's started
already.*

"You'll hear more of the old tales tonight," Oak
laughed. "There's nothing like wine to lubricate song
and story, and Goibniu of the Sacred Vat be witness,
we've plenty of *that* to go with the roast venison and
pastries. All we needed to do for grapes was prune, pick
and crush."

"Chief," Edain said abruptly, raising his binoculars for
a moment; one of his dogs had looked up and whined,
then the other pair came to their feet and pointed southward. "One of our scouts is headed back our way, and in
a bit of a hurry."

CHAPTER TWENTY-TWO

Everyone went from genial to cold cat-alert at the tone. The Bow-Captain of the High King's Archers was two years younger than her father and looked a bit older, a broad-shouldered weathered man of middle height who shaved his square chin, unlike most clansfolk his age. He made a slight imperative gesture, and the Archers all slipped off their horses and strung their great yellow yew bows with a brace and pull and flex; the beasts were for getting them about where bicycles weren't practical, but you needed your feet on the ground to use the Mackenzie weapon.

The sound of a horse at a gallop came before the scout reappeared around a clump of oaks, and the muffled thud of a saber-scabbard against a leather-clad thigh and then the rattle of arrows in a quiver. Órlaith saw out of the corner of her eye that Heuradys had leaned over and was giving sharp concise orders to a varlet, who ran for the pack-train, but her main attention was concentrated on the messenger.

The quarter horse was lathered as she drew rein, with foam speckling her light mail shirt. Órlaith recognized her; her father had always said you should know as many names as possible. Nohemi Hierro, a wiry brown-skinned, black-haired young woman from the CORA territories around Bend, on the dry side of the High Cascades. A Rancher's retainer by birth, with a hawk-nose and a small gold ring in one ear and a dandified trio of coyote-tails at the back of her helmet, spending a few years in the Royal service to see the world and build a stake.

"Your Majesty," she said, raising her recurve bow in salute and offering a folded message. She pronounced it more like *Yer Maj'sty*, in the manner of her folk.

"Give us the verbal précis," he said as he opened it.

Órlaith could see a sketch-map on the paper. Her father gave it a single flickering glance and handed it to her; he had an uncanny grasp of the terrain anywhere in the High Kingdom, as if he could summon up maps in his head or see the living land from a bird's-eye view.

The sketch was concise enough, and everyone in the High Kingdom's forces used the same set of symbols for landscape features. There was the marshy strip of beaver-dams and reeds and dense tangled willow-alder-sycamore-cottonwood forest along the river laced together with wild vines, the ruins of ancient Napa town, which were now a wood too, with bits of building sticking up through it, open country just to its north. An X at the western end of two parallel stretches of woods, and an arrow pointing towards it. She memorized and handed it back to Edain, and he to the rest.

The scout obeyed, raising her voice so all the officers and squad-leaders crowding close could hear clearly:

"Captain Hellman reports two groups of outlanders are fighting each other to the south of here, about three miles. There's at least one beached ship, it's burning, you'll be able to see the smoke soon. He thinks two more beyond it, no more than a light watch on either."

"How many blades?" her father said crisply.

"More than one hundred, less than two, both sides together, but one side outnumbers the other two, three to one. Some of them are Haida—"

There was a growl and a hiss and a rattle from the High King's party; seaborne raiders from those northern isles had been a plague to the coasts of Montival since not long after the Change, despite defenses and punitive expeditions. They had little enough in common with the ancient tribe except the name, but they were pirates for certain, and vicious enough and to spare, and their hit-and-run attacks were the one problem Montival had never really been able to solve completely.

"But there are two other groups, different gear and banners, nothing we've ever seen or heard of. One lot is fighting side by side with the Haida against the third bunch."

"Well, that simplifies things, just a bit; we'll judge each by the company they keep, for the present."

The scout nodded. "Captain Hellman is keeping them all under observation and holding us out of sight; we went in on foot and stealthy to get the information, once we spotted them on our way back from the Bay. They're not paying much attention to anything but each other. He says that if you want to intervene, you'd best be quick; the fight won't last much longer."

"He's wise to wait, with no more than a dozen scouts. Back with you, tell him I'm following in your tracks and he's to meet and brief me, screening as he does. Prepare for action."

He turned to Oak. "How many bows can Dun Barstow muster?"

"Who're listed for the First Levy? Two-score and three; the folk here are mostly young and fit. Except for me," he added with a grim smile. "And I'm fit enough. We've bicycles enough for them all. Like old times, eh?"

"If it's all the same to you I'd rather watch sheep eat grass. Turn them out and follow quick as you can, with the usual cautions."

Oak nodded without bothering to speak, and he and his snatched up their weapons and headed off westward at a run. Most Mackenzies were a loquacious folk by inclination, and loved argument and debate, but they knew when to shut up as well.

The High King went on, writing on his own order pad, tearing off the sheet and holding it out: "Sir Aleaume! A rider to Castle Rutherford. The commander to order a general alert, word to all the settlements in the valley, and his ready company to move out at once. And I want both his gliders in the air, I need reconnaissance of this whole area."

The knight barked an order, and a messenger in the leathers of a courier took the paper, stuffed it under his helmet-lining and took off northward towards that half-completed fortress, leading two remounts at a gallop. Edain put his bow in front of his monarch's horse as it turned to a shift of its rider's balance.

"Arm up first, Chief. And the rest o' the lobsters.

We're not in such a hurry you can't spare that much time."

Her father snorted, said: "Yes, mother," and slipped off his mount.

Órlaith did likewise, speaking before the guard-captain could:

"And if you say *the little princess had best stay behind* I'll clout you, old wolf. I've taken valor"—which meant qualifying for the First Levy, among the Clan—"and earned the golden spurs as well."

Her mother Mathilda was Lady Protector of the Portland Protective Association as well as High Queen, and the old north-realm was the home of chivalry.

"You were the age I am now when you went east on the Quest, too, that you were," she finished.

"Which is the truth, and I wouldn't dream of saying anything like that," Edain said, with a wry twist of his mouth.

And patent untruth; he'd been guardian to her all her life, even more than to her brothers and sisters. His own children had laughed to her more than once how glad they were he wasn't such a clucking mother hen with *them*.

Her father stood with arms outstretched, and the High King's squires rushed forward lugging heavy canvas sacks full of armor before they helped each other.

You couldn't don full plate by yourself without time and contortions, and Órlaith was too recently a knight herself to have a squire of her own. Heuradys didn't either, since her duties as junior household knight made it difficult; that was a substantial responsibility, one they both took seriously. Instead they would help each other on with the gear; that was nearly as fast as having a squire do it.

Heuradys' eyes were shining. "This is it," she whispered. "I told you back when we were little girls that I'd be your liege-knight and fight by your side someday."

"You called it, liegewoman," Órlaith nodded.

They put their hands on each other's shoulders. Heuradys closed her eyes for a moment and spoke, with none of the usual hint of mockery in her voice:

"Shining war-maid, Gray-Eyed One of the piercing glance, I pray to you. Precision and unmuddled thought grant to me, surety and conviction, quick wit and quick action and unbaffled sight. Protector of the City, let me protect my King and her to whom I have sworn my oath, though my life be the cost."

Órlaith hesitated for a moment. Then: "Dark Mother, in whatever form I need You most, come to me now, that I be worthy of my oaths and honor and the land that looks to my blood for guardianship. And what price You ask, that I shall pay without withholding."

Something seemed to pass across her eyes. She blinked and it was gone. The rest of the lancers were on the ground too, assisting each other to complete the additions to the half armor they usually rode in to spare the horses.

Oh, Powers, she thought an instant later as they efficiently stripped the gear out of the padded bags. *If Heuradys doesn't make it, I'd have to go tell Lady Delia and her family!*

It would be easier just to get killed yourself, but she pushed the thought aside. The arming doublet went over her head in a brief moment of blindness and the smell of stale sweat that never came out of the padding after the first use—cynics called it the scent of chivalry. Deft fingers doubled her fighting braid and tied it around her head; Heuradys just used a knitted cap for hers. Metal clattered and weight came on shoulder and hip, calming and reassuring and familiar.

She shook herself to seat it all properly when it was finished, and she and Heuradys touched the knuckles of their armored gauntlets and shook hand-to-wrist. Then she took the flared sallet helm and settled it on her head with her palms on either side of the low dome, making sure the six pads gripped firmly but not too tightly before she fastened the chin-cup. She left the curved visor up, like the bill of a cap. You didn't want to view the world through a vision slit until you had to, the way it muffled sound was bad enough.

The fan of Golden Eagle feathers on the crest caught the breeze with a faint rippling sound. Heuradys wore a similar V-shaped wedge on hers, but it was fashioned from the black-scalloped white feathers of the Harfang, the Great Snowy Owl. Somehow the act of putting on your helm made you feel different. More *focused*, as if you were now *about* something more limited, more primal. Like the metal on the edge of a blade.

"What could this be about?" Órlaith said, looking south.

My first battle, perhaps, at the least, she thought, swallowing a mixture of dry-mouthed eagerness and a sinking in the belly as an involuntary flash of doubt over how she'd show went through her mind.

She'd been trained for it all her life that she could remember. Intensively so by the finest teachers since it became obvious she had the inclination and would grow into the heft for the business. Her own father was the foremost warrior of his day, and that with his own hands as much as commanding armies. Her mother had been a knight, a rare thing for a woman up in the Association territories, and a good one. Órlaith had hunted boar and bear and tiger, of course, and flown gliders and gone rock climbing, and tournaments weren't exactly *safe*, not when a lancehead came at you travelling thirty miles an hour, even a blunt and rebated one.

But how could you really know how you'd greet the Red Hag before you met Her?

"That's what we should find out," her father said, answering her last words and unintentionally echoing her thought. "There are Haida this far south, which is bad, and foreigners making free with their steel on our land, the which I will not have. And if the Haida have made a foreign alliance, we must know of it."

Varlets had switched their riding saddles for the heavier, longer-stirruped war type. Órlaith checked the girths—some things you just didn't leave to someone else, even if you trusted them implicitly—took a skipping step and vaulted up. Doing that in armor was one of the tests of knighthood among Associates; not as difficult as it looked, since the fifty pounds of steel was well-distributed, but not easy either and it made you look a proper fool if you missed. Her father got into his with a plain businesslike lift and swing.

She settled into the saddle and accepted the four-foot kite-shaped shield. It was blazoned with the undifferenced Crowned Mountain and Sword that only she and her father could bear; she ducked her head beneath the strap and ran her left forearm through the loop set on the inside. The grip for her hand was at the upper right corner and she held it loosely for now, taking the reins around two fingers.

Riding in full plate was different, there was a lot less contact with the mount, but their horses were well trained and of the tall muscular breed called coursers— what knights rode in battle when they weren't using the far more specialized and expensive destriers.

"Forward," her father said calmly when everyone was ready, slanting his left gauntlet to the front for a moment.

Dancer fidgeted a little, sensing her nervousness. She made herself draw her breath deep, holding it and then releasing slowly while thinking of a pond of still clear water, a technique she'd been taught during a stay at Chenrezi Monastery far off eastward in the Valley of the Sun. It worked just the way the monks of the Noble Eightfold Path said, and she found herself taut but calmer. The Archers spread out in a double line and loped off southwards along the scout's track.

Heuradys reined her mount Toad in on her right, Órlaith's vulnerable shieldless side, and just a little back.

"I've got your flank here, Órry," she said. "Just keep your eyes ahead."

The High King spared his daughter a brief glance and a grim smile that was mostly a narrowing of the eyes, accompanied by a small slight nod. Her heart swelled; she'd *imagined* going into battle by his side a thousand times, and a fierce determination not to fail him or the others helped quell the butterflies that seemed to be nesting below her breastbone.

The Archers were moving southward at a steady trot with their kilts swirling around their knees, drawing a little ahead before the heavy horse followed. They all wore Mackenzie war-gear, the brigantine of little plates riveted between two layers of soft green leather, bow and quiver, short sword and buckler and dirk, though the blazon on their chests was the Crowned Mountain, not the Moon-and-Antlers. Not every one was actually of the Clan; to be accepted into that oldest of the Guard units all you had to do was pass some stringent tests, be very good with the bow to begin with . . . and swear fealty before the bearer of the Sword of the Lady, who could see into your innermost soul as you pledged.

A few came from as far away as the kingdom called Norrheim on the far eastern ocean where her father had paused and found allies during the Quest in his youth.

The plate-armored knights and squires and men-at-arms followed with their horses at a quick walk, keeping in double column. The varlets brought up the rear, save for a few left with the provisions and tents, sumpter-mules and remounts. They weren't fighters by trade, but they were armed and everyone in the High King's train was expected to turn their hand to what was needful. The healer and her two assistants came last.

Órlaith could hear a soft murmur from her father beside her, of prayer to his patron and hers, the Goddess in Her form as the Lady of the Crows, the Dark Mother. It ended with:

"And if this be the day when the King must die for the people, then know that I go to You most willing, as to a joyful feast."

She knew that one, but she'd never heard him speak it before. It was the prayer before battle, and the King's prayer at that. When she spoke she tried for lightness:

"It'll be a skirmish only, surely, Da? Compared to all the great battles you've fought."

His grin was hard. "My heart, when men fight to kill, there's no such thing as a *small* battle. Not for the ones killing and dying, at least. Nor is it the less hard afterwards to tell a mother why the one she remembers as a child at her breast will not be coming home, or a child why they're an orphan."

Abashed, she looked down at her horse's head for a moment. His expression turned gentle, and his voice soft.

"My treasure, Edain or Sir Aleaume could manage this fight as well as I. For that matter, Father Ignatius could, even with his beard gone white—and for the rest of the daily work, he's a better administrator than I, or even than your mother is or her mother was, and that is saying a very great deal."

"But there's more than either to being High King." She'd known that, but right now it felt as if she was learning it all over again. "That's why you're going yourself."

"Aye. Your mother's faith and ours share a deep truth: that from sacrifice springs great power, and the greatest of all from the one who walks to it with open eyes, knowing their fate and consenting. Didn't their God's only begotten Son give himself to it? And that was a deed whose echo resounds down the ages; so also the One-Eyed gave Himself to Himself to win the wisdom he needed. So it is with the very Lord, who dies each year when the yellow corn falls before the reaper's steel, that humankind may eat and live."

"And He rises again in the spring to wed the Maiden."

"Aye; we rest, and we return, but that doesn't make the dying any less real. Your mother and I bound our very selves to this land and all its peoples and kindreds at the Kingmaking on the shores of Lost Lake, with the Sword of the Lady and a drop of our mingled blood. You were beneath her heart at that moment; through you we bound all our descendants to the King's fate. One day *my* day will come. And one day . . . may it be distant . . . so you too will walk to the Dark Mother, your eyes open to the falling blade."

"May it be distant for you too, Da!"

He laughed, and out of the corners of her eye she could see men in the column looking at each other and grinning to see the High King merry before a fight. They were alone enough to keep the conversation private if they spoke quietly, but in full view. Her father went on:

"From your mouth to ears of the Three who spin Fate, my heart. But we must always be ready for it. We of the royal kin are those whose blood renews the land."

Seriously, with a brisk tone: "Now, you know what you'll be about, girl, and take my word for it that you're a warrior born and have learned your lessons well. They're written in your bone and muscle now. Just listen to the wisdom of the body, and remember this: when a man takes a spear in his hand and comes up against you, he accepts his death and leaves you clean of it, just as you do for him. So strike hard and don't hesitate."

He looked beyond her to Heuradys. "And as for you, knight, you bear proud arms on your shield. Let's just say I'm as happy to have you on my daughter's shieldless side as I would have been to have your second mother in her prime. Which is to say a great deal."

Captain Hellman trotted up and reined in, a rawboned man in his thirties with a weathered face and short-cropped brown beard, followed by his troop. His birth-place was east of the Rockies themselves in the kingdom's farthest marches short of the Lakota lands, and there was a sharp High-Line plainsman's twang in his voice when he saluted and spoke, pointing:

"They'll be visible just beyond that clump of eucalyp-tus around the ruined farmhouse, sire. The ones under attack are making a stand on a slight rise—it's open to the east, flanked by woods, and at the west end there are some low snags of brick wall they're using, I'd say they were making for the mountains and that was as far as they got before the others caught them. There's about thirty or forty of them left. Three times that of the attackers. Four-score dead and wounded on both sides. They're se-rious about this, no prisoners I could see. Nobody else within an hour's walk unless they're lying on their backs in the swamp breathing through reeds."

"How much time?" the High King asked.

He's thinking of Oak, Órlaith knew. *With his Dun Bar-stow levy, we'd have the numbers on our side.*

"None. The next rush will overrun them, sire," Hell-man said stolidly.

"What's the ground like, just there?"

"Grass, mostly, leadin' up to the ruins. Looks like it was open grazing land or what did they call it, a lawn, and the snags of walls are long enough to have been a knight's manor or a fair-sized Rancher's home-place, but nothing much above waist-high now. None of these damned vine-stumps between those two tongues of woodland, and they've trampled it pretty flat. It looks solid, I'd take it at a gallop. Even on them big beasts you're riding."

"Gear?"

"Mixed. The foreigners on the hill all have pretty good armor and what looked like longbows and curved swords like the Kyklos use. They're in dense formation around a banner but I couldn't see what was on it. The Haida, the usual light gear. Looks like the strangers with them have mail, mostly; and they all have helmets. Pole arms and recurve bows, chopping swords. Some shields. They're in fair order but it's no Bearkiller phalanx."

The High King blew out a breath. "Hasty approach, then." He cocked an eye at their surroundings. "Not dry enough for much dust, they may not spot us until we're upon them. The which would be a *good* thing."

He thought for a moment, right hand caressing the pommel of the Sword, then went on calmly: "They'll break for their ships if they can when they're beaten . . . you lead in on my signal, then extend our flank to the left, Captain Hellman. Block them when they run, we'll have none leaving to alert others who may be about. We can snap up their ships afterwards. Sir Aleaume, we'll let the light horse and the Archers soften them a little, and then give them the lance when they're on the back foot. Edain, deploy on either side of the men-at-arms, riddle them, then follow us in when we charge."

Edain grunted. "Where's that battery of field catapults when you need them?" he said.

Rudi grinned. "Why not wish for that band of Mc-Clintocks we were offered when we guested at their Chief's hall south of Ashland? Likely lads and lasses they looked, if a bit . . . *rambunctious and independent*, as you might say."

"Or *a pack of drunken fookin' savages* . . . as you might

say. Covered in tattoos, as well. But I wish we had them, Chief, that I do."

High King Artos heeled his horse a little forward and turned as he stood in the stirrups for a second, speaking to carry:

"Strangers have come with weapons in hand to make war on Montival's land. It's the King's work to ward his folk from such. Are you with me, brothers and sisters?"

"Artos and Montival!"

Órlaith found herself shouting as loud as the rest, and echoing the growl within the cry. Her father raised a hand, and silence fell.

"All right, let's be about it. Hellman, move out. Edain, follow at fifty yards."

The light cavalry reined about. Edain wet a finger and held it up, then called to his command.

"The wind will be in our teeth and a little from the left, but not too bad. Remember you'll lose ten paces range and correct for drift. We'll start dropping shafts on their heads at ten-score and fifty paces and advance with walking fire; use your bodkins first and we'll clear a path for the lobsters. They need it, the puir darlin's."

Many of the High King's Archers grinned, and some of the men-at-arms scowled. *Lobster* was Mackenzie slang for the plate-armored heavy cavalry of the Association, and not a compliment.

Edain went on: "Shoot fast and listen for the word. Take surrenders if they're offered at the last but don't take any risks about it. Now follow me."

CHAPTER TWENTY-THREE

The High King's force slid south. Time seemed to pass with shocking speed for Órlaith though she was achingly conscious of every second; she made herself let her shield drop a little so the guige-strap could take its fifteen-pound weight and keep that arm limber for when she needed to move it swiftly. She could see a plume of smoke now from ahead and to the left, dirty-brown wisps rising and blowing towards them; that must be the burning ship the scout had mentioned.

"I wonder why it is that folk always set things on fire during a fight?" her father mused calmly. "Because they do, so. Whether there's a reason or not. I've seen horizons afire from one edge to the other, rick and cot and tree, when armies passed through."

Then they were past the last roll of land—even what looked like flat terrain could be deceptive that way—and the clamor of voices and a hard banging clatter came on the wind. She could see the strangers as they turned west,

a cluster of tiny figures at the end of a long alley of trampled tall grass no more than a bowshot across. A chant
was building amid a rhythmic clash of wood and metal,
probably the attackers nerving themselves for another
rush . . . though she couldn't be sure.

It's confusing, she thought. *Well, thank the Crone and
the Keeper-of-Laws I'm not in charge. Twenty minutes ago
all I was looking forward to was a Beltane feast at Dun
Barstow and findin' out what roast ostrich tastes like!*

Órlaith thrust her right hand out.

"Lance!"

The squire who'd armed her father pushed the lance
into her palm. She closed her hand around the ashwood
of the grip below the dish-shaped guard, the hide binding
rough even through the leather palm of her steel gauntlet, resting the butt on her thigh with a *click* of metal on
metal. The sound and the feel of the tapering twelve-foot
shaft were familiar, but everything was strange, as if she
were seeing the world clear yet distant through a sheet of
salvaged glass.

"Noisy bastards," Heuradys said quietly to her side, as
Toad tossed his head and champed at his bit until foam
drooled from his jaws. "But this is good ground for a
knight's battle. Very good. Auntie Tiph always said pick-
ing the right ground was half way to winning."

Her father made another gesture with his left hand
and called: "*Now*, Hellman."

The horse-archers all dropped their knotted reins on
their horses' necks, reached over their shoulder for a shaft
and leaned forward. Their mounts rocked up to a canter
and then a gallop, abruptly shrinking away forward. Another shout of *Artos and Montival!* went up from them,

and then a chorus of yelping, yipping cries, like mad coyotes or files on metal or both.

The High King hadn't taken his lance yet, and used that hand to raise binoculars to his eyes. He barked a laugh.

"Da?" she said, startled.

"They're just now noticing us. There's a Haida chief in a sealskin jacket sewn with iron rings running up and down shouting at them to look to their rear . . . yes, and kicking their backsides too, by way of getting their attention."

Even Sir Aleaume, who was a bit stiff, chuckled at that.

"*So* sorry, are we *interrupting* something private and intimate?" Heuradys added, and there were more harsh barks of amusement.

They were closer now, close enough to see the enemy formation writhe and shake as the first flight of arrows from the horse-archers slashed into them, just as they tried to turn their attention to the rear. The light horsemen rose in their stirrups and went into a fast nock-draw-loose rhythm as they charged.

The war cries from the strangers were suddenly interspersed with shrieks of raw pain as arrows driven by the springy horn-and-sinew bows slammed down out of the sky; and the beleaguered group in the ruins rose and started shooting at their foemen again too. The horse-archers broke to the right at fifty yards from the enemy front— you could only aim ahead, behind and to the left from horseback—and raced down their ranks, loosing with flat aimed shots at close range in a ripple that emptied their quivers. Arrows came back at them, but few and hasty; then they were turning away, twisting in the saddle to shoot a last shaft or two behind them. They thundered by the rest of the Montivallan party to the right, whooping triumph and waving their bows in the air, looping around to refill from the packhorses led by the varlets.

"Nicely done, almost like a drill," her father said judiciously. "Hellman knows his business." A little louder: "When you think the range is right, Bow-Captain."

Another dozen paces, and Edain's voice cracked out: *"Draw!"*

His command halted and the yew staves bent, the Archers sinking into the wide-braced, whole-body, arse-down style that the Clan's longbowmen practiced from the age of six, what they called drawing *in the bow*. The points of the bodkins glittered as they rose to a forty-five-degree angle, and the drawing-hands went back until they were behind the angle of the jaw. Behind the Archers their piper cut loose with the keening menace of the "Ravens Pibroch"; bringing along a battery of Lambeg drums would have been excessive with less than a tenth of the guard-regiment here, but you wouldn't find forty Mackenzies without at least one set of bagpipes.

Edain's voice punched through the savage wail of the *píob mhór*:

"Let the gray geese fly! Wholly together—shoot!"

There were twice twenty and one of the High King's Archers here, counting their commander. That wasn't enough longbows to generate the sort of sky-darkening arrowstorm that had smashed armies on the battlefields of the Prophet's War. Though the target was a lot smaller too, if nicely packed, and these were picked experts who could loose a shaft every three or four seconds and put it exactly where they wished. Forty scythed down into the foreigners in the first volley, then a flickering stream as each bowman walked four paces, shot, walked, shot . . .

Órlaith swallowed; she was close enough now to see men screaming and staggering with an arrow through the face or writhing on the ground trying to pull out one that had punched through armor into chest or belly or groin, or just lying still with their eyes open wide. With the wind in her face she thought she could smell that tang of salt and iron too, like being in a garth in the autumn at pig-slaughtering time . . . except that there was no one standing by with a bucket of oatmeal to catch the blood for sausages.

When her father spoke his voice had the flat judiciousness of a landsman looking at a yellow field of grain he'd plowed and sown and tended, rubbing a handful of ripe ears between his hands before tasting the kernels and nodding satisfaction that it was time to send in the reapers.

"We surprised them right enough. Now they're dung for our pitchforks, the careless bastards. Let's not let them get their balance back."

Even with her nerves thrumming-taut Órlaith shivered a little. Her father was a gentle and forbearing man, slow to anger and quick to laugh and endlessly patient in composing the quarrels of which Montival's wildly varied peoples had an abundance.

One of her earliest memories was clinging to his back with a tiny fallen bird in her free hand as they climbed a tree to put it back in the nest. He would make a three weeks' ride in the dead of winter to be sure of the facts in an appeal to the Crown's justice, when a death sentence was at stake. This was a side of him she hadn't seen much of before, and suddenly the tales of the man who'd broken the Prophet's hordes and forged a kingdom took on a new light.

It had been a *sword* that the Lady had given him on the magic isle, after all.

"Sir Aleaume!" he said crisply, as he extended his hand for his lance and a squire leaned forward to fill it. "Advance to contact!"

The baron's son nodded to his signaler. That young man raised the long Portlander trumpet slung across his body and put the mouthpiece to his lips.

The men-at-arms knocked down their visors with the edge of their shields as he raised the *oliphant*. Órlaith did the same; darkness fell with a *click* as the metal snapped into its catch, and the world shrank to a long narrow slit of brightness, like a painting or a tapestry. Her father's visor and hers were both drawn down to points at chin level, suggesting a beak: his was scored and inlaid with black niello like his helm, echoing the feathers of the Raven that was his sept totem. The markings on hers were threads of pure burnished gold, for the great hunting eagle that had come to her on her spirit-quest. Something of that raptor's intensity seemed to fill her, as if she were a vessel of movement and focus stooping from a great height.

"Chevaliers, *haro*!" Aleaume shouted. "For Artos and Montival . . . *à l'outrance, charge!*"

The silver scream of the *oliphant* echoed the command, like a white flash in the mind. Their coursers were as well trained as the men, and scarcely needed rein or spur or even the riders' shift of balance. The dozen armored men-at-arms spread out into a close-spaced line and their horses moved up the pace. Walk . . . trot . . . a long rocking canter . . . and the pennants began to snap and flutter in the speed of their hoof-drumming rush.

They passed where the archers had halted in easy range of the enemy, a score on either side; the arrows were still going by overhead, focused now on the spot where the lanceheads would go home. Apparently the foemen knew something about receiving a cavalry charge, for they were trying to pack together and present a hedge of points to the horses; trying and failing, falling or throwing up shields to stop the rain of gray-feathered cloth-yard shafts.

Closer, a hundred yards, and then the trumpet shrieked again for the gallop—a close-held controlled hand-gallop, not the wild dash that would scatter them like hailstones on a roof. Her instructors had hammered home that the shock of a charge depended on all the lances striking at the same moment. Her father's lance came down, and she couched her own; the rest followed in a ripple, the black-gold-silver of Heuradys' pennant rattling and cracking a yard to the right and twelve inches behind her own.

The foot-long blades of the heads pointed down at breast-height on a standing man, wavering only a little as the hooves pounded and the horses' heads pumped up and down. She raised her left fist to just below her chin, and that put the curved upper rim of her shield right below the level of her eyes.

It didn't feel heavy now, just comfortingly solid. Arrows shot by the men facing them went by with a nasty *whpppt* sound, one glanced with a *tick* against the side of her helmet like a quick rap with a hammer, and then three smashed into the shield *crack-crack-crack*, punching

through the thin sheet-steel facing and into the bullhide
and plywood beneath.

Someone is trying to kill *me!* went through her mind.

She knew it was absurd even as she thought it, but that
didn't remove the sense of *indignation*, and it carried the
faint memory of a scolding and swat on the bottom she'd
gotten when she was six and pointed a half-drawn bow at
someone.

The impact of the arrows hammered against her, but
the grip of the high-cantled war saddle kept her firm and
she braced her legs in the long stirrups. What was about
to happen would be much worse. Hitting things at speed
with a lance she knew about.

Pick your man, a harsh remembered voice spoke at the
back of her mind. *Pick him the moment you couch the lance
and your horse goes up to the gallop.*

It had been an old knight from County Molalla, with
a wrinkled brown face like a scar-map of campaigns and
lumpy with ancient badly healed bone-breaks. He lec-
tured the young squires in his charge with the combination of vehemence and boredom used for vital truths told
a thousand times, and he'd spared none of them an iota
for birth or rank or sex:

*You can't change your mind once you're committed and
you get only one chance with a lance. Don't waste it.*

A mailed figure ahead of her with a spike atop a conical
helmet that spread in a lobster-tail fan over his neck was
waving his square-tipped blade and screaming a war cry
that sounded something like *jew-che* as he tried to rally his
men. She let the point dip towards him; a touch of the
rein to neck and the alignment of the lance itself brought
the last ounce of effort from Dancer. The man snarled

with his eyes wide and swept the sword back, suddenly close enough to see a mole beside his mouth—

Thud!

Impact, massive and somehow soft and heavy at the same time, wrenching savagely at her arm and shoulder and slamming her lower torso against the curved cantle of the saddle. Near two thousand pounds of horse and armored rider moving *fast*, all packed behind the hard steel point. You could knock yourself head over heels off the horse if you did it wrong, but she came back upright as the lance broke across and she made her hand unclench and toss away the stub. The man in the pointed helm was down, with the lancehead driven right through his body and three feet of the shaft standing out of his chest.

He's dead, she thought suddenly. *I killed him.* Then her father's voice: *Don't hesitate.*

Her hand pulled the war hammer loose from the straps at her saddlebow, a yard of steel shaft with a serrated head on one side and a thick curved spike on the other. A Haida warrior with an orca painted on his round shield tried to come in stooping low and hack at the horse's legs. Dancer came up in a perfect running *levade* and lashed out with both forehooves. Her body flexed again, and her teeth went *click* as the horse stamped on over the prostrate body.

She blocked a spearhead with the point of her shield and lashed down with the war hammer on the top of the man's helmet: metal dented and bone cracked beneath, the feeling vibrating up the shaft and into her hand.

"Morrigú!" her father's voice shouted.

"Scathatch!" her own replied in a keening shriek as she hacked down to the right with the spike.

And that was most strange, some distant part of her mind noted. He had named the Crow Goddess, the aspect of Her that watched over warriors; for She was all things, the gentle Mother-of-All who gave life and the Red Hag who reaped men on a bloody field as well.

Órlaith had called instead on the Dark Mother in Her most terrible form: Scathatch.

The Devouring Shadow Beneath.

She Who Brings Fear.

For a moment there was nothing but chaos, the knights ramping through the mass like steel-clad tigers, sword and hammer and lashing hooves, the Archers running up and firing point-blank before throwing down their bows and wading in with buckler and short sword. A man leveled a crossbow at her, but an already-bloodied lancepoint tore into his throat with savage force and a deadly precision.

"Alale alala!" Heuradys screamed, tossing the lance aside and drawing her sword. *"Alale alala!"*

Then the beleaguered foreigners who'd been facing certain death before the Montivallans arrived rose from among the ruins and charged into the disordered mass. There were only thirty on their feet, many wounded, but they came in a disciplined armored mass of points and swords, a red-and-white banner fluttering in their midst and a harsh baying throat-tearing chorus sounding in time to the pounding of their boots:

"Tennōheika banzai! Banzai! Banzai! *Banzai!"*

The newcomers fell upon their foemen with terrifying intensity and skilled fury, like a blizzard of dancing butcher knives. The enemy broke then, south and west, screaming in terror and throwing away their weapons to run the faster. Hellman's light cavalry looped effortlessly around them and deployed, though there seemed to be two less of them. The ten drawn up in a semicircle with their stiff bows pulled to the ear were enough, though. The foemen stopped and milled about; one or two drove daggers into their own throats, or each other's. Those were the surviving Haida—they seldom let themselves be taken alive, which saved the Montivallans the trouble of hanging them for piracy.

Órlaith turned Dancer and followed her father without conscious thought. For an instant her attention went to what clotted and dripped on the head of her war hammer; she gulped a little and dragged it through a bush as she passed.

"Odd," her father said. "That war cry the enemy were using—it meant *self-reliance*, more or less. An admirable quality, but not what you'd expect on a battlefield."

"What were the . . . well, the other lot of foreigners saying?"

"Mmmm . . . more or less literally . . . *To the Heavenly Sovereign Majesty, ten thousand years!* Or *Long Live the Emperor* for short; it's a polished and compact phrase."

He halted and spoke to the captives, in a language Órlaith didn't even recognize. That was another gift of the Sword of the Lady; the bearer could speak the tongues that were needful to the High King's work. The foreigners cast their weapons and helms away and knelt, their hands on their heads.

The Montivallan party were around them now, and she could see the first of Dun Barstow's levy coming up, jumping off their bicycles and trotting forward with arrows on the string. One fresh-faced Archer of the guard

younger than she spoke *sotto voce* to a veteran who had a
scar like a thin white mustache crumpling the dark skin of
his upper lip:

"Is it always that easy, so?" the youngster said, trying
to be nonchalant and not quite suppressing a quaver; the
freckles stood out against a face gone pale.

"It's easy enough when you catch them with their kilts
up and Little Jack in hand, laddie," the older man said, a
little indistinctly and making an illustrative pumping motion with his right. "And when the Morrigú doesn't get up
to any of Her little tricks. When they're waiting for you,
and things do go wrong . . . then it gets very hard. Enjoy
this while you can, for you'll not see the like often. The
Ard Rí and our Old Wolf did a nice neat job o' work, I'll
say that for any to hear."

It hadn't been easy for everyone; two of Hellman's
troopers were laying out a third. It was the one who'd
brought the message, Noemi Hierro, lying still with an
arrow sunk fletching-deep under her right armpit and an
expression of surprise on her face beneath the blood and
her twenty-first year never to be completed. Órlaith felt a
little winded at the sight; that had been someone she
knew, fairly well after weeks of travel together, and liked.

So sudden, she thought, a little dazed; the young man
who'd closed her eyes looked even more stunned—not in
an anguish of grief yet, just . . . disbelieving.

The healers were busy with several others, including
some from both lots of foreigners—that was part of their
oath to Brigit, to care for all Her children first and put
everything else second when they saw the need. Though
sometimes all that could be done was a massive dose of
morphine.

The hale prisoners were all men, mostly youngish and stocky-muscular though not large. With their helmets off she could see that they were all of very much the same physical type, which itself was slightly odd to Montivallan eyes. Their skins were of a pale umber a little darker than hers when she had a summer tan, and they had sharply slanted dark eyes—shaped like Sir Aleaume's, but more so—and short snub noses and close-cropped raven hair, faces high-cheeked and rather flat and sparse of beard where they had any. That combination of features was known in Montival though not common in pure form these days, and she knew that they stemmed originally from the other side of the Pacific.

Her father spoke again, then dropped back into English for her: "I've promised them their lives if they behave," he said, pitching his voice to carry to his followers. "We'll need to question them, of course."

To her, more quietly: "But now let's see to our friends . . . or at least, the enemies of our enemies."

Heuradys wiped and sheathed her sword and passed a canteen to Órlaith; she sucked greedily at it, suddenly conscious of how her mouth was dusty-dry and gummy at once. The water was cut one-fifth with harsh red wine, and it tasted better than anything she'd ever drunk. The High King took two long swallows when she offered to him, and sighed.

"You forget what thirsty work this is, you do."

The other group of strangers had halted when the Montivallans indicated they should—though there weren't any living foemen behind them. She recognized the armor they wore now that they were close. It was more complex than that of the men they'd been fighting,

built up from many enameled steel plates held together
with silk cord, and helmets with broad flares and sometimes contorted masks over the face like visors. Several
had banners flying from small poles fixed in holders on
their backs.

"*Nihon* style," Órlaith murmured, and one of them
close enough to hear gave her a sharp look, plainly recognizing the word. "And we thought nobody survived
there!"

"They speak *Nihongo* as well as wearing the gear;
they're *Nihonjin*, right enough. Japanese, the ancients
would have said," her father said.

The phalanx of . . . Japanese . . . murmured a little
among themselves, evidently remarking on the fact that
they'd been recognized. She and her father dismounted,
removing their helmets; at his gesture the squires unfas-
tened the King's *bevoir*, the piece that protected throat
and chin but made conversation with anyone unaccus-
tomed to them a little difficult.

The strangers—could they really be from the fabled
land of Japan?—removed their helms as well and bowed,
a uniform formal-looking gesture held for a second before they came erect again; they were of the same race as
the other party of strangers but looked very different,
with their hair shaven in a broad strip up the center of the
pate and then curled into a tight topknot behind. Some
wore white headbands with a single red dot flanked by
spiky script as well. Their faces were set, without any of
the grins or whooping she'd have expected from a like
number of Mackenzies. There were others in Montival
who cultivated a similar stoic manner, of course; Bearkillers, for example.

Órlaith's brows went up. The last of the Nihonjin had taken off his helmet. . . .

No, her *helmet. A woman, and about my own age . . . somewhere between my age and Herry's, maybe.* The features were strong but delicate. *Not wearing that strange hairdo, either, though she does have the headband.*

She wore the same armor as the others, and she carried a naginata, a long curved blade on the end of an eight-foot bamboo shaft. There was blood on the tip, too. She began to speak slowly in what Órlaith recognized as an attempt at English . . . probably grammatically correct English, but with the sounds so badly rendered that it was incomprehensible except for the odd word.

". . . *senkkyu Beddi Mach,*" she finished.

Was that "thank you very much"? Órlaith wondered.

Her father responded with a bow of his own and spoke Nihongo in a barking staccato manner, to the evident vast relief of the newcomers. They seemed astonished, too. They bowed again when he indicated himself and said something that ended with:

". . . *koutei* Dai-Montival."

Then the whole party turned with a clatter and a united gasp. Two more of the Nipponese were approaching, carrying the body of a third between them.

"Ouch," Heuradys said softly just behind her ear. "No way he's going to live with that just there."

She nodded agreement. An arrow stood in his torso; her training calculated the position and put it down as far too near the big clutch of blood vessels above the heart.

You had only to nick something there and the body cavity would fill with blood in a minute or less. . . . The woman gave a small shocked cry as they laid the dead man down and called out what might be a name.

"That was their ruler, their *Tennō*," her father murmured to her. "Heavenly Sovereign, their Emperor. And the father of that young woman."

Órlaith made a small shocked sound of her own, throttled down out of consideration, not to intrude on grief.

Mother-of-All, be merciful to her! she thought. *The poor lass, to come so close to safety and then lose her Da so! Hard, hard, very hard indeed.*

"That's not one of our arrows, praise and thanks to Lugh of the Long Hand," her father said quietly. "Accidents of that sort can happen more often than is comfortable, in a scramblin' fight like this."

"No, it's fletched with gull feathers and shafted with some sort of reed," she agreed, wincing at the thought.

All the rest of the Nihonjin sank to their knees and then bowed forward towards the dead man, forehead to ground with their hands flat on the earth and fingertips touching. When they sat back on their heels their impassive countenances were like tragic masks. One of them nearest the young woman had a square scarred face that underneath the differences might have been Edain Aylward's to the life, and a single tear trickled down his cheek. He slowly reached for the short curved sword at his right hip, twin to the longer blade tucked edge-up through the sash he wore, touching the clasps of his armor at with the other hand.

The young woman unfroze and made a sharp chopping gesture, and spoke in a commanding tone without a break in it, though her own eyes were glistening. The man said something in a pleading tone, and she repeated the order.

Her father leaned close to Órlaith and murmured. "She just denied him permission to kill himself in apology for failure. *No*, she said. *I forbid it. I forbid you all. I will need your living swords, and you may not desert me or our people. Our need is too great.*"

Órlaith nodded respectfully. The middle-aged Nihonjin looked at his ruler's daughter for a long moment. He made the same gesture of obeisance to her that he had to the dead man; the others followed him. Then with hands upflung he barked out a short phrase; she thought it had a word something like *jotei* in it, used several times with another from the war cry as well. The others repeated it and took it up, chanting for a moment, ignoring the eyes of the Montivallans. Her father translated in the same low murmur:

"Hail to the Heavenly Sovereign Empress! Daughter of the Sun Goddess! To the Empress, Ten Thousand Years!"

He shook his head, and continued almost as softly: "And here I thought we'd achieved a nice, boring, uneventful life!"

The High King and his daughter waited courteously until the ritual ran its course, then stepped forward. Artos spoke again when the . . .

"Well, I suppose she's an empress now, though of what we don't know," Órlaith murmured.

"Maybe a country, maybe of one village and a pet ox," Heuradys replied almost inaudibly sotto voce.

News travelled across the great ocean, but slowly and fitfully and mostly from the southern parts of Asia whence came a trickle of trade. Everyone had just assumed Japan was a total wreck, like most of Europe or the coastal parts of China. Too many big cities too close together.

. . . the empress rose and faced him.

Movement, and a shout. Órlaith spun on one heel and froze for an instant. One of the kneeling prisoners was *grinning* at her, and his eyes . . . were solid black, emptiness with only a rim of white around the outside. She'd heard of the like, but never thought to see it herself.

"I . . . see . . . you . . ." he said, in a voice from the surface of a dead star.

Existence itself wavered. She looked into those eyes, and through them into a universe where matter itself perished with a whimpering squeal, absolute cold, utter black forever and everywhere, where nothing happened and nothing ever would. She could not move, for nothing did. . . .

The prisoner's hands went down from his bristle-shaven head to the back of his collar. A bodkin-headed arrow plowed into his forehead and sank inches deep with a wet splintering crack of bone, and Edain was cursing as he reached for another with blurring speed and half a dozen of the Archers shot too and men-at-arms were charging with their swords raised, but the dead man's hands flashed forward. Two streaks of silver went through the air.

Time slowed, like a spoon through honey. The thick-set man beside the foreign empress flung a hand out in a desperate reach like a baseball outfielder. It went between his charge and the weapon, and suddenly a small slim blade was standing out of his palm. Her father grabbed at Órlaith, throwing her backward with huge and desperate

strength as he dove between her and the threat and Heuradys' shield came around before her.

And she knew he'd started to move an instant *before*
the attacker.

As he did he jerked his own right arm up, the shield-
bearing arm that reflex would put in the way of a threat.
The flash of silver went over it by the merest fraction, and
then he was falling backward beside her, his hand clasped
to his throat and the dimpled bone hilt of the throwing-
knife standing between the fingers. Blood welled out over
the hand and from his mouth. Time unfroze, and she
checked her lunge forward. The angle meant that anything she did would make things worse.

A few seconds ticked by like years. Faces gathered
about where she knelt by her father, but they were more
distant than the Moon. He reached with his other hand,
fumbling, and she saw what he was doing and helped,
bringing the Sword up until it lay on his breast, with her
hand over his on the hilt. Light flared in the crystal pommel. For a moment she hoped wildly and then—

"Hello, my darling girl, my heart, my treasure," he said
gently.

They were standing in the trampled meadow, but the
grass nodded undisturbed instead of lying flat, and there
were neither men nor weapons nor blood. Her father was
in a simple kilt and shirt, smiling at her as the wind ruf-
fled his bright hair.

That expression turned rueful as he looked down at his
right hand, flexing the arm and opening and closing the
long shapely fingers.

"I was told at the time that Cutter arrow in my right

shoulder would be the death of me. And so it was, with a twenty-year stay of execution. Just a fraction of a second too slow for me to make old bones. Well, I had it on the best of authorities I'd not see my beard go gray . . . and I noticed the first gray hair six months ago."

"Da!"

His arms went about her, comforting and strong as she wept. "Ah, lass, it's sorry I am to leave you. So, so. Grieve, but not too long; it's the way of nature for a child to bury her parents."

A thought penetrated even her sorrow. "Oh, Goddess, I'll have to tell Mother!"

She could feel his head shake. "No. She is High Queen. We were linked to the land, and to each other. She'll have known.

"Tell your mother that I will wait for her, in the world beyond the world."

He held her at arm's length with his hands on her shoulders. "You and I will meet once more, my heart, in this cycle of the world; long ago for me, not too long in the future for you. By Lost Lake."

A thread of eeriness penetrated her misery. That was where the Kingmaking took place. Nobody went there but a new made High King . . . or High Queen.

Then the world crashed in on her once more. Her father lay with his eyes closed, comely even with the blood bright on this throat and lips, years vanished from his face. She stood, slowly, the Sword of the Lady in her hand. Always before it had seemed a little heavy, a little large, as a blade sized for her father would.

Now it was perfect, alive in her grip at the exact weight

her wrist and arm could wield, and her fingers closed around it as if it had been fashioned for her at the place where the world began. Somehow that made the moment real, as even her father's face relaxed in death could not.

Slowly she raised the Sword on high. Heuradys fell to her knees, head bowed, and the others did in a ripple outward like the fall of petals from flowers.

"I am my father's heir," she called, her voice strange and harsh in her ears. "And for him and for Montival, for the land that he has watered with his blood . . . I swear vengeance on those who did this deed!"

ALSO AVAILABLE FROM
New York Times bestselling author

S. M. STIRLING

"FIRST-RATE ADVENTURE ALL THE WAY."
—HARRY TURTLEDOVE

Available wherever books are sold or at
penguin.com

s922